Jı

Jukebox

By

Saira Viola

Fahrenheit Press

Sold me out for chicken change…
The Payback, *James Brown*

Crime butchers innocence to secure a throne,
and innocence struggles with all its might
against the attempts of crime.
Maximilien Robespierre

Chapter One: Legalize It

'Screw you, you fucking Jew! Eat shit and die and get the fuck out of my life. *Rrot Kard*!' She strutted down the street in latex and leopard skin cussing under her breath in a smattering of Balkan dialects.

It was 7 a.m. on a grim grey Monday. The pigeons were pooling the pavements, feasting on curried chips and MSG, as Mel Greenberg was hustling heavies and skinning strippers – just another fleece and fold morning.

'I'll give you one tip for free,' spewed Mel, wiping the blood away from his mouth. 'I've tasted every kind of bitch there is, but there's nothing like a desperate bitch and that's the best fucking bitch you'll find.'

With him were Mickey Gold Tooth and Solomon (Sal) Leif, his accountant.

'Nothing like a blonde on heat, eh? She spat blood on your face … And I think she called you a dickhead in Albanian.'

'She'll get what's coming to her Sal … trying to dumb me over, stealing punters and thieving cash. Fuck that bitch.'

'You already have.'

'Her pussy's a sewer. Fucking slut. I'll teach her some fucking respect. Bitch.'

'Easy.'

'She's a fucking racist whore Sal and she's gonna get slapped.'

'Maybe now's not the right time. Let it go.'

'Mickey, would *you* let it go?'

'Fuck no, boss, but Sal's right, there's a time, a place, and a way to get even.'

'She pickles my gut, making me feel like I was nothing. Making out I was a no one.'

'Easy, Mel. Why you so sensitive all of a sudden?'

'You know me Sal I'm as sensitive as a new born pup when it comes to my money especially when some fucking Albanian scrubber is being racist and mugging me off.'

'I dunno, Mel. You've got to calm down.' He scratched his ear and said: 'you're Jewish, I'm Jewish. That's not racist. She's just stating the obvious. Let it go.'

'You fuckin' taking her side, Sal, eh?'

'Come on, Mel.'

'She was being fucking racist – trying to make out I was worse than a fucking animal.'

'A lot of Jewish people come from Albania.' Sal looked at Mickey like he was a prize wally.

Mel ignored the remark, his eyes were red and cruel.

'She was acting like a fucking bitch. I'll pimp her out, fuck her, then slug her till she's on her fucking knees – bitch.'

Sal started fiddling with his ring nervously, worried that matters might escalate out of control.

'Why don't you go back to the flat, get some sleep, freshen up, and I'll come back for you around noon.'

'Can't just let that slut walk Sal.'

'Look, all I said was, the profits were down with her takings. It would have been nice to start the week without a fucking jam bust.'

The three men started down Portpool Lane, past Pier Studios and onto the market where they disappeared into the morning crowd.

Nick Stringer, a trainee solicitor was walking on the opposite side of the road, getting ready for court. A tattered copy of *American Psycho* in his pocket. Nick rented a small basement flat in Theobald's Road and had split from his Ukrainian girlfriend a year ago. She'd left him with a smashed heart and drunk in debt.

Shut down from the noisy live-it-up office crowd, he was piling every penny to save his big dream, fighting the temptation to kick it all in and bash his cash on cheap sex and vintage whisky.

Stringer was crossing the busy Fleet Street end of Chancery Lane when he spied a group of dance DJs and a well-known music producer. They were dressed all the same: designer denim, Adidas trainers, and Boss shirts streaked with easy-cum easy-go shades of yesterday.

'Oi, Oi,' shouted one.

Nick looked behind him – yes, they were definitely speaking to *him*. He checked over his shoulder again, convinced the guy wanted someone else.

'I'm Ritchie – You're with that law firm, aren't ya, on Clerkenwell Road?'

'Yeah, I'm sorry, I'm not sure who …' started Nick with a squirrel jitter. He was Hush-Puppy sweet, unaccustomed to talking to such a copacetic crowd. To him, people like that were above and apart from the jobbing mainstream. *I'm just a bumbling geek with stick-up hair and skin the colour of raw chicken – what do they want with me.* He fretted, his messy locks had shot up in a wiry fuzz all over his temple making him look like a frazzled cartoon loon.

'You know my cousin, Julian. You had a night out with him at Faces in Enfield about a week ago.' He spoke with a pronounced North London cant, ubiquitous in black-taxi drivers and insurance scammers. He was a large hulk of a man with acute halitosis and an awkward mop of hair that crowned his sallow face.

He had 'Popeye the Sailor' lips and capped teeth, reminding Nick of Harpo Marx. The truth was that Nick had no memory of a night out at Faces, but he faked recollection.

As far as he knew, Faces was a Hoddesdon dive playing wall-to-wall smoove groove rammed with toilet-chic babes hooked on Malibu and Pineapple, prinked up in Primark not Prada.

'Oh yeah, right, I'm … er … on my way to court, but here's my card.' Nick held out a small cream-coloured business card, printed in blue roman lettering, which read: *Nick Stringer Trainee Solicitor Fisher Fowler & Ferret LLP.* Ritchie took it with predictable indifference, but then:

'Oh, I like your bizzo card. Yeah, nice combination blue and neutral – yeah, that's clarrrsh that is.'

It was an *American Psycho* film tag but the irony was lost on the dumb-faced BMW-fuelled lifestyle of the London D J collective. Nick nodded politely while the others in the group were gassing about football, drugs, and a billboard blonde. He was glad to get away – Ritchie's egg-smell breath had left him funking for air.

Nick hurried to the Royal Courts of Justice in stress mode, listening to the burning rhythms of The Prodigy. Gibson guitars, electronic hard beats and the grainy sound of The Libertines were all calling out to him. Ever since he'd heard 'All Along the Watchtower', he'd wanted more than anything to start his own record label and make music move the moment. He'd stumbled into the legal profession upon his uncle's say-so, a barrister's clerk, but Nick hated the pedestrian lifestyle of the law. He hated lawyers and their sneaking artifice. He hated their formality; he hated their pseudo respectability; he hated their smug little lives, and their crowing greed. Most of all, Nick hated himself for agreeing to become a lawyer in the first place.

But Nick's father was battling Alzheimer's; slowly losing his mind, which lay trapped in the sweet underlay of nowheresville, so Nick had promised his mother he would get a respectable job and live a chip-and-pin existence with a guaranteed pension and two weeks in the sun and one on the snow every year.

'Fuck! Fuck! Fuck!' He uttered the expletive with a

staccato cadence, all of his papers sinking into the nearby pothole at the corner of the road. He scooped them up and parked himself in the security line at the entrance of the court.

Once through, the gothic splendour and sculpted arches of the imposing building did little to calm his nerves. He rushed with bullet speed to Room E101: East Wing: Queen's Bench Division. He'd no intention of being late for a jelly-belly judge with an ego twice the size of an African bush elephant.

Outside the grey lacquered door was an officious-looking law clerk robed in black, sporting ink-blue varnish and MAC's Fuchsia Fix lip tint. She wore a knife pleat skirt with a tailored white shirt. She was civil-servant hot. She handed him a form to complete. He filled in all that was relevant and returned it with a dimpled grin and polite handshake waiting anxiously for his adversary to arrive, pacing the marble floors and staring at the oak-panelled ceilings while fluffing a fake call. He popped some Trident Fresh into his mouth, humming the chorus of 'A Town Called Malice.' Misery glutted his mind. He needed to escape the spread of rotting conformity.

His chafing gloom suddenly rattled by the sexy click-click of patent stilettos. A strawberry blonde with a look, look and look again stride came towards him. She exuded charm-school grace and a wine-press smile.

Nick had done his homework on Ms. Wheately: She had a double first in Classics, from Cambridge and was in her first six at one of the best chambers in London. "*On track to becoming* one *of the leading lights of the legal profession*" A direct quote Nick had read from her showcase CV, proudly profiled on her web link. Nick tried hard not to strip her with his eyes, ripple his tongue over those blue-chip curves and fuck her dirty.

'You must be Mr Stringer.' She spoke with moneyed arrogance.

Nick put his hand out as a professional courtesy ready to

exchange official hellos.

She ignored it, stepping aside and keeping her distance, then she gabbled on in her *Horse* and *Hound* yap.

'We won't be settling for anything less. We intend giving your client a bloody nose.'

Nick was bored of her beefy aggression. He said quietly:

'Let's see what the Master has to say.'

What a strange name for a judge, 'Master'. Another quirky eccentricity of the English legal system and a punching reminder of constitutional tradition – still drowning in medieval jargon. It had no place in modern society. Such a ball and chain existence. He sighed with Miles Davis melancholy.

Master Swinebottom was a real corker of a man with pink butterball hands and a fleshy pockmarked jowl. He was trussed up in a tight pinstripe suit. His meaty stomach made Nick think of an overstuffed turkey at Christmas. He wore pince-nez eyeglasses and peered with hawkish intent at the two individuals before him as if they were exhibits on show at the Tate Modern.

'Please, Master. My name is Lucinda Jane Wheatley.' She bowed with priggish familiarity.

'I appear on behalf of the claimant in this application, which is an application for summary judgement. I've set out the grounds in my witness statement, Master, and would be grateful if I could take you through it, sir.'

The Master listened courteously as she presented the facts in issue. Then he turned to Nick.

'I didn't quite catch your name Mr … er … could you spell it for me, please?'

'It's on the form I submitted to you, sir,' Nick answered wearily.

'Yeees, your handwriting is very squiggly and I can't read it,' he replied acidly, his lips were stern and purple with dried spittle around the sides of his mouth.

'My apologies, Master. My name is Nick Stringer, and I appear on behalf of the defendant in this action.'

'Yes. Well what do you have to say, Mr …, … Mr

Stringer, about the claimant's arguments?'

'Well, Sir, I strongly disagree, and if you would be so kind as to take a look at the arguments in my submission, I believe the defendant still has a strong case and has a right to be heard.'

Nick passed his papers forward, and handed a copy to Ms Wheatley with a playful wink.

'I'm quite a quick reader Mr Stringer, so if you'll allow me a few moments …'

'Yes, of course,' responded Nick with deceptive civility.

After about fifteen minutes, he delivered his judgement.

'On consideration of the facts,.....yessss..."

He spoke as if he were a lisping cobra ready to pounce.

'And after hearing both Ms Wheatley for the claimant and Mr Stringer for the defendant, I make the following order for the defendant that on the pleadings before me there is a case to answer …'

The Master continued with his byzantine spout, interrupted by the grousing rumble of Ms Wheatley:

'I would like to appeal your order now, Master,' she raged.

'Make the appropriate application. That is all.'

Nick left the court with a super-jock smirk and later that evening beat the drum with some Panama Red.

Chapter Two: Shake Your Money Maker

It was a flat Tuesday afternoon. Chords of broken sunlight gilded the long bay windows and the acoustic gravel of James Blunt was dulling the air with scales of yellow tedium. There were no punters around except for Ryan, an ex-con stewed on coke and weed.

He ordered a beer from the Lithuanian bartender. She was gym bunny fresh with a gentle inflexion in her voice and hold-me-tight eyes.

'A Pint of Stella, please, darlin'. He spoke with a whisky knot, his voice a snuff-coloured wheeze that hushed the cutting squall of the police siren outside.

'Coming right up,' she cruised.

Nick sat alone reading a copy of *The Independent*. Cocaine socialists were trying their hardest to juice up Britain's economy with super casinos, twenty-four-hour pub licensing and tax relief for the suits in Whitehall. Millionaire donors were trading boardrooms for bikinis, and reality TV had become the preferred drug of choice for the George Clooney obsessed housewives strung out on empty promises and splintered dreams – the call of the suburbs had deadened his spark, forcing him back to the monochrome certainty of the scuzzy bar.

Nick looked up and Ryan sat down. He was a stab-and-jab yard bird with a Costa del Sol glow and hair like George Peppard in *Breakfast at Tiffany's*.

'Alright my son, let's have a light ale. I need to talk to you.'

'Sure – yeah, thanks.' Nick knew Ryan was an old-time crook with solid backing, a fiercely independent streak, and a hit 'em hard attitude. Ryan had never joined a mob ring or organised gang because he refused to take orders from any 'racist bastards' who acted 'worse than savages'. He spoke in a slow steady drone:

'The buzz on the street is that you're getting it on with Mel and his firm.'

Nick could feel his cheeks redden. He lowered his eyes and started jabbing his fingers into his palms.

How could anyone know about a meeting that hadn't taken place? He had agreed to see Mel after a brief telephone conversation with Ritchie in the morning. Just a hook-up, nothing definite.

'I promised your family I'd look out for you. I'm just saying, son, keep your nose clean. They're prime time. Have as little as possible to do with them and keep it strictly business. Make no deals and no promises, or I'll chop your balls off.'

Nick wormed uncomfortably in his seat.

'Come on now. Don't get all shy, boy. Just be careful.'

'Yeah, sure. Thanks for the warning Ryan.'

'Gotta keep up to snuff. Now, you know where you're going – just by Farringdon Station – or are you heading to big G's first?'

'Big …?'

'Are you going to Mel's now?'

'I was, yeah,'

'Well be careful, son.'

Nick left Deux Beers with a mixture of verve and Radio Head *dread*.

It took less than twenty minutes to get to Mel's. Just as he was about to reach the door, his phone rang. It was his mother.

'Hi, Mum. Is everything okay?'

'I don't know where your father's wandered off to. Sorry Nick, but you'll have to come home and help look for him. I can't cope on my own, it's just too much,' she blubbered.

'Oh crap, I was just about to head off to a meeting.' Then, a long over-stressed pause. 'Okay, I'll be there in ten, maybe twenty minutes, depending on the traffic.'

He turned around and hailed a cab. It was an automatic I'll-be-there response. Everything was on standby when his father went walkabout.

'I'm sorry dear. I know this is hard on you with work, but it's hard for all of us, and I do need your help.'

'Just give me a few minutes Mum, I'm in the cab now. Please – no tears.'

Neither wanted to be tied to this torturous situation, but both were knee-deep in family loyalty and obligation.

Nick's father, Graham, once a stalwart of the civil service, was now a floundering skeletal glitch, reduced to recycling every day greetings and staring into space for hours at a time. Graham had been diagnosed with the disease six months ago, and Nick had been forced to watch his father's macabre transformation as if he were a life exhibit at the V&A. General outlook: not promising.

The taxi was looping in and out of traffic like a yoyo, breaking sharply at every red light, causing him to jerk forward.

'Legally you should 'ave your seat belt on mate,' nagged the cabbie.

'Yeah, sorry. I … um … I'm feeling a bit iffy.'

'Best roll the winders down. There are automatic buttons on the side. You just press it –_don't want you messing up my cab.'

'Yeah, sure, okay.'

Finally, Nick spotted his mother traipsing around the front of the house.

He met her at the door of the cab. She was wearing old trackie bottoms and a wrinkled blouse. Her face: an uneasy mix of lines and creases, echoing the shape of her sinking frame and greying hair. She was all slump and sag, her spirit withering like a tuckering weed shambling for a way out. Her voice was strained:

'I'm sorry Nick, I'm so worried. God knows where he's drifted off to now.'

'I would have been here quicker, but you know the traffic's really bad towards Islington at this time.'

'Okay, that'll be £10 exactly guv.'

'Keep the change,' Nick shoved £15 through the window.

Once the cab had sped off, Nick entered the small bungalow and headed straight for his mother's car keys.

'You coming with me?'

'No dear, I'll wait here. It's best if someone stays at home. He may wander back himself.'

'Okay. Call me if there's any news.'

Every day she loses a bit more of herself, every day another nail in her coffin – house payments, medical bills, and middle aged isolation. Martyrdom is a lonely business.

He clambered into the car, adjusted the seat position, front and rear mirrors, buckled up, turned the radio on and sped off towards Islington High Street. Slowing down to a leisurely crawl he zigzagged around the surrounding streets, little pockets of tree-lined suburbia masking the secrets of the middle classes. Nick knew that behind the manicured lawns and groomed symmetry lay a fractured dawn of false promises and never-ending yesterdays.

Nick's father had always been his sparkling paradigm, the man who believed in the day, and someone he could count on, someone who was strong enough to give a damn and make everything matter.

Why now, why after six long decades? It left him feeling bitter. *Dad always put family first never bothered with himself. He was just a yes sir, no sir, and three bloody bags full sir kind of man. Not one risk, not one gamble, not one moment of self-indulgent pleasure and now the ultimate sacrifice . . .*

Nick admired his father's selfless devotion but still

thought he was a bit of a soft touch. He never seemed to have any regrets, and there was no ugly aftertaste in his life of altruism, but he must have had some lusty vices, some secret he never wanted to share. There was nothing Nick could think of; he had always been faithful to his mother, they very rarely argued, and when they did it was over in seconds, smiles out in minutes.

Now what would happen? He was plagued with uncertainty. One thing that did annoy Nick, was that his father hated his arty indulgences, seeing them as nothing more than the idle pursuits of the well-to to-do.

'You can't afford to waste your time on a drum kit, Nick, can't afford to spend hours learning the guitar. There's only one in a million who get to follow their dream and you're not *that* one.'

How he hated this closed-door mind-set, and yet, now more than ever, he missed his sobering practicality. Nick's father believed in toil and struggle, not pipe dreams or the beauty of Byron.

'Now, Nicholas, you know what time it is don't you?' he would scold.

'Yes, Dad,'

'Time is the devil's playmate. Unless you're working, boy, you have nothing in life, and where does nothing lead, Nicholas?'

'Nowhere,' Nick would whisper, then hide away his guitar and pack up his drum kit bought for him with his mother's pride.

Scouring the neatly packed streets and side roads, Nick came to a large clearing and parked the car, choosing to continue his search by foot.

He walked along the cul-de-sacs and byways, arriving at a small gated garden. It was covered with long thick grass and overgrown plants, as well as hundreds of white Gerbera daisies. There in front of him he saw a thin bent figure sitting on a roughened bench.

Yes, there he was – his dear old dad staring into a vast sea of nothing, and where did that get him: nowhere.

'Dad,' he choked.

There was no recognition, no memory, just space: dead space in his sickly blue eyes. He wiped away his tears, afraid of letting his father see him in such a pitiable state. He quickened his pace, but there was still nothing, his father fixated on an empty horizon. He was Duke Ellington blue and no one could stir him from that zombie state.

'It's me, Dad. Nicholas. It's Nick. I've come to take you home.' He held him by the arm.

'We'd better get you back. Mum's been so worried.'

His father, dressed comfortably in corduroys and a V-neck sweater, allowed him to guide him back to the car. Nick, trying to erase the awkward silences with a rolling discourse on the state of English cricket, the price of a pint at his local and the popularity of *Twitter*, the social networking site.

'Yeah, everyone's doing it, Dad. Even the politicians tweet. All the stars are at it, and you can talk to almost anyone on Twitter.'

As they drove back, Nick turned on the radio. Smooth FM was one of his father's favourites; he liked the jazz, Motown and old blues records. Nick thought it might switch the mood from grey to violet: from despair to hope. 'Tears of a Clown' by Smokey Robinson came on. He looked at his father now less than a shadow of what he once was. Alone and lifeless, this was the face of a man, with nothing to cling to.

They drove on with Smokey's soulful lament cleansing the fuggy air.

Once Nick had dropped his father home, he called Mel to reschedule their appointment.

'Hi, Mel. It's me, Nick. I'm running late. Can we put our meeting back to this evening, I had—'

'Family problems to take care of.'

'Yeah, how did … how did you know?'

'Don't worry about it. I'll see you around six. Be on time.' The phone cut out.

Nick was spooked but had no time to waste if he wanted to make it for six. He darted back to the office, got out his latest files and began dictating letters, drafting court documents and litigation briefs, hoping to clear the backlog before his boss returned.

Over at the Purple Turtle, Mel Greenberg was getting ready to hire another schmuck for his Bernie Madoff style Ponzi scheme. At fifty-five years old, he'd been through two wives and a dozen trial separations. Now he'd settled on a Thai princess, a squeal-and-deal kind of girl who was always giggling at the quirkiness of English life. Then, every third day of the month, he'd visit a Somali model he'd set up in a flat in Holland Park. She was skinnier than a gazelle with the fine, sculpted bone structure of the Queen of Sheba.

Mel had come from a background of tailors and goldsmiths but had chosen another career path when details of his father's infidelities came to light and had caused a family rift that still scarred the right side of his cheek today. With the instincts of an alley cat and the needle precision of a brain surgeon, he had escaped the attention of the law and was now the self-styled Gordon Gecko of North London's Jewish community, taking care of their financial investments, stock portfolios, shares, mortgage payments and pension plans – basically shafting the hell out of them. Mel was big and heavyset with a stubborn bulge of belly fat he sometimes concealed with a man girdle.

With a weekly spray tan and his light-brown tufts of hair styled in a sharp angular quiff, he looked more like Mike Score front man of pop band Flock of Seagulls rather than Hollywood heartthrob Michael Douglas. It was, however, always a talking point and somehow managed to complement his olive skin tone.

A fan of baubles and bling, Mel wore solid-gold, high-carat jewellery on his hands and his chest, a 1960s' Rolex Submariner watch and enough Paco Rabanne aftershave to scare off any competition. He didn't like shopping and didn't do Sundays.

The office 'clerk' who had responded to the ad for a dynamic salesman was a gangly, buck-toothed Asian lad of around nineteen years old. He had straight dark hair, small-rimmed wire spectacles and a geeky charm that Mel was drawn to.

'Wasn't sure I got the right address.'

'Come in. Sit down,' he blustered as the boy entered the room timidly.

'The club belongs to a friend of the family and sometimes I hold bizzo meets here.' Mel was sifting through cheque stubs and till receipts. 'Your name's Mushi, right?'

'Yeah. My real name's Mushtaq, but everyone calls me Mushi.'

Mushi had a way of talking that made his nostrils flare and his gums protrude, giving him the permanent look of a distressed guinea pig.

'I've been looking at your CV and you appear to have had considerable experience with face-to-face selling. It says here you've worked at Carphone Warehouse, call centres, and your latest job: flogging Sky TV. How's that going?'

'Yeah, great. We keep our own diary and our own hours, but I've been working in sales since I left college, and I'm looking for more of a challenge now. A chance to make some real money,' he explained, keen to impress, unaware he was dealing with London's answer to John Gotti.

'I understand. It's great you have the determination to go for what you want now. If you keep that focus and do what I tell you, I reckon there's a strong chance you'll be on your way to making serious cash.'

'That sounds good.'

'It'll be more than good.' Mel grinned. Wearing a smart Saville Row suit, classic silk tie, solid-gold cufflinks, pink argyle socks and handcrafted English brogues, he believed in overstated chic and label glamour that was a million miles away from his working-class roots. He still spoke with a definite North London tartness and had a weakness for gold which he hoarded for pleasure.

'Okay, now this is what you'll have to do. Drum up business in your community, people who you know, people who want safe investments for their future, and people who you think will be able to invest at least a few grand at a time.'

'Well, I've got lots of contacts through family and friends.'

'Yeah, that's a good place to start. How it works is we buy all kinds of commodities for our clients like … industrial products – gold and precious metals. Then we manage that for them so, when a client joins up their money is invested, and they get a return on their investment after a certain time.'

'So, we take their money- invest it and manage it for them so it makes a profit.'

'Exactly, but the scheme only works if you have lots of clients and lots of money. There must be plenty of people in your rabble who have capital sitting around in banks and safes not doing anything. Speculate to accumulate – get it?'

'Yeah totally, I know loads of people who may be interested. Most of the Asian community are professionals. They usually opt for traditional financial products, but I can try to make them join the company,' Mushi spoke with fresh enthusiasm.

Of course that was the bite – the hook. Mel knew that Mushi would have absolutely no problem bending the arm of friendly 'aunties' and 'uncles' who would be only too pleased to support him in his business endeavours. Who could resist a face like Mushi's? He was a human Labrador.

'Right then, no time to waste. We'll start you off tomorrow. Turn up at that address. I'll get your desk and bizzo cards ready, and let's make some moolah. Tonight, get all your contacts ready, and we'll arrange your pitch-and-sell for the morning, take them out to lunch, schmooze them – rope them in and hang 'em.'

'That's it?' asked Mushi, a little unsure of what had just happened.

'Yeah, for now, but I'm expecting great things from you Mushi, great things. I'll sort you with a Blackberry, latest gizmos, social media promotion, face book twitter and all that malarkey. You'll start on a basic salary of £50k and I'll even throw in a company car for ya. How's that?'

'I-I don't need that much, Mr Greenberg.'

'It's not about what you need, Mushi. It's about what you can get away with. Oh, call me Mel, and *smile* – you just got the equivalent of a BJ, a steak and a model girlfriend. Bish bash bosh. All sorted.'

'Okay then, Mel. See you tomorrow.'

Mushi hurried to the door, a little pensive but still holding onto that feel good vibe all the way home from Farringdon to Hounslow. It was Pet Shop Boys fantastic! That was one of Mushi's favourite eighties bands and the only way to explain the fizzy thoughts colouring his brain, which had turned a glowing shade of pink.

Now that Mel had recruited another numpty for his Ponzi hybrid swindle, he was in a cheerful mood quoting Voltaire to himself lip-synching to an invisible audience: 'Those who can make you believe absurdities can make you commit atrocities.'

Mel had started the hustle about seven months ago, spurred on by the success of Bernie Madoff, and he believed it was a nice, safe, respectable swindle that could generate a healthy profit. When he began the scam there were only two of them but now it had grown to over 1,000, each person recruiting more and more, and each person paying an initial recruitment fee of just £10. Then that person recruited another ten, and on and on it went until Mel was top of the pyramid chain. It would only be a matter of time before the scheme fell apart, and he wanted to milk it just a tad longer. He was winging it, promising high returns to his more educated clientele and easy cash to those on the straight pyramid. It was a win-win situation for him and a double loss for them. Mel would seduce clients with guaranteed profits on their money but not really specify *how* that money was invested. At the moment he was taking money off Peter to pay Paul, so their 'returns' were just investment monies from other clients. New money paying off old. The pyramid aspect worked on its own, but with no products being sold, no investments being made, and only so many recruiters joining, this would be the first scheme to go belly up. Mel made all his recruits for these businesses either solicit new blood through special investment clubs or sell products with no obvious market value and then recruit further numbers to join the scheme.

Luckily for Mel he wasn't solely reliant on the fraud racket he was running and controlled a wealthy crime syndicate that included illegal gambling, prostitution, ID theft and the sale of bootleg alcohol made in a local 'distillery', which was resold as genuine branded vodka to high-end clubs and bars all over West End central and Europe. On average they were producing around twenty-four bottles every minute in a twenty-four-hour cycle. Mel had employed a Polish workforce to man the operation.

The bootleg booze helped build Mel's Marbella mansion, fund a stately home in Pau, made it possible for his kids to go to private school and netted a privileged lifestyle for his wife, black mistress and a massage therapist addicted to caviar and fried liver.

Sal, had worked out that Mel had personally defrauded the tax man of millions in VAT and unpaid duty. It gave them a chuckling delight to know they had deprived the tax cats of such an enormous sum.

Now Mel was diversifying into the music bizz he had

tagged a prime target for his latest racket: Nick Stringer, illegitimate grandchild of his own dear father and offspring of his half-brother, now afflicted with Alzheimer's. Well, in the interests of family unity and all that, he wanted to help the lad achieve his full potential. Why not? He had been keeping a protective eye out for Nick ever since he had been told he was his nephew and part of the Greenberg tribe.

Nick got a cab from work and slumped to the back of the seat. His suit was all scrunched up but he'd managed to change his shirt and spritz himself with some Right Guard and a dab of Davidoff. He stared at his phone. There were no missed calls, no voicemails, no sign of anyone wanting to contact him. He scrolled lazily through the names, and realised that there really was no one for him to call except his mother. Of course, he had around 752 Facebook 'friends', but how many of those could he rely on? With only three close friends he could count on, none of whom were around now, he felt very much alone. Nick never had time to think about Anichka since she'd left but at moments like this, in between snatched seconds of Van Gogh beauty, when the sun was setting, and the night was dotted with stars, and the moon buttered with Virgil's poetry, he knew only *she* would appreciate the melody of the skies.

Mel was sitting inside his small office, chatting on the phone:

'Yeah, I'm cool about that. No problemo. We'll pick up the conversation later. Yeah, yeah.'

He beckoned Nick into the room.

'Okay. Good, good. We'll wrap it up next week. Yeah, great talking to you.'

He slammed the phone down whilst mouthing the word 'wanker' and winking at Nick as he signalled him to sit.

'Bloody moron doesn't know his arse from his Morgan Stanley. Trying to tell me where to invest money.' He shook his head, tutting and swearing in Yiddish.

Nick smiled, showing only his lower teeth. He was a bit antsy. *Don't wanna balls this up.*

'So, Richie called me up, said you're a trainee solicitor, and what you really, really want is to run your own music business, have your own label, that kind of thing?'

'Yeah, I don't know Richie that well, but he knows the law firm I work for, and some of his contacts know me, so he told me to call you after we'd had a chat. He said you might be the right guy to lend me some seed money for a record business and my own band.'

'Yeah, and what were you thinking? What sort of bands did you want to join this new set-up?'

'I want like a proper rock band, an all-girl group, a bit of rebellion grime, that kind of thing. Eventually I want to work exclusively in music try and keep my band together and leave the legal profession altogether.' Mel jerked his head forward and spoke sternly.

'No, you have to stay at the firm. That's where the action is. All those acts you sign up, they need lawyers, not just for contracts, agreements and artist bullshit, they need 'em for driving offences, drug offences, and marriage aggro. A good lawyer serves you from the cradle to the grave, Nick.'

'I had intended to give it up. It—'

'No, No, No,' Mel quacked, waggling his big fat finger in Nick's face. It was as large as a sausage and twice as pink. 'You can't give up the law. It's an income stream, boy. It's your retirement egg. No, you can run both businesses, and be in your band. How long before you qualify?'

'Well, I'm in the last year of my training contract, so I'll have another six months and then—'

'And then you'll be let loose on the public for good, eh?'

'Yeah, I suppose so. It's just that I wanted to quit the law for good.'

'No, you can't do that. You've invested too much time, too much money, in becoming a lawyer. It won't be long now before you qualify, and having a legal business is like having your own sweet shop, D'ya understand? You can do whatever you want fronting a law firm.'

'I'm sorry I don't—'

Mel cut him off.

'Look at it this way. If you wanna be major league, run a successful record company, what's the main part of your bizzo?'

'Well, finding the artists and—'

'No, no, that's bullshit. The main part of the business and any business at all, is the law. I'll have no problem giving you finance, provided you qualify. It's only a few poxy months. Why would you fuck that up for yourself? This way you get to do it all. I'll present myself at your offices on Monday as one of your new clients. Then your boss will know he's got a real safe investment for his firm. A retainer of around £200,000 should put you in his good books, eh, and then the real bizzo can begin what d'ya think?'

'But what about—?'

Mel's face turned a viperous shade of red. 'Stop being a clown. Use your noodle boy.

Listen, you have a good thing going with this law firm. You know the best way for any music business to be successful is to have a lawyer on standby. Think long term. You have to stay on at the firm, qualify, and then you can specialise. For now, you'll have to deal with all my legal affairs. It's the only way. I'm not Lloyds Bank, son, I need more than a handshake to make this work, understand?'

'Or?'

'Or you become like a million others: big talk, big dreams, and big nothing at the end of it all.'

'I'll think about it,' Nick bleated.

'Better to take a wrong rather than no turn at all Nick. If you fuck around, you always stay in a rut. My offer's simple. Take £200,000. Use the money to invest in the business, make a change, get a life, or stay exactly as you are, but don't come crying to me when you hit fifty and all you have is a cruise booked for two and a couple of kids who hate your guts. D'ya understand me, Nick?'

Nick was feeling it. Mel had tripped him into panic mode. What he couldn't be – wouldn't be – was exactly like his old man: a jingle-brained washout existing on the crumbs of life.

'Here, let me show you something,' Mel's tone softened. 'Recognise this man?'

It was an old black and white of his father, Mel, and other family members. It was more than nostalgia. His father looked different, hopeful, someone who was destined for better than he had.

'Such a shame to look at him now. Can't even make his own breakfast without thinking about it for half a day. Yeah he's got you, he's got dear sweet Rebecca, but do you know what your father really wanted?'

Nick had no idea that Mel was so close to his father, so this was a little unsettling.

'No,' he answered, shaking his head.

'He wanted to be Marc Bolan.'

Mel paused for a while, let it sink in. Then carried on:

'Marc Bolan was the—'

'I know who Marc Bolan was.'

'From Marc Bolan to the ageing safety of nowhere, it's as easy as A … B … C.'

'Look, I get it. I *understand*. I still have to think about it. I- I'm not sure. It's a big risk.'

'Yeah, that much is true, Nick. It is a big risk, a big fucking risk *I'm* taking on you.'

Nick's experience of the criminal world was limited to small time shoplifters, teenage pot dealers, and on occasion petty grifters. They would turn up at the office with a charge sheet and a request for charitable donations to help them with travelling expenses. They usually got bail, suspended sentences, and were repeat offenders. None of them were on the scale of what he was about to get involved with.

Chapter Three: In Perpetuity

Fisher, Fowler, and Ferret were a traditional law firm. The three partners built it from scratch after serving their apprenticeships in solid, first-rate practices. They believed in the justice system because they had no reason to doubt it. In their world, integrity and respect were as sacrosanct as truth and liberty. Starch-pressed and clean-cut, they ran their offices with apple-pie order. Their taxes were always paid on time, as were their legal dues, company insurance and so on. They were more than professionally compliant, they were an exemplar to others and could recite verbatim the entire contents of the Professional Conduct Rules for Solicitors. They had never fallen foul of any of any of their governing regulations and prided themselves on the fact that not even one client had lodged a complaint against the firm in almost fifteen years of practice.

Edward Fisher was a tall balding man with frog eyes knock- knees and a sharp angular face that predicted doom and gloom. He lacked the social graces of polite society, having hideously bitten fingernails and a nasty dry skin irritation, which left his eyebrows riddled with sore patches and his scalp permanently flaky. He was approaching fifty and looking forward to retirement. Fisher specialised in business ventures and tax law. Married to a South American doctor whom he met on the internet he was the proud father of two. He eyed Mel with a mixture of greed and disdain.

'Mr Fisher, sir, I'd like to introduce you to Mel Greenberg. He's a record producer, venture capitalist and entrepreneur, as well as being one of the biggest land developers in London.'

'A pleasure to meet you, Mr Greenberg. I hope Fisher, Fowler and Ferret will prove most useful in your business endeavours.' When Fisher spoke his lips were wafer thin.

Mel was wearing a heritage two-button Gucci suit. It was a luxury blend of dark grey silk mixed with soft lamb's wool and had an elaborate monogram print lining. It was beautifully cut and styled for drama.

In that suit, Mel knew he looked better than Philip Green after a sun splurge and richer than Donald Trump. He had masked his brawny stomach with a man girdle, giving him a leaner, taller silhouette. He wore a baby-blue open neck, shirt embossed with signature Versace buttons, and a pair of Oliver Sweeney Serpentine shoes

Fisher, in comparison, wore an Ede and Ravenscroft bespoke flannel suit, white herringbone shirt, plain silk pocket square, and a Prince of Wales check tie, with gold lozenge cufflinks and handcrafted, hand-sewn Grenson brown leather brogues. He had no time for frippery and fuss.

'Pleasure's all mine,' Mel chortled like an overgrown meathead. He may have been one of London's most astute con men, but didn't possess that cultivated intelligence that comes from years of education and ivory tower privilege.

Fisher stayed with Nick in the boardroom alongside Mel to work out the fine print of their undertaking. Nick said nothing when the phrase 'in perpetuity' cropped up at least seven times. Well, he was getting fifty thousand pounds, and the practice was benefitting to the tune of one hundred and fifty thousand pounds directly.

'I've got a few immediate matters I'd like the firm to deal with.'

'Of course, Mr Greenberg, you can just see Nick when it's convenient.'

Mel snickered, clicking his tongue, shoving a cigar in his

mouth like Archie Bunker while he waited for the documents to be reviewed.

Fisher was still poring over the documentation with falcon-like intensity, his fingers scrolling the words like talons of prey.

'Clause 4.2b seems to be a little restrictive, Mr Greenberg.'

'I'm putting up all the capital for this venture.'

'Yes, quite. I'm just saying it makes young Nick here very – how can I put this delicately? – indentured, should he fall foul of his obligations. Still, ultimately, it's his choice.'

'Well, it's a shot in the dark with *my* money. Nick has no previous experience running a record label. It's not an even wager by any standards. I'm taking a header with no guarantee of return.'

'True, but he's a young lad. If things get complicated, this clause ties him to you for life." Fisher's monotone voice muffled the atmosphere with doubt. Mel was firm:

'He has nothing now, nothing at all. He can't afford to pass on this.' Nick's eyes became earnest:

'I think the clause has to be there for Mr Greenberg's protection,' He wanted to clinch the deal without any hiccups or legal headaches.

Nick knew that Fisher was leeching the situation by faking concern for him.

It was the same old story: push more paper, pad out the bills. Old Fisher was just like Mel, sharking for victims in the same pond but with different MO.

'Mr Greenberg – I'll arrange for the papers to be forwarded to you by the end of the week, so if you'll excuse me, I have some other matters that need my attention.' Fisher nodded and left the room.

'What a royal plonker. Sorry Nick, no offence, but the man's a real dick. I mean, I'm giving it to you on a platter, like a geisha in a tea house, and he's treating me like a class-

A villain. I mean fuck me – I just handed your smarmy law firm hundreds and thousands of pounds and that fuckwit treats me like a regular Mr Small balls a shrivel fuck. It's not right. Nick, come 'ere son.' Nick seemed abashed by Mel's colourful language but said nothing.

Mel inched closer. Nick could see the little red veins mapping the bridge of his nose circling towards his large open mouth. He felt like a clam in the jaws of a raccoon. Still, he managed to look interested rather than unnerved.

'One thing, Nick, you must always remember: you don't screw family, and you don't screw anyone who screws harder than you. Understand?'

Nick arched his head forward in a kind of embarrassed acquiescence, only to have Mel reach up and plant a smacker straight on his lips. Nick pulled away, his cheeks flushing beetroot and his eyes lowering.

'Come on, boy, let's celebrate. You've got a record company and you're a lawyer. Anything's possible! Listen, I'll be sending some associates of mine over who need your legal expertise after lunch. Make sure you sort them out. In the meantime, let's go and have a slap-up meal at Scalini's in Knightsbridge. Best Italian food on the planet. Just like mamma used to make.' He beamed, flashing his Hollywood fangs.

Scalini's, a favourite of the footballer, the wag in training and the recycled celeb. With a homely, Italian charm, it was a great place to get boozed, and loaded on lobster. Mel was a regular and, as with all regulars, enjoyed a welcome reserved for VIPs and English royalty. They were seated by a large bay window on small cushioned chairs.

'Oh dear, oh dear – you would 'ave thought they could make these chairs a little bigger.

I need more room. They pack too many tables too close together.' Mel's blubber belly was squished up in front of him like a set blancmange.

Nick pretended to sympathise but his eyes were focused on the photo gallery of the rich, the famous, the has-beens and the unknowns. Stacks of pictures framed the ceiling; snapshots of time freezing each second, for now and ever more.

Well I suppose they're a good talking point if you're stuck with someone like Mel for lunch. He moved the table closer to him to give Mel more legroom.

'Ah, you're checking out all the celebs, eh, Nick? Bit of a punter are you?'

'Yeah, I was just thinking, the way they've placed all the photos is really clever because you still get a lot of light from the ceiling.'

'Yeah, it has a wonderful airiness to it, like eating in a conservatory. I do enjoy that aspect of the place, very nice.'

'Do you come here because it's the place to be seen or because of the food?'

'Both. It's a fantastic place to do business. I've sealed many a deal here, and of course it has some of the best Italian south of Turin,' responded Mel, as if he'd been asked this question several times before.

'There's so much to choose from,' Nick said politely trying his best to fill dead air.

He hated passing the time with inane chit-chat, especially with Mel. He didn't want to think too deeply about what was in store for him.

'What's your favourite food?'

'Steak.'

'They do a lovely T-bone here, melts in your mouth. Just slides off the plate.' Mel curled his fingers into a circle, kissing them like a showy gourmet chef. 'Beautiful steak, lovely.'

'What are you going to have?'

'Oh, my usual.'

Of course, Mel would have a usual.

'And what's that?'

'To start, I'll 'ave the avocado *caldo*, then I'll 'ave the

Megadiloni di manzo Stefano. Later, if there's room, the tiramisu.'

'Sounds good.'

I don't understand the pull of this place. It looks like a tarted-up version of a high street bistro. Tabloid glitterati doesn't make it cool. I hope the food's fucking amazing. The walls are all full of somebodies trying hard to be more than nobody, but in the end we're all just ourselves. Why do we need public validation? What's the point of it? That kind of love isn't real love. That kind of love is nobody's love.

The waitress came over. She was cherry-pie sweet, with a golden tan, flutter-furl eyelashes, and a gutsy full-bodied Italian accent:

'*Buongiorno*, what can I get for you today?'

'You know what I want don't ya, darling?'

'Yes, of course, Mr Mel, and what will you be drinking today?'

He turned to Nick. 'In the mood for a tipple?'

'Sure.'

'Let's have a couple of Stolis?'

'Certainly.'

'And what would you like?'

Nick was dreading this moment, unsure of whether to do a two-bit cornball attempt at pronouncing the dishes in Italian, or opting for the safe English version written underneath. He decided to stick to what he knew.

'I'll have the T-bone. And to start – the *Ca-la-mari* …'

'*Luciana*, *si*, that's my favourite,' she blossomed. 'How would you like the steak cooked?'

'Medium rare please.'

'*Bene.*'

The menus were taken away and Nick started to relax a little, listening to the clink and clatter of polished cutlery and glassware.

As they were enjoying their starters, Mel kicked off with another preachy pep talk.

'It's like this, Nick. What you have to do now is keep focused, keep your eye on the ball.'

Nick loathed these sporting terms. Not a keen footballer, he had no chummy affiliations to any one team. He listened politely, bowing to Mel's seasoned *savoir faire*.

Mel was waving his fork in the air and in between mouthfuls of beef chomped his words out.

'I'm sending over … like I say … a couple of people, you know … they've been a little bit silly, a little bit reckless … and I just want you to tell them straight. Understand? Tell them … exactly what to expect … if they get booked.'

'Booked?'

'Yeah … if they get charged, you know, if the boys in blue come knocking.'

'Well, I'm not really a criminal lawyer, I specialise—'

Mel banged the side of the table with his hand stopping Nick mid-sentence and rattling the tableware. 'Don't be a muppet, Nick. Doesn't matter what you "specialise" in, you're a lawyer, that's enough – read up on it, do what you have to do, just tell them. Understand?'

Nick couldn't refuse. He felt Mel's grip tighten around him.

'I'll do what I can.'

'You'll do what you're told, boy,' Mel chunked in between mouthfuls of food.

'Now raise your glass. Lechayim, lechayim!'

Nick chugged his vodka down with medicinal fury. It was too late to back out. His stomach turned over and his hands grew shaky as he tried to grip his spoon. *What the fuck have I signed up to? It can't be that bad*, he kept repeating to himself like a holy mantra. *It can't be that bad.*

'I run a small import-export business – had two jobbies on the take. Now they've ended up in the soup. I'll let them explain when they come see you. Crawled back to me, they did, made up some bullshit about what they were up to, but I knew, Nick. I knew exactly where they'd been and what they'd been up to.'

'Yeah.'

'Eat up, boy, don't waste good food. How's your mother

and your old man doing?'

'Okay,' shrugged Nick. This small talk with Mel was worse than watching reruns of Judge Judy on daytime TV.

'Well, think of what you can treat 'em to now, eh? Think of all the good times you can have. Maybe you can get one of those private nurses to help your poor mother. Your dad … must drive her barmy 'aving to keep watch over 'im all the time.'

'I'll talk to her about it. She's under a lot of pressure. It's hard for us all.' Nick's mind was fixed on who these ex-associates might be and the extent of their shady dealings. He might have to set up a whole new criminal department and make everything at least appear perfectly legitimate.

'Excuse me for a moment while I visit the gents.'

'Yeah, sure.'

Mel reappeared a few moments later.

'See Nick, I've given that firm of yours a monster wad of cash, bubbeleh. It's monster, and now I get all my legal work done without having to pay one lawyer for this and another for that. All the work done in the same place, just like family, Nick, just like family.' Nick peered at him nervously like a tabby cat:

'Yeah,'

'Hypothetically speaking, what's the worst you can get for say, distribution of a class-A drug?' Mel had coked himself up in the toilets and was getting ready for lift off.

'Um, I'm not sure. I'd have to look it up. You know the law changes, but it's definitely five years or more.'

'Yeah, that's what I thought, a five-year stretch, maybe longer.'

'How long depends on how much – you know, the quantity.'

'Did you hear about Eres, one of our more devout brethren?'

'No.'

'He was caught with hundreds of thousands of pills. Recruited young Hassidim – you know, the Hassidic community – to smuggle pure grams of MDMA all across the world.'

'I heard something about that but never knew the guy's name.'

'Why would you, bubbeleh, why would you? Drink up. Then it's back to the office for you. I have another two property clients and a couple of villains I need you to see, then later this evening, bubbeleh, you can concentrate on your music projects. How does that sound?'

'Good,' Nick mewled, surprised at how quiet his voice had become.

Now Mel was talking front-page drug deals and Hassidic crime cartels. *Am I in a Seth Rogen comedy, or has this man seriously asked me about organised mob syndicates? How many suitcases of gold will buy a man's soul?*

'*Il conto, per fervore*, sweetheart.' Mel scrolled the air with his index finger as if he were writing a cheque. A dimpled brunette hurriedly prepared the bill and bought it over.

'Not a lot of change out of a monkey, but it's okay, we're celebrating. Welcome to the family, Nick.' Mel put his arms out, smiling broadly and hugged him again. Nick inadvertently flinched, but this went unnoticed by Mel, who was coking the day away thinking of his next hustle.

'Get your list together,' Mel guzzled, as he shoved a wad of Orbit in his mouth.

'My list?'

'Yeah, you know, who we gonna sign first, any hot punk bands. I like a bit of fetish diva – bit of attitude. Then we got to sign a dance act, you know, 'cos all the—'

Nick, who had been trying his best to ignore Mel's incessant patter, suddenly stopped and raised his hand.

'No. No fucking way. The extra criminal clients – fine. The property clients – okay, but no fucking way are you gonna interfere in the music side of things. Either … either it's my way, my bands, my project – my bag exclusively – or the deal's off.' Nick was fuming, his eyes squinching and his cheeks smoking red.

'Relax, relax, you just tell me who you wanna sign and we'll take them on. So long as you don't slush the cash on useless Emo shit eh?'

'I-I'm sorry, it's just I feel really strongly about it.'

'I understand, bubbeleh – don't stress yourself. Calm, stay calm. Get your acts, we'll sign them.'

Nick loosened his tie and walked out of Scalini's with a fresh attitude – a kind of bravado that scared him a little. Like a watered-down version of Michael Corleone. He was experiencing a little of the dark side, and it felt better than cool – it felt almost real.

Chapter Four: Communication Breakdown

Matt, the naked guitarist, was strumming his days away on a toxic blend of Facebook fiction and bottles of Jack. A PPE student at LSE, he shared a small flat with Hermes, the roach who lived behind his refrigerator, and a homeless Tabby. He called her Nikita, in tribute to Elton John and a Moscow exchange student he'd enjoyed a summer fling with.

Matt modelled himself on Robert Plant and Jimi Hendrix. With his shaggy blond hair and leather fringed coat, he looked more like a fucked-up version of Bjorn Borg, the 1970s' tennis star. Matt walked with a pimp limp and often wore super tight denim and stacked Cuban heels. Originally from Huddersfield, he finished his sentences with the word 'man', which he repeated in a long, West Coast American drawl. He was jossing out on incense and ganja when the phone rang.

'Heeey, man.'

'You okay?'

'Heeey, Nick, good to hear from you, maaan. Thought you were the landlord dicing me for cash.'

'No, dude. Now listen up, I've got some cool news – great news in fact.'

'Shoot.'

'You know that deal I was trying to land – the music deal?'

'Yeahhh, maaan.'

'Well it's done.'

'Like done as in you've got more business meetings to attend to and various people to screw? Or done like the needle's on the record?'

'Yeah. The deal's done. The money's in the firm's account, and we're ready to rock and groove.'

'Sooo, what you mean—'

'Not joking, dude, I have loads-a-money to play with.'

'As in Simon Cowell loads—'

'Please don't mention that pop puppeteer of plastic in this divine moment of peace. Get ready to jam. We need to celebrate. Our number's come up! This is everything we wanted now we can have complete artistic control of our own stuff and run a label.'

'You're serious?'

'Deadly.'

'Hmmm, careful Nick. If you've been given a stack of cash, whose bitch are you? Who do you belong to for that kind of loot?'

'Nobody, it's a me-myself-and-I deal.' Nick gritted his teeth and rubbed his brow, a silent drama brewing in his head.

Of course, I belong to Mel now, but that doesn't mean I can't do good with this money. I can make a change with this money. I can be free with this money.

'I decide the project, I decide the ride. In fact, the crazier the concept, the easier it will be to make it happen.'

'I don't like the way you're talking, Nicholas. You sound a little powered-up, a little fucking insane, and it's only 8.30 a.m.'

'Time money – money time. Bands need money. We got to hit now.'

'Let me finish my pizza.'

'It's 8.30 in the fucking morning and you're trolling pizza down your gut?'

'Yeah, why, did you power pack sushi or some kind of

Tibetan elixir?'

'No, but pizza at this time is kind of sketchy.'

'Look man, I was on Facebook until 3 a.m. posting the usual combination of sex, lies and cyber trash. I have 4,562 "fans" and need to keep them happy. Domino's had a special deal, a two-for-one meat combo.'

'Dude, you're a twenty-seven-year-old post-grad student living in a studio on a perennial government grant. You need to step away from the internet and focus.'

Shit, he used that word – the Mel word – focus. He really shouldn't have used that word, but Matt knew how to rock his chain.

'Er, it's a post-grad scholarship actually, and Domino's and FB hit the right note.'

'Okay, whatever, dude, but you gotta listen. That guy I told you about – Melvin Maurice Greenberg?'

'Yeah.'

'Well, he delivered. Came over to the office and in front of old Fisher stuck £200,000 spondoolicks on the table. Even get the title of VP.'

'VP, as in visible prat who shows his panty line?'

'Shut up – look, are you in or what?'

'You're scared as hell aren't you?'

Once again Matt had him sussed. Nick downplayed his concern.

'Yeah, of course I'm a little apprehensive. Mel Greenberg's like a cheap version of Al Capone without the Italian pizzazz.'

'That's heavy duty. He doesn't need pizzazz. He seems to have what it takes to get the party started. What's his cut?'

'Well, he said he just needs the names of the bands I wanna take on, and I have to deal with some of his extra work.'

'Yeah, – extra as in first rate gangsters, drugs, prostitution, God only knows what else. Sounds like you'll be knee-deep with the fishes. Don't do it. Back out.'

'Too late. I've signed the deal and taken the hit.'

'Shit, you even sound like Mafiosi now – you've taken the hit! Listen to yourself, Nick.'

'Look, all I know is I signed the papers and we have the money.'

C'mon Nick - you know the score. This Mel guy has probably got zero interest in what bands you sign or any of that – he just needs a squeaky clean law firm to front his dodgy dealings and legitimise his shifty business plans. You were ripe for the picking.'

It's a sound deal Matt don't be so negative.'

'You sure you never signed a clause for your first born in there? And what about us?'

'You mean the band?'

'Yeah. Or did you forget about us?'

'Look we'll sign us both to the label that way I can still jam and rehearse with you guys and we can all get paid and wasted. Sound good?'

'Biggest sell-out ever- Nicholas. You fucked up. You signed the three-sixty deal. A piece of everything you ever do will always get signed away. Fair play to Mr Greenberg. He stitched you up like a kippah.'

'I know what risks I'm taking – You can't stand around like a fucking tourist all your life. Sometimes Matt, you got to get messy.'

'Sell out.'

'Listen if you wanna be on a big label or any label, you have to sell a little piece of yourself. You got to do what's necessary Matt.'

'Necessary and right aren't the same thing.'

'Meet me later. There's a gig at The Cuckoo Club – a girl band – we can discuss this properly then. I'll put your name on the door.'

'Fuck off Nick. You sound like a proper twat.'

'It's a closed gig. I need to let them know who's coming. Look Matt It's about adapting if you want your dreams to become real and not confined to stories before bedtime – you just have to roll with it.'

'Whatever, dude. See you later, it will take much more than a promise of major finance to get me to bend over and sign my life away. One thing I have is artistic integrity, and I don't belong to anyone.'

He clicked off. Away from cyber vision, Matt was eating TV dinners at dawn, smoking cigarettes and stewing his nights away on half-baked promises and lies. He was almost desperate for a break but refused to cave. Matt was holding out for the big one, the mother of all record deals, because he knew he was worth more.

I'll work on him later. Nick needs me like a hook needs a baseline.

Chapter Five: When a Man loves a Woman

Since Mel had graced the firm with such a handsome retainer, Nick had been provided with a swanky new office (strictly reserved for the highest earners) and a secretary of his own, Sylvie Wildfire. She had Betty Boo curves and smoky eyes. Today she was dressed in a tight-fitting wrap dress cinched at the waist with a black leather belt. She wore patent red stilettos and had an infectious Brook Street giggle. Originally from sunny Queensland, she took dictation at lightning speed, could type over one hundred words a minute, and was always chewing gum.

'Hey there, Mr Stringer, my name's Sylvie Wildfire – you can call me Sylvie.'

'Great – Nick's fine.'

'Okie dokie. I've organised your diary. Mr Greenberg has sent along two gentlemen to see you. They never had appointments, but Mr Greenberg was insistent that you see them today. They're in reception.'

'Okay, do you have their names or any other information?'

'Yep, it's all in the file I opened on your desk, but they refused to explain what it was about. They said it was personal.'

'No problem. How long have they been waiting?'

'Oh, only about ten minutes or so.'

'Okay, send them in. Thanks Sylvie.'

She wiggled away, swerving her hips in a Mae West crush.

'Check 'er out, she's a sort,' Ronnie tittered.

'Yeah, very tasty,' heaved Steve coughing loudly.

The two men were in their late forties and spoke with burnt cackles. Ronnie had silver-tipped dark hair that he slicked to the side in a Brylcreem mess. His scalp was caked with tiny pink sores which he tried to conceal with a mass of bristling waves that formed an uneven greasy snake pattern on his crown. All he needed was some sensitive shampoo to treat it, but he was too set in his ways to try it. He wore size XXL denim with an adjustable waistband and a baggy green sports shirt covered by a cheap leather jacket that was lined in polyester and made in China. It was slim-cut, cuffed at the sleeves and hemmed with ribbed elastic, causing his chubby gut to flab awkwardly in front of him.

Steve sat opposite, he was scrawny with a cleft chin a distinguishing feature he believed gave him a film-star polish, but in truth it looked like a hollow groove denting the centre of his face. His powder-blue eyes weeping and watery due to persistent conjunctivitis caused by an acute allergy to his cat, Omelette. Steve wore a Next suit that boasted Italian design and high-quality cloth, but, due to its starched simplicity and his lanky frame, exuded more of a Tesco vibe. He had a foamy white head of hair barking back to his glory punk days, streaked with luminescent hints of solid platinum that gave him an Andy Warhol sheen. Secretly he thought he was a dead ringer for Billy Idol, but this was definitely wishful thinking on his part. His chalky hue and whitish eyelashes evoked concern and sympathy from strangers, who thought him jaundiced, anaemic, or worse.

They entered Nick's office with a use them and loose them arrogance as if they had seen off hundreds of lawyers before and would do so again.

'Please sit down.'

Jesus they look like extras from Layer Cake.

'I'm Nick Stringer. You can just call me Nick.'

First Ronnie, and then Steve, stood up to shake Nick's hand. Ronnie's grip was hard and tight, his salmon-coloured fingers and dry scabby nails callousing Nick's smooth touch. Steve's hands were ice cold; they felt like steel spindles spiking his skin.

Both stared at him intently as if he was the cause of all their misfortune.

'So, Mr Greenberg arranged the appointment. I hope you didn't have a long wait?'

'Nah,' Steve winced, his leather face chapped with pain.

'Are you okay?'

'It's the IBS – stomach cramps – it'll pass.'

'Would you like some water or?'

'No – get used to it – you was sayin?'

'Mel – Mr Greenberg – said something about you both being charged with Grievous Bodily Harm, both of you facing the same charge. Is that right?'

'Yep,' Ronnie sniffed and wiped his nose.

'Okay, well, perhaps you can tell me what happened and who it was you allegedly attacked.'

Nick was all too aware of his position: on the one hand, he had to contend with two obvious psychotic morons, and on the other he had to get some sort of 'result' to appease Mel, hovering in the background like a ticking time bomb.

'You tell it, Ronnie while I catch me breath.'

'Well it was silly really. We were boozing over at PT's and 'ad just done a bizzo deal. Everyone was tanked-up and ready to go when I get this call.'

'Sorry, what's PT's?'

'The Purple Turtle.'

'Right.'

'Well it's me old dear on the blower and it was me ex what turned up on 'er doorstep effing and blinding and wielding a hammer to my muvvah's door. I mean, fuckin"ell, a fucking hammer to my muvvah's door!' Ronnie lifted his arms to demonstrate.

'His muvvah is a darlin', she's a – beautiful woman.'

'I could 'ear 'er screamin' down the phone, so I get 'old of Steve and we leg it down there.'

'Right,' Nick nodded.

'When we got there we found my ex's new fella trying it on with me mum. 'E's got her hostage while the pair of 'em are going round the 'ouse grabbing stuff. You know, flat-screen telly electrics, some jewellery, a couple of quality antiques and my stereo.'

Nick was making notes, occasionally looking up at a natural break in the conversation.

'I see.'

'Well, it was the ultimate disrespect.' Ronnie let out a long sigh. 'I got 'er free.'

'And . . . um, how did you do that?'

'I gave the ex's fella a slap while Steve held 'er back.'

'Sorry, you'll have to give me a little more information.'

'I whacked him in the face with my fists until he was bleedin' all over my hands, and then I warned 'im if 'e ever ever disrespects my muvvah again I'll fuckin' kill 'im. We let 'em go but the ex called the old bill on us, and next thing we know we've been arrested and are down the cop shop.'

'Did you have a duty solicitor Ronnie?' Nick continued.

'No we 'ad a brilliant brief who got us bail. Told them how my old dear, seventy-five years old and registered disabled 'cos of her gammy knee, was terrified out of 'er brain, so we was bailed but still charged with GBH.'

'Do you have a charge sheet or any other documentation?'

'Nah, but the name of the brief is Robbie Gunner.'

Nick had heard of him. He had a sterling rep for getting the young, hot, and dangerous out of trouble. He was a super league lawyer and always got the right result. *I'm just being used to mop up the slops,* Nick thought dismally.

'I'll get the papers. You were obviously released on police bail, so can you remember when you have to go back?'

Ronnie looked at Steve and back at Nick: 'Nah, Gunner's

got all the info. He's retiring soon or somethin', so 'e'll be expecting your call.'

'Okay.'

'What's the worst that can 'appen?' Asked Steve

'Well, I'll have to check the charge sheet to see exactly what you've been charged with. If it's a section 20 we should be able to come up with a convincing defence. If it's a section 18 it could be tricky.'

'Yeah, section 18 of the Offences Against the Person Act 1861, also referred to as 'wounding with intent' or 'causing GBH with intent'. Very serious and likely to be detained at HM leisure for many moons to come.' Ronnie puffed putting on a posh-snot accent.

'Unlikely we was charged under sec 18. We wouldn't 'ave made bail otherwise.'

Nick wasn't impressed by their legal know-how. Steve probed further:

'No offence or nuthin', but we was expecting top-drawer service.'

'Don't worry. I'll do what it takes to get the right result,' Nick replied, surprised at his own confidence. He started drumming the table, whistling the Stealers Wheels tune, 'Clowns to the left of me, jokers to the right, here I am, stuck …'

Neither Steve nor Ronnie spotted it.

Steve continued: 'Glad to 'ear it. Mel said you was good.'

Then Ronnie piped up:

'Yeah, we don't mean any disrespect. We was expecting someone – 'ow can I put this – a bit more mature. Someone who's bin round the block a bit. We don't need a textbook brief. We need a proper lawyer who'll tell us 'ow to get off.'

'I can't make any promises. I have to see what you've been charged with and take it from there. It all depends on the evidence. Did the vict—. Did the individual … um … was he hospitalised for his injuries, do you know?'

'I should bloody well hope so!' steamed Ronnie.

'We was taken to the nick, that's all we know,' Steve

surmised.

'Okay, leave it with me. I'll give you a call in a couple of days.'

'Nice doing bizzo with you, Nick. Mel knows 'ow to get in touch with us c'mon Steve we got bizzo to do.'

The two men got up at the same time leaving the door ajar.

So these were Mel's gangsters. Could they escape a GBH charge? He could try self-defence – better if they just disappeared altogether.

'It's Mr Greenberg on the line, sir.' Sylvie had interrupted Nick's corrosive train of thought.

'So you've met Mumbo and Jumbo then?'

'Er, Mumb—, sorry I—'

'You know. Red Ronnie, Soppy Steve – cries over all those Disney flicks – soppy bastard.'

'Oh yes, yes. They've just this minute left.'

'What are their chances, or do they 'ave to go on a nice long holiday?'

'They said their papers were with their other solicitor, a Mr Gunner?'

'I'll 'ave them sent to you pronto.'

'Once I've had a look at all the documents, I can have a better understanding of the case and assess their chances.'

'What does your gut instinct tell ya, boy?' Nick was reluctant to respond but decided to be frank.

'My instinct tells me they're both going down.'

'That's what I needed to hear. You're learning, Nicholas, you're learning.'

Later that day, Nick received the file from Gunner and a handwritten note that read: '*Satisfaction is annihilation.*' He thought about it for a while and then called Matt. They agreed to meet around eight.

'Sylvie, can you get a list of serviced offices around here and get these new letterheads to the printers?'

'Oooh, very swish. Is this for your new record label?'

'Yeah.'

'I like the logo. Who did that?'

'Superman's always been my inspiration, so Soopa Records makes perfect sense.'

'Very cool.'

'Well it's bold, distinctive – smacks you in the face.'

'I'll get to it straight away.'

'I've also done a tape on the two clients from this morning – here's their file. Oh, and send out the ad copy I've drafted for *NME*, *Mojo*, and *The Stage*. For the web: all territories, all publications. It's on the end of the tape.'

'Okay – fine I'll run it by you first and then get it in for print and online.'

'Sylvie, there's also a stack of files on various other matters that I've left on your desk.'

'On it.'

Nick was sourcing another office space for the record company, sending out trade ads for new personnel and emerging talent. His mind was jammed with fresh swag. The question was, could he deliver?

If someone tried to attack my mother, I'd probably do the necessary, he thought. Then with an involuntary shrug of his shoulders he conceded, *No, if someone tried to attack my mother, I'd knock his bloody head off.*

Chapter Six: I Like to Boogie

The laboured decadence of The Cuckoo Club repelled Matt into bitchy overdrive.

'Ugh, can't stand these pink curtains, they're like cast-offs from an Alan Carr charity bash, all chintz and chav. This décor is sooo nouveau masquerading as cool.'

His date, super-hot, super-privileged, and super-bratty, was dressed in leather, lace, and lascivious eye make-up. She was a brooding combo of Winehouse eroticism mixed with the marbled perfection of Dita Von Teese. With her blood-kissed lips and sultry stare, she knew she brought the heat and could turn it on and off to perfection. She spoke in a lush-hush combo of LA and Moscow.

'I quite like eeeit.'

'Yeah, exactly. Over-bred self-indulgent glitzy crap.'

The cocktail waitress was dressed in a fetish-inspired rubber number, rocked with zips, studs, and metal rivets, but the themed reticence of it made her look like an elongated sex dummy with vocals.

'Please be seated. There's a free bar, and two beetroot Martinis for you to try,' she had a husky velvet voice.

'Thanks,' Matt answered for both of them.

'And now ladies, gents, esteemed members of the paparazzi, boys and girls of the music press, moochers, star liggers and premium hangers-on, please give a warm welcome to the *Kandy Sluts*, the coolest female line-up since

Siouxsie and The Banshees.'

'Matt! You made it!' Nick was wearing a Clash tee-shirt and some faded jeans ripped at the knee. His hair was tussled with fresh highlights, turning him from legal dork to Hollywood crush.

'Whoa, look at you. Last week you were about as attractive as Ricky Gervais with piles, and now look at you, a hunk of destruction. Ladies, beware, Nick has arrived!'

'Shut the fuck up Matt you're embarrassing me. Seriously, who's this?'

'No intro needed for the divine, the delectable, the daring Dominica Mordashov,' rolled Matt, as if announcing a circus act.

'Charmed to make your acquaintance.' She put out her delicate little paw hooked with falsies and a rock the size of her nose.

'Likewise.'

'Nick's breaking new talent. He's got a record label.'

'Cool.'

'Yeah, Nick wants to be the next Simon Cowell.'

'Fuck off Matt.'

'Is this your band?' asked Dominica.

'They want me to manage them.'

'Cool.'

'We'll see.'

Eight bottles of Cris later, upstairs in the VIP room where management had set up a karaoke machine, Matt, Nick and their trailing entourage were getting loaded.

'All I see is suits, sunglasses, and oversized handbags,' Nick complained.

'You should have elves here dispensing cocaine. Now that's coolalicious.'

'Earth to Matt are you in fucking Fraggle Rock?'

'Just making the point, to make this gig super sick you need coke-dispensing elves. Guaranteed to be the most talked about rave in town. Elves always turn an event into a happening." Nick shook his head and cleared his throat:

'It's time to parteee!' He bellowed. Tanked-up and ready to rumble, he had lost his shy-boy edge.

'Billie Jean's not my love, she's just a girl that claims that I am the one, on the dance … ow!'

Thrusting his groin and gooching the dance floor like a deranged jack-in-the-box, he was whacking out to the music and finking the beat like a pro, his voice cutting through the booze-ripped air like a switchblade on ice.

Dominica joined him, crumping around like a ghetto babe, complete with exaggerated booty humps and over-stressed arm waves.

'Billie Jean's not my lover … whooo yeah, whooo yeah … she's just a girl that claims that I am the one … on the dance, whooo!' She honked while showboating her moves. He spun her round and threw her in the air. Now the floor was filling up with other scenesters, keen to get their piece of bad.

'You can really move it,' gushed an energised indie chick, too laid-back to be hip, but with enough urban slickness to blend in. She wore pencil-slim skinny jeans and a dip-dyed silver tee. With her multi-buckle platforms, cosmic-blue hair, and Crayola-gold nail polish, she was in a class of her own. Nudging forward, she strut-looped and criss-crossed in front of Nick until they were only inches apart.

'So, are you like in a band or something?'

Before Nick could answer, Dominica butted in.

'No, he's a manager, owns Soopa Records, so he's actually very boring.'

'And you are?'

'Dominica.'

'Riiight, are you and …?'

'Nick,' she chimed, with cut-throat superiority.

'Are you and Nick together?'

'We're not fucking, but I like him,'

'I don't need that kind of hassle,' the indie chick turned her back on Dominica.

'Wait, don't go yet.' Nick pulled her arm gently then

shouted out to Matt.

'Matt, get over here.'

Matt was oblivious, doing lines of coke with three burlesque dancers.

'Not now man. I'm busy.'

'Listen … er, Nick. I'm just here to get wasted on the music. I really don't need any complications.'

'Don't stress it. There's nothing going on between me and that frosty princess. Come on, have a drink with me.'

Dominica arched her eyebrows and flounced off to Matt's table, leaving them alone.

'My name's Nick … well, you know that already —'

'I know your … er …'

'Yeah, the Russian Rottweiler. I just met her. She's with a friend of mine. She's very forward. Has Paris Hilton delusions.'

'Ahhh, but whereas Paris is kind of cool, she comes off as a spoilt Tori Spelling minus the humanity.'

'You're pretty funny, you know that?'

'I have to be, it's my USP.'

'Oh yeah?'

'Yeah, what's yours?'

'What's my what?'

'Your thing … your unique selling point.'

'Ha, I guess that would be my ultra-nerdish perspective on life.'

'I don't think that counts.'

'No?'

'Nope. It's a little hard seeing you that way. I mean, you're in one of London's most exclusive hangouts, you have your pick of deluxe hotties, your own record label, and this whole show was put on for the benefit of a group *you* may manage, so I don't think you can honestly call yourself a nerd.'

'I'm just starting out, you know.'

'Yeah sure.'

'Now you think you know all about me – what about

you?'

'My day job, you mean?'

'If you like.'

'I'm a journo.'

'You are?'

'Yeah, I work for *The Daily Post.*'

'Enjoying it?'

'I'm a junior reporter. It's my second year.'

'Great.'

'Yeah – still looking for my Watergate.'

'You'll find it. It just takes time and a lot of digging.'

'Well, I have my shovel ready.'

They smiled at each other.

'I'm not going to sleep with you. I wouldn't like to take advantage of a guy in club – anyway you seem pretty blitzed.'

'That's true. I'm bombed … feel invincible. I wasn't going to ask you home.'

'Hmmm, maybe not tonight. Call me, okay? 702 3415. And so you won't forget, I'll write it on this.' She scrawled her number on the back of a condom packet and placed it in the inside of Nick's jacket.

'Aww, don't leave yet, we'll be winding down soon – there's only a few more minutes. If you hang around, I'll sing for you.'

'Something dreamy?'

'Sure.'

The mellow warmth of the night was growing on them. People were slow jiving and chilling out.

'Hey, I never asked your name.'

'Avery.'

'Ahhhh Avery just rolls of the tongue. '

'Blame it on Captain Sisko. '

'Star Trek- Deep Space Nine – of course. '

Avery's eyes were bright, shiny, fixed on Nick. No one had ever made the connection before. She was named after an American TV star.

'We have time for one more song Nick – will you do the

honours?' The MC turned to face him.

Silence hit the room and Nick slid in for the final track of the night. It was close to 3 a.m. Matt was propped up by the bar, the Kandy Sluts were in the front row and Dominica was lounging on a table snogging an Argentine polo player, while Avery leant forward, her chin, in her hands floating the moment.

'I know the routine. Put another nickel in that there machine … Feeling so bad …'

Melting the stillness of dawn, Nick's rendition of the Sinatra classic was exquisitely raw, bruised with hurt and a baking honesty. Nick knew he could sing, but away from the alcohol he never had enough spunk to try. As he held the last note, he thought of Anicha, once more the tender ruffle of his voice lifting him to cloud nine.

'Fuck me, love it when the boy sings!' Matt was clapping and wolf whistling, kicking off a chain reaction of drunken applause and hoots of appreciation from the VIP crowd.

Nick stumbled off the stage, making his way back to the bar.

Avery was on her feet cheering wildly.

'You have an amazing voice.'

'It's not that great. I have to be pretty laced to get through a song.'

'You should be a pro. Your voice is beautiful.'

'Hey, I appreciate the compliments, but I'm slammed with work. Gotta run. Perhaps we can hook up this week?'

'Perhaps.' Then she kissed him full on the lips.

Nick saw the danger in her eyes he knew Avery was trouble with a capital T.

Chapter Seven: A Hard Day's Night

Mel was on the phone, in Pau. He had organised a big job, importing several kilos of coke and some grass. With him were Jimmy Squash, Terry Carroll (Tezza) and Buster the boxer pup. Terry had a buzz cut combo, the back clipped to the length of around half an inch and the front an Elvis quiff slick backed with Dax wax. With his thuggish oversized lips and close-set piggy-piggy eyes, he looked like a top brass mobster. He was around five foot eight and had a squat-rot complexion pitted with scars. His face was shadowed with five days' fuzz. He wore a button down Ralph Lauren shirt and navy-blue trousers from Reiss. He was fish cold and spoke with a distinctive 'sauf London' spit, chucking vowels and syllables in the air and dropping his aitches with feisty aplomb. Terry had personally been responsible for the grisly killing of at least ten people caught up in Mel's dirty cons. alongside him stood Jimmy Squash, a large freckle-faced man with a square-set head dusted with orange stubble. He was a terrifying hybrid of 1950s' Frankenstein mixed with mythical Minotaur, his face a sand ball of ginger floss and zits. Jimmy had earned his colourful soubriquet not because of his peachy hue but because he could squash a man's skull in less than a minute flat.

Mel was trafficking cocaine and cannabis across the French–Spanish border and had handpicked his crew, but of course he relied on a network of traffickers who controlled the border between France and Spain, keeping in close contact with key members of the Guardia Civil.

Mel already had a deal in place with the Spanish police. It was a simple and highly effective strategy. One car serves as a 'ringer', a vehicle that's deliberately tugged by border control. It was a tried and tested con: bribe the officer on guard, agree to target a specific car, prearrange the time it would be stopped, and ensure that, there's only a limited amount of gear in the ringer, leaving the rest of the haul free to pass security, with no checks.

Mel had three British cars with 13 kilos of uncut cocaine. He was looking at a street value of hundreds of thousands of pounds. Mel would send it off to a distribution hub where it was mixed with cheaper stimulants like speed, caffeine, and, on occasion, veterinary worming tablets and pain killers. The Spanish rental car – the ringer – was rigged with 15 kilos of cannabis earmarked for a customs seize. Mel had run the con several times before without any hassle.

'We got a problem.'

Mel was flicking dandruff from his collar then, burying his fat mitt in Boxers' coat.

'Everything's gone through, but the ringer had young Phil and his girlfriend as driver and passenger.'

'Fuckin' 'ell, Phil 'the pill' Drummond and his fiancée. Michael's gonna blow it. 'E'll go fuckin' ballistic.'

'Always statin' the obvious aren't ya, Jimmy.'

''Ow did this 'appen Boss?'

'You tell me Tezza. Both of you fuckin' morons let me down. I told everyone what car should go through and that we needed someone drivin' the car who knows the ropes, not a fuckin' cabbage with girlfriend in tow.'

'I don't understand it – Michael cleared it 'is end. Said it was all okay - the grass would be tugged. We sorted it and double-checked everything didn't we Tezza?' Jimmy looked flummoxed.

'Where was the drop?'

'Collection point boss – opposite KFC, -underground car

park near Estepona,' Jimmy replied with robotic precision. Terry put both of his hands on the side of his head.

'Yeah, we left the keys, package, the lot, at the KFC in Fuengirola.'

'Well, lads, according to Phil's lot, 'e was takin' his bird across the border for a secret getaway and now they're both busted, sitting pretty in Pau, Nick.' Mel stuck a match in his mouth and began chewing the tip.

Phil was the eldest son of one of England's most notorious crime families. A self-confessed hippie who had no stomach for his father's mob ring. He was an unrepentant romantic in love with his childhood sweetheart Lindsay. 'D'you fink Phil's bird was in on it boss?' Mel looked at Jimmy as if he was a sovereign numbskull.

'She's nineteen years old, works as beautician in the suburbs. Thinks Phil's old man got 'is money from buying and selling houses and renting student flats. Course she wasn't in on it.'

'What about the others, boss?'

'They're all safe.'

'Michael will be going nuts, with his pride and joy locked up in some French clink for months on end.'

'Leave Michael to me Tezza. Phil and Lindsay will just 'ave to lump it. Now, get me that Kim Li over tonight, will ya.'

'Again?'

'You know me, always fancy a bit of Chinese. Oh, and, get Stringer on the phone, it's time he started earning his keep. Tezza, I want you and Jimmy to accompany our legal beaver over 'ere and explain 'e has to use all 'is charms to convince our two young lovers to keep their mouths shut.'

'Got it boss.'

Mel spent the rest of the night rock-socking Kim Li. Terry and Jimmy left on Easy Jet and were back in London before midnight. The following day Nick got an urgent text from

Mel: *Mr Carroll will come by the office at 10 p.m. Call me on his arrival.*

Terry landed at Nick's office soon after. Clumping through reception, he was stopped by security.

'Yes, sah.' The security guard, a tall Nigerian man with glossy ebony-rich skin and an overly genteel manner, was not used to dealing with such ruffians, especially so late in the evening.

'Can I help you, sah?'

'I need to see Stringer.'

'Ah yes, Mr Stringer from …?'

'Yeah, Stringer.'

Terry tried to make a beeline for the lift.

'One moment, sah. I can't just let you up without being announced. You have to take your security badge with you and sign your name in the visitah's book, sah. All standard procedure, sah.'

'You havin' a laugh? I don't 'ave time to be monkeying around with all this shit.' Tezza rubbed the dust from his eyes.

'Excuse me, sah.'

'No offence, I didn't … what I meant was, I don't have time for this bollocks.'

'There is no need for such rude and offensive language, sah. I will let Mr Nick know you are here, but you must sign in.'

'Fine.'

'Now, sah. First, please fill in the information: name, parpose of business, and who you are here to see.'

'You know who I'm 'ere to see.'

'You has to write it in ze book, sah. All standard procedure, sah.'

'You got a pen? This is ridiculous … you 'ear me, fuckin ridiculous.'

'Just security, sah. All standard procedure, sah. Here is theee pen, sah.'

'Right.' With a flourish of the black ballpoint handed to

him, Terry stabbed under the marked headings. *Name: Mickey Mouse. Purpose of business: Disney ride. Who are you here to see: Donald Duck.*

'Done,' he corked.

'Thank you, sah.'

The security guard, whose name was stencilled in large white letters on a formal-looking ID badge – George Adebayo Sunday – took the visitor's log and slowly read out the entries.

'I'm sorry, sah.'

'What?'

'I can't write theees on the visitor's badge. This cannot be logged.'

'Why not?'

'Eeeet is a lie, sah.'

'A lie?'

'Yes, sah, I cannot put the parpose of your visit is to see Donald Duck, and I cannot write that you are Mickey Mouse. Eeit is not true. Eeit is a lie.'

'Just ring up and tell Stringer I'm here.'

'You have to fill in da form first.'

'I suggest you get Stringer now before I do a bit of stringing on my own,' he fumed.

'No sah, I can't do it, not unless you put in your full name and fill in the rest of the information properly.'

'Listen, you get on that phone now and bring Stringer down.'

George leant back on his stool, folded his arms, and shook his head.

'Look, sah, I don't want any trouble. I'm not a person who likes confrontation, but you are making fun of me, and I have a job to do just like you, sah. I know you think I am a person of no value, but my father told me, *Son, a tiger does not have to proclaim its tigritude.*'

'Right, yeah, all very good, George,' he snarled, spying his name badge. 'But I need to see Stringer now, not Christmas.'

'Then pleeese just tell me your name and I will do the

rest.'

'Terry.'

'Oh very good, Mr Terry,' he smiled widely flashing his perfectly symmetrical teeth. Quickly, he tore off the plastic ID card and finally rang Nick's office.

'You can go straight up sah. Fourth floor.'

'Jesus H. Christ that was such a fuckin' waste of time.'

Nick was already at the door.

'Hi, I'm N—'

'I know who you are. Fucking' twat downstairs wouldn't let me up.' Terry barged in, ignoring Nick's offer of a handshake.

'Please come in Mr …?'

'It's Terry C – Just call me Tezza. The C stands for Carroll.'

'Of course.'

'We should call Mel. Now.'

'Right.'

He pulled a phone out of his pocket, pressed automatic redial, and signalled Nick to get on the line.

'I'm wiv 'im now boss. Tosser downstairs wasted a fuckin' moon tellin' me about Nigerian proverbs – don't worry about it.'

'Nick? We need you in Pau. We'll discuss what you have to say when you get here. French lawyer will get you up to speed. You got two clients. It's a drug bust. You're travelling with Terry. It's a direct flight and then from there a short drive to me. Terry will fill you in. There's a lot riding on this. We're counting on you. You'll be travelling with Tezza and Jimmy.'

'I'll have to clear it with the French legal system. I have to notify them of my visit as a matter of professional courtesy and then arrange a formal visit. I—'

'All done, Nick.'

'How? I—'

'When you get here, I'll explain. Now, put me back on to Tezza.'

'Stick with 'im. Understand? Watch 'is every move wherever, whatever, whenever – I wanna know. Bell me back just before you leave 'is office.'

'Right, boss.'

Terry sat down and took out a pack of Mayfair Superkings.

'You can't light up in here. Smoke alarms will go off.'

'Do I look like I give a shit?'

Nick reeled back, angst-ridden.

'Don't worry. I'll put it out in five minutes.'

'I'd appreciate it.'

'I'm gonna be hangin' around for a bit. We 'ave to buzz Mel again before we leave tonight. What time do you clock off?'

'I have to go through some papers and stuff. Should be done in about ten minutes or so.'

'Got a key for this gaff?'

'A key?'

'Yeah, I don't intend waltzing around the Nigerian soothsayer just to get in the fuckin' room.'

Nick was jumpy.

'I-I don't think I can just give you a key. I mean, there's other partners here. I just can't hand out a key. There's valuable stuff in here, commercially sensitive documents and private property that belong to clients. I don't think I can—'

''Ow do the cleaners get in?'

'They have a key.'

'Exactly – welcome to your new personal cleaning assistant. Now go get me a key.'

'I suppose it will be alright – if it's only until we leave for Pau.'

'Yeah, whatever.'

Nick slumped off to Sylvie's desk and removed the spare key fob from her file tray.

Terry was smoking in the boardroom, with the door wide open. His feet stretched out on the long conference table, his left hand hiked above his head, eyeing Nick like a raven eyes a dead squirrel.

'This isn't some schoolboy outing. This is show time. You need to deliver.'

Terry was fond of this chalk-talk. It seemed to have little effect on Nick.

'Ta very much,' he ribbed, jabbing the key into his top pocket. 'You got a booze cupboard here?'

'I don't have the … er … it's locked. The drinks cabinet is actually locked.' Nick started waving the smoke away from the ceiling. 'Please can you put that out now – don't want security in here – the smoke could spark the alarm.'

'Alright – alright keep your hair on.' Terry stubbed out the cigarette with stagy sincerity.

'Now, go open the booze cupboard.'

'Fucking crap.'

'What d'ya say, Nick?'

'Nothing – have you got through to Mel yet?' Despondency flattened Nick's eyes and slowly spread over his entire face.

'It's ringin'. Hold up.' Terry was doodling on the boardroom blotter.

'Boss – got the key to the gaff, and Nick knows 'e's got to be ready to fly ASAP.' Terry leaned into the back of the chair as if he was top dog.

''Ere you are, want another word?'

'Hi. Yeah, I understand the protocol. I guess I'll just file the paperwork with Pau prison and confirm that a lawyer's visit has been arranged.'

'I'm relying on you Nick – understand?'

'Yeah.'

'Put Tezza back on.'

Nick handed the phone to Terry he shared a joke with Mel and hung up. Terry stood up stretched his arms and said:

'Right, I'm off. I'll see you in a couple of days.'

'Fine.'

Nick saw him out and rode the lift to the top floor. He was jouncing like a jelly and needed five minutes to kill the pressure of the night. He reached inside his jacket pocket for his shrooms and got ready to unwind.

I'm nothing more than Mel's pussy whipped whore George the security guard has more rope than me.

He opened the exit door to the roof, the fear of the Mistral wind sharking his back. He felt like a phoney, tied to the undergrowth with no way out. He pulled out his phone and punched redial.

'Hi, Mum. Hope everything's okay love you.' Once he'd left the message he clicked off.

He had a missed call from a number he didn't recognise and three messages from Matt. He sat on the ledge and took a dose letting his mind trip into shroom mode. This had been his preferred method of dealing with stress ever since he had tried, albeit unsuccessfully, to smoke Banana Strings at college, believing the urban myth about bananadine. Then, after reading the *Anarchist Cook Book* six times, he was convinced he could filter out the negative energies in his life via astral projections and psychoactive grooves. He had around five grams of caps, spliced with MDMA, guaranteed to give him a flower fizz. Shrooming was risky for two main reasons: under current drug laws, possession of psilocybin mushrooms had been upgraded to a class-A, which meant up to seven years in prison and, or, an unlimited fine. Add to the mix he was a practicing lawyer, and Nick was looking at serious jail time. Watching the night crawl of the traffic, he waited for his psychedelic kick. After about thirty minutes he checked his phone again, his sensory overload about to hit.

Think I'll try this number.

'Hi – It's Nick Stringer.'

The voice that curled back was soft, infused with a Courvoisier break.

'Nick –it's Avery.'

Thinking about her got Nick steamed.

'Hey Avery– what's up?'

'Just thought I'd say hi, and maybe you could buy me that drink you promised?'

'You know, it's a … I'm a …'

'Yes,' she scorched back.

'I'm on a rooftop and I've just ingested three grams of dried mushrooms,' he blurted out.

'Whoa, really?'

'Yeah.'

'So Where you at?'

'I'm at the top of my building. It's 63 Clerkenwell Road.'

'What have you got, regular liberty caps, or those fairy tale red and whites?'

'Yeah. Straight-up psilocybin, baby.' Nick was surfing loose.

'Maybe you should come down off the roof. I'm heading over.'

'Don't worry, I won't fly off. As Bill Hicks said, if I thought I could fly I'd start from the ground.'

'Pretty selfish of you to call me now. We could have tripped this one together.'

'How long will you be?'

'Give me fifteen minutes.'

'When you get here, sign in on the automatic key/fob. Just press 411 and follow the signs to the roof.'

Half an hour later, Avery appeared wearing a dove-white dress and sneakers. 'Hi...'

'Over here,' Nick whispered, drunk by the music in her voice.

They carried on talking well into the night, polychromatic city lights meshing into patches of orange and yellow sky. Nick drifted away from the conversation. His mind spangled on neon brightness, and disco bonfire swirls that were sparking the London skyline, his heart somersaulting on streams of vibrancy. Nick was blitzed on complex shapes and dot-like matrices which were freewheeling the arc of his mind. It was a manic fusion of Vegas glitz and Blackpool kitsch, his subconscious, a garden of mosaic intensity. He switched off his mobile, allowing himself to stud his groove with rivers of purple and turquoise, flecked with gold and red.

I'm skating on animated pixels. I see blocks of smarties and lollipops, the waves of sound looping around zoetic sublime. I hear angels of cacophony. Nick was submerged by the city. It was as if London was alive. He barely noticed when Avery tapped him on the shoulder:

'I need the loo.'

'What – oh yeah, it's one floor down next to the boardroom.'

She hopped in the lift and got out at the floor below. She noticed the boardroom door was ajar. Naturally curious, she saw a brown envelope sticking out of a bundle of papers. She turned it over.

'Mel Greenberg … I recognise that name.'

She was about to leave it on the desk when she heard a loud clump as if someone else was there too.

She shoved the envelope in her bag and hurried out. She left through the front entrance, whistling at Nick.

'Going home now! Catch you tomorrow! She blew him a kiss and ran off.

On Mel's orders, Terry was watching the office and Ryan was watching them both. Terry tailed Avery home, snuck in through an open window and snatched the envelope back.

Nick continued his shroom vibe, watching tail lights stretching across the horizon, morphing the road into an oasis of multi-coloured comets, fanning the city with long pleats of light that fluted the night air with kites of harmony. He would deal with everything tomorrow.

Chapter Eight: I Fought the Law and the Law Won

It was 8.30 a.m. The sun was greasing the skies with fried dirt larded with yesterday's Chinese and Indian takeout. XFM was blaring from the car radio. Nick downloaded a new track from a promising new vocalist. She had an Adele hue to her voice but was morphine grubby. Nick was juiced at the prospect of signing her. She was a keeper. Her voice charred with pain and haunted with regret. Every word she sang froze the air with drama. She was on target for an industry award and plenty of inside accolades, he was sure.

He pulled into the office car park and slammed on the brakes. Just ahead of him in his spot was Terry. *Not him again*. He opened the front window.

''Allo, guv.'

'Mr Carroll.'

'I told you – call me Tezza. Thought we could get some brekkie and 'ave a nice sit down. I'll fill you in. Mel will be in touch soon. Then we 'ave to hit the road.'

'I'm-I'm not sure, I still have to check with the Pau legal authorities that they have everything first.'

'All done, Nick. All taken care of. Mel's got the Pau lawyer on standby at the airport.'

'Well, we should just go upstairs then – make sure nothing urgent's cropped up.'

'No can do, Nick. I've agreed to meet Jimmy at a restaurant in Smithfield Market. We'll 'ave a nice breakfast and a long chat.

'Fine, I'll let the office know I'm available on my mobile and I'll be in Pau for a few days.'

'Yeah, you do that.' Terry lurched, his breath a stale mix of KP nuts and morning tar.

Nick opened the passenger door and let him in, as he dialled Sylvie.

'Hi … it's Nick … how's it going today?'

'Yeah, good thanks. You have seven messages about the Harrison case and a young lady called Avery rang. She'd like you to call her on her mobile. Mr Fisher has scheduled a staff meeting for four o'clock and there are two new cases from Mr Greenberg.'

'Okay, could you kindly reschedule my diary and let Mr Fisher know I'm away on business with a new matter. I'll be in Pau. I'm not sure for how long – just clear my diary for a few days. You can reach me on my mobile if it's urgent.'

'No worries, I'll just put your appointments back until next week and let the partners know you're working a new case.'

'Thanks Sylvie – be in touch soon.'

He ended the call.

Terry was picking nose hairs in the front mirror with tweezers then tossing them out of the window. *Fucking animal, that's disgusting. I mean who the fuck does that?* Of course, Nick said nothing and Terry continued to pull his wires.

"Jimmy – will be coming along too. Top geezer. You may 'ave seen him about?' Nick nodded.

'Oi, turn this up, it's a blindin' track.'

Nick was only too glad to drown out his barroom banter with the sweltering heat of James Brown. They ran a red light, dodged an old lady on a zebra crossing, and finally got to Smith's a few seconds later.

'Don't ya just love the breakfasts they do in' ere?'

Nick blanked him. He figured that was the best approach for now.

A young blonde armed with a pencil, menu and Cape

Town tan came over to take their order. She spoke with an upturned inflexion so every second word was like a question. 'Hey there, lovely morning?'

'Yeah, fantasticccch,' Terry ripped back, his gravel-tipped wheeze settling on the newly laid out cutlery.

'I'll order for us and Jimmy too.' He turned to the waitress. 'There'll be another one of us along shortly.'

'Okay, no problem. So what are you in the mood for today?'

'We'll all 'ave the full English with black puddin's and porridge for starters.'

'I don't want any black pudding,' moaned Nick. *Fucking cunt is even choosing what I eat. Fuck that shit. I'm not his fucking bitch.*

'It's good for yer, black pudding.'

'I don't like it,' Nick bitched.

'That's alright then, no black pudding for 'im.'

'Excellent,' she chirped, sweeping the menus away.

Terry folded his arms on the table, itching to light up.

'Tezza, I don't think you can smoke in here either.'

'I know, I know – I ain't. It's one of those nicotine subs – a fake ciggie. That's all, a pretend fag.'

'Thought it was real.' Nick shrugged his shoulders as if they were buckled to an invisible strait jacket. He was struggling with heartburn.

'So what d'ya do after I left?'

Nick was in no mood for small talk. He didn't want Terry knowing about his shroom and boom romp with Avery.

'Nothing much – caught up with some paperwork.'

'Saw you on the roof.'

'What?'

'Yeah, I saw you on the fuckin' roof.'

'I-I had to get some air.'

This Orwellian voyeurism is suffocating. Fucking Terry is omnipresent.

'You know we got your back.'

He tilted his chair forward, roughing up his trouser leg

with his hand as he rubbed his shin.

'And your front, ha!' Jimmy clacked as he strutted over.

'We've ordered the full English.'

'Tasty.'

'And the food ain't bad either.'

Nick was tired of their tabloid lechery, and a little embarrassed. Their caricatured crassness would have been laughable had it not been for the fact that they bought into it lock, stock and barrel.

The waitress set their food down. 'This will put hairs on your chest. Be careful, Nick, you don't know what could happen in the middle of the night on the fucking roof,' Terry hooted.

Nick responded with yet another shoulder shrug. He wished he could shoot them both in the head.

'Now, Nick, it works like this. You owe us, see?' Terry's eyes were clamped on his.

'Yeah, I know.'

'That means wherever, whenever whatever, you're always there. Not on a roof, not on voicemail, not taking your grandma to tea. Your balls belong to the family, understand?'

Nick was doing his best not to buckle into fits of laughter. He wondered whether the recycled wherever–whatever phrase was like a brainwashing technique Mel had instilled in them. He wanted to explain it was an ad line for a hotel chain but decided against it.

Let's just play it their way.

'I get it.'

'Good, let's eat.'

Jimmy motioned the waitress over.

'More tea please, darlin'.'

'Right away.'

'You know why we're sending you to Pau?'

'Yeah.'

'We need you to get word to the two muppets inside to keep schtum. Phil's the first born of one of the biggest crime families in Europe, but 'e's not fit for the job. Phil's what you might call a dreamer. 'Asn't got a bad bone in 'is body, but truth is Phil can't be trusted to keep 'is gob shut.' Terry poured more tea into his cup.

'Yeah, and as for Ms Hill, aka Lindsay the loudmouth, she don't know much about nuffing except hair extensions and sun beds. Finks Phil's part of a really wealthy family who got their money buyin' and sellin' luxury homes.'

'Right, I see.'

'So stick to the script and stress silence is golden.'

'I'll do what's required Tezza.'

'Good lad.'

'They're not the brightest of people are they Jimmy eh? And they'll be under pressure. I mean, Mel has sorted it so they're well looked after inside, but they'll 'ave to be told by someone like you that the best thing they can do is keep quiet, keep their heads down and just count the days. Let them know their real reward comes after they've served their sentences.'

I'm in the fucking circle of evil – the nine rings of hell.

'Fine.'

They shoved their food down noisily, even Nick, who was trying to retain a dignified civility.

'C'mon Nick drink up.'

Jimmy smacked his lips together like a yawning hound, a little egg yolk dripping onto his shirt. He wiped it off, showing the back of his hand, which had a knife scar running from the start of his wrist to the tip of his little finger. 'And pass the hot sauce.'

'Fank you, squire,' he blinked.

Terry spread his hands across the table and grinned: 'She played you.'

'Who?'

'That sort you was with on the roof, who d'ya fink?'

He cleared his plate and wiped his mouth clean.

'I never touched her,' Nick said quietly, averting Terry's gaze and staring at the ceiling.

'After you never touched 'er, she 'ad a nosey around. She

went to the boardroom on the way out and pocketed these.'

Terry pulled out a stash of papers relating to Mel and the firm.

'I-I don't understand. How?'

'Doesn't matter. You gotta keep on the ball – always three steps ahead.'

Nick took the papers and stuffed them in his briefcase. He was sorely disconcerted by his lapse of judgement and didn't want them thinking he was a sap. He racked his brain trying to work out when Avery could have nabbed the papers and how they knew about it. *Must have been when she asked where the bathroom was.*

Terry slurped the remnants of his tea.

'We'll be off soon, so eat up, son. Put some meat on those bones, eh.'

Outside, the industrial skies were heaving with muted shadows of grey. It was all around them, this flat solid canvas of sober granite, as if their very souls were entombed in it. Nick felt the cut of the cold, stinging his eyes.

'It's freezing,' Nick's face was tightening as the wind gnawed his back and sides. Terry pulled up his coat collar and stuck some gum in his mouth.

'Come on, we 'aven't got time to kill.'

They left the leaded horizon of Clerkenwell and headed west.

Chapter Nine: She's a Lady

Avery was working full time as a junior reporter for *The Daily Post*. She had impressed the editor with her expert knowledge of football and had been a summer intern at the paper while a uni- student. She was well liked in the office and good at her job but wanted to write about stuff that mattered, not showbiz gossip and inane trivia. After hours, she had been working on some private leads of her own and compiling data on one of the most notorious criminal tycoons to ever bloody London's streets. It was pure coincidence she had stumbled across *that* envelope in Nick's boardroom. She recognised Mel's name and had to have a peek inside. She knew she was crossing a line when she stole the documents but her competitive streak kicked in. She had no idea that, Nick was Mel's lawyer. Fate had thrown them together. She was determined to cut through the rot and ride her train. She liked Nick – he seemed warm, kind of mellow, like an easy Sunday. She hoped he was free of Mel's rotting feculence. Nick had poochie-pup eyes that made her melt. She could easily fall for him.

I won't take sides … I'll tell it as it is.

'I can't find it anywhere.' She was sucking a cough drop, sweet cherry red. It made her tongue fizz and the inside of her mouth warm and soft. Spiked with menthol and eucalyptus, it gave her a clean feel.

'What you lookin' fer?' buzzed Ollie the intern. He was

tall and scuffed with ink stains. He had close puckered lips, a Bieber boy haircut and whippet thin hands etched with noticeably blue veins. He spoke with a distinctive, northern smack to his accent: an unsteady mix of TV Americana blended with Mancunian rock star.

'Not now, Ollie – really, really busy.'

'I was only askin'. I might be able to help, you know?'

'Doubt that,' she scoffed.

She rattled the bottom of her file drawer, unable to find the bundle of papers she had pilfered from Nick's Law Firm. She straightened her blouse, running her hands from the collar to the hem, neatening the folds of her mind and brushing away the fluff and dust. She clicked her fingers and crunched the remains of her throat lozenge. Ollie moved over to the photocopier.

Have to be careful how I play him, else he'll complain to his father and probably get me fired.

There had been six redundancies that month alone, and jobs like hers were hard to keep.

'Actually, Ollie, you may be able to help. Would you be a sweetheart and get me a coffee?'

'Sure, that's really gonna 'elp me learn the trade,' he snapped.

'Coffee first, it will make us all feel better.' She broke into a demi smile and Ollie's baby-buck eyes softened her mood.

How can I resist such innocence! Yes, he annoys the crap out of me, but he's just a kid. Why not help him?

'Later, I'll show you some basic subediting and explain why doing law at university could prove very useful.'

Ollie reminded her of a harmless string puppet with an over-coiffed hairpiece.

'Th-thanks '

'You're just a stutter mutter of cute aren't you Ollie?'

'Only at the outset once you get to know me it's a different story,' his floppy fringe covering his left eye as he scampered across the room.

Avery swivelled her chair around and opened her make-up mirror. She was pegged out, her mascara flaking and her lipstick smudged. Her eyes were rimmed with blue gunk and the top of her cupid's bow lined with Clinique's Pink Spice. It gave her a slutty magnetism she was unaware of. Her washed-out inky-blue tresses remain tinged with colour on the tips, creating a violet gloss. She clicked some numbers on her mobile.

'Hi, can I speak to Mr Stringer?' She spoke with fake brevity, polite but curt.

'Yeah, can I ask who's calling please?'

'Avery'

'Avery who?'

'Just Avery… um, he knows me. Actually, can I schedule an appointment with Nick for this afternoon?'

'Hmmm, that might be tricky. He's out of the country on urgent business.'

'Oh, I see. Right. Okay.'

'I can always leave a message or schedule an appointment for next week?'

'No … no, that's okay. I'll try him on his mobile.' Avery was stumped. The papers in the envelope had gone from the bag, but nothing else. She was sure she had them when she left Nick's office, but she'd also misplaced her earrings too. It made no sense to her.

'I got you a mocha latte.'

'Ooh, great. Love the choccie sprinkles. Nice touch.' She drained her cup with a deep satisfying sigh. 'Ahh, that was really good.'

'You're welcome.'

'Now, go get the story you've been working on.'

Ollie strolled over to his desk and pulled out a heavy doodled file, covered, with caricatures of manga chicks and superheroes.

'The trick with subediting is making it tighter and cleaner, so that it flows and reads like newsprint.'

'I get it.'

'Now, let me take a look.'

She got out a red marker and started scrawling all over it, inserting corrections and substituting words and phrases.

'You need to basically rewrite the whole piece. Make it short and tidy so your copy is tight.'

Ollie re-read it aloud.

'Wow, it works as a story now!'

'Yeah, it's not bad. You got a good flow with your lingo, Ollie!'

'Thanks.'

Secretly, that was a pile of piffle. Ollie might be a wizard with IT, but his reporting skills needed a lot more work.

'Have you done any legal seminars or shadowed anyone on interview?'

'No, not yet.'

'Well, good interview technique is all about trust and asking the right questions. You need to structure it right, just like a story, so that the subject in the interview doesn't go off tangent, you know. I learnt the old-fashioned way, the five C's.'

'Yeah, my dad's always repeating those to me. Be clear, concise, consistent, comprehensible and correct.'

'That's right.'

Fuck, if even half the journos on gossip mags and online tried at least two of those, there wouldn't be any fluff at all. It's a shame we're all tempted by big-money stories and celeb excess.

She reached into her desk drawer and pulled out various bundles. One, headed *The Freedom of Information Act*, was a voluminous thickly bound legal document.

'This allows you to make information requests from any publicly funded organisation – your old school, your doctor, your college. It's also great for small presses and has been used very effectively in print journalism. Golden rule: ask, ask, ask and ask again.'

Ollie took the bulging bundle of bureaucratic papers and looked downcast.

'That's why a law degree is really handy. Most of what you write has to be accurate and balanced.'

If only news reporters could stop their red and blue bias, there might be some way of salvaging the art of telling a great story.

'Whatever you do, especially in a really emotive piece like this, you have to look at things from both sides. Be fair. Gain the trust of the people you're pumping info from.'

'I get it. I'm doin' this story on knife crime, and although I'm rooting for the victims, I still have to report on the perpetrators.'

'Kind of. If there's a reason for the attack, put it forward, but it cuts deeper than that. You have to be accurate, truthful, and balanced. Who are you working the story with?'

'Jez.'

'He's a good reporter.'

Jez. Yeah, gay, privileged, perfectionist, and rising fast, but he's a poster child for puffery. He and I shouldn't collide.

Avery was fireball ambitious, plotting her way to the top like a comic strip heroine. Ollie was an easy target.

'When you're done with that, what about doing some good *old-school* style detective work?'

'Sure.'

Avery watched as Ollie sat at his desk leafing through pics of manga chicks. She could tell by his glazed look that he was somewhere else. Just then Joe walked in:

'Ollie?'

He didn't answer and it was only the thump of his father's hand on his shoulder, which brought him back to the buzz of the newsroom.

'Oh hi, Dad.'

'Alright, son. Not being a pain are you?'

'Nooo.'

'Avery my office, five minutes, please.'

'Yes sir, Mr Gander.'

Joe Gander was a bellyache of a man. He had learnt the newspaper trade the hard way and believed in the traditional values of journalism: integrity, honesty and independence.

He was doing his best to keep the paper alive, but the spread of celebrity gossip on the web and the wave of digital and online publications masquerading as news had bled the paper dry. With his tufts of white hair, pork-belly stomach and sun-gnarled complexion, he looked like a cross between Jeff Bridges and a post-dated Alec Baldwin. The lines on his face cockled with vodka and gin. He carried a boiling resentment for the *now generation*, blaming them for the paper's struggles. He had to save it. The paper was more than his place of work, it was his lifeline – the reason he woke up every morning, the reason that made everything worthwhile. He put his hands above his head and leant back in his plush chair, the quilted leather harnessing his bulky frame and mirroring the folds of his skin on his forehead.

'Come in Avery. Sit down.' His voice was looped with honey and bourbon. He pointed to the chair with his hand. It was strong, brawny, and freckled, with a thatch of blond knuckle hair. Crossing her legs like a Parisian escort, Avery showed just enough thigh to tease but was careful not to reveal too much flesh.

'You like working here don't you?'

'Yes, sir, Mr Gander, I really do.'

'How would you feel if I gave you a little more responsibility, more delegation?'

'Fine.'

Maybe that was too quick. Should she have thought about it more?

'Good, you can keep churning out the showbiz and celebrity trivia, but start working on a new weekly topic for the online version of the paper – city desk crime, that will be your beat, and we'll see how you do. Get Ollie to help with all the techno stuff – Twitter, Facebook apps and so on. He's an SEO whiz kid.'

He bit down on a bic biro, showing rows of smoke-stained teeth, and then settled back in his chair, ploughing through invoices and phone bills. He read her easy. She was ripe for slut-bugging, but Joe never fooled around with the help. He liked to keep his professional space free from law whores and complications. He was part of the old guard and it would take more than a hint of pussy to get him to turn.

She left his room and rang Ollie. After placing requests for online help and tech support, she thrust a list in his hand.

'Your dad says this is priority.'

'Oh yeah, right.' He yawned and shuffled back to his PC. After drafting and editing some pieces on sub rate celebs, Avery pulled out a thick paper journal. Thumbing through the pages, she found the number for Mimi Deepridge, former centrefold hottie, reality TV chick, glamour model, soft porn star, and now dethroned mistress of Mel Greenberg.

Chapter Ten: Tour de France

Pau is in the south-west of France and is best known as one of the chain of mountain villages that link each stage of the famous Tour de France bike race. Typically picturesque, it is girded by the Alps to the north and the Pyrenees to the south, bordering Spain. Dotted with charming little walkways and cobbled streets, it's a popular holiday spot, famous for its cultural and historical landmarks and a firm favourite with the criminal glitterati.

Mel was in good shape, the mountain air refining his cheeks with a fresh bloom. He was holed up in his luxury hideout with several of his cronies, waiting for Nick.

They touched down around 7 p.m. local time after a direct flight from London City Airport. At the arrivals gate they were greeted by a sober little man in his fifties. Conservatively dressed, carrying a black attaché case, he was holding a sign that read: Avocat Stringer. He had oiled black hair, neatly parted, a pigeon chest and stabbing blue eyes.

Nick waved him over. With Jimmy and Terry on either side, he felt confident, almost in control.

'Mr Strinnngerrr?' His voice was infused with the hills of Andalucía, rich and melodic but tightly controlled. He rolled his R's and clung to his S's.

'Yes, sir.'

Terry and Jimmy nodded in unison.

'I'm Eduardo Cortesss. I understand you've been retained by Misss Hill and Mr Drummond in their case?'

'Yes, sir.'

'Good. If you follow me I will take you to the office. From there you will take thessse papersss in thisss bag I am holding, and then after you have dinner we will see each other again in the morning.'

Nick nodded, still wondering how close to trouble he was but trumped with adrenalin all the same.

'Here are the documents that enable you to see your clients and allow you to address the judge. I have, asss a professional courtesy, arranged everything for you. If you are uncertain about anything, please don't hesitate to call me. I will give you a cell phone when we get to the office.'

Jimmy and Terry looked on while Eduardo walked briskly to the exit. They followed him out.

They were given a red rental: a Citroen C4 about five years old.

'Not a bad motor, eh Eduardo?' razzed Terry as if they were sharing a private joke. Eduardo handed the keys to him.

'It's a bad situation, Tezza. He better be good. Now keep following me until we get to my office. You can call Mel from there.'

'Got it.'

Jimmy, Nick, and Terry scrambled into the car with Nick and Terry in the front.

'Oi, Tezza, got any good tunes?' grumbled Jimmy.

'Wait up. 'Aven't even started yet.'

'From what I can remember, it's at least a two-hour drive to the office and then another thirty minutes from there.'

'No, it's only about an 'our's drive to Ed's office through Pau past the pretty castle, and then we hit Mel's about twenty minutes after that. Piece of cake – now buckle up.'

Nick was checking his Blackberry for messages. Avery had called three times. Terry put the radio on. Power ballads were driving the beat. Nick was in no mood for Jennifer

Rush or Celine Dion clicking his teeth he groaned:

'Terry what the fuck is this shit?'

'This is Paul!'

Terry and Jimmy started laughing, aping the lyrics with exaggerated hand movements and pained expressions to Dion's version of *The Power of Love*.

'Seriously, this music is fucking crap. It reminds me of drunk, menopausal women. I hate it. Stop it, change the station.'

'Just enjoy the scenery,' Terry twinkled, pointing out the lush rolling hills and kaleidoscopic flowers.

'Breathe that in, Nick, breathe it in.'

Nick slammed his iPod into gear. If he was going to get through this he would need the company of the inimitable master bluesman Robert Johnson.

Well if anyone can understand me, he can. The devil's always hogging the world for souls.

After about forty minutes they arrived at the Holiday Inn. Nick looked confused:

'I thought we were going to the lawyer's office?'

'This is it,' Terry replied.

They pulled into the car park and steered the car adjacent to Eduardo's modest Peugeot. Eduardo tapped on the front window on the driver's side. Terry rolled down the window.

'Just give me a few minutes. I'll phone when I'm ready and let you have the room number.'

'Right.'

Nick was quiet, surveying the scene in front of him, locked between two psychopaths and about to get instructions from a third. The Faustian fist of excess was pushing him to the edge.

I'm not even close to control. I'm just scraping a living off the family jewels. Nothing more than Mel's schlemiel.

Just then, Terry's phone rang.

'Holaaar,' he goofed in a Benidorm Essex bend.

'Yes, Eduardo. Okay, yep, I'll send him up. Yeah, will do. He swivelled round to face Nick head on.

'He's in room 513, top floor. He says get off on the fourth floor and he'll meet you in the stairwell – a precaution.'

'Precaution for what?'

'Dunno, but it's best to do what 'e says. Meantime, I'll call Mel.'

'Aren't you and Jimmy coming?'

'No, but we'll be in the car waitin'.'

Nick got out of the car slowly with a hush-hush kind of stealth that was clearly overplayed. Terry shook his head and called him back. 'Nick come back now. What you doin? Stop doin' that. You look really obvious. Act natural.'

'Alright,' snapped Nick, combing his fingers through his hair and wiping the sweat away from his forehead. He walked over to the hotel trying to be as casual as possible.

There were lots of families, couples, and business execs milling around in the foyer. Generic wall paintings of nondescript still-life and dim wall lights created an eerie pumpkin feeling, as if Nick were on the set of a cheap horror flick. He waited for the lift and got off on the fourth floor. He turned left through a fire exit and saw Eduardo approaching.

'Pleasse come this way,' Nick followed him up another flight of stairs to his hotel room.

'Close the door behind you. Pleasse sit down. I have everything you need in *that bag*.' He pointed to a leather holdall on the floor. Then he rummaged through it and pulled out a wad of papers and a prepaid Nokia phone. He inserted the sim card and entered some numbers from his own mobile.

'Okay, so you now have an untraceable cell, my number, the prison numbers and Mel's all programmed in.'

'Right.'

Shit- am I up to this?

'Everything's in there.' Eduardo pointed to the bag again. 'Check inside, please.'

Nick picked up the bag and put it on a chair. He felt

around carefully, removing a thick padded envelope. It had his name scrawled on it. Nick opened it, revealing thousands of euros.

'All there – 5,000 now and 5,000 after you see them.'

There was something about the way that money felt in Nick's hands. Touching it made him rock hard.

'Monday morning at 9 a.m. you will appear in court as the advocate for both clients. This is your certificate allowing you to present yourself to the court and speak on their behalf.' Eduardo gave Nick a long formal document.

'Right.'

'As for protocol, it's much the same as in other prisons. You turn up, hand in your paperwork and wait for the clients – pretty straightforward, but you won't have time to see them properly until midweek. Most likely you'll get a few minutes at the hearing.'

'Yes, I understand.'

'This is more background on the case and the prosecution outline. The judge isn't a fool, so be careful. My advice: don't improvise.'

'Thanks.'

Eduardo shoved the bag beneath Nick's arm and showed him out.

As a trainee, Nick was still a novice with an L-plate and a backseat pass. He was soft in the gut, unaccustomed to such power play. He needed to muscle up.

Finally, after almost an hour of puke tunes courtesy of Bonnie Tyler, Roxette and Barbara Streisand, they reached *Chateau de Rose*, Mel's impressive-looking home, gated and set within its own spectacular grounds. Yet, in a crude, unseemly display, Mel had desecrated the fourteenth century mansion with a garish daffy sign, wrecking the quiet refinery of the exclusive French countryside, and maiming the subdued elegance of the elite purlieu it read: *Welcome to Chateau de Rose, Mel's Monster Palace.*

Complete with stone-built columns, period wrought-iron doors and a steep terracotta roof, it was characteristic of most of the houses in the region and dated back to the reign of Gaston Fébus, the Prince of Béarn. With five bedrooms and three bathrooms, it was comfortable enough for Mel and his brood during summer and made a good hideaway for the rest of the year.

Typical Mel – not bad for an uneducated blockhead, but who sticks flash-trash crap on a piece of fucking history? Mel owns a slice of French aristocracy and mullers it with flo glo kitsch. Mel's king pimp, a sucker ball of greed with a self-made Forbes *entry. Where's the justice? Why should I stand by watching my mother grow old with worry. Debt and sadness stitching the remains of her broken existence?*

Mel was at the door, standing guard like a highly trained Alsatian.

'Nick, Jimmy, Tezza.'

They piled into the entrance. It was bling digity suave. The polished mahogany floors, reflecting the natural light that bounced off the ceilings, adding a lustrous oyster patina to the furniture, and wall hangings. Nick was transfixed by the contemporary art, lavish light fittings and a bizarre bronze head resting on its own plinth. It was hideously deformed, torn at the waist with one misshapen horn. Mel's noisy voice extricating him from its deadening allure.

'Right, you lot go freshen up. Nick, yours is up two flights of stairs, first on the left. Jimmy, Tezza, you're in the usual. Now look lively. No time to be wastin.' We got court Monday. When you're ready, we'll go 'ave a chat and somefin' to eat.'

As Nick climbed the stairs, he thought of his mother's smile, petal soft, lifting him through the crevices of his darkening world.

Time to get baseline nasty. *If Mel could have all this, imagine what I could have if I played to win.*

Chapter Eleven: Hell on my Trail

Matt had spent his teen years with a guitar on his lap. His cobalt-blue Les Paul was a fixture that became synonymous with Matt himself. After his mother's brutal murder when he was only nine, he had been spoiled and indulged by his devoted father, who left him a handsome trust fund to play with and a swelling addiction to feed. Matt spent the bulk of his time locked in his room playing for six or seven hours at a clip without noticing that day had fallen to dusk. The thick sweet smell of reefer roped the air, a gift to the rock gods and a way for him to express the metaphoric avowal of his soul as he became one with his guitar, all-consuming and all-embracing. For him it was all about creating that perfect sound, pushing until he could hear the notes of purity in his crunching melodies.

Matt had known Nick since pre-school and they had formed a solid and impenetrable friendship ever since. They were so close that Matt paid off Nick's gambling debts and stripper tab when Anichka left, so close that Matt took the blame when Nick was fined for a drink-drive offence, so close they knew each other's exact birth times and had matching Latin tattoos inscribed on their torsos, *Amicitias Immortales Esse Oportet*. Matt had silver dollar talent but lacked the cold determination needed to 'make it'. He enjoyed all the trappings of a clichéd rock star life without any public endorsement. He needed to amp up his real world for big name stardom.

When Matt played, all else would fade from sight. His head hung over the nape of his guitar, his shaggy curls dangling just above the pick-ups. He was alone, in a better world. Often Nick would just leave without saying goodbye.

Nick took up bass that summer. He knew it would cement their bond if he could tie in with Matt and give them more time to hang out. Nick often spoke of rock's big league, dreamt of packed arenas and limos filled with hot pussy. This talk never prompted more than a dismissive laugh from Matt. It wasn't about fantasising for him. He was a guitar nerd, an audiophile. He had memorised every riff Hendrix had ever put on record. For Matt it was like religion, sacred. It sanctified him. Some people see rock-'n'-roll from the outside, the seductive pull of razzle dazzle, the effect it has on others and the anarchy it creates. They approach it like dissecting a frog or a maths problem. This view was all upside down and backwards to Matt. For him it came from the inside out, a necessity like eating or breathing. He had little choice in that. It was never about money or fame, it was more about how Dave Navarro got a certain note to bend and ring, like the solo to 'Been Caught Stealing'. Or how Bob Marley up-picked his rhythms, and the magic that created. These were the types of things he'd reflected on while riding the bus to school when they were kids, or walking home from the nearby record shop. It was still, years later, the same unadulterated simplicity that controlled his compulsion.

Matt had been badly beaten by his drug-fucked girlfriend after a long night of infidelity. It started with a Brazilian waitress at Source Below Zero, a private karaoke bar, and ended with a Tequila tongue job courtesy of a bathroom babe in KoKo. He had downed an almost lethal combo of oxys and Klonopin, he'd bought off the web and was feeling morbid gross. The hook-ups made Matt feel needed and helped him blank out his hang-ups. He had been involved with Isobel for over two years, but neither were believers in the conventional rules of commitment, although they had a magnetic, almost infectious, attraction to each other. Inside the basement of his mind, Matt still felt like a scuz ball whenever they played this sordid game. Every time they shared a moment of intimacy, he would remember the endless nights of easy fucks, cheap booze and copious drug use. It was only a matter of time before someone or something would drive a wedge between them forever. Matt blamed Nick. He needed him now – needed to make sense of it all. He had recognised something new in his best friend, something he didn't like. Nick looked different, stamped with venom as if the sins of his clients were blotting his face. Matt had to convince him that Mel was a jinx, the bastard of genius; an architect of evil. He needed to win Nick back and free him from Mel's sucking teat, to somehow reclaim their childhood paradise. Mel was the cause of his stewing blues. He decided to give Nick a call.

'Nick?'

'Matt. I can't talk for long. I'm in Pau.'

'Where?'

'Never mind … what's up?'

'I need you. I've got a little stalkie problem.'

'I'll be back in a few days. How bad is it?'

'Well, this morning I had twenty-seven missed calls and eighteen messages on my Facebook wall.'

'Who is it?'

'Her name's Viktoria. She's been tailing me for days. I've nicknamed her Stalker Ella Vicky."

'Yeah right. Try and hang low till Monday. Message me if it gets really bad. We'll get together when I get back -book some band time. Don't antagonise her."

'I won't. Thanks, bro.'

Matt was being hounded by a Lithuanian call girl. They had stripper sex in the back seat of her beaten-up Ford when foolishly Matt had given her his number. For two weeks now she had been calling, texting, and Face booking. Matt was actually enjoying all the attention but grew wary of the repetitious references to his physical similarity to various rock supremoes. Nick would sort it out and that would give him a chance to see how tight he was cuffed to Mel.

He thought back to easier times before Mel, when they were kids, when it was just him and Nick drowning reality away in a nirvana sea.

It was orgasmic. I kicked straight through that cheap amp. Hated that clean sterile twang. A tiny rip in the speaker led to a buzzing sound like a Hendrix Marshall stack, and a life of guitar licks tighter than virgin pussy. Major distortion – and I was finally free to strum the walls of my bedroom with pure sex.

Chapter Twelve: You Can Leave Your Hat On

The wailing hump of the police siren broke the delicacy of the night. Avery was uptight. She rang the number again and slipped back onto the taxi seat.

'Hi, Ms Deepridge, it's Avery Cross. You agreed to meet me tonight after your set?'

'Oh yes, Avery from the newspaper. What's it called again?' The voice she was greeted with was soft, with a deep rich tone, not affected, but cool, understated, and a little cagey.

'Yeah, *The Daily Post*.'

'Yes, I remember. Everything's arranged for you. I'm on stage around 11:30 and we can talk after that.'

'Great, thank you. I'll be there.'

That was a relief. Her name had been left with reception and a seat reserved for her so she could catch the show and then do the interview. She was actually there to tap Mimi about Mel, but Mimi was a goldmine of info in her own right. She flicked through her notes: a Catholic-born burlesque dancer who dated a Jewish gangster with a feline obsession for fur. She could already see banner headlines.

Madame Jojo's was an iconic part of British club land and a Mecca for the T-generation – that would be trannies, transvestites, transsexuals, and the transgendered. Hosting one of its hot-blooded burlesque nights was the infamous Levi Louch. Ever since the 1950s this famous spot in Central

London had been a hotbed of vice and vainglorious decadence. Now it was home to Soho's lost and found bohemian elite.

Burlesque night was a chance for Mimi to radiate: a combo of *Vogue* superstar Tracy Trinita and the famed androgyny of Andrej Pejić, she was a looker, mixing urban slinky and R-rated sin. With her Coke-bottle hips and blowfish lips, she had an off-kilter pulpiness that intoxicated. Today her hair was rolled in a Lauren Bacall demi wave and her Harley Street implants were hanging heavy. She was all touch but no feel, a simmering siren of want. Mimi was a lesson in unrivalled seduction, someone everyone needed. Her voice was low, misted with smoke and a hint of self-deprecation. Mimi was a make-it-and-rake-it babe. She always got what she needed, fucking her way into the cream of British society. Everyone loved her exquisite bone structure, her lean legs and frisky-kitty lashes.

A long queue spiralled from Brewer Street to Walker's Court. It was a hip neighbourhood reminding Avery of the Meatpacking District in NYC, crawling with slut-fucks, art whores, and the laid-back luxe of the super-rich. People who had time to blow on Soho coffees, cakes and cocaine. At night, the tinselled sparkle of its go – go streets gave it an amplified decadence. Once inside, Avery found herself knee-deep in models, showbiz types and media bores. She noticed a group of ageing celebs and post-pubescent male strippers lounging around, mouthing the lyrics to a steady stream of Vegas show tunes. There were also lots of Japanese tourists and some wholesome Canadians in the audience. Then the tempo changed and the houselights were dimmed. On stage, Mimi Deepridge mirror primped: part fifties' showgirl, part Vegas diva in sequins and smiles carrying a Dolce Vita insouciance. She had a driving magnetism that drew everyone in. Her own kind of sentimental melodrama that kept the crowd hooked. Avery found the performance strangely compelling, even touching. She drunk her vodka and headed backstage.

'It's okay, let her through.' Mimi was ordering the burly beef heads around.

'Come on in, we can talk while I take this off.' Mimi was wiggling around in feathers and stilettos, removing a long hairpiece and peeling off layers of face paint. Avery was fascinated.

'Do you mind if I turn on the tape recorder?'

'No, go ahead.'

'Thanks,' she said, smiling.

'So, I had intended this to be a story about women in the glamour trade and how they're treated in the industry. Whether they can effectively use their sexuality, almost, like a weapon to get ahead.'

'Yes, some women do get head, darling. Lots of head.'

Avery squirmed. This woman was smarter than her, more beautiful than she could ever be, and now cracking double entendres mid-interview.

'But I thought on my way over here I could ask you about something else. Firstly, though, perhaps you could explain why you chose this profession. I mean, what makes a woman decide she wants to be a burlesque dancer?'

'Well you could say it chose me. I was fifteen years old and a runaway – very strict Catholic upbringing. I met a Madam in Soho and she turned me on to this. I've never looked back and I've been independent for over two decades. This work pays.'

As Mimi was wiping and cleansing, she was exposing more than open pores. Avery glimpsed a tiny Adam's apple underneath her velvet choker.

Avery couldn't help but stare. She had an inkling, of course but it was still unsettling: Mimi was so much of a woman: she was a man

'It freaks everyone out dahling. I'm a pre-op trannie, so I take female hormones and very soon I'm gonna go for the chop.'

'I … er, I had no idea. I mean, you're so …'

'Womanly?'

'Kind of surprising. I really did think you were female.'

'Well I am, sweetie, here.' She pointed to her chest and head. 'But not down here.' She pressed her hands between her thighs.

'So what d'you think about the fact that you're earning money by being objectified in a purely sexual way? Isn't dance hall camp just patriarchal T and A?' The irony wasn't lost on Avery— now interviewing a tri-sexual diva in a Soho revue show that had a blue rep for sex and smut.

'Well, honey, I'm not being chased around the office by a man in a suit or being told how short my skirt should be at work.'

Mimi's voice had an undertone of contempt:

'I do this show on my terms with my rules, unlike other women who have the "respectability" of a routine gig. The truth is, I think any woman who can get away with using their sexuality as a tool to get ahead will … and honestly, men expect it. I don't think it matters what kind of business you're in. I know female journalists like yourself, women doctors and women lawyers, who hump their way to the top.'

'Do you think it's right?'

'I think it's primitive – survival – and it's bullshit if you don't believe it happens.'

'What do you think that says about women?'

'It says more about the society *we've* created – we pay people, reward them for greed and sleaze. When a sex tape gets made, a star is born with a publicity agent on speed dial, a six-figure pay cheque, a reality TV gig and a tacky lingerie line in the works. It's a marketing scam: selling filth so you can get your face on *Time* magazine.'

'So what you're saying is women are responding to their environment?'

'In a way, yes. If a woman can fuck her way to success she's gonna do it.'

Avery paused the tape and looked around her. The atmosphere was tight with tease.

I wonder if she – he – knows what I'm really here for.

'Just checking the recording.'

'Course, basically, women – all women – need to feel wanted and useful, and one of the easiest ways to do that is through their sexuality.'

'Sexuality to secure promotion. It's a simple sell.'

'Yes, it's easy to oversimplify things, but take your job, for instance. I bet you've thought about nailing a really good story, maybe putting on some extra slap, a pair of stilettos and some sexy nylons.'

'Well, it's a people person kind of job.'

'Course it is, luvvie.'

'I mean, you know, I meet people all the time … anyway, this is about *you* and what *you* think about women in the workplace using their charms, especially with what *you* do.'

'I always tell the truth, that's my problem. I see something I don't like, or hear something I don't agree with, and I make an issue about it. I've always stuck up for the underdog – always been a fighter – I was born that way.'

'Yes, I can see that.'

'Do you think that women can really handle *your* job? I mean, it can get nasty – serious investigative reporting. There aren't many top – should I say senior? – female journalists who can handle that kind of pressure.'

Did Mimi know why she was there – was this a veiled threat?

'Sure, I think that's true in a way. Some editors, and even other women journalists, believe there's a vulnerable side to this job -that women can't take care of themselves.'

'Exactly my point. Sometimes it takes a real woman to do a man's job.' She revealed a perfect set of pearly whites.

That got Avery thinking of Patty Maddock, former queen of London's Fleet Street. She could definitely see her snagging a scoop with a sweep of her fox-coloured mane. *A little flirt and fool was all part of the job, right?*

'Um, is it okay if a photographer comes over next week to take some shots?' She looked up as Mimi started pulling off fake beauty moles and dousing her skin in Evian water spray.

'And are you comfortable talking about the romantic side of your life?'

'Absolutely.'

'Is there a special someone?' Avery leaned forward in her chair as Mimi removed strings of faux pearls and supersized flash-trash earrings.

'There was …' Mimi's voice trailed the perfumed air with sorrow.

'And?'

'Well, like so many others, he was disgusted when he found out. I mean, really found out. There was a part of him that hated me and a part of him that wanted more. He knew I was taboo, out of reach, forbidden to him, and that left him gagging for more. He faked it, of course, but I knew, he *needed* me. We had it, that chemistry. It was real. My feelings were real, and after a while, like any rainy day cliché, he just walked.'

'I'm sorry, can you … tell me anything else about him?'

'Darling, if you knew all there was to know about *him*, you probably wouldn't be walking straight in the morning.'

'You mean he's—'

'Very well hung? Yes, that too … but no, he's extremely well connected, sweetie.'

'When he left for good, how did that make you feel?'

'Like shit – I mean it's rejection over and over again. I knew he was married, I understood the Jewish thing. He was a real gentleman, you know. I'd get beautiful flowers before and after a set, exquisite jewellery, and he'd do the most amazing things for me, then, finally, after a few weeks I got the courage to tell him outright.'

'Sorry? A-a few weeks!'

'He said he was in love with me, and you know, we never saw each other every day. We went slowly at first – there was this incredible energy between us – and then we climaxed! Twenty-four-hours of pleasure. After that it was never the same. We did everything together, ate breakfast, read the

Sunday papers, laughed in the park, we even baked biscuits while listening to Nina Simone. We were like a proper couple. Every touch every look, everything we did was: love. The intimacy between us was more than working. It was honest. He opened up to me, showed me stuff, you know, personal stuff. I felt completely natural with him. I thought he was *it*.'

Avery was empathetic but couldn't believe that Mel 'the monster' Greenberg could ever care about anyone but himself.

'What did he do ... I mean what kind of work did he do?'

'He wasn't an angel, but I never realised how many lives he stole. I didn't think he was a bastard, just an opportunist. There's a difference, you know.'

'Yeah.'

'I mean, if I thought like a man, which I don't, I'd have been able to read him better. He's unnaturally vicious.'

'How so?' Mimi threw Avery a look of irritation.

'Look, you said you wanted to ask me something else – what is it?'

'The man you're alluding to.'

'Yes?'

'I'm piecing together a story – a big story – and the reason I'm here, the real reason I'm here, is not for some enlightening piece on the female moral code, although that's interesting in itself. The reason I came here tonight was to try and find out more about *him*.'

'You want to run a piece on Mel Greenberg?' Mimi was rubbing hand lotion on her fingers.

'Yeah, I want to rock the newsroom with some serious shit.'

Avery felt liberated by her confession. Mimi was non-committal. She seemed worried.

'I'm not sure, I ... he's a very dangerous man, Avery. You wouldn't want to mess with him, and I couldn't be implicated. I don't want this on me. I'll have to think this through, really think it through. Can you get some real money for the story?'

'Possibly, if what we get is an exclusive. Maybe we can meet up next week and discuss it then?'

'Sure, but right now I have to meet someone and I'm running late.'

'Thank you, I really appreciate this.'

Avery left Madame Jojo's sauced with that can-do feeling, the kind that drives you to the top.

Chapter Thirteen: Which Side Are You On?

Nick was in a booze haze. He had tried to resist but it was all cancan la la and a wild memory of three boudoir brunettes – blood-red lipstick and a one-eyed Hungarian pimp. He checked the left side of his cheek. It felt raw, kind of serrated. Yes, a long cat scratch had raised itself on his freshly shaved face.

Shit, I'd better go fix it.

'Où est la toilette?' he asked, parroting a typically uncultured Brit abroad.

'To your right, and then left,' a court official replied in perfect English. She looked like a definitive Hitchcock blonde, with an obvious Gallic charm. Her hair brushed back in a neat pony tail and her big blue eyes reeling him in.

Nick had no time to think of how he might, could, would, do her – he had to get his game on. After trying to salve his cut with lip balm, he adjusted his shirt and tie, clocking Mel on his way in. Nodding, he saw both clients seated silently in the defendant's area. There were three judges on the bench, which was apparently the norm in France. Nick was pissed.

Everyone knows foreign nationals won't get bail. Why the fuck has Mel put me through this? It's a sham.

It was over in minutes. Eduardo Cortes was clearly embarrassed. He jammed a heap of papers under Nick's arm and was all too aware that Nick had been roped in only for theatrical effect. Still, at least appointments had been made to see both Drummond and Hill, and Nick was saved from further humiliation by the prosecution, by explaining that there were unforeseen developments regarding a potential plea bargain, thus rendering their bail application redundant.

There was some kind of deal being brokered, and as usual Nick was the last to know. It centred on the fact that if they were able to lessen the charge then they could probably work out a deal at the discretion of the Prosecution. The procedure only worked for certain crimes and was ostensibly a technical strategy that theoretically at least, resulted in less jail time.

Later that week, Nick was driven to Pau prison. He was wilting under the pressure. He knew conditions in French jails were not as modern as those in the rest of Europe, and many inmates were subject to cruel and degrading treatment, many driven to slicing depression due to boredom and tension and many on suicide watch. He was briefed before breakfast by Mel.

'Make sure you let 'em know they 'ave to keep their gobs shut. They'll be well looked after, inside and out. Got it? We'll 'ave dinner with Cortes after.' He dropped Nick off outside:

So this was the birthplace of human rights. It's like a scene from Papillion.

Nick was frisked down and let through. It stank of toilet bleach, stale cigarette smoke, and famished yesterdays. The walls were shitted with scaling plaster and sweaty night tremors.

Phil 'the pill' Drummond was not what Nick expected. As a prisoner on remand he was entitled to certain privileges, but even Nick was unprepared for what he saw. Phil had only been inside, at the most, two weeks. He was carcass thin and unshaved. His eyes blistered with red blood spots and his hair matted and tangled falling past his shoulders. His skin was splotched with regret and large burgundy-coloured wheals that circled his cheeks and nose. He looked close to death, really close.

'Phil – Nick, Nick Stringer.' Nick pulled his chair back and sat down.

'Nice to meet you, Nick. When are they getting us out?' Phil's voice was flat and small.

'Your dad's working on it. I've arranged with the guards for you to have some stuff. You'll be okay. There's some vitamins, an iPod and other things you may need. It's going to be alright, I promise.'

Nick was torn up. Phil wasn't much older than he was. *Karma's a bitch. Is this it piss-slapped hands and schitzy prison guards? This is bad.*

'I'm not sleeping well. I need something to help me sleep. Can they put me in the medical unit or something?'

'I'll see what we can do.'

'How's Lindsay doin'? Is she alright? She never knew anything. I don't know if she'll get through it. You know what I'm sayin'?' Phil was biting his nails, his eyes drilling into Nick's soul.

'She's fine. Everything's going to be fine. You just have to keep quiet.'

'Fucking keep quiet. I can't even take a fucking crap in 'ere without someone behind me. They said we'd be looked after inside. I don't feel fucking safe. Tell those cunts if they want me to keep quiet they 'ave to fucking pay for that privilege. Bastards just left us to rot.'

'No that's not true. Honestly, everyone is working to get you out. It's a little complicated.'

'Look at me, you fucking dingbat, just look at me. I've got fucking mites in my hair. I can feel them crawling on me at night, they're fucking crawling all over me. I can't stand it. My cell-mate, 'e's Arab, 'e's teaching me Arabic. It gives me somefing to do. Muslims, they rule inside 'ere. There's no fucking bitch boy this or that, but as you can see it's not exactly The Ritz in 'ere. 'E's been more fucking 'elp than any of you lot. And you know what? I'm fucking finding the morning prayers quite calming too. Tell that to Mel. Tell 'im converting. Fucking bastard got me in 'ere. Wait till I'm out. I'm gonna fucking 'ave him.'

Phil's breath smelt of blood and bile in that order. Nick was queasy.

Phil motioned the guard over, an overweight gut butt with two missing front teeth and a Marseille tan.

'Ready.'

Well that went down like a Pope at the Folies Bergère. He would tell Mel it was A-Okay but Phil wouldn't last four months in there let alone four years.

About twenty minutes later, Nick appeared at the female prison which was located opposite the male one. It had the same flaking walls and a shabby-looking French flag, ripped with prison neglect.

Nobody gives a fuck, not Mel, not the inmates, not the guards. I'm going to report these jails to a human rights group. Even dogs are treated better.

Lindsay still had a curve and swerve kind of prettiness, but her eyes were sore from crying.

'I'm Lindsay.' She spoke with an Essex loop.

'Nick.' He tried looking upbeat.

If anything, this is worse. The stench of fear is so overwhelming I can feel it on my clothes and my skin. It grips you by the neck and reins you in …

'I know they've got the wrong people. It's mistaken identity or somefing.'

Nick nodded.

'Everyone's working to get you out of here – hopefully it won't be long.'

'Yeah. Did you get the list of things I need? It's mostly okay except late at night. All you can 'ear is cryin', cryin' all the time. Does your 'ead in. Way I see it, like an adventure, a challenge. Who'd have thought I'd go from stressin' over my hair extensions and Malibu fake bake to this? You'd never have thought would ya? Probably be able to sell the story to *Hello* magazine though, what d'ya think?'

Nick was boosted by her stoic spirit. She was almost sunny. Of course, her artless simplicity helped her. *If she knew she could be facing four long years inside this hellhole, her outlook might be different. Still at least she believes in the sell and tell.*

'That's the best way to look at it.'

'How's Phil doin'? Poor darlin'. He's such a sensitive soul. Gets homesick after a couple of days away, and that's when we're in five-star luxury.'

'He's doing great.'

'Good, that's good, got to keep his strength up. I got a letter from my sister Natalie, and she says everyone at home is alright. I've done some of the girls' hair, you know. 'Cos I'm a beauty therapist. Breaks the ice a bit. There's one girl got done in by some French gangster. It's such a shame. Lovely girl she is.'

Yep, these were people just like him and now they were Mel's drug toads.

'I'll make sure you get a visit every two weeks. Mel's arranging for your sis' to come over.'

'Yeah, an adventure. Life's one adventure.'

Later that night Nick got so trashed he could barely remember his own name. He vomited on Mel's flabby thigh while Mel was driving, and then flopped into a foetal ball. He was exhausted with shame. He sobbed:

'Night, night, Mel,'

'Night, Nick. We'll talk in the mornin' mate.'

The silver-threaded skies were awash with stars and people's dreams but Mel's sprawling subterfuge was casting a Stygian gloom over everything, yoking Nick to the grain.

Chapter Fourteen: Career Opportunities

Joe was pressure popped. He had been asked to make another round of layoffs, look into advertising programmes, raise revenue for the paper and make numerous staff changes.

He yawned, his eyes squinting in the afternoon sunshine, which threw trellis- like patterns on his desk. Sweat rings circled his shirt sleeves and collar.

'Mr Gander.' Avery made a beeline for his desk.

'Yep.'

'That story I was working on?'

'What, the Trannie-Annie piece?'

'Well, it's changed – the paper needs a big story and I think I can get it.'

'Yeah – shazam! You're the answer we've been looking for.'

'Look, Mr Gander, I know things aren't going so well with the paper's finances, but this story, the one I'm working on, is potentially explosive. It features one of the biggest crime mobsters in the country, a former Tory cabinet minister and a pre-op transsexual who can potentially expose this man's criminal activities, and tap into his network of the criminal elite.'

Well I had to pitch it right so Gander would buy it

'What's the story?'

'It's not there yet, I'm still working on it, but the witness requires payment – some sort of protection and anonymity.'

'Hmmm.' Joe checked his watch then asked:

'How hot, how exclusive … on a scale of one to ten?'

Avery fixed her eyes on the vein at the top of his forehead.

'Right now it'd be a seven.'

'How reliable is the source?'

'Very. She was the subject's former lover and has intimated she may have access to some of his most personal documents and papers that could potentially destroy him.'

'So this is what you're up to, is it? Tired of lightweight stuff, want to get in the trenches, do you, Avery?'

'I'd like to take a shot, sir.'

'There's no moral high ground when it comes to the crunch, Avery.'

'Sir?'

'Witnesses can be notoriously unreliable. The information has to be in the public interest to justify the story.'

'Yes, sir.'

'If, after a full briefing, I decide it's worth running at some stage, if I decide it's sound, have you thought about how you're going to get the material you need?'

'Well, I thought that we could give the source a tape recorder, and she could use it undercover. Very simple low tech, but proven in its efficiency. I think the source still has access to this mobster by the way she talks about him. It's a gut feeling.'

'It needs to be an exclusive and we need to cover our arses. We don't want to be sued over this. You're gonna need more than your gut.'

'I understand.'

'You have to be in complete control, Avery. You have to take the lead and dictate the pace. It's a trust thing. You have to earn her trust.'

'Yes, sir. I've agreed to meet her later this week and am working on ways to persuade her it's the right move to make.'

'You need a tight game plan. This isn't the movies, not some scripted reality TV show. If you fuck up it's real peoples pay-packets on the line. We're not a huge money-making enterprise, Avery. We built this paper up from nothing, and what I always stick to, what I always believe in, is the truth.'

'Yes, sir.'

'Now, your source wants the story out there, right?'

'Yes, sir.'

'But she doesn't want to be identified?'

'Mmmmhmmm. But she wants payment, protection, and anonymity.'

'Shit. What else does she want, a fucking suite at The Savoy?'

'She's solid, sir.'

'I'll need to meet her, of course, when you're ready. This is high stakes Avery.'

'I know, sir. I won't put the paper at risk.'

'Papers have to "justify" their stories, Avery. They can't just be there for the sake of screwing someone over. There's got to be a bigger principle – a reason why the public should know about it.'

'Yes, sir.'

'The trouble with paying punters, is that sometimes they tell porkies to sustain their own story, or worse they hold back, so you have to make sure she's in the bag first Avery.'

'Yes, sir.'

'I like the idea – two big pieces, one about this woman-slash-man's life with this crime don and one about her life since leaving him etc. I'll also check some points with Legal.'

He slid back in his chair and tapped a memo on his Blackberry, and then spun round.

'Avery, get some real evidence too. The target can always sue, dismiss the story as malicious gossip from a spurned lover. Check her out. If she's a former junkie her story won't be worth that much and she'll get badly burnt.'

Fuck, I should have done that right at the very beginning.

'Yes, sir.'

'It's not enough just hooking her in, Avery, if we run this story, we want to bring the target down and get a pat on the back for it.'

'Yes, sir.'

'Well, what are you waiting for? You got plenty to do.'

'Yes, Mr Gander.'

Avery left his office, thoughts zooming around her brain. *When the going gets tough, the tough get creative.*

Chapter Fifteen: Yeah I Used to Love Her, But It's All Over Now

It was a flavourless day compressed with monotony.

'Hi, Mimi, it's …'

'Avery.'

'Yeah, how's you?'

'Fitter than a four foot flying monkey.'

Always the wit, always the smart gun.

'Can't say I've ever seen a real flying monkey.'

'Well it's a sight, dahling, especially if they're bald with creeping veins.'

'I'll be sure to keep a watch out.'

'You do that. Now, where we at?'

'Well, I've spoken to my editor and he's agreed we can do the story, but I think we should obviously have a meeting and clear up a few issues.'

'Yes, of course. Can we have it somewhere chi chi, a high tea perhaps?'

'Absolutely.'

Wonder where she'll want to go for that …?

'Now the main issue we have is how you're going to get Mel to talk. Do you—'

'Leave Mel to me. I know what pushes his buttons. You just give me the necessaries to do what I have to.'

'How long has it been since you were last together?'

'About six months. I know he's not seeing anyone, just a few working girls, nobody special.'

'Right.'

'Look, what I'm worried about, potentially, is the risk I face if Mel finds out it was me who fucked him over. He has lots of squealers on his payroll – they're terrified of him. I know he's nasty when he needs to be and I want the paper to secure my protection.'

'I understand. We have to handle it very carefully. Why don't we speak again when I've arranged something?'

'Sounds good.'

'Bye, Mimi.'

'Bye, Avery.'

The best way to protect Mimi, of course, would be for her to be kept completely off the record, but it was likely Mel would still know. I could run the story without names. Leveson has made it almost impossible to run a story without pulling out the legal armoury, as everyone's paranoid about getting gagged.

Avery got out her jotter and started drafting a legal affidavit for the company lawyer.

What we really need is a telephone recording or text message to pin him with.

She then wrote an email to her boss.

From: Avery Cross

To: Joe Gander

Re: Mel Greenberg Story – Mimi Deepridge.

Arranging further meeting and drafted affidavit for source. Will send to legal after lunch. Source has confirmed she can get Mel to reveal information of a criminal and commercially sensitive nature. Points for discussion: source's legal protection – can we run story anonymously with affidavit evidence from her? If she spoke 'on the record', the story carries more gravitas. Will need at least 2–4 weeks for story to work as source has to reconnect with MG and strategy has to be planned. Will update further after meeting.

Avery

There are so many angles to this story: the fact that Mel is Jewish and keeps connections in the community is significant. The orthodoxy would not only frown on his spiralling crime ring, but the relationship with Mimi is explosive in itself. I've got to get this story cut right.

'Ollie,' she hollered.

'Yeahhh.'

'Can you do me a favour please?'

'Depends.'

'On what?'

'On what you can do for me.'

'How about I don't rat on you for being a prick.'

'Only joking, Avery Jeez.'

'Yeah, well, the newspaper world is full of pricks, Ollie. You don't want to end up being a loudmouthed news prick. It's such a stereotype.'

'What do you need?'

'A new life, but in the meantime can you do some spot research on cool places to have afternoon tea in London.'

'Sure. Places to have high tea,' he grinned, clicking on Google.

'Don't mock it. Research is crucial in this job. Are you okay - you look a little out of it?'

'Yeah it's the Red bull and two bags of cheesy wotsits

I've just consumed. This "high tea", palaver a bit la-di-da isn't it?'

'Maybe, but what the lady wants, the lady gets,' Avery said impatiently.

'Who is she?'

'A woman who is in essence a true gent.'

'What?'

'A feature I'm working on, and the source needs to be well treated, as she has an unbelievable story and we want it.'

'Fuck, there're tons of places to have a tea party.'

'Anywhere with a sense of style and a little theatricality?'

'Yeah, loads. There's a Mad Hatter thing over at The Sanderson.'

'Anything else?'

'Well, can't do better than Claridge's. Fit for any queen. It's traditional, classy, and as well as forty different teas, they offer freshly baked apple scones, pastries, and finger sandwiches – top drawer.'

'Hmmm, who do we know at Claridge's?'

'Can't we just book it?'

'No, these places have got a waiting list as long as your arm, and they're very strict about reservations – easier to book a flight to a war zone – I'm being serious.'

'So now what?'

'Now it's time to tap into your thespian side and *Method* by telling a teensy little lie. Call them up. Now sit back and watch and learn …'

Ollie dialled the number. Then Avery grabbed the phone from him and put it on speaker.

'Hi, I'd like to talk with David?' she squealed in a high-pitched American accent.

'Good afternoon, madam. David who?'

'You know, David and Frederick, the owners.'

'I'm sorry, madam, if you're referring to David and Frederick Barclay, they aren't here. Can we help you in any way?'

'We met David last week at the grand prix and—'

'Sorry madam, if I may interrupt, who might you be?'

'I'm Nicola Jennings PA to Ms. Knowles and we'd like to arrange two for tea.'

'Er … Ms Knowles?'

'Bianca Jade Knowles.'

'Well, you'll have to go through reservations.'

'Sure.'

'One moment please, madam.'

There was a brief pause. Ollie was mouthing something. Avery scribbled, *Write it down on a post-it note*. He pencilled: *Bianca's Twitter feed says she is looking forward to Chime for Change Benefit gig. Not here*! Avery placed her hand on the receiver and spoke in a hushed tone.

'They won't know her exact itinerary. Look, blagging is a routine part of the job and this is the easiest kind of thing to blag. Ssshh.'

'Ms Jenkins, my name's Kristian Smalls I'm the—'

'General Manager, yes I know. You have gorgeous eyes.'

'Well, thank you. I don't recall ever meeting you.'

'A while back now last Fall. I'd like to make a reservation for Ms Knowles and a friend for next week.'

'I see, and this is for?'

'Afternoon tea: Ms Knowles and Ms Cross.'

'Certainly, if you'd just like to confirm that by fax with the date.'

'Of course.'

'Upon receipt of the fax, we'll telephone to double-check the booking for you.'

'Thank you so much, your discretion is very much appreciated.'

'Of course.'

Avery hung up.

'How you gonna get a fax to them. Isn't that illegal?' razzed Ollie making a sarcastic face.

'No, the fax will just say from AC. PR, or something like that, with this fax number, that we wish to confirm tea for two next Friday as arranged. Provided we don't mention who for etc. and it will be signed by me as Avery Cross.'

'Seems a lot of bullshit to go through to blag a table at Claridge's.'

'Well, to be honest, it's just an example of the lowest kind of blagging, and were it not for the fact we need to schmooze our source, it would be completely unnecessary.'

'But, isn't all blagging unethical and illegal Avery – my dad says it is.'

'Yeah, your dad's right. I mean, blagging personal info like phone bills, bank statements, health records and serious stuff like that is a complete no-no. The area can get very shadowy once the line is crossed. You can read all about it in The Data Protection Act.'

'And what you just did?'

'A confidence trick used to get access to an over-subscribed tea room. It's no biggie.'

Ollie wasn't buying it.

'Why not admit you're the paper and do it that way?'

'Because places like Claridges are famous for their exclusivity and would most likely have snubbed a humble paper.'

'Maybe, but at least you'd have told the truth. Now we have to do a fax and make it all formal.'

'Yeah, we do, so get to it, and use my mobile as a direct dial contact number, okay?'

'Fine.'

Tutting and frowning, Ollie shuffled over to his desk and started working on the fake document.

Joe was fending off another head office cull. They had asked him to seek a fifteen per cent reduction of the paper's staff in an attempt to overhaul the company. Buyouts, layoffs, everything was on the table. Somehow he just couldn't face losing all his photographic staff, but with everyone able to pop a pic from their phone, they were a luxury he must now do without. He knew this was an inevitable consequence of the internet era; real lives relegated to little more than collateral damage. Later that afternoon Avery rang Mimi:

'Mimi its Avery. We're hoping to get a table at Claridges for tea. If that's cool with you – maybe next week?'

'That would be lovely otherwise you can always find me at Verve not so glam but it's convenient -a night club. I nearly always end up there before or after gigs. Maybe easier?'

'Okay. I'll be in touch.'

' Can you believe after all our creative tinkering Mimi the magnificent may not even take us up on the invite to Claridges and suggested somewhere else instead - Verve?'

Ollie shrugged his shoulders.

'Really going off the newspaper biz. Might try being a DJ instead.'

'Part and parcel of the job Ollie don't sweat it.'

Once the email had been sent to Joe and the fax fired off anyway, Avery tried Nick's mobile. She had a VIP invite to a luxe event at the 02 Arena, perfect for a little bait and switch with Nick. There was no answer, so she sent him a text and carried on working.

Chapter Sixteen: Can I get a Witness

Mel, Nick and the others flew back to London with poison guts and a bad feeling. Mel had a lot to take care of and only a little time.

Nick agreed to see Matt later that evening and do music. It was a welcome break from the grit-shit of the last few days, and he was relieved to hear him on the phone.

'I want you to meet someone tonight, maybe you already have.' Matt was wrapped in a blue foil fantasy, day tripping away to the Grand Caymans and Seven Mile beach.

'Sure, who?'

'Just someone. He's well … you'll see …' he floated.

With him was Buddha Christ Mohammed, also known as BCM, six foot four with a rippled, sunburnt torso and poker straight hair, his eyes the colour of blue cactus. In his hand he carried a long stick and a faded leather satchel full of potions and homemade concoctions. A reflective mix of Gandalf and a young Tommy Lee Jones, he had an imposing dignity frayed with the weariness of a man who's seen too much. BCM had seen more than any mortal should, – seen things that the world wanted to hide. With a smart, sharp wit, he made a great friend and an even greater enemy.

Matt first came across this enigmatic traveller when he stumbled on a bloody hit and run. A young boy had been launched into the road by a joy rider who quickly fled the scene. The child was weeping and badly hurt. 'BCM' was leaning over his wounded body attempting to comfort him. Although it was a busy West London street, police and medical help were slow off the mark. Crowds started gathering. Shocked passers-by and a gaggle of do-gooders just clouded the atmosphere. BCM and the bleeding boy remained unaffected, as if cocooned from the chaos. BCM reached into his bag, removed a stick of sage and calmly asked a bystander to light it and hold it for him. He slowly took the child's hurt leg with his left hand as he used his right to cover his own eyes, tilting his head to the skies. You could see the agony on the child's face. Then, all at once, BCM cried out, 'Shem de la Shem de le shog!' Matt had watched as a gentle equilibrium coddled the boy. With a white cloth from his satchel, BCM had stopped all the bleeding before the medics had arrived, and beyond all reason the suffering child lay in the street exuding a rosy peace. BCM leaned in close saying something to the child that made him laugh. There, in the middle of a crash scene, surrounded by raised voices and emergency sirens, BCM had somehow managed to erase the child's pain and shelter him from darkness. Then he picked the child up, carried him to the pavement and sat by his side until the ambulance finally arrived. The child was saved. It was unbelievable. A miracle moment. Matt met him again several times after that, and they became close friends.

Matt's man crush on BCM was borderline obsessive, but BCM was easy about it.

'That was him.'

'Your friend – Nick?'

'Yeah, the one I want you to talk to. The one I want you to heal.'

'What exactly is the problem?'

'Well, it started a few weeks back. He met a businessman, a big-league mobster, and he's been different ever since – seems to have lost his morality – we've got gigs coming up for the band too and he seems different. I think the power's swallowed him whole.'

Talking like this to BCM felt right. BCM stretched out his long, lean legs and eased his spliff to his lips, tokin' it fat.

'This friend of yours. He the lawyer?'

Matt nodded.

'You know what the power of a lawyer is?'

'What?' BCM raised his hands behind his head and blew deep through his nose.

'A lawyer can **create** the truth – even the greatest artist can't do that.'

Matt watched in awe, as BCM fluted the air with a kind of prayer. Matt closed his eyes and sank back onto the sofa, oblivious to the sound of the street. The hypnotic chant lulling him to sleep as the room fell silent.

BCM left Matt snoozing and scribbled a message for him on the back of a toffee wrapper. It read: *Luck falls where it needs to see you. Buddha Christ Mohammed.*

He opened the door, eyeing a fat knucklehead with flattop hair. They locked eyes.

'Oi, you fuckin' weirdo, what the fuck you lookin at?' he globbed, spit bubbles smearing his upper lip. 'Are you Matt? Mel's got a message for you. Stay away from Nick.'

BCM was unnerved.

'Oi, you listening? Stay away or else.'

BCM continued to walk towards him, speaking firmly. 'Don't do anything you'll regret, friend.'

'I ain't your friend. Do you know who you're fucking with? I'll kill you!'

'I don't think so.' BCM stood solid.

And then came the blow, a clumsy wayward punch that did little. BCM fenced it off with a strong hand and a steely look. Fat fist took a swipe, and tripped into a clownish heap, knocking his head on the ground.

BCM leant down and felt for his pulse;

'In the sleep of eternity, you shall find the lesson of life.'

Outside, the sky was running through a *Dulux* palette of

blues, greys and pinks that splattered the eastern horizon like Japanese pop art. It was a symphony of painted optimism. BCM reached into his satchel and took out a small compass-like object with markings and symbols engraved into the metal. He pointed it forward, the arrows jumped north-west. He walked ahead towards Hatton Garden. He was only a few blocks away from Nick's flat and minutes from Mel's local.

Outside Deux Beers, BCM chalked the pavement with a circle and stepped inside, reciting an incantation, tapped his left cowboy boot three times and then entered the bar. It was insanely surreal for a Monday night. Inside, the slaving ebb of pushy bar staff and the clink-drink chatter of pissed office workers created a whirring buzz. BCM moved away from the numbers to a darkened part of the dive. Although smoking was banned and had been for some time now, the pub still stank of ash, toilet bleach and cheap rotisserie chicken – the generic kind: chicken that smells of cabbage. He pulled the chair back and sat down, watching the scene before him unfold. A curvy brunette with slip and slide hips sauntered over. She wore a low-cut blouse and a tight-fitting skirt, her jacket bunched in her arm like a stale afterthought. She slid her tongue between her teeth and opened her mouth tossing her head back.

'You're a little different from the usual,' she giggled showing her gums.

BCM just nodded as if he were engaging with a harmless animal. He sensed she would be a handful.

'Do you mind if I sit here,' she prattled, oblivious to his response, setting her duck-butt down. BCM kept quiet.

'Oooh, your eyes are gorgeous.'

BCM looked away. He found her over-forward and had no time for recreational pussy. He tried a polite brush off: 'I'm not into this today – not feeling good, sorry.'

'Aww, darlin', I know just the thing that'll make you feel better.' She scrunched her face, stiffening her make-up. Her hair was clamped into a work bun. She undid it, faking a slo-mo TV ad, shaking loads of head flakes onto the table. It was awkward, but the woman was too boozed to care. 'Oops, sorry. Only a bit of hair floss.'

BCM was expressionless.

'What's your name, handsome?'

'Buddha Christ Mohammed.'

She looked at him with a foreign disquiet.

'You're not one of those converts are ya?'

'My name's Buddha Christ Mohammed,' he repeated.

'Oi, Si,' she belched. 'We got one of *them* 'ere.'

A red-nosed lard-head with a jiggle-belly and hairy chest came thumping over. The sweat stains gassing the arms of his white shirt had become yellow. He spit–spoke, spraying saliva everywhere.

'Whhhhat?'

'Guess what this man's name is?' She burped.

'Dunno.'

'Go on, tell him.'

'Buddha Christ Mohammed.'

'Fuckin' hell. What a fuckin' mouthful.'

'I think he's an Islamist Si'. One of those, you know, crazy terrorists.'

'Yeah, wif a name like that – but isn't Buddhism peaceful? Richard … actor fellow … you know, what's his name … yeah, Richard Gere, that's it, 'e's one,' Si replied.

BCM looked at them with a wry stare:

'Are you guys just dumb or do your brains need a rest?'

Si put his arms behind him and scowled.

'Are you being funny?'

'Do you find that funny?'

'What?'

'Think you're a right comedian, don't ya?'

'There's plenty better Si? But I always think laughing's easier for a fool.'

'Fuck you. You takin' the piss?'

'Last time I checked, no.'

'You fink you're a fucking someone.' Si lurched closer.

'Trust me, spending the evening with you and your

associates really brings it home to me that I'm really no one.'

'Oi, listen up, there's a fuckin' Islamist in 'ere … a fuckin' terrorist.'

Everybody in the bar turned towards them, the dumbness of the statement hushing the bar still. The words hung in the air like an invisible block of iron. BCM attempted to get up. Si blocked him with his beer-stained mitt. BCM swiped his hand away, with the ease of a young Bruce Lee. Then, deftly disposed of seven other try-hards. He left a trail of broken noses, splintered wrists, and bruised egos. BCM slipped the bartender some cash for the damage and whispered: 'There are many kinds of people that annoy me, but ignorance and no sense of humour annoys me the most.'

Chapter Seventeen: Move On Up

Avery was vibing the boom, boom, boogie of the night. She felt like Gena Rowlands in *Gloria* – ready willing and able. She double-checked herself in the mirror and brushed away an eyelash hair, wishing on it for luck. She popped her supa-pimped spy phone in her purse, bought for Mimi, to extract as much intel as she could on Mel. It worked very simply by acting as a 'dead phone', one that appeared to be broken or drained of battery power, but as soon as it rang, it answered automatically in silent mode. It came installed with an internal, self-charging optimum power battery that lasted for days. Once it was activated, the caller was able to hear and record everything. Avery herself, had a more primitive version that only recorded a limited amount of data but was pretty effective and looked just like an ordinary Blackberry.

She speed dialled Mimi.

'Hi, it's Avery. How's everything?'

'All going to plan. Mel's come back from a trip to Pau. He has a place over there, so he must have been up to something. One of his heels told me he'd be at *Stringfellows* around eleven. I'll be in Verve first around half ten so we could meet then?'

'Great.'

'Hasn't Mel got his own strip club?'

'Yeah but for down time he goes to Stringie's.'

'Of course, where else would he be but Stringie's,

frequented by soap stars and middle-aged account execs called Nigel.'

'Got lots of friends who've worked there. Not all of them are happy though.'

'That's the thing with table dancing. It can be big money but there's not much dignity in stripping off for twenty quid and paying management fees for the privilege of getting your kit off.'

'I know, dahling, but it's one of the oldest professions around, just revamped now and again. The idea is that you make enough to take home, so it doesn't eat into your savings. Eventually it all catches up with you. 'Avery was irritable but stayed on topic.

'All this fucking freedom and women in the West oinking on about equality, but the truth is they're still being pimped for profit. I mean, they should regulate businesses like that so people aren't fucking exploited.'

'It's still very much a male preserve dahling. And of course a club like that dictates how you look, who you dance for … same old sexism tarted up as female empowerment. What's so liberating about slutting yourself out to a sleaze ball who controls every fucking moment of your life and takes a huge slice of your earnings?'

Avery wasn't up to a stirring soliloquy on the downside of stripping but let Mimi continue.

'Yeah, and the other way they tap cash from the dancers is to fine them for shit like being in the loos too long, not turning up to meetings and even having a bad hair day!'

'If the sex and skin biz was better regulated, women might have more control.'

'Mel was quite good to his dancers from what I saw.'

Avery quickly wrapped up the conversation with a meet time to hand over the phone.

'Okay, so I'll see you around 10.30 at Verve.'

'You can't miss it cheap repro furniture and a big chandelier in the middle of the bar. It's perfect for those Barbette phonies all chewing gum, looking dumb with hi –

res spa-tans and nowhere plans.'

'You could write a song.'

'I could do many things, my dear, but I'm staying low for now. Mel can be tricky.'

'We'll have a final chat when we meet, but it'll be okay. I've got another event at the 02 first, so it's gonna be a busy night. Everything's gonna be fine I promise.'

'If promises were gold, dahling, I'd be richer than Tori Black.'

'Hmmm, well, it's a start. See you later.' Avery had no idea who Tori Black was and threw the name out of her mind.

'Okay.'

Avery was undecided. *If I take a friend, I'll be babysitting all night. If I take Ollie, he'll ask too many questions. I'll go alone and see what I can cream out of Nick.*

A little while later She called a cab and left a message for Nick: *Hi, it's me, just making sure we're on for tonight use my name to get in and I'll see you soon.* She waited at the entrance of her apartment block. Outside, London town was filling up with the bad, the beautiful and the buzzed, while weary office workers and grad students made their way home. The lamps by the River Thames were bouncing cords of light across the pavements, bathing the streets with pastel luminosity. The air was barbed with the rinky-dink-dink of party laughs, the sound of car brakes, mobile phones and drunken chit-chat. It was pump and bump for a loaded Friday night.

As she pulled up to the entrance of the O2, Avery realised why she'd bagged tickets for this star-studded bash. No one else wanted to cover it. She loathed Russell 'I'm-a-rock-star without-a-band' Brand. Just the sight of him in skin tight leather layered with beads and New Age knuckle rings made her gag. Avery didn't quite understand her feelings about Brand but thought Nick would make a welcome distraction from the romantic frilly shirts, pre-Raphaelite curls and over-sauced mockney twang. Security was tight – there were men in black with clipboards and walkie-talkies ushering people in and checking faces and passes. This was the only perk of working showbiz events: freebies.

Deftly passing Helen Mirren, classy in ocelot, she glimpsed Brand and Claudia Schiffer to her right. Schiffer resplendent in a floor-length nude gown, channelled retro charm, leaving Brand overshadowed in a plain suit with trademark designer stubble. Once inside, she found Nick already mixing with cast and crew.

'Hi.'

'Thanks so much for inviting me here Avery I love Brand.'

'I'm so glad.'

'I never knew there were so many big stars in this movie.'

'Ssshh, we can talk after.'

The lights dimmed and the rustle of snack wrappers and programmes could be heard. After about forty minutes Avery, bored shitless, found herself yawning.

'Oh my God, this is crap.'

'I know.'

'Let's hit it.'

It was hard to navigate the auditorium in the dark, but eventually they broke through the surveillance wall and exited the building. Avery's face was full of excitement.

'What a fucking disaster. Can't believe he did that!

'You mean the film in general or that last scene?'

'No, the whole thing. I mean the people in there can't possibly think that was an achievement?'

'Piece of performance art.'

'Let's go get drinks at Verve.'

'Why there?'

'Got a little bizzo to take care of.'

'Sure. I haven't told you by the way, you look terrific.'

'Aww thanks very much.' *Glad I wore black, chic, understated. So me.*

'Taxi!'

'Easy, Nick.' She leaned over and pulled him away from the road._'You've got to stick your hand in the air too, otherwise they ignore you.'

The cab was warm inside, free from the elitist dinosaurs and cocktail chickstas posing for press and paparazzi. Avery flopped into her seat, stretching her legs and tossing her heels to the side.

'Oh, that's much better.'

'There's a reason they call them killer heels,' smiled Nick, shaking his head.

'Yeah I'd like to see you try.' She thrust a shoe at him.

Nick swirled them around in his hand, checking their label whistling his appreciation. 'Nicceee.'

'Yeah, the price wasn't nice.'

'They do look stunning though.'

'Thanks.'

'So, been working on any cool stories?'

'Not really. I've got something cooking, but morale is low. Loads of people at the paper have been laid off and there's more cuts to come.'

'Sorry. Isn't that just the sign of the times?'

'Maybe I dunno. They got rid of a whole fucking department like a tsunami First the "shooters" get wiped out, then it's only a matter of time before more of us get the chop. They may have saved heaps of money, but it means that we have to take snappy snaps when we're working a story. It's not the same, and it's killing a serious part of news journalism. Blame it on the selfie generation. How about you?' Avery reached inside her bag and discreetly turned on the Blackberry, activating record.

'I was in Pau visiting two young drug runners.'

'Drugs, Pau? I thought you were an entertainment lawyer, music biz, that kind of thing?'

'Yeah, I wear lots of hats.'

'Don't you need to specialise in crime and European law at least?'

'Guess it helps, but as a solicitor I'm trained to do it all.'

'Like a family doctor?'

'Yeah, like that.'

'So, how was it?'

Nick paused for a moment.

'It was like looking into a bucket of dead dreams.'

'Shit, that's heavy.'

'Yeah there's no way of hiding it. Two young lives thrown away.'

'Did they know what they were doing, what risk they were taking?'

'The guy knew … kind of, but not his girlfriend.'

'Pressure.'

'Yeah, if it doesn't work out for them, they'll lose more than just physical freedom, they'll lose their minds. It's a heavy price to pay.'

'Wow, that place really affected you.'

'It was suffocating. That feeling, that death was better than being under lock and key twenty-four-seven.

'Yeah I get you – must be really hard to switch off – lucky not all your clients are banged up.'

'Yeah that's true. I mean, I'm happier doing the less emotive stuff, music artist agreements and contracts.'

'I thought Fisher Fowler and Ferret were like corporate bigwigs.'

'Yeah, they do have a rep for being tax wizards: saving millions for fat cat companies but I mainly do other stuff.'

'What else? I mean apart from the fringe criminal work and the music stuff?'

'I'm kind of tied up with one special client, and he offloads all manner of shit on me.'

'Right.' Avery knew exactly who Nick was talking about but faked distraction when her phone rang.

'Excuse me, I've got to take this.'

'Sure.'

'Hi. Yeah, I'm on my way. Be there in like ten minutes. Okay, okay, relax.'

'Trouble?'

'This individual I'm meeting, she's a little jittery.'

'Why's that?'

'She's helping me with a story. She's nervous.'

'Oh, right.'

'So you were saying about this one client who brings all this work your way?'

'Yeah, he's a Jewish entrepreneur – kind of Alan Sugar meets Scarface.'

Avery made a sarcastic throat sound.

'Yeah, I wish I was joking.'

'Are you Jewish? I only ask because I saw the Star of David tat on your wrist.'

'I've got other tats too but to answer your question, technically I am Jewish, as my mother's Jewish, but my father's mixed, so I guess you could say the dreamier half of me is Jewish.'

'I think Jewish men are great,' Avery fluttered, trying to break the heaviness of the conversation.

'Why's that?'

'Don't pretend – you know why.'

'Oh that.'

'Ah, so coy.'

'No, just intrigued.'

Finally, they got to Verve, the cab circling around for a few minutes.

'I'll get it. Think of it as a company expense.' Avery dived into her purse and took out a crumpled £20.

'Keep the change,' she twirled, as if knee deep in money.

They found Mimi holding court at a centre table. She wore a classic Hervé Leger body –con stretch dress. Draping each curve like plastic wrap, she shone. She had backcombed her hair, parting her fringe, which fell to one side in a flirt flick. As Avery walked up to her, Mimi leapt from her chair and tattled:

'Dahling, over here, precious, '

'Ohhh kay, I'm going to get a drink while you … er … go do your bizzo chat with …'

'Yeah, words failed me too when I first met Mimi. I'll come get you at the bar.'

Avery was playing it tight with Nick at the bar and Mimi on display. It was slippery ground.

'So who's he?' asked Mimi looking Nick up and down.

'Just a friend.'

'Mmmm, fab hair.'

Avery clocked the table. It was full of random guys, drunk and hot-faced – quite literally steaming testosterone. Avery needed to get Mimi alone and show her how to use the phone. She signalled: the ladies.

'Excuse me, gentlemen. I have to pop to the loo, and then if anyone's up for it I'm off to Stringie's.'

They tottered off to the loos, their heels scraping the floor with a dozen eyes trailing their wiggle and jiggle. They knew they were being watched and gave the guys an eyeful.

Avery looked around. No one else was in there so she squeezed them both into a cubicle.

'Is this really necessary, dahling?'

'Yes, ssshh, now listen.' She took out the phone and held it in her left hand.

'Right, now, see this button.' She pointed.

'Yes.'

'This is the automatic button and this is the number you dial from your regular phone. It will answer and activate record automatically. Got it?'

'Yes.'

'All you have to do is leave the phone on and put it in Mel's jacket pocket.'

'I'll do my best.'

'Great. Now, what time do you think you might see him?'

'I was told he'd be at Stringie's around eleven.'

'Okay. Any problems, any worries, just buzz me.'

'Got it.'

'Good luck Mimi, I'll speak to you in a couple of days, yeah?'

'Fine.'

Avery made her way back through the bar and found Nick getting progressively drunk.

'Why don't we finish this at my place?'

'Whoa, right to it, eh? I like a woman who doesn't play games.'

'I don't believe in the slow dance. You like something, you gotta go for it, right?'

'I agree. Let's dump the small talk. It's a waste of time.'

'The way I see it – small talk, small minds, small - everything.'

'In that case you're heading in the right direction. No need to worry about small minds or small "anything" tonight. Let's go shall we?'

Nick chugged down his whisky and they left the bar together. Avery was fluffing, pretending to be over-tipsy, touching his face and rolling her fingers through his hair. Both of them were acting wasted and both were semi-sober. Each had a reason not to trust the other but both were attracted to each other. It was a double bluff.

Inside the cab, Avery made the first move. Lying in the back seat, half-strewn across Nick, face to face, she grabbed the underside of his thigh, squeezing firmly. At the same time, Nick's hand slapped her tight behind. Kind of surprised, she volleyed back as if they were in a competition, cupping her hand over his cock.

Breathless, she whispered: 'No small anything here. Can't wait for *that* in my mouth.' Either Avery was giving an Oscar-worthy performance or was hotter than a hellcat. She slid over him, the cab seats squeaking noisily while he kissed the back of her neck and reached underneath her dress, his hand between her legs, lifting her slightly. He was horny and ready for the draw. She was wet through her silk knickers. They were fever pitch high. Nick murmured: 'Mmm, that feels good.'

The driver snuck a glance in the rear mirror.

'Where to Gov?' Hearing his voice Nick abruptly pulled away. Avery answered while patting down her hair and straightening her clothes her voice was faint: 'Britten Street, EC1.' The cabbie steered his attention back on the road.

Avery got out her compact and reapplied some lip gloss.

'Well, that was a little awkward, I had forgotten we weren't alone.'

'We had a nice moment.'

'Hang on to that thought. We'll be at my flat soon.' She kissed him hard, pinching his bottom lip between hers, giving him a taste of what was to come. They rode the rest of the way almost in silence, except for the occasional caress. Casual conversation seemed false after such a heated tryst.

After a few minutes, the cab slowed to the kerb in front of Avery's apartment. Nick hit the driver with a fifty through the front window of the cab. 'Keep the change.'

Looking wilder than a four-balled tomcat, he raced towards her, stumbling on a step.

Avery covered her mouth as she laughed.

'Don't hurt yourself before we reach the top. This is all yours tonight.' She ran her hands across her body like an *FHM* model. He sped up the staircase just the same, crashing into her at the top and taking her into his arms as they disappeared behind the doorway.

Got to keep this together. Got to get information on Mel – another voice hit back – *No harm in having a little fun on the job. Guys do it all the time.* It was settled in her mind. Nick flipped her by the hips.

'Are you alright, babe?' His concern warmed her but not enough to lose control.

'I'm fine, gorgeous,' she simmered running her fingers through his hair. He guided her through the door and slid her against it. Taking her head in his hands as he kissed her over and over. She wrapped her legs around him, drawing him in tight. Slammed against the wall they were pulling at each other's clothes, frenzied with lust. Avery stopped and placed her fingers over Nick's mouth. Leaning forward, she looked at him with please-me-tease–me eyes and turned towards the bedroom. They tumbled to the side of the bed. Nick hiked her dress to her thigh. With a wolfish growl he snapped her G –string, ripping it in half in one startling motion.

Avery gasped as he reached for her warm, wet pussy. With a shy smile she pulled back and dropped to the bed, seated. Legs akimbo, she fumbled at Nick's belt, pulling down his jeans, pausing for a second. Nick grinned as she yanked his boxers off, his cock falling right in front of her face – three-quarters firm and growing. She took it in her hand, raising it to her lips, opening her mouth, gagging slightly as it hit her throat. Nick tugged her head back as she sucked harder. He pushed her to the bed, slowly climbing between her thighs, spreading her legs wide. Avery knew better than to trust a guy about to unload. She was breathless:

'I hope . . . you don't think . . . that's going inside me before . . . you wrap it.'

'Oh fuck, course not. Just lost my head there for a minute. You got any?'

Avery turned over and reached for the drawer on her night stand. Grappling around in the dark she snagged a handful.

'This is your lucky day. You got a choice – go all night or super flavours?'

'I'll go with staying power.'

Nick slid the condom on.

'Don't you turn back around on me now.'

He grabbed her hips and pulled her to him, kissing her navel. As she drew him into her swollen pussy, she let out the sweetest sigh. Coke-spurred, he thrust into her a second time, their bodies entwined in a warm steamy haze. Avery was in a daze, finally remembering she was there to extract Intel. *Wow, he's a stud.*

Nick pulled Avery on top, their eyes meeting. As if reading her mind, he commented,

'Bet you never expected things to go down like this.' He paused trying to keep the eagerness out of his voice.

'I haven't felt this good in a long time.'

Avery spread out on the bed and edged away from him.

'Don't pretend you're not in the middle of one of the best shags of your life.'

A few minutes later, she groped for her emergency cigs on her nightstand.

'Wanna smoke?'

'No you go ahead.' She snuggled up close. Nestled in his arms, she followed the smoke rings up towards the ceiling. They kissed the dawn away, their minds adrift.

Something was happening; the fun part was over and Avery had some sleuthing to do. It felt good and bad, but mostly bad.

Chapter Eighteen: Satta Massagana

BCM felt the tug of his spirit guide. Ever since he was a child he had been gifted this way. When his parents died, it was his grandfather, a highly revered shaman of the Lakota tribe, who told him that this would follow him throughout his life, prompting him to seek the wisdom of his ancestors. An important message was waiting for him from the other side. He just needed an opportunity to pierce the veil. He craved peace and serenity. He needed to get back to nature and knew just the right spot. Every summer he would visit Highgate Cemetery, a little hilly haven he felt close to. His girlfriend Aria was buried there. They met in Brazil, and he had followed her to London only to witness her gruesome death in a railway accident. He started off on the eastern side, a tourist hot spot, famous for the interment of Karl Marx. He paused and read the inscription.

It was a soft sultry evening, shadows eclipsing the thickets with mysterious shapes, the lyre of birdsong corralling the grounds. He walked slowly to Aria's small well-tended grave. He kept his visitor's card with him at all times. The grounds were so popular with the living they were closed off to the public except for guided tours and prearranged appointments.

A refuge for souls has become a cheap Disney attraction. He placed a single pink rose on the fresh ripened soil. A sublime vista of green, gold and orange flamed the graves with a blissful arc of light. *My home, my future, I find no sorrow, no disappointment, no pain – peace branches these veins of life.*

By his side was a child of four or five, laughing gently, her spirit gliding through the trees. *Truth comes first to those whose minds are free, but gradually truth comes to all.* He watched the child disappear into the woods and continued to recite prayers: *Let us stop worshipping the votaries of sin, stop idolatry, of celebrities and gold. Let us sever the hanging necktie of bigotry and take comfort in the ultimate light of celestial purity. Light upon light, let us unshackle the chain of ignorance and reveal the fountain of truth.* BCM was sitting underneath a shaded oak in dove-like solitude. What he liked best about this site was the diversity of faiths and ethnicities represented. Be they Muslim, Catholic, Christian or Jew, they had all found solace in this wooded sanctum.

He ambled across the paths, checking headstones and memorials. Some ornate and grand, others more humble and modest, all a tablet reminder of lost lives. Nourished by his abstract ruminations and soulful reflection of Aria, he continued west to Egyptian Avenue, flanked by two columns and circled by cherry laurels in full bloom, their lush flowers guarding the gate to the entrance. Through the avenue and past the family vaults, steering clear of French and Japanese coach parties, he followed the path north to the Circle of Lebanon, another imposing area of funerary architecture. Gothic and classical styles competed with Egyptian examples of burial grandeur. There by the Terrace Catacombs he stopped underneath a magnificent cedar spanning three centuries, perfected by time and nature. He looked around him and continued climbing a small hill, spotting a tiny parcel of bushes and trees cut off from the public pathway. As he got closer to the greenery, he saw a swift white light skim past the corner of his eye, like a comet – the shaman's version of 'call waiting'. He braced himself and crawled through an overgrown thicket. There he found a beautifully remote and tranquil opening marked by one solitary willow tree, its wavy branches creating a natural shield.

This is perfect. BCM rested his back as he began to rifle through his satchel. There was only one entheogenic plant that would do the trick. A smokable form of DMT, a must for any shaman on the go. DMT, derived from jungle vines in the Amazon and dubbed the spirit molecule by Western scientists, was the star ingredient in ayahuasca: a lethal concoction dating back thousands of years, used by medicine men to help them escape everyday life. Now, it was the favoured choice of hipsters, college grads and psychedelic thrill junkies looking for legitimate ways to mind manifest. For BCM it was something more than a subliminal high. He took out a small glass vial, ready to blast off. He only needed a little. He cautiously sprinkled a pinch of the golden shale-like powder into his trusted wooden pipe. Taking his first hit, he let out a billow of thick white smoke as he flexed his spine and relaxed against the tree. Then another hit, this one a little deeper, holding the smoke in his lungs a bit longer than the first time. He felt vibrations strumming his brain and a slight spin. He knew he was close. He took one last drag, making sure to ignite all the DMT left. Deep into his diaphragm he breathed, holding it for as long as his lungs would allow.

'Whooo!' Exhaling, he sped into orbit. Before he even expelled the smoke he was whirring through the stratosphere. *I'm the rocket man. Fireworks are spiralling.* BCM felt the energy of his body surge upward through twisting geometric patterns that were ablaze with colour. He broke through a fluorescent green cloud and dived into an emerald city. He recognised Aztec imagery and saw shrines made of luminescent glass.

Got to calm down, take one breath at a time. He took a series of deep breaths to steady his nerves as an electrifying drum-thump blanketed his vision. He heard thunder in the distance. It was tribal and primitive. He moved with that beat, swaying his body from side to side as he became one on a trippadelic ride. A small iridescent flame began to flicker at the centre of the horizon. With each beat it grew closer, heading straight for him along a crystalline causeway. Finally the flame was only inches away. Within it a figure emerged. He could sense it was a woman by the shape of the body.

'Sacred spirit of the vine, I didn't expect *you*.'

'Don't dissuade yourself, my son.' When the apparition spoke he recognised the lyrical beauty that flowed from her lips. It sounded like his great-grandmother. As she floated before him, he was submerged in her velvet embrace. She leaned closer, raising her hand, pressing the centre of his brow with her finger. Just then a jaguar leapt from the darkness – claws bared, teeth gnashing, swiping at his chest.

'Awwwooo!'

Growling with such toxic intensity, BCM cowered, as it set itself up for another attack.

This is a malevolent sign. What now? He nodded at the large cat, who just sat there eyeing him with rage. Winding his head down, the animal's face morphed for a brief second into that of man's. There was no mistaking it. It was the face of evil scarped with Satan's fork. To BCM it was a warning of some kind, that's why he let it blot his mind. Hissing and spitting, the jaguar pawed the ground. *I don't see you. I don't see you* – he knew better than to toy with this beast from the other side. He relaxed and took several more deep breaths.

Just behind the big cat was a youngling eager to play, but it was clearly in the older one's clutches. The cub tried to tumble with BCM, but the older cat wouldn't allow it and seizing his chance struck the little whelp with a vicious blow. The cub tried to jump out of reach, landing on BCM's chest. Face to face, its features were sliding into another person – male. Again, he didn't recognise who it was but was struck by the innocence of his eyes. He knew from past encounters he'd see them again. With a slashing cry the cub faded away. The larger cat remained, pacing its territory. With a menacing stare it placed itself directly at BCM's feet. He looked away and noticed that the ground beneath the jaguar had started to seep blood – thick warm blood oozing through its paws, the cat's evil grin spreading like a giant clown's mouth. A red pool flooded the scene until his entire vision – the ground, the flowers, the shrubs – were submerged in a violent red mass, until finally the sky bled red.

BCM made eye contact with the jaguar once more, both of them trying to stare each other out. Then, with a final ear-splitting scream, it lashed out and dissolved into the night.

As he came to, it started to rain. BCM was left with more questions than answers. He pulled his collar up as the downpour got heavier and denser, and then he saw it in a blip of a second, a juvenile pipistrelle bruising the horizon with its deadly squawk. The bat swooped closer, circling his head with its flapping leather wings, and then flew away haunting the skies with dread.

BCM looked around and dusted himself off. Highgate village wasn't far from the park. He'd find a place for the night and then head over to Matt's later.

As he trekked on, lightning struck. He found himself outside The Flask tavern, a traditional old English pub. Sitting alone at one of the tables was a nerdy Asian guy wearing specs. He was nursing a warm beer when BCM joined him.

'May I?'

'Sure, why not.'

'I've had a long day.'

'I hear you man.'

'To friendship.'

They clinked glasses.

'What do you, er …?'

'Do for a living?'

'Yeah.'

'I'm trying to work that one out. My new boss hired me, telling me I'd be selling financial products to a sophisticated market.'

'And?'

'And so far no one's buying – after friends and family

gave me the cold shoulder, my only leads now are an eighty-five-year-old grandma who lives off her pension, a couple of hard-up students who earn less than me, and a redundant fire-fighter laid off after injury. None of them seem the investing type but my boss wants me to sign them all up.'

'Seems like your boss has a different perspective.'

'Yeah. How about you, what do you do? Nice cane, never seen one that detailed.'

'It's very old and from China. Bamboo from China.

'Wow, that's cool.'

'It has its moments.'

'So what line of business are you in?'

'I'm a guide. Yeah, a life guide.'

'What, like one of those life coaches?'

'In a way. Life can't be coached from the outside. The real coach is inside of you or he may just be lost on holiday or playing World of Warcraft twenty-four-seven.

'Yeah.' He nodded. 'So you give people advice on what decisions to make and what shirt looks best with their trousers, is that it?'

'Not quite, but that could be useful to some.'

'Yeah, makes you wonder though what kind of prat needs to hire someone to choose and style their wardrobe.'

'I don't know, jogging suits and plaid shirts don't suit everyone. And what's with the obsession with stripes? They're fucking everywhere.'

'Yeah, that's true nautical chic. It's like you don't have a boat but you got deck shoes. Ha! Good luck to them if they've got money to spend on shit like that. Did you hear about that guy from India? He was drenched in gold, had all these Western devotees and was like some kind of guru. He made them wear signs, like 'do not speak', and they weren't allowed to speak for, say, ten days. Fucking ridiculous. He's made a fortune out of this shit. I mean, people pay him for this shit.'

'Maybe *they* need that kind of shit?'

'Maybe, especially if they're all decked out in stripes.'

BCM knew that people saw him in the same way: a New Age bounty hunter stalking for souls. He let it ride. The old creaking floors, pure wood panelling and sloping ceilings made him feel comfy, almost as if he were in a different time.

'Just going to the gents.'

'Sure.'

A few minutes later BCM reappeared settled back in his chair and took another swig:

'Very respectable.'

'What?'

'The gents, they were in excellent condition.'

'Oh, yeah right, the publican likes to keep a clean house.'

'Indeed.'

'So how's the life – whatever it is you actually do – working out for you?'

'It's working …'

'Great.' The nerdy guy smiled amiably.

'I like the ceilings in here.' BCM angled his head up.

'Yeah, it's the original building from way back when.'

'Yes.'

'Sorry, I didn't catch your name.'

'I didn't give it to you.'

'No, sorry. I'll go first -name's Mushtaq – Mushi – Saddique. '

'Buddha Christ Mohammed.'

In between sips of beer, Mushi spluttered: 'What?' And almost toppled off his chair.

'Buddha Christ Mohammed.'

'Seriously, your parents, called you that at birth?'

'My parents are dead.'

'Sorry mate. What a fucking spectacular name though, Buddha Christ Mohammed.'

'It can be a talking point.'

'I bet. I can honestly say I've never met anyone called that before.'

'And you're unlikely to again.'

'Yep.'

'Buddha Christ Mohammed – what about your surname?'

'It's not important.'

'Seriously, do you sign your credit card bills with Buddha Christ Mohammed on there?'

'Everything is signed with my name.'

'Course it is, yeah, fuck me …'

'So what about you – heart in the right place?

'Think so, maybe – I dunno, why?'

'Had a vision this bar would burn to the ground tonight – no survivors – but if your heart's in the right place …'

'Are you fucking serious?'

'Almost never.'

BCM started to smile and Mushi grinned nervously. They continued spilling the time away and then BCM's eyes lost their mischievous glint and he became more serious.

'I need a favour.'

'I'd like to help, but obviously if it's a financial kind of favour I wouldn't be able to. You know, I just started my …'

'I need you to listen - not say anything else for the next ten minutes, just listen to what I have to say. Can you do that Mushtaq?'

Mushi's eyes became cautious *This wacko comes into the boozer, takes a pew at my table, and now he wants me to listen. So mysterious, as if the world's gonna end.*

'I don't know I was meant to meet my girlfriend for a twilight stroll of the cemetery – I should get back. She'll be waiting.'

'The cemetery?'

'She's quirky like that – a bit of a Goth appreciates the dark side of life. The romance of the supernatural – that's why I suggested the walk.'

'Ah I see. Well if you listen to what I say both of you may learn something. What's the harm?'

This guy's a little weird but seems harmless – just a hippie. What the hell, it will be a good story to tell if nothing else. May as well let the kook spill.

'Yeah why not, ten minutes. So long as it's not about weird shit or creepy stripes.'

'It's just a little life guidance, dude.'

'I'm all ears.'

Later that night when Mushi got home, he crept upstairs to his room and never spoke to a soul. He tossed and turned, unable to sleep. Darkness surrounded him like a prison wall, vast and voracious, swallowing him whole. Shaken, he leapt up and turned on the light.

This isn't fucking rational. I must be tripping. He walked to the window, opened it, and breathed in the smoky air. It felt good to taste that concrete familiarity. Close by, office lights were streaking the dawn with brilliance.

He's either a lunatic, a guru of some sort, or more likely blasted on crack. I'll just sleep on it.

BCM spent the night at the pub in a room upstairs. Fast asleep in the shadow of a spider's web, he escaped into inky seclusion with ease and enveloped himself into a solitary trance, with the faces of good and evil defining his dreams.

Chapter Nineteen: Daddy I've Fallen for a Monster

Mimi hit Stringie's with old school poise, trailing behind her a group of work jerks too pissed to know she was a he and too rocket-charged to care. Mimi was playing tease and touch. The dancers looked on, catting for space. All these guys and no one was taking the bait.

'Watch me,' Mimi purred, then pressed her long, soft fingers to her mouth and let her tongue slide across her hand, beckoning one of the girls over, a classic stripper: Benidorm blonde with puffer-fish lips and a pay-me-now scowl. She was viper slut sexy and had a need to please. Mimi licked the note and stuck her finger in her mouth while the guys ogled. She sucked it again, tracing the note past her neck and onto the crest of her cleavage. She was having fun, but for one man it was all too much.

Before she could sidestep away, Mel, who had been watching this kinky spectacle from the corner of the stage, whisked her off to a VIP booth. Mimi was right on cue. She knew how Mel worked, and how to greenlight his gaze.

'Jesus fucking Christ girl, what the fuck you doin' here?'

'I was looking for a fuck.'

'You came to the right place.' He couldn't stop – couldn't, wouldn't. Mel had to have one more try at Mimi. No one else came close. *Chemistry, it's fucking chemistry.*

'Do you miss me, big boy?'

'Yeah I fuckin' do. Jesus, you look good. I mean, Jesus

fucking Christ, what's a man to do?'

'Go with it.'

'Come here.' They'd been sitting a few spaces apart, then Mimi edged closer. Mel was all over her, tonguing her tightly, stroking her legs, feeling the softness of her thighs. A few moments later a dancer pulled back the drape and started a slow erotica waltz, pulsating her body before them, unhooking her sequin bra, peeling off her G string, while Mimi fed Mel's lust, a wall of smut covering him. After the dancer had left, she deftly placed the phone into his jacket pocket and continued kissing him deep and heavy on the lips.

'Let's go to mine,' His voice was soft and low. Mel was in a porn haze. Nothing mattered to him now except Mimi. He wanted all of her. They left the club through the back door, away from prying eyes and nosey showbiz reporters. Mel's right arm was circling her waist and his left hand cupping her breasts.

'Stop a minute, let me look at you.' He spoke as if he owned her. Instinctively she stalled. 'You do something to me.'

She said nothing. Her eyes spoke for her. They were pleading for mercy. He looked away, staring at the folded jets of black sky rocking his pain like an open grave.

'I'll tell you straight, Mimi, tell you how it is. I'm a simple man. I'm a man who doesn't like talking sentimental shit, but you do something to me. Jesus you do.'

Mimi was biting her lip, playing for time. All she knew was Mel's eyes were lying. He looked down at her, exquisitely fragile under the star shot light. He reached into his trouser pocket and pulled out the phone.

'Fucking hell, this isn't mine. I must have left mine at the club.'

'Well it's not mine either.'

'Must belong to one of the guys. I'll see whose it is.' He switched it on. Mimi tried distracting him.

'Don't bother with that now. Everything we need is right

here: the moon, the night, each other.' She wrapped her fingers around his and looked up at him. Caught by the romantic tenderness of her gaze, he stopped fidgeting with the mobile, placing it back in his jacket pocket.

'I wanted you, whatever, I thought you could be …'

'Ssshh, let's not talk, let's just enjoy this.' She placed her hand across his mouth. He took her fingers, kissing each one, and then he pulled away from her.

'I believed you Mimi. I fucking trusted you.'

'You still can.'

'No. You played me like a fucking violin. Everyone knew, the guys, the girls at the club, everyone knew except me.'

'I didn't want you to leave. You knew I was different – don't deny it, Mel – I … please, I love you.'

'Fucking love is for fucking pussies. If you fucking had one you'd know. You'd understand. I wouldn't 'ave to spell it out for you. You know nothing about love.' His eyes were hard boiled and cruel. 'Jesus Mimi, am I talking to a man, a woman, or fucking both of you right now? Help me Mimi. What the fuck are you? I'll tell you shall I? You're a man playing dress-up. A freak, Mimi, that's what you are, a fucking freak, and there can be no comeback ever. Understand me, never.'

He pushed her off him. She started sobbing, and he moved away from her. Mel needed complete control. Underneath that flabby gut and stinking lard, he was numb with grief for a love he could never have.

'Get in. Come on, get in. I'll take you home.' He couldn't let go. He wanted to flush her out, but something pulled him back, a feeling so intense he wanted to scream.

'It's okay,' she sniffed, wiping away tears with a lacy handkerchief.

'Come on, I'll take you.' He helped her up. Once inside the car he whipped the radio on. Gladys Knight smoothing the tension away as Mel swerved left into the oncoming traffic, his oversized banana hands grabbing the wheel as he spun a right onto High Holborn. Mimi was still blubbing and scrolling through her phone messages. They had around twenty minutes of drive time to kill, so Mel tried talking to clear the air.

'How you getting along with everything?'

'Work and gigs are great. I meant to – well, if it's not too weird – to … ask you something?'

'Yeah, you know I'll sort it. Whatever you want, just tell me.'

'I'm thinking of starting an escort agency.'

'Right, you going into competition with Mel's Blue Angels?'

'No, no. It's for people like me, girls who are guys who are girls.'

'Oh, a trannie escort agency.'

'Yeah, and I'd like you to sort out the protection and the venue, and of course, you'd get your cut.'

'Course I'll get my cut. I always get my cut.' Even when Mel was on downtime he was deal-busting. Like a true pro he never let sentimental smush skewer a good bizzo opportunity.

'I've got just the right place for that too.'

'Yeah?'

'Yep. Nice little mews office in Soho.'

'Great.'

'Leave it with me. I'll set it up, the company, the premises, the works.'

'Do you have a good lawyer?'

'Mimi, do I …'

'What?'

'Sometimes you're so naïve, aren't you, eh? I pull the strings. It's my show and you ask me that! D'you think I'm a shumck?'

'I don't understand.'

'Do I have a good lawyer? Mimi, I've only got the best fucking law firm in London covering my arse: Fisher Fowler and Ferret.'

'Well I don't know – haven't seen you for months. How

do I know who your lawyers are?'

They pulled up in front of Mimi's apartment.

'Well you should. How else do I run all my businesses, eh? Got to have top-drawer legal brass in your pocket or else you can't do nothing. And it doesn't stop there. You need judges, QCs and all the coppers you can get.'

Mimi was feeling a little uncertain about everything, but when Mel sprang for the chance to be involved in her project, she felt she'd won a little ground. She had planted the bug, sorted out security for her start-up and was home in one piece before 4 a.m.

'I would invite you up, but …'

'Never say never, eh?'

'Maybe another time.'

'Yeah. I'll have Sal call you in the week about the escort bizzo and we'll see how things pan out.'

'Thanks, Mel.'

'Yeah, stay out of trouble.' He kissed her lightly on the cheek and let her out. She jived up the drive and blew him a kiss goodnight. Once inside, she dialled Avery.

'Hi, it's Mimi. It's done. I wasn't sure about this evening. I'd like to meet up and go over a few things. Call me when you get this.'

She slumped onto the sofa, her hand trembling and her throat dry. She knew only too well what Mel was *really* thinking. She was running out of time.

Mel had flipped the script again. Seeing Mimi, all those old feelings came over him. He knew she needed to be nixed but he didn't have the balls to do it. *All that talk about me being **the** man. I'm too much of a pussy to whack her. I just need one bullet and the job's done.*

He parked off Southampton Row. They called it Midtown. It was dominated by banks, office blocks and bars. He got out, paced the pavement, and stood by the car. He took out a cigar from his pocket and put it in his mouth. Just then, a Land Rover luxe bunked up behind him. Inside were Terry and Mickey. They climbed out and stood next to him.

'We couldn't get you on the phone, boss. We waited around but she stayed in her flat.'

'Don't stress it. We just have to take our time.'

'I wanted to get it over today, boss, but Tezza said we'd better wait until you gave the green light.'

'Yeah. Smart call, Tezza.'

'Well boss, I know things are a little complicated.'

'No, not complicated. Just delicate, Tezza, just delicate.'

'Could have done it today. Do you wanna light for that boss?' He gestured to the cigar.

He handed him a matchbook and Mel lit up and inhaled.

'Thanks Tezza go back and keep an eye on her. Come round tomorrow and we'll sort it, work out something simple – nice and tidy is how I want it.'

'Yes, boss,' they answered together.

'Well you two can get off now I'll stay and enjoy this for a bit.' Terry and Mickey drove off and Mel stood alone with a distant look in his eyes. After a warm, satisfying smoke Mel got back in the car and winged it home. He wanted to catch his wife before her Pilates class and bonk her brainless.

Chapter Twenty: Mista Lova

The sun was shaving the blinds with stripes of light. Avery was nude sexy, lying on her side with her long, tanned legs wrapped around a pillow. Blinking the sleep away from her eyes, she woke up and looked around. There was no sign of Nick anywhere, but a flo-glow post-it note on her night stand read: *Thanx for an incredible night. Call me. Nick x.*

She was glad he'd slunk out early. *Great, no need for crap chats and awkward smiles.* She dashed into the shower and set it to *rain*. Singing to Prince's 'Raspberry Beret', she had tummy growlies and an after sesh grin. *What a guy,* she sighed. *Can't get too close, but one of the foxes of Fleet Street did say that if you want a scoop, stick on some red lipstick. I'm just doing what women all over the world do. I'm winning.*

Her conscience suitably assuaged, she brushed and flossed, backcombed her hair Bardot style and put on a simple black bodycon dress. Super stretchy, it sculpted her curves to precision, the one per cent spandex guaranteeing a smooth scissor-sharp silhouette. She wore cranberry-red Estee Lauder lip stain and dabbed it on the apples of her cheeks. She fastened her stockings and slung on her Tory Burch leather pumps. A last-minute spritz of Cashmere Mist and she was out the door, ready for her meeting at the paper.

Joe's budget meetings were run with tyrannical efficiency.

Today he had a nasty abscess and his mood was triple blue.

'Over the last five days we have amassed a whole bunch of shit. There are two major murder trials, a teenage abduction and a motorway pile-up. We need copy on everything. I want you lot to turn in your stories no later than seven. I need timelines on when copy's ready as there's two pages to fill and I want winning stories. I want stuff that sells, but that isn't an excuse to turn in crap.'

Ollie and Jez were having a private conversation, rustling papers and whispering, but it was still a distraction.

'If both of you don't shut the fuck up, you can leave now.'

Ollie blushed red. Jez offered a feeble excuse.

'So sorry, Mr Gander, sir. I was just confirming the name of a source for another story.'

'Yeah, course you were, Jez – do it later. Now, have you got that memo? I don't know what you're still doing here. Natalie's signed in sick and we emailed you details of the court you're meant to be at – the verdict's due in thirty minutes. Why the fuck are you here?'

'Yes. I—'

'Not now – what are you waiting for, a fucking flying carpet? You'll need one if the traffic is anything to go by. Shit – have we any bodies in the area to cover while you're prancing around?'

Jez fixed his tie and left. About five or six other journos were seated at the long table and each one had articles and stories to turn in. They used to put the paper to bed around midnight, but a spate of cost-cutting meant they now shared their printing presses with three other publications and were forced to publish much earlier than before.

'Jack, I've told you about these photos already. If you can't operate your phone properly, take Ollie with you. He's a whizz on the camera phones and can take all the snappy snaps you need. We can't use this, it's not up to scratch. Ollie, get the info from Jack and go take a couple of photos for this piece. I need about three, and I need them in an hour.'

Jack and Ollie both got up, heading for Jack's desk.

'Okay – nearly done. Lucy, have you reworked your story?'

'Almost, sir.'

'Almost doesn't cut it, Lucy. You asked for home and social affairs. That's your beat. You deal with it. I want it on my desk in the next twenty minutes.'

'Yes, sir.'

'Right, I have half a page of space left – Chris, anything?'

'Yep.'

'Let's have it then.'

'Right here, sir.'

Joe skimmed the piece with an expert eye.

'How about that. According to Bolivian news sources, the oldest man alive eats lizards to stay fit. I'll use it, great.'

Chris and the remaining hacks stayed seated while Joe wound down:

'I'm assigning the abduction and the Marsden trial to Chris and Jack. If anyone else has anything else they need to talk to me about, I have ten minutes after this meeting, otherwise let's get to work. Thank you very much, ladies and gents.'

Everyone filed out of the room.

'Hi, Chris.'

'Hi, Avery.' She nodded to a group of her fellow colleagues as they brushed past. Avery went straight to her desk and listened to the recordings on the dummy phone. She scribbled down dates and times and made notes. Then she dialled Mimi.

'Hi, Mimi – Avery.'

'Hi, Avery.'

'I've just listened to some of it – great, it's really good. Well done.'

'I'm glad.'

Mimi sounded deflated.

'Mimi, is everything okay, you sound a little out of it?'

'No. I need to speak to you. I want out. I want out of this.'

'Okay, okay, calm down. Let's meet later tomorrow for lunch.'

'Where?'

'Carluccios, St Christopher's Place – not too far from your club.'

'Okay.'

Avery dialled the dummy phone again hoping for more intel. She left another voicemail for Nick and then sent him a text:

Hi it's me. How's things? Thanx 4 a fab evening. A X.

It was not even 10 a.m. and already Mel was on the boil. Nick was lusting after Avery when he rang.

'Where are you? You're not at your office. Where the fuck are you?'

He dropped Mel's call three times and let it go to voicemail until,

'I need you at your desk, you fucking joke – hope you're listening to me. I need you to do some proper legal work, schmuck. Understand me, no phone calls, no pussy. Playtime's over. You need to keep grafting. Work's on your desk, where you should be.'

When Nick finally got to his office, he found his table swamped with papers and a large brown envelope with a handwritten infantile scribble, obviously from Mel, that read:

All my online businesses are suffering – adult entertainment, gambling etc. from illegal downloads. I want you to bash out 20,000 letters and ask these punters to pay up – it's perfectly legal and it works. Each letter raises around £750, and as it's my businesses I expect my cut to be 50 per cent of all the monies recouped. People panic, they worry about being associated to porn and gambling sites, so they don't ask questions. I am losing a lot of revenue and don't like being mugged off. As my lawyer, I want you to take action. Tell me when you've sent out the letters.

What a wanker. He wants me to send out speculative fee letters – Fucking breach of the code of conduct and I doubt whether Fisher Fowler and Ferret have ever done them before. Worse, he knows exactly how this sordid con works and wants me to enter into a fucking fee arrangement with him. Billing would be tricky in those circumstances.

He buzzed old Fisher.

'Mr Fisher?'

'Yes, Nicholas.'

'I was just wondering. One of my clients wants me to send some speculative fee letters. I was …'

'It's flimflam, Nick. Don't tell me that ghastly Mel Greenberg chap is involved?'

'Yes.'

'Oh dear, that's not the way things are done, Nicholas. What's he want?'

'He's left papers on my desk, sir. Claims there are breaches of the Copyright and Data Protection Act 1988 by illegal file sharing.'

'Doubt that. Seems like a classic con and the firm is being used as a vehicle to perpetrate the sting.'

'I see, sir. How is it wrong exactly?'

'I'll explain it as simply as I can. You send out a letter to person A, accuse them of illegal downloads and they have to pay up by noon Friday, but person A turns out to be a five-year-old child or a college student who is piggybacking his Wi-Fi connection on someone else's internet or, worse, a blind widow who has no internet. Get my point? The whole problem with this type of allegation is that you can't be sure that person A is illegally downloading anything. In short, it's a typical numbers game. The way it works is the law firm sends out as many letters to the presumed owners of a host of IP addresses stating that they are protecting their client's copyright and the alleged perp' must pay up or else face court action. Of course, the hope is that the recipient of the letter won't respond at all, and there will be a surge in 'default' payments where people have been unable to state their case or where people just pay to get rid of the problem. It's a very crooked practice and not one that this firm condones.'

'I understand, sir.'

'Read about it in the Solicitors Disciplinary Findings. A firm has already been caught doing precisely that.'

'Yes, so, sir, it's sort of like saying that if someone steals your car and then commits a crime in it, you're guilty for not fitting an alarm.'

'Yes, if we start claiming that XYZ have illegally downloaded whatever it is from the net, but there is no real evidence to back it up and the person denies it, they cannot be held liable without proof. It is speculative and abhorrent, and IP addresses are notoriously difficult to pin down. They may be fake, non-existent, or shared. Anyway, it is not permitted under the professional rules. That's it, tell him no. Remember, Nick – integrity and independence are never for sale.'

'Yes, sir.'

How the fuck am I gonna tell that … greedy cunt … no, maybe I'll just lie. Why should I risk my professional career for him? If I

don't, he'll come at me with worse. Maybe I'll just do a few and keep
him off my back. What am I doing? Why won't he just fuck off?

Later that afternoon Nick drafted a claim letter from his
personal laptop demanding payment of £750 or else. He
chose one hundred random names to send the demands to.
He felt sordid, but not enough to stop.

What makes you any different from any other con artist?

I was instructed by my client to help curtail the significant loss he
was suffering as a result of unlawful file sharing.

Wow, who am I kidding? I've been hired to bilk people out of their
savings Mel calls it business. To everyone else, it's extortion – legal
blackmail.

'Sylvie.'

'Nick.'

'There's a load of addresses on my desk. These letters
need to be posted to all of them.'

'No worries.'

While she was pasting and posting, Sylvie mistakenly put
one of the letters in Mrs Stringer's birthday envelope. It
didn't compute with her, as she wasn't reading, just stuffing
envelopes with paper. By ten that evening, all one hundred
letters had been sent to random members of the public,
including Nick's own mother.

After wasting the day on dodgy legal shit, Nick was
wacked and thought he'd surprise Avery with a visit. At
around 11 p.m., he texted her:_Hi thanx 4 txt was great hearing_
from u – know it's late but maybe we can meet up tonight? N X.

Avery was about to text back but was busy listening to
Mel from the dummy phone that was still in his jacket
pocket.

'Fucking schmuck, I gave him some fucking proper work
to do, fool that he is. I told him, have those letters done by
today. Who does he think he is? He belongs to me. All
lawyers are fucking con merchants. That's why they play the
game in the first place. They enjoy breaking the law. Oh, and

Mickey?'

'Yeah?'

'Find out who was on the roster for Blue …'

Avery couldn't make out the rest of the conversation but heard a definite wheeze in the background. She left the audio running and texted Nick back: *Bit slammed today but maybe tomorrow A x.*

Mel was sparking abuse at his wife, the punters in his strip club, and an in-house plumber. After another six minutes or so of backchat, Mel rummaged through his jacket pocket, pulled out the phone and stared at it. It took him back to his one on one with Mimi. He thought about those bedroom curves and their heated frisson. His anger turned to shame and gave way to something else, a carnal need that defied his logic. He remembered the first night when he made his move reaching for her pussy. He remembered her eyes when he pulled back. He tabbed her, unwanted, forbidden. Did that make him gay? *I've screwed hundreds of women, so I'm not a fag, but Mimi's not a real man. What the fuck does that make me?*

He stuffed the phone back in his jacket pocket as he tasted every part of Mimi in the cavern of his mind.

Avery heard a few doors open and shut and then silence. Mel was balling his turf but Avery was on his sack.

Chapter Twenty-One: What's My Name?

'Jesus Christ. What the fuck am I doing?' Nick was in the underground car park next door to his office. He put his head in hands and bashed the hood of his Porsche three times with his briefcase. There was no one around. The security staff and valets had long gone and the only sound was the soft whir of a car padding the surrounding streets in the distance. He found an ounce of coke in his jacket pocket and kept his hand on it as if he were guarding a secret. He dialled Matt:

'Yo, it's me. What you doing?'

'I was meditating.'

'That's bullshit, because if you were on the Zen trail you wouldn't answer the phone.'

'Fine, I was watching TV. Crap programme about fucking train robbers and gangsters glorifying infamy. Same old, same old.'

'The British love elevating criminals to rock star status. It's kind of annoying. You never get iconic images of the victims though, like a bloodied corpse in B Minor or a fucking rape victim under the title 'Work in Progress.'

'Are you high?'

'Not yet.'

'Wanna come over?'

'No. Meet me at the Tardis.'

'Are they still up over there?'

'Yeah. They're artistes. Sleeping is for the common man. They don't do that kind of thing.'

'What, sleep?'

'Yeah, they're too busy being creative. They're above all that. Anyway, I'll be bringing some blow to the party. It's a great equaliser.'

'I don't know. It will take me at least twenty minutes to get there.'

'Up to you. I'm walking over now.'

'Okay. See you in a bit.'

'Cool, and Matt …'

'Yeah?'

'Leave the petty jealousy at home.'

'What?'

'The shit about gangsters and thieves being thoroughly respected …'

'Oh yeah, sure. Wouldn't want to offend any of them.'

'Bye.'

Nick and Matt had befriended a media darling years ago whose father had been one of the most celebrated gangsters in the world and part of the legendary counterculture of the Brit cool clique. He was a combo of Sal Dali and Ronald McDonald. A fringe celeb wheeled out for TV appearances and guest slots on his *father's* life or the 'art' work he had conceived about his *father's* life. He had an annoying habit of believing his own hype and possessed a suitably self-deluded grandeur that dominated his six-foot frame. He was a perfect example of a fame-obsessed milieu where the spectre of mediocrity is trumpeted as something rare and original. Nick and Matt nicknamed him Slick Dick the Dicksta and it had stuck with him ever since. Slick Dick described himself as a 'conceptual artist', but all Nick had ever seen him do was fashion papier-mâché figurines, masks and casts and then work them over in different textures and materials. To Nick it was little more than an art con. Ironic really, as Slick Dick's dad was a sovereign thief. Papier-mâché was first used in

Egypt and then Europe. The technique itself was easily learnt and could be successfully replicated by a child of five or six. Of course, the showbiz columnists and art editors lapped it up like the Second Coming, and suddenly Slick Dick was a cause célèbre, monetising the nauseating nepotism of his father's infamy through his crude depictions of real-life gangsters. Of course that's not a cultural cliché, that's art.

'Nick, good to see you.'

'Dicksta.'

They laughed and hugged. Dick knew Nick would have some gear on him. He almost expected it – a sense of entitlement that comes with minor celeb status.

'Where's George?'

'He's in the bar.'

The Tardis had its own fully stocked bar. Most of the drinks were donated free because the Tardis had charity status and was the prime spot for hosting the city's most illustrious showbiz events. George was the owner/director of the place, allowing Dick some space to 'create' and sleep in an outdoor shed with a bed. It was kind of surreal but seemed to work for them both. Of course, Dick's real home was the sunny island of Antigua. He was a white black man with black credibility and a luxuriously indulgent 'white' lifestyle.

'Cool. I phoned Matt. He should be here soon.'

'Cool.'

'Yeah. I'm starting some music projects now.'

'Really?'

'Yeah.'

Of course, Dicksta knew all about music. Not only was he an artist, he played the harmonica as if he was Sonny Boy Williamson.

'That's fucking great, man.'

'Yeah.'

'So what you gonna do? Have you thought about who you might start collaborating with and shit?'

'Yeah. Matt's band which I'm part of but he's a hard sell, he wants his pound of flesh and there's a new girl band I just signed.'

'Cool.'

'Yeah, Matt had three major gigs. I should have been there but it wasn't meant to be.'

'Shit, really, three?'

'Yeah.'

Dick was also in a band. It had a suitably hip name and secured major success by featuring one of its songs as the main soundtrack to a popular TV gangster show – another cute little irony not lost on the Dicksta, who often mentioned it at dinner parties and soirées in front of adoring American actresses easily duped by the Dicksta and his tall tales of royalty, riches, and princely affirmation. Nick still liked hanging out with him, as he had an affable charm and didn't ask questions. Nick continued chatting:

'So you hit all the festivals and stuff.'

'Yeah, the usual. Fucking amazing though.'

George, hearing voices bustled over.

Nick never understood the relationship between Dick and George. They were always together and were affiliated to loads of left-wing political groups, especially ones that featured glam models or witty thespians. It was a kind of retro boho existence, one that Nick secretly coveted.

How fucking cool to get up in the morning and just think about creating shit and not have to worry about anyone or anything, just how to work a fucking piece of plaster of paris. What a fucking joke. His life is piss easy.

'Alright, Nick – looking a bit tired.'

'Yeah, lots of late nights, early mornings.'

'Come and take a pew.'

'Thanks, George.'

Nick got out the coke. It was a given. George had a razor ready. Nick gave him the bag. George emptied the blow onto a mat on the table and then started racking it into fine lines, cutting through the grains of white powder with the grace of a heart surgeon.

'Well done, George.' Nick grinned from ear to ear.

'Here's a fifty,' First George, then Nick and finally Dick all took a shot snorting the zone. Matt arrived about fifteen minutes later and Dick let him in.

'Matt.' Dick spoke with a coke croak.

'Hey, Dick. Saw you in the *Evening Standard*. Nice piece about you and your dad.'

As if it would be about anything else.

'Oh cool, did you see that? It was the fortieth anniversary of the heist, and they did a celebration piece on it.'

'Right – yeah. I was just watching ITV4 and saw you on that too. About how your *dad* went to the same cobblers as the queen.'

'Yeah, he had an expensive eye.'

'Good job, he was a robber then.'

'We just had some gear. You want some?'

'Yeah, why not?'

Matt followed him through to the room where they were all sitting.

'I now understand why they call this the Tardis. There's fucking doors everywhere.'

'Yeah, it's a really odd building. Part of Clerkenwell's art heritage.'

'So tell me, what's the difference between papier-mâché what five-year-olds do and what you do, Dickie boy?'

'I'm a sculptor.'

Sensing an artistic face-off between Dick and Matt, Nick tried to diffuse the mounting tension: 'I've always thought that seeing things with a child's eye creates a kind of magical innocence about art.'

'I've always thought unmade beds, puerile script notes on the back of envelopes and stuff of that ilk is just hobby-horse stuff,' Matt sniped back.

'Yeah?'

'Yeah.'

Matt and Dick were each convinced of their own bona fides as avant-garde romantics, each doubting the other's artistic credentials, but to Nick they were both pretty much the same, and the reason he liked the Tardis was the sheer diversity of people that could be found there: from topless go-go dancers to poets and gangsters – it was a private oasis of bohemian eternity, its blue door a visible reminder that in the midst of all the shady sleaze of the metropolis, there was a waiting wonderland to be explored.

'It's all art, regardless, because art is in the eye of the beholder.'

'Very diplomatic.'

'We got a rock fiend on one side, a sculptor on the other, and a humanitarian in the middle. Whose side you gonna take, Nick?'

'No one's. My side. I'm always on my side. I don't stick my neck out for anyone.'

'Yeah, steer clear of the middle man,' clipped Matt, who appeared hurt by Nick's coldness.

'Why you only gonna take your side Nick?'

'You can never trust a middle man George.'

This spiteful repartee continued for another ten minutes, when the doorbell rang.

'Who's that George?'

'Not expecting anyone Dick it's quarter to five in the morning,'

'Let's ignore it.'

'No, it could be important.'

'Alright I'll go.'

Nick and Matt continued their nugatory ramblings. George wanted to play some music.

'Everyone here likes a bit of Mick Jagger, don't they?'

Matt shook his head:

'Nah, not me, George. I find him toxic. He's been aping black music for the best part of fifty years and parodying the blues. I find the whole chicken strut – big-lipped stage shit –

really fucking annoying. He has great taste in women though – Bianca, Jerry. Then there was that Marie from Hawaii.''

Yeah, I'm with Matt on this one, Jagger's been duping the public for years. Can't stand him.'

'Okay, no Stones.'

'But I won't say no to Hendrix.'

'Yeah, good choice Nick everyone needs a Hendrix hit.' Dicksta came back into the lounge:

'It's Rafique, the kid from the cab office.' George was still loading the Stones track:

'Right. What's he want?'

'Wants to know when the painters should come round.'

Nick stifled a yawn: 'Painters?'

Matt looked puzzled:

'He's just a school kid.'

George was defensive:

'He's legal.'

A scrawny Bangladeshi child scooched into the room armed with a pail and brush.

'Seriously George, he looks about twelve. Are you running a sweat shop, an underage slave labour camp or something?'

'No, nothing like that Nick, some kids want to do the painting. I'm letting them do it. Course we pay them.'

'Right.' Nick raised his eyebrow sarcastically at Matt.

What the fuck. I know they live outside the norms of society, but really? Getting kids to paint at that time – kind of fucking ridiculous.

Ding, ding. Another blast of the bell broke the surreal chit-chat.

'Now what?'

'Dick, who is it? Rafique left. Trotting behind him was a supersized ageing blonde covered up in a beige rain mac and red stilettos.

'Sorry, guyyys.' She spoke with a charming East End oomph.

'Alright. It's Trixie,' George announced as if everyone should know who Trixie was. She behaved younger than she was and blew giant gum bubbles when she talked.

'Fuck me, is fhat blow on the table, George?'

'Maybe, care for some?'

'Nah, I'm still buzzin' from last night.'

'What's a pretty young thing like you doing here?' smirked Matt.

'We got a photo shoot 'ere.'

'Oh right.'

'Yeah, it's for *Front* magazine – football, fantasy and felines.'

Do you get paid for hiring the venue out, George?' Matt cut in ignoring the woman's rehearsed sales patter.

'Sometimes, but Trixie's an old friend and wanted to do it here.'

'Right.'

Nick had gone to the Tardis to escape the scuz of work and try and get back a sense of his worth, but now he felt worse.

Child workers, glamour models past their prime. It's as if I'm in Fagin's lair. What the fuck is going on?

'Did you know the Dickens museum is just up the road? Ironic really, as all the class criminarti are in Clerkenwell,' Matt continued.

Trixie looked nonplussed.

'Criminarttttti?'

'Just made it up. Criminals who have been prettified by the media for public consumption.'

George interrupted:

'This is Nick he's a lawyer.'

'How many lawyers does it take to chaaange a light bulb?' Trixie giggled.

'Five.'

'Oh, you 'eard fhat one?'

''Eard them all, and yeah, that's my cue to head back to the office now. You coming, Matt?'

'Yeah. Good to see you, Dick, George. Nice to meet you, Trixie. Break a leg and all that.'

They got up and Dick saw them out. As they walked into the dawn a black cat was circling the building and the road lights came on.

'Fuck me, he's got child labour, cougar pussy, and he wanted to stick on the Stones.'

'Fucking Nuts.'

'Yeah.'

'Imagine, if all the media tarts knew what really goes on at places like this, I don't think they'd be tuned into Slick Dick's party machine.'

'Listen Matt, Mel's asked me to do something that's not quite legit.'

'What d'ya mean not quite?'

'It's a fee hustle. I asked the partner to make sure, and it breaches the conduct rules.'

'Well don't fucking do it.'

'It's not that easy, Matt. Mel's paid a lot of money to the firm, and he makes me do all his personal criminal work. He'll know if I don't do it.'

'Tell him it's a breach and you'll lose your licence to practice.'

'I've checked. The penalty's a suspension or a fine.'

'Would you fucking stop and listen to yourself – just a suspension or a fine! It's wrong. It compromises who you are. You didn't break your back for seven years to be Mel's poodle. Your mum and dad slaved three jobs for you to go to law school, Nick. Remember, they SLAVED so you could have a fucking life. Cleaned people's floors so you wouldn't have to – think about that, Nick. It's not just a suspension or a fine, it's a fucking stain on your mother's heart.'

'I do drugs and that's not legit.'

'Yeah, but that's not hurting anyone, just you. You're not a con man. You're a fucking lawyer, for God's sake.'

The Law is like a jungle – only the strongest survive

'I know, Matt but it's like a one-time thing.'

'A one time thing? No, it's just the beginning. I wouldn't fucking do it. Not for Mel Greenberg.'

They walked back to the office, subdued, Nick stewing about what he'd already done and Matt planning an emergency meet with BCM. As they crossed the road, a sparrow was run over. Blood sprayed the pavements, and matted feathers and a broken wing lay wedged in a sewer cap. They continued in silence. It was only 8 a.m. and already the day was scarred with death and regret.

Chapter Twenty-Two: Armageddon Time

It was lunch hour on a rainy Friday, the clouds a choppy combo of black and grey. Trust fund babies, coke sluts and bankers were fleecing their feathers on London's Bond Street when … crash, crash, chink, splat, the front window of *Chanel* was smashed. The onsite alarm kicked in as chunks of glass fractured the floor.

'Oh my God, Pierre, panic button now!' screamed Yvette, a tall statuesque blonde with immaculate nails and *jus*-dipped lips, stubbing her toe in stilettos as she tripped to the floor, glass shards coating her dress and chignon hair.

'Get the fuck down. No one move or we'll fucking shoot!'

Yvette was terrified, unable to speak. She shushed her staff with her finger and lay quivering on the floor.

Two masked men had rammed the upscale boutique with a power scooter. One stayed seated while the other, brandishing what looked like a gun, grabbed everything he saw, making a beeline for the cash register, emptying it and filling his duffle bag with jewellery, watches, and diamonds.

'Everyone stay down or we'll fucking take you out!' he honked. There was only one customer in the store, cowering by the changing rooms, and three staff members, including Pierre, who had failed to push the panic switch in time. All of them were scared shitless. Outside, a crowd was gathering.

'C'mon, hurry the fuck up! That's it. Let's go.'

It was over in minutes. They had swiped enough merchandise to feed a small African village for a week: sunglasses, clothes, shoes, and money from the till. They scrambled the streets at top speed, clocking up to a hundred miles per hour at one point.

'Fuck me. I thought that security nonce was gonna be a bit of bother!'

'Fucking still shaking.'

They darted through the traffic, dodging red lights and pedestrians until finally they reached Essex Road, Islington.

They were part of a ten-man crew who had been responsible for a spate of robberies targeting the capital's premier boutiques. They parked the bike and offloaded the gear in an outside lock-up waiting for a text message from Stevie D, the twenty-year-old in charge.

'All done. We 'ave to meet up at The Old Monk, High Holborn at seven.'

'Cool.'

Later that evening, Terry and Mickey were doing a little extracurricular bizzo of their own. They had teamed up with the couture heist gang and were awaiting the arrival of Stevie outside the pub.

Terry stared ahead: 'Aw, yeah, look at this geezer. What a fucking fool. Flashy cap and Gucci loafers, loads of fucking chains. Better not be part of Stevie's lot.'

'Nah, they can't be that stupid. Anyway 'es comin' alone. These flash cunts are all a little too obvious eh Tezza?''

'You think?'

'It's alright, 'es 'eading for the bookies.'

'Look at that sort. She's a bit of alright eh Mickey?'

'Yeah, right out of your league.'

'Fuck me, look who she's with.'

They spotted an old balding gent, with a pink freckled face and a fish-eye stare.

'Well, she would be with a fella like that. He's probably raking it in.'

Terry's mobile rang. It was the Soprano's soundtrack.

'Boss.'

He nodded his head and made hand signs to Mickey.

'Yeah, boss, no problem. We'll be there. Just sorting some other bizzo. Yeah, boss, got it.'

'He wants us to be at the club around eleven. Let's ring this prick again.'

'Temper, Tezza, be calm. I'm the one what's loaned them the bikes.'

'Yeah, well, why the fuck is 'e taking so long? Seven, 'e said. We can't hang about all fucking night now, can we?'

'Hold up, 'ere 'e is. I see 'im now.' A smart, casually dressed guy entered the pub. At that moment, Mickey got a text on his phone. It read:

In the pub now wearing dark trousers and Ralph Lauren shirt, got a new diamond stud in my ear, carrying my LV man purse.

'Who's that then?'

Mickey started laughing.

Terry leaned forward: 'What?'

'You ain't gonna believe the text I just got. It's fucking ridiculous.'

'Go on.'

'You won't believe it Tezza -. Fucking instructions as if I'm on a fucking date.'

'You serious?'

'Unfortunately.'

Mickey held up the phone and read out the message verbatim, ending with a stinging emphasis on the phrase *man purse.*

'What a fucking idiot. 'E should delete that message. It's so fucking poncey. What a fucking numpty.'

'I'm fucking deleting it now Tezza, and then 'im when I get in the fucking pub.'

'C'mon, let's get inside and check out 'ow much this moron 'as got in 'is LV man purse.'

They entered the pub from the back, Terry ready to knock his brains out. Stevie was at the bar chatting up the barmaid.

Terry cut in:

'Nice to see you, lad.'

Stevie wasn't expecting them so soon. He gave a parting smile to the barmaid and walked over to a booth. When they were all seated, Terry was the first to speak.

'Listen, Stevie, don't ever send shitty little texts like that, ok?'

Stevie shrugged his shoulders. 'I was just letting Mick—'

'Shut it.'

'I deleted the text and I want you to lose my number pronto.'

Stevie nodded, losing all sense of his big boy bravado.

'I didn't mean nothing Mickey I just wanted you to know I was 'ere.'

'"We ain't your fucking friends, understand. You're only 'ere 'cos of Mel, and we certainly don't give a fuck about your new fucking earring or your fucking man bag. What the fuck do you think this is, *Blind Fucking Date?*'

'I didn't mean nuffing,' he winced. Terry slid closer and whispered:

'Lucky for you they know us in this boozer. Upstairs there's a room and a brown envelope in the first drawer. Take your fucking man fag up there and give us what you owe. You did five stores today and used our bikes in all of 'em. You're on Mel's manor, so you better cough up if you wanna carry on with your enterprising little venture.'

Stevie scurried up the stairs, his face a wet rag of tension, and placed five grand in the envelope. He thrust it into Mickey's palm.

'Cheers mate. Next time it'll be double, and no fucking man bag shit.'

Stevie skedaddled while Mickey and Terry ordered more drinks and flushed the cash on horses and whores.

Chapter Twenty-Three: Drop It

Mel was auditioning girls for the club. He liked to know who and what he was taking on. With him was his trusted 'house mother' Esther, a fifty-plus glamour gran and one of the key figures in Mel's adult entertainment bizzo. Esther was smart, sweet and a skilled negotiator. She had started at the club in the late eighties and slipped into her current matriarchal role over time. The first girl on the list was eighteen-year-old Maya, a Romanian student.

'Hi, my name's Esther, and this is Mel. He owns this place.'

Mel's butt gut was larding the leather settee. He pushed himself up in an attempt to look semi-interested.

'Don't worry. Don't be nervous. The DJ will play your track and you can make use of the pole if you want. The whole space is yours.'

'Thanks.'

The girl had answered an ad for an *exotic dancer* in her local paper. She had chosen a cheesy Madonna number to strut the stage. She was awkward as fuck, clunking around like an automated droid, her arms, legs and body out of synch and her feet hammered in six-inch plastic.

'Okay, cut the track.' Esther took her aside.

'Take your time, feel the rhythm and make your movements as natural as possible.'

'Sorry, - first time.'

'Don't force it. Just let your body speak for you.'

'I try.'

They laced the track again. This time she took it slow, feeling the pulse of the music circle her hips, straddle the dip of her breasts, and finally cop her creamy lips.

'Right there – she's got it.'

'I get job?'

'Yes, you start tonight. Be here at 9 p.m. Now there's lots of things you need to know, so if you wait backstage, I'll run through it all with you. Anything you need, I can get for you – dresses, make-up, shoes – and you can pay later.'

The girl nodded and smiled, relieved she had made the cut. With newbies, Esther didn't like taking tips or money up front. She wanted the girls to get a few jobs under their belts first, but it was customary for strippers to scoop tips to the house mother, who could be relied upon to do anything from finding nail gloss to dumping nuisance boyfriends. Being on good terms with the house mother was essential for a dancer. Mel's main criteria when judging the girls was simple: is she ballsy enough to take her kit off, and will the punters like her? Maya was a sure bet.

He called Esther over. 'I think you should explain how it all works to her now. She looks like she's in a hurry.'

'Okay.'

'Maya, dear, come with me.' She led her to a small tidy back office and made her sit down.

'Here's your contract that says you're working for the club. You can sign that later and hand it in tonight. I'll just go through some of the admin /penalty fees on there. A to D are the amounts you have to pay so that you can dance here: house fees, £30 a night from your earnings, then discretionary tips to the DJ and myself, and penalties if you get drunk or breach house rules, which are listed on the other page. We encourage you to have a good time. If you get your clients to buy champagne, we give you a cut of the cost of the bottle. The more they buy, the more you make. Are you getting this?'

'Yes.'

'You want to focus on lap dances, one to one. The stage doesn't earn you much. Private dances can be bought in the Stallion room. No sex ever – you don't give it away. You make £20 a dance. We waive house fees on slow nights, so it's best to turn up. You decide how much you make. It's all about the right attitude: be friendly, look interested, and keep eye contact. Tony and Pete are the managers – the guys standing at the door. They'll keep you safe from any dodgy punters, okay? A couple of practical tips: don't douse yourself in body oil – it's great for the beach but makes the floor surface very slippery, and there have already been some nasty falls, so no body oil. We recommend you keep a garter on and your money wrapped inside with elastic. It's safe, sexy, and won't get stolen. Any questions?'

'Yes, if customer wants sex, how much?'

'Sex is not permitted on the premises. We aren't selling sex. It's not a brothel, it's a club, understand? No sex on the premises ever.'

'Okay.' Maya didn't look convinced, but Esther over-stressed the point again just to make doubly sure she understood.

'Maya – no screwing on the side. Keep your honour locked up tight, yeah?'

'Okay, I come at nine tonight. I have to go other job now.'

'Right, where you working?'

'I get job as sales assistant in Chanel boutique.'

'Bond Street?'

'Yes.'

'Okay then, see you tonight.'

Maya bounced out the club, bumping her booty and winking. Her nerves had disappeared completely.

Mel stayed around for a few more auditions, jaded by all the T and A on display. None of them could hump the drum like Mimi. He took out the phone he'd found the night he'd seen her and casually opened and shut it. He stuck it back in his pocket, wrapping his fingers around it tightly. He'd hang on to it for now. He had a five o'clock with his cyber team and wanted to be on time.

'Right, I'm off, Esther. Let me know about Friday night. I want Nicole and Tamsin on as I've got a meeting with some guys from Dubai. They love blondes with big bazookas, and the added bonus is they're twins – double the pleasure, double the fun.'

'No problem.'

Mel's early lotto had come in a European bank heist, targeting over ten countries. He was meeting with the key players in the cartel later that evening and hoping to net at least fifteen mil from the deal.

At around eight, Mel appeared in his suite at The Dorchester, where he did his premium bizzo, away from the cock and bull of low-level scams and gangster shit. He had a silver service butler on hand and had arranged a luxury supper for his guests, two of the world's finest hackers. He'd slapped on some Paco Rabanne, slicked his hair back with gel and fixed his tie, when the butler buzzed up two guys. One was lanky, with blonde wispy hair, wore glasses, a UCLA hoodie and checked Bermuda's. The other was short, Chinese, had geometric red and black spiky hair and was wearing faded denim and a plaid shirt.

'Mr Wai and Mr Evans, sir.'

'Thank you, Horace.'

'Sir.'

Robert Wai and Tim Evans were two of the most celebrated Californian hackers on the circuit. Together they could penetrate any bank system and withdraw millions. It was bloodless, high tech and not a ski mask in sight. *This is the future and now I'm part of it.*

'Come on, make yourselves at home. You boys been travelling long?'

'We just got back from Amsterdam.'

They both spoke in low register, laid back Kalifornia.

'Great place Robert,' agreed Mel. 'Well, what would you like to drink?'

'Jack and Coke for me,' Tim smiled.

'Milk with a shot of bourbon.'

'Horace, you heard the lads … and a Greenwich Sour.'

'Coming right up, sir. Dinner will be served in ten minutes.'

Horace bustled out while Mel and the guys sat down. They picked at hors d'oeuvres and nibbled sticks of bread and cheese. Then Horace returned with a king-size duck and all the trimmings.

'Wow that looks amazing.' Robert's eyes lit up.

'I asked Tim what your fave nosh was, so we're having duck, and chocolate cake for dessert.'

'That's great, Mel.'

'Yeah. Wanted you to have some pucker grub.'

'I think you're gonna like what you see.'

'I'm counting on it Robbie.' Mel started eating.

'Well we really enjoyed this project. We're white hat hackers, you know – we don't do this just for the money. I mean, we get seriously psyched by the challenge of breaking the system, downloading the data and encrypting the cards. It's not about hurting anyone. It's about the vibe and riding the hacking wave.' Mel's eyes became cynical.

'Let me tell you something, Tim. When I was a young man all I wanted was loads of money and to be loved. Of course, now I'm older I know for a fact that money is all that really matters. You can wishy wash your way into thinking it's not purely about the money and wear the white hat and 'ave an adventure, but trust me, it's always about the money always.'

'Yeah, we don't really think too much about that. You know, we get our thrills from the illicit taste of prohibition. You know, when you break a system or jam a virus it throws your mind, man.'

They continued talking and eating, polishing off their dessert with minted tea and biscuits.

'Now let's get to bizzo. What you got for me?' asked Mel.

'Well, they do say, save the best for last.'

'Yes, indeed Robbie - let's have the pièce de résistance.' Mel beamed, rubbing his fat hands in anticipation.

Tim took out his Sony Experia Z and laid it out on the table.

'Watch this.'

There were JPEGs of cash machines and ATMs all across the capital and major cities in Europe being skimmed. Hundreds and thousands of pounds and euros being shoved into holdalls and rucksacks by an army of cashers on the ground as if it were Monopoly money. Mel scrolled through the images one by one in horror.

The mood in the suite turned sour. Mel stared intently at Tim:

'What the fuck. Where were these pictures taken? What kind of fucking jug head has his photo taken with the money? A fucking muppet with a beanie hat on his head, bags full of cash and his face on full show.'

Tim leant forward and tried to move the cursor away from the page but …

'What else you got there? Give me that. Fucking great-pictures with fucking backpacks and rucksacks. Why not wear a fucking sticker across your forehead saying, "I did it, come get me"?'

Robert's eyes began to bulge and Tim started chewing his nails.

'You might be God's answer to life in your fucked up universe, but you know fuck all about a fast shuffle … or *they* know nothin' about it. What the fuck were the cashers doing posing with the money? They'll be nabbed.' Tim was apologetic his pacific coast drawl tempering the mood.

'Okaaay, so we told them to take discreet photos to show that everything went to plan, and that way everyone could be sure of their cut. We said, you know, be discreet, don't face the camera, just show enough so we know it's all done,'

'Yeah, you gotta believe us, we were very careful about

that. We told them to be low-key and not to draw any attention to themselves. We—'

'Does that look like a fucking low-key picture Robbie? He's smiling to the fucking camera with a pile of cash in his cock. What the fuck were you cretins thinking?'

'Sorry Me—'

'Dearie me, white hat, bollocks – nonsense. I thought you were fucking pros. This is worse than amateur night at the Portland Arms and that's saying something.'

'White hat is like a phrase – they wore, like, black hats and white hats in Westerns and it kind of … so anyways, just saying, we did make it clear they should be on the down low.'

'Tim, do I look like I give a fuck about what fucking hat you're wearing? Seems to me you two brainiacs got a lot to learn. You might be brilliant hackers, but intellectuals like you are of almost no use to me.'

They looked at him in utter bewilderment.

'Almost, lads, almost …'

'There's no way this can get back to us.'

'Well, if that's the case Robbie no need to worry eh? If any of you do get nicked, I'll fucking slice you up in little pieces and post your ugly mugs on your fucking Facebook page. There's a pic to remember, eh? What kind of hat would that be?'

Robbie and Tim stared at each other in horror and then at Mel.

'Only joking lads having a little fun. Don't you intellectuals 'ave a sense of humour?'

The two were wimping out at the table, unsure of what to do next. They had fallen for the whole glamour chic gangsta sales pitch Mel had been pedalling and were now seriously off-kilter. The seduction had begun when they'd first met. He had wowed them with Russian hotties, unrestricted access to hip celebs, and enough white lobster to fill a yacht in Puerto Banús. Now they were faced with a violent sociopath ready to shoot.

'Okay, gents, let's toast your genius – Horace readyyy.'

Horace scuttled in with a tray. On top was a shallow bowl of crushed ice with a tin of beluga alongside three dainty mother-of-pearl spoons and some neat bread strips.

'Oh man, is that for real?'

'Yes, Timothy, this is the real deal. The rarest sturgeon in the Caspian Sea – took almost twenty years to produce these eggs. Let's scarf it in one.'

'Oh man, I've never tried it. Looks frickin' amazinnng.'

'Use the spoon to spread it on and … Mmmm … that's pure fucking luxury, that's what I'm talking about …'

Robert, and then Tim, delicately spread the caviar on the bread and placed it in their mouths, chewing very slowly. Tim took a sip of water:

'Man, it's salty, but it tastes good.'

'Has forty-seven vitamins and minerals. It's fantastic for your health, boys. C'mon Rob, get it down.' Robbie looked on awkwardly too polite to spit it out.

'It's a little over-salty for me.'

'I love it,'

'Easy, not too much, just a little is enough,' cautioned Mel as Tim helped himself to more.

'Right, then I've got more work to do and you fellas can go back to wearing your hats and all that bananas. I'll be in touch. Here's your VIP card for the clubs. Bring your mates along too. Let 'em 'ave a taste of Mel's world.'

Horace escorted them out and Mel bought Sal over for some serious number crunching. Mel had framed the deal a few months ago. It had taken time – two months – to source the right card processors and a few weeks to tap other players. It was an elegant con. *All's well that ends well. The hired help have been dropped from the sting by their own unbelievable stupidity, and none of 'em will dare grass me up. Fuck the suckers.*

Later that evening Mel got a delivery of eight bags. Inside them around ten mill'. He would whisk some through Nick for legal expenses and the rest he'd bank in Switzerland. Mel was gaming hard and in for the win.

Chapter Twenty-Four: Police and Thieves

'Nick, it's me, your Uncle Mel. Open the door.' Mel was in the reception area of Nick's building shouting on the phone. Reception and security were concerned.

'Don't be arsing around with name badges,' he barked as he tried to get past George.

'I probably pay your fucking wages, mate, so don't be asking me my fucking name.'

George called for assistance via a discreet black button underneath the desk, and old Fisher came down.

'What seems to be all the fuss, what's going on?'

'Ah, Fisher, good. I need to see Nick – now.'

'There's no need to start a ruckus, Mr Greenberg. I'm sure Nick will see you soon. Now, if you just wait here, for a few moments his secretary will be along shortly. '

Mel sucked in his gut and sat down, unaccustomed to waiting for anyone or anything. A few seconds later he was called up, and Wildfire came down to escort him to the office.

'Sorry for your wait. Nick had a problem with his car, which is why he's running a little late. Can I get you a coffee or tea?'

'Yeah, coffee black, no frills.'

'Okay, be right in, and if you just make your way to the office, Nick's waiting for you.'

'Nick! What the fuck? If I say I'm coming in for eight, don't leave me downstairs like a fucking lemon.'

'Sorry Mel, had some issue with the car – all sorted now.'

'You should've phoned me, plonker.'

'Yeah, sorry.'

'Right, got a bag here full of money.'

'Yes.'

'For legal expenses and shit. I want you to start work on a new file – let's call it Mel's Investments.'

'Right.'

'And then guess what?'

'What?'

'Mel's Investments goes kaput.'

'I-I don't get you.'

'Nah, course you don't. Just start the file, and here's the cash, run it through, yeah. I'm giving you £100k up front.'

'Okay.'

'Now, obviously, if the transactions are abortive and don't go through, you'll give me my money back, right?'

'Right.'

Wildfire knocked. Nick let her in and she set the coffees on the desk.

'Thanks.'

'Thanks, darlin'.'

'Nick, about that other bizzo – the infringement of my copyright?'

'Yes, I haven't been able to do them all.'

'No?'

'No – but I've done some, and we should see the responses for those this week.'

'I want them all done, Nick.'

'I'll get to it when I can.'

'I want every single one by close of play Friday. Is that clear, Nicholas?'

'I'll do my best, Mel.'

'Good. Now I'll be back in a few weeks for my money on *Mel's Investments*.'

Nick got up to see him out. When he shook his hand, Mel bent his fingers all the way back to the bone and seethed,

'Listen, Nick, be a good boy and don't fuck with me.'

Nick's heart was racing. He was pretty sure he'd been asked to launder the cash, but Mel's ugly assault had left him cold. He bolted the door of his office, took out a bin bag and puked his guts out. Wildfire belled his private line.

'Is everything okay, Nick?'

'Yeah, fine, just got a stomach bug, I'll be fine. Can you nip down to the chemist and get me some Gaviscon?'

'Yeah, give me five minutes.'

'Thanks.'

Avery was on text: *Meet me later at The Eagle A x*

Be cool to see Avery again.

I'll be there around 8 N X.

With Nick's plans for the evening set, he went and used the office bathroom to spruce up. He would call the Ethics Line later and find out more about the monies upfront crap.

More fucking bullshit Mel wants to tie me up with.

Wildfire returned with Gaviscon and some natural indigestion pills.

'I use these too,' she gave him a comforting mumsy look.

'Thanks, Sylvie. Can you hold the fort for a while? I've got a meeting I need to get to.'

'Sure, but there's nothing scheduled in the diary …'

'Yeah, it's not in there, it's up here.' He tapped his forehead.

Just need some space to think.

As he was leaving, Fisher tried to grab him.

'Sorry, sir, got to dash, important meeting.'

He'd become an expert at avoiding people since he'd joined the practice and adept at lying whenever necessary since Mel's arrival. He couldn't shake the image of Phil and Lindsay petty pawns in Mel's lust for more.

I spent seven fucking years training, and what for, so some fat fucking moron can sit on my balls all day – might as well join the army. All I do is take orders twenty four seven. I'm not honourable enough to be a soldier. They believe in a cause. I'll just hit Mel where it hurts, right in the fucking pocket. He flagged a cab and headed home hoping to net some band time.

Chapter Twenty-Five: Death or Glory

'Avery speaking.'

'It's Mimi.'

'Hi, Mimi. We said we'd meet for lunch later in the week?'

'It can't wait.'

'Okay, where are you?'

'In the ladies room on the third floor.'

Avery looked up from her desk and leaned back on her recliner.

'You mean the third floor of our building? You're in the ladies room in our building?'

'Yes.'

'I'll be right up, hold on.'

'No, I don't want to see anyone. I've been really tense. I can't be sure, but I think Mel's got some of his people following me, Avery . . . I'm scared.'

'Don't move. I'm a floor away.' While Mimi was talking, Avery had been climbing the stairs, afraid to lose her signal in the lift. At last she reached the third floor, made a left and a right, then entered the female cloakroom. Luckily, they were alone. Mimi was in a cubicle.

'I'm here. It's okay, you can come out.'

'Avery?'

'Yes. Would you please come out or do you wanna have this conversation in the toilets?'

'I just needed to be sure it was you.' Mimi opened the

door of the lav. She was dressed like an extra from The Rocky Horror Show: stage make-up and cabaret chic, her hair in a glossy sock bun favoured by the Hollywood elite and London's It chicks.

'You look fabulous.'

'Thanks, but I haven't been sleeping or eating since I planted that wire and I'm pretty sure I've developed a stress lump.' She pressed her palm to her brow and twisted her face, keeping her head bowed.

'Look, let's go somewhere else and discuss this, come on.' Avery led her out of the washroom and walked beside her slowly and calmly.

'There's a very small coffee shop about five minutes from here. C'mon.'

They rode the lift to the ground floor.

Outside, Mickey and Terry were parked in a black Range Rover, watching them leave.

'Fancy a walkabout, Mickey?'

'If Mimi sees us, the game's up. I reckon we should just wait.'

'If we just sit 'ere, 'ow are we gonna find out who that other piece really is? Same sort who stole the papers from Nick's office.'

'Well, it's a news building. It ain't rocket science, Sherlock. She's probably a reporter.'

'They don't look very chatty. Mimi keeps checking over 'er shoulder.'

'Maybe she's getting some girl on girl action.' He winked.

'Don't you ever think about anything else?'

'What? Just saying.'

'Check out their body language. Mimi looks all Pete' Purvis and the other bird's 'ands are flying about as if she's explaining somethin' to 'er.'

'Well, would you listen to you! Been watching those dodgy psychology shows again?'

'No, but anyone can tell they're not a couple.'

'I think I'll go and 'ave a word with security. Get the disabled badge out. I may be a while and I don't want a fucking ticket. It's a double yellow.' Mickey reached into the side pocket on the passenger seat and took out an authentic-looking, disabled person's car permit, allowing the recipient to park in restrictive areas.

'Right, you wait 'ere, Mick, and I'll go and see what I can find out.'

'Okay, mate. On your way back, can you get me a cheese sarnie? I'm starved.'

'Yeah, yeah. I'll nip into the café after.'

Terry left Mickey doing the crossword in *The Sun*.

The café Avery had taken Mimi to offered special discounts to staff at the paper and Avery always wangled the best. She was well known, liked, and her patronage favourably rewarded by the husband and wife team who owned it.

'Avery darliink, *Sei bellissima*!' Pierro was around fifty with greying temples and a soft sun-beaten face. He had playful blue eyes and a generous good-life paunch which he covered with baggy shirts and overlarge tees.

'Hey, Pierro.'

'What a beauty you bring with you today. She is really something – the two of you together, mmmmwah!' He kissed his fingertips and gestured them to a table.

'Thanks, Pierro, you're always so sweet. I'll have one mozzarella on rye, one bresaola and avocado, two cappuccinos and a blueberry cheesecake.'

'*Eccellente* – be about five minutes.'

'Thanks, Pierro.'

Mimi was crouched in a corner sitting at the back of the café with her nicotine inhaler at the ready.

'Do those things actually work?'

'Well, I only really need it for when I'm majorly stressed.'

'Sure. So you think Mel suspects you're up to something or he's just covering his bases or … I mean … how did it all

---

178

go when you met?'

Mimi checked to her left and her right, then bent her head closer.

'It was fucking great, Avery, but I know Mel and I don't think I'm enough. I don't think he can stand the shame of loving me.'

'I know this is hard, Mimi, but you wanted a little payback and I'm halfway through the info. This will be spectacular.'

'Maybe, but at what cost? I don't think you understand just how much I screwed with his head. He fell for me.'

'Well, yeah. So what makes you think he wants to harm you?'

'It's to do with respect, an old-fashioned kind of honour. Mel's complicated, Avery, but when you peel away the layers, there's a simplicity there. A man who has a very traditional approach to women, and he expects a woman to be a woman in *every* sense.'

'I know you care a lot for him, but think of how worthless he made you feel.'

'Avery, I get that you want your story, I just don't think Mel will let this go.'

'Mimi, I'll be frank. I think the public have the right to know about Mel. I think it's in the public interest because he has so many people in his control, and I know you're scared and it's tough on you – it is – but if you stick with it just a little longer it will work.'

'What?'

'You'll get even.'

'At first, that's what mattered, but after seeing him again and planting that bug, I feel bad. I feel shitty, I feel cheap.'

Avery hadn't anticipated such schmaltz from Mimi but pressed harder.

'Mimi, you're in this now and it's important you see it through.'

'What, so you can sell more sleaze?'

'Mimi, it's not about the paper or me or even you, it's

179

about what's right.' Mimi looked at her quizzically with her head cocked to the side and said demurely:

'Avery, have you ever been in love?'

'Maybe … once … it's hard to define.'

'That's a no. Love is the moment you don't exist anymore. You become part of someone else. Love is red, gold and black – crazy addictive. Love means you'll pull the trigger if he asks.'

'I get it, Mimi, but I like to think there's always a hint of reason in madness. You and Mel weren't meant to be, but if we can show his dark side, maybe he'll become a better man.'

'I don't want anyone, especially a person like me, to feel so, so …' her words wobbled as she started to sob.

Avery stood up and went to the opposite side of the table. She put a comforting arm around her.

'He abandoned me because of what I am, and conflicted as I am, I'll keep going, but it's not easy betraying the man you love.'

Avery did her best to reassure her but was concerned about her safety. With all the intel she had been gathering on Mel, she knew Mimi was definitely a target.

'I'll ask my editor if we can get some security for you. He might agree. If not, you're welcome to stay at mine.'

'No, that's really kind of you, Avery, and I appreciate the gesture. I'll see if I can ask around. The trouble is, most of the guys I know are all connected to Mel.'

'Don't worry too much. We'll work it out, okay? Now, please finish your cheesecake or Pierro will be rightly pissed.'

'Thanks, Avery.' They toyed with their food, neither in the mood to finish, and killed the afternoon sunshine with acetic gloom.

Terry had turned up trumps.

'Well?'

'She's twenty-five, Avery Cross junior reporter. 'Asn't got

a steady fella, but she's been seeing some city lawyer called Nick and does features. There's your sarnie.'

'Thank God. I was starvin' marvin. What did you get?'

'Ham and pickle.'

'Mmmm, maybe I should 'ave gone for that.'

'What is it with you, eh Mickey, you always want what I've got.'

'At the time I felt like cheese.'

'Tell you what, let's split it. You gimme one of yours and you can 'ave one of mine.'

'Cheers Tezza.'

''Ere look, they're back, and Mimi's on the go.'

They were stuffing their faces as they spoke. Terry shifted into gear.

'I do like 'er motor. It's quite nifty for town.'

'Yeah, not bad Tezza but I prefer something a bit more lively. So who d'ya get all that info from then?'

'Old boy at reception. 'E 'ears everything and says nuffing, except when you shove a monkey in his mitt, then you can't shut 'im up.'

'So, this Avery bird …?'

'Yeah, same one from Nick's roof, and now she's tied in with Mimi. Quite a busy bee.'

'So, same bird, Nick's the fella and Avery…'

'Yeah, Colombo, join the dots. She's obviously working on a story or something. We'll give Mel the rundown tonight.'

'Yeah.'

Terry tuned the radio to Magic FM and let Randy Crawford seal the day with love.

Chapter Twenty-Six: That's Alright Now Mamma

'Nick, it's so lovely to have you home. Come on in, bubbeleh. Your father's at his check-up.' Nick set his briefcase down in the hallway, tossed his jacket aside and then plonked himself down on the small settee in the living room. It smelt of mothballs and gefilte fish. Nick tried to get home every other Friday. It soothed his conscience and satisfied his mother, who always kept some braised brisket on standby. Nick liked the tradition of his parent's home life, even though his father's illness had ruptured the family portrait on occasion.

'Well now, what's been happening at work? Tell me all about it.'

'Work? What do you mean?'

'I haven't seen you in two weeks? What have you been doing, bubbeleh?'

Scamming clients, ingesting obscene amounts of cocaine, and having wanton sex with beautiful women.

'Nothing much to tell, Mum, just boring legal shtick.'

'I ran into the senior partner, Mr Fisher, about a week ago, and he says you had such a demanding schedule. You were flown to France on a special assignment and you have been working all hours right into the night and are doing very well for the firm.'

Fucking Fisher, always spouting crap.

'He's exaggerating. I had a different style of case, Mum,

but it's been the same drill day in, day out.'

'Oh bubbeleh, don't be so jaded. Remember when you graduated? You were so happy. Your father was so proud. He couldn't stop smiling all day, remember?'

Nick didn't answer.

'I have the album – just a second – of you in your cap and gown on graduation. It was wonderful. Wait a minute and I'll go get it. So adorable you were in your outfit.'

'Mum that was ages ago.' The last thing Nick needed was to be reminded of how far he'd fallen.

'Won't be a minute. Go and lay the table. I'll be right back.'

'Mum, just so you know, I can't stay the whole night,' he yelled. Mrs Stringer returned, clutching a bulky green leather photo album.

'Look, so innocent and sweet. Remember how you were going to take on the world, bubbeleh, and rid it of corruption?' She smiled and her whole face shone.

One picture caught his eye. He was around twelve with Matt and some other kids from school. They were in uniform on Brighton Pier and he was cradling a pet monkey.

Nothing changes. Still got a monkey on my back. Ha!

The two of them sat down and were just about to tuck in when there was a loud knock on the door.

'Must be the postman or maybe the window cleaner. Help yourself to the brisket and I'll be in soon.'

There it was again, only louder.

'Alright, I'm coming,' she yammered, muttering phrases in Yiddish.

'Oh my goodness, it's you!' She unchained the lock and flung it open, rooted to the spot.

'Well I never! How long has it been? Come on in, we're just carving the brisket.'

'Rebecca, so good to see you. It's been too long. I meant to come earlier. I meant to visit when Graham was diagnosed, but life gets in the way.' They were standing in the corridor, within earshot of the dining room.

'Come on now, don't be silly, you're always welcome, you know that, always.' Nick recognised the aftershave first. It tacked his senses like a noxious gas. It was a struggle for him to breathe. Then the boom-blast voice cracking the normality of the scene.

'Oh, that smells wonderful, Becca.'

There was no mistaking it, Mel was in his home. Nick peeked into the living room just to be sure. Mel hauled his burly frame onto his father's chair.

'You don't mind, do you Becca?' The way he said his mother's name made Nick retch.

'Of course not. Graham is at the doctor's, but Nick and I were just about to eat, so please stay and join us.' She called out to him. 'Nicholas, look who's popped in for a visit.'

Nick's first urge was to bolt. Instead, he limped into the room with his teeth clenched.

'Here he is.' She gleamed as if broadcasting the fact on primetime TV.

'Just the boy I need to see,' rocked Mel.

Nick's face dropped. He was sinking – he could feel Mel shake his soul. 'Uncle Melvin.'

'Nick. How you doin'? I have more work for you, son.'

'I appreciate that.'

'Our Nicholas is doing so well at his law firm. We were just going through some old snaps before you got here.' She reached for the photo album and leafed through the pages.

'Look, there you are with me and Graham, and there's Catherine with you. Oh, those were happy times.'

Mel held the pic to the light and nodded, but Nick was curious.

'Mum, you never did say what happened to Aunt Cathy.'

'Oh, she was your uncle's first wife and you were too young then to be told the whole story but she well …'

Mel interrupted with a belligerent air:

'Catherine was my first wife. She died during childbirth, and my son never made it – a long time ago, before you was even born.'

184

'Sorry to hear that, Uncle Mel,' Nick gulled him into believing he gave a shit.

'All in the past now, and we're going to have a lovely dinner, so come on, let's get to it, I could eat for all of Tottenham.'

The three of them entered the dining room, Nick wondering if he had stumbled on Mel's Achilles heel as he chomped on in silence while Nick regaled his mother with fake office stories and court victories. After about an hour, Nick and Mel left together.

'Family first, Nick, family first. Got a special job for you in the morning, so be on time.' He sped off, leaving Nick pondering his next move.

Chapter Twenty-Seven: Smoking Menthol

Avery was a regular at The Eagle, the self-styled gastro pub on Farringdon Road, an existentialist nirvana that served fab food, favoured by London hipsters, Clerkenwell's intelligentsia, fashion flies and art students but was still popular with locals and night owls. Office emos and beer bankers were stirring the scene and there was a continuous buzz that looped the air.

'Sorry Avery, can't get any more of it. Times have changed. It's too risky.'

'You sound like I'm asking for crack, for God's sake. You do realise that half the US has legalised weed now and I'm only after an eighth. Even school kids can score an eighth.'

'Well, maybe you better find a prepubescent dealer and hook up with one of them.'

'Maybe I will.' They both laughed. Avery continued sipping her drink. She was twiddling with her straw, making air bubbles, and kept turning to the door every few seconds.

'Waiting for someone?'

'That obvious?'

'They don't call me Shifty-eye Pete for nothing. I've been a barman for too long not to spot the obvious. He's probably a no-show.'

'Says the man who couldn't pull a stripper in Stringie's.'

'Oh, you heard about that too?'

'Everyone this side of the river knows about that, Pete.'

'She was already taken.'

'They always are.'

Nick rolled in from the back exit, and, seeing Avery in mid-conversation, snuck up behind her.

'I don't know, there's still a few available,' he chirped.

'Nick!' She sprang to her feet and gave him a warm hug. 'Let's go grab a table.'

'Sure thing. So Avery, how's the week been for ya?'

'Really good. I've been working this story, and I think it's developing now.'

That's terrific, Avery, – pleased for you.'

Well, we'll see. I'm still researching and putting stuff together, you know, but I got a hit on an unexpected lead and I made a lot of headway, so yeah, making progress.' Avery had been digging around and had unearthed some major intel from a techie pal of hers about an international cyber heist. She wasn't about to spill – not yet, Nick may be too close to Mel.

'How have you been? Still stuck with nasty scammers and gangstas?'

'Absolutely, the cream of the criminarti.'

'Oh, very droll.'

'Are you sticking around for the late-night hustle?'

'The what? Sounds like some fifties dance craze.'

'No, it's an unlicensed poker game. Starts around 2 a.m.'

Avery was thrown.

'Here at the Eagle?'

'Yeah, I played last month and the month before.'

Guess I'm not a regular at all. Not that kind.

'Mmm, you haven't got a drink yet.'

'Pete will sort me out. I've got a tab. Vodka and Red Bull.'

'Oh, is this is your local too?'

'All the bars and clubs from here to King's Cross and West End Central.'

'You never said. I mean, you don't come across as a barfly.'

'Not a barfly, Avery. I just like drinking.'

'Be right back.' She slid back to the bar in flirt mode.

'Hey, Pete, could I get a vodka and Red Bull and another pint of Guinness?'

'Coming straight up.'

'So you never said you knew Nick?'

'Everyone knows Nick. They call him the Prince of Clerkenwell.'

'You serious?'

'Yes, he's extremely well connected, an overgenerous tipper. An all-round good guy, very princely.'

'Who else does he knock around with then?'

'The usual Clerkenwell crew: models, gangsters, architects, you lot, aspiring piss artists, showbiz types – all sorts.'

'Yeah?'

'He's a lawyer, knows lots of people, and I've never heard a bad word spoken about him.'

'Thanks.' She smiled and balanced the drinks back to the table.

'Thank you, gorgeous. Have to say you look dangerously hot tonight. That skirt is … well …'

Avery lowered her gaze and started playing with her hair and the strap of her stilettos, Nick's charm popping her cheeks pink.

'Bet you say that to all the girls you've had a one-nighter with.'

'No, only the ones I want to see more of.' He leaned in. 'You feel that?'

'What?'

'It's chemistry – naked passion.'

Avery knew it was risky getting involved with Nick. He was Mel's lawyer and things could get messy very quickly, but there was something about him. She got goose bumps every time he got close, and although she was serious about scoring info from him, she was honest enough to admit she wanted to get to know him better. *We definitely have chemistry.*

Why not see what happens.

They chatted some more, downed a few rounds and got tipsy. Around one thirty, Pete came over.

'Will you both be joining us when we shut up shop?'

'Yes,' they answered in giggle burps.

'Great. Couple of locals and a few new faces – should be a fun night. Even got some Yanks in the game. Could be interesting.'

Pete started packing away the pub clobber, like dirty glasses, napkins and wads of nicotine gum. He latched the front doors and waited for the regulars to come via the side door.

They sat at a round table in the centre of the bar.

'Nicki, Nick, lookin' good – who you got there, then?'

'Avery, this is Terry and Mickey … um, sorry, not sure … who?'

'Yeah, we got Robert – we call 'im Robbie – and Tim. Our visitors from America.'

'Nice to meet you both.' Smiled Nick.

They nodded.

Two new faces broke the ice. They were college kids, book smart and overly polite – Karen and Martin.

'Hey everyone, I'm Karen and this is Martin.'

Martin was in his twenties with preppy boy hair and dimples, and Karen was a similar age, with strawberry blonde curls and batten bow lips. They looked like novices but both were well connected and had been grinding poker tables since their late teens. Everyone there had a tie-up to Mel. He had a fifty-one per cent stake in the pub and used the monthly game to talent-spot players for high-stakes games in Vegas. With no limits on stakes or winnings and no casino licence, the pub was in breach of the Gambling Act 2005, but the misfits at the table weren't bothered.

'Now that everyone's acquainted, let's play.'

Terry took the lead. They each got two cards face down and five community cards. They were playing No Limit Texas Hold'em Poker, but as with every game of poker, they were playing the player not the game. Avery dropped early. She wasn't a card player and her instincts failed her. One by one they were chewed up until only Nick, Karen, and Tim remained.

'I'll see your three thousand and raise you two thousand.'

Tim started rapping his fingers on the table.

'I don't wanna piss you guys off but I gotta move my hands.'

Karen wasn't fazed. 'Well?'

'Yeah, I'm all the way out like a midget in quicksand.'

Karen and Nick were still locked in.

Let me call it. Nick was confident.

'I call.'

Nick fanned his cards across the table. He showed a full house, but Karen had it nailed with a royal flush. Nick was beaten but brushed it off. They downed some more booze and said their goodbyes.

Avery and Nick spent the night together folding the dawn away with starlight kisses.

Chapter Twenty-Eight: Imagine

Matt and BCM were half-asleep. Matt was sporting three days stubble and BCM a craggy goatee and mussed-up locks that were de rigueur with the peacenik party crowd that had been blazing the wire for the last two days. It was the morning after the night before the morning after. The sun was trailing dust balls and cat hair on the settee through the open window, chalking BCM's face with mirrored heat. He lay there with a small blanket wrapped over him, his long legs hanging over the end of the couch and his eyes still closed. Matt crept into the room, blinking, in boxers and a tee-shirt.

Quietly, he put on his jeans, hoodie and sneakers. He scrambled for change and found a twenty in his pocket, rubbed his chin and crept out of the apartment heading for Bea's of Bloomsbury, his regular coffee shop for take away breakfast.

Meanwhile, BCM had risen and after a shower and change had spent the last few minutes cleaning up, his arms buried in beer cans, rizzla papers and coffee cups. He found a spot in the lounge and sat down cross-legged on a large mat, aligning his back, neck and head in a straight line. Facing east, he took five deep breaths and closed his eyes, clearing his mind of abstractions. He concentrated on an image and inhaled and then exhaled until he found his rhythm. Gradually the whole room was draped in serenity.

Matt let himself in, puzzled at the cleanliness that greeted him.

'Hey man, you didn't have to do that. I bought us breakfast.'

'It was easy, no problem at all. What d'ya get?'

'Muffins, coffee and fruit pots.'

'Great.'

Matt went and grabbed some cutlery and plates and set it down on the table. They talked while they ate.

'I tried calling Nick. Wanted to invite him over for breakfast. Thought it might be a good time for you to talk, you know?'

'Yeah.' BCM looked at him kindly.

'I couldn't reach him, so …'

'Don't stress it. I'll be around for a while, and when the time's right we'll meet.'

'Sure. I worry about him. He's been missing rehearsals flunking out on the band he's changing. I know he has a good heart, but he's being drawn to the wall.'

Matt tagged the sympathy in BCM's eyes. He wanted him to know that Nick had slipped into depravity.

'I saw him a few days ago and he told me he was strung in with a mobster client, Mel. He keeps pushing him further and further …'

'Even if I do get to speak to him, and even if he listens, there's no guarantee he's gonna switch and see the light. You have to want it to change it.'

'I hear you, brother – just hope it's not too late.'

'The wheel of life keeps turning, but it's all illusion. That's how I see it. All I can do is try to see the honesty in everything I do.'

'It's a loaded concept, honesty.'

Matt started rolling a fatty spliff. It helped him unwind when talking like this with no boundaries.

'When did you start, really helping people?'

'Well, I don't know that I help so much as stick a lighted candle in the mix. I just have a knack of changing messed-up situations. My grandfather was a real spiritual leader. But things are very different in London. There's a scam a second and you have to be alert to it.'

'Yep. It's all fucked up. You can't be sure of anything, just death.'

'Yeah, death is a promise every soul will keep, so you might as well live in the now.'

'True, the art of God is an unfinished canvas.'

'Matt, lighten up, you sound like a clergyman about to enter a strip bar.'

'Just saying, man. I'm a believer.'

Matt was tuned into BCM's vibe and enjoying their quirky talk.

'I'm only ever really at peace when I'm playing,' Matt orbed.

'That's cool. Music can change the fucking world, man. I respect your dedication.'

'Well, I was gonna sign with Nick. He's part of the band when he wants to be. I probably will, still sign with him as it's got nothing to do with his legal business, and he'll give me complete artistic control, which is what every singer-songwriter secretly wants. Enough money to make creative decisions and keep hold of my artistic integrity.'

'If you can do that it would be priceless. You'd probably be hated though.'

'Yeah, the curse of the fan. I mean, I don't wanna blow on about all the manufactured puppets pimped around in the biz, but I've never been able to understand that desire, that need for riches and bitches. Success is awesome, but being tabloid fodder doesn't turn me on, you know?' Matt frizzed.

They were toking the day away, consumed by the ganja cloud that engulfed the room. BCM walked over to the windows and opened them wider.

'Here it is, London's carousel of life: Paradise, Purgatory, Hell. A nonstop freak show all in one take.'

Matt looked on, bleary-eyed.

'What's the date today, bro?'

'Twentieth.'

'Got an anti-war gig tomorrow. Texted Nick about it already – do you wanna come?'

'That's righteous, man. Sure. War or civilisation, how can man fund both? To me, war is never a "necessary" evil, it always ends in further bloodshed, further conflict and further away from the truth.'

'Yeah, I feel like I wear my tee-shirt and wave my banner, but in the end none of it matters as the people at the top, the people in control, they just do what lines their pockets best. To hell with the innocents.'

'I hear you brother. The higher up you crawl, the more people you have to buy to stay there, but at least you give a shit. That matters.'

'Guess that's better than being a fucking pedestrian on life's highway – sit back, consume, consume, consume – watch, don't get involved. You ain't living unless you're in it.'

'Yeah, it's a fine balance between standing on the sidelines and immersing yourself in the thick of it. In the end it's what feels right and how trashed you are midweek.'

'Amen to that.'

They rounded off their abstract discussion with more profundity and some killer bud.

Chapter Twenty-Nine: High Hopes

Avery was transcribing her tape from Mel's phone. She had drawn an elaborate mind map listing all her potential sources and her basic hypothesis. She was sifting through all her data and was on top form, collating intel from the wire, her cyber grass and doing extensive documentary research. Mel had a vast and highly impressive property portfolio with over a hundred different companies, all of which registered Solomon Leif (Sal) and himself as either director or secretary at some point. Mel had resigned from all but three, and everything appeared to be tied to an off shore account in Liechtenstein. Apart from the companies stretching from gourmet restaurants to capital real estate, Mel had also amassed an extraordinary collection of fine art, which was stored in a special warehouse in London's Ludgate Hill. Mel kept the building at a constant 65 degrees with 47 per cent humidity. The art was wrapped face to back and museum framed in a vertical position. Mel had covered the windows with UV filter film. With premium surveillance and a twenty-four-hour concierge, Sal had used this address as the company registered office for many of the offshoot businesses, and this is where Avery planned to wing an unofficial stakeout. There was a highly publicised art auction taking place next week. Mel was bound to send one of his crew as a proxy bidder. Avery would keep track and follow the booty back to Ludgate Hill.

'Shit, this coffee is bad.'

'Is that from downstairs?' asked Ollie.

'Yeah, tastes gross. What you up to next Tuesday?' She took another swig and flinched.

'Zilch.'

'Well, you are now. You're accompanying me to Bonhams Auctioneers, so swot up on your Bratby and your Procktor.'

'What's this fer, your big exposé?'

'Yeees, it's for my red letter moment and may give us more ammo' to nail this guy.'

'Sure.'

'How good are you on secret cameras and undercover microphones?'

'Pretty good. Everyone thinks it's piss easy to operate them, but to track good audio and get clear footage it's all about preparation and positioning.'

Avery had compiled a detailed list of all the previous works bought through Mel's company and cross-referenced them to similar works on sale at the auction. She handed a copy to Ollie.

'Here you go. Give you a taster of what we're gonna be looking at. If we find the fence who's ringing this stuff in for Mel, we may be able to find more on him. I think we have to follow all leads.'

'Gotcha. What makes you so sure he's gonna be there?'

'I'm not. Just acting on impulse.'

'Riiight, journo on a mission.'

'Well, he's tricky. All the clubs, bars and restaurants are in legitimate company names, but I've requisitioned his company accounts, as they're a matter of public record, and we'll see what they show.'

'Have you thought about using a PI?'

'Shit, yeah. I'd love to hack the fucker's phone and seal the scoop. But that kind of technique is no longer encouraged. Your dad would go bananas. Good PIs are at a premium and in short supply.'

'Yeah. Guess you're right.'

'Probably in breach of the new Bribery Act. All this fucking red tape makes it really hard to tackle smart crooks.'

'I'll go get a copy of the act.'

'Yeah, do that.'

Avery did have an excellent police insider she could use, but if word got out to a local bobby on Mel's turf, her story would be blown. She would steer clear for now. Instead, she focused her attention on more data sources and undertook a simple Land Registry search of all the properties she had stumbled across in her research. The owners were listed as Melvin Maurice Greenberg and Mo Holdings. She then checked the Companies Register for Mo Holdings and requested key documents including details of capital, mortgages, previous directors and accounts records. She yawned.

'This part of the puzzle is painstakingly slow,' she moaned.

'Yeah, well, there's masses of stuff you can't do now thanks to the Bribery Act,' Ollie ribbed.

'Fucking great. Bring on bribes, blaggers and bull shitters and let's just rifle through it.'

'It's frustrating if you're working a hard story like this. No one's likely to give up info freely or grass up a criminal without payment protection or both. The act makes a lot of sense for useless gossip, but if you need to nozzle a source, how you gonna do it if you don't pay them?'

'Exactly. Whether you're a whistle-blower in Whitehall or a prostitute in Pimlico, you won't blab without being paid. Ironic really, first it takes a good year of your life to make these fucking contacts, and now you might not even be able to use any of 'em because of the Bribery Act.'

Avery thumbed through the act methodically, and then after about ten minutes turned to Ollie and concluded,

'Do you realise that it would now be illegal for journalists at *The Sunday Telegraph* to buy that stolen disk – the smoking gun revealing all those MP's fraudulent expenses.'

'Yeah, it would be illegal under the Bribery Act, and a story that exposed corruption and illegality itself would never have seen the light of day, and the money crunchers in Whitehall would still be stealing from the public purse.'

'Hmmm, I wonder if early Crimbo pressies can be construed as bribery.'

'Seems to me, the more we want to tell, the tighter the law and legal shit to deal with.'

'So much for a free press – how to nab a criminal without becoming one in the process – all these restrictions on what we can, but, more importantly, what we can't do.'

'I know. Most of the world's greatest journos have been rule breakers.'

'I'm glad you feel that way, Ollie, as we may have some rule breaking of our own to do.'

'So long as it's for the greater good and stops Justin Bieber headlining news, I'm in.'

Avery shook her head impatiently: 'Tabloid excess has stolen the integrity of newspapers, but these regulations could kill off the press completely.'

'And on that sombre note, shall we go grab lunch?'

'No. I'm still snooping and searching, but you can get me a cheese sanga if you want?'

'Okay, on my way back, yeah?'

'Cool.'

Avery spun her chair back to her desk and continued digging out data. It was going to be a bitch of an afternoon.

Chapter Thirty: It's All Yellow

Due to Mel's largesse, his local synagogue had benefitted to the tune of one million pounds. It had been a comforting feature of the British landscape for over two hundred years, and Mel had always made a point of visiting regularly.

As he parked in front of the ornate building, he stared at the picture-perfect clouds swirling across the sky.

It's a beautiful day for atonement. He climbed the stairs to the lobby and waited in reception.

'Rabbi Weinberg is in his office, second floor.' A peachy admin clerk with shiny hair and sensible shoes led him part of the way.

'Just at the end there.'

Mel hadn't slept properly the last couple of days. Mimi's face puckered his dreams. He wanted answers.

Rabbi Weinberg was a scholarly sort, patient and prone to impromptu speeches about the meaning of life. Mel just wanted to feel better.

'Come in, come in.'

'Thank you, Rabbi.'

'You don't look well. Please sit down, Melvin.'

Mel pushed the small chair towards him. His man girdle was pinching, making him sweat. He sat down with his elbows on the desk, hunched forward, his eyes rimmed red and grey, bagging his skin like a Shar Pei.

'I'm very confused, Rabbi. I need answers.'

'Tell me what's going on.'

'There's a woman from my past, Rabbi. I saw her recently and I felt all those old feelings resurface.'

'But you're recently married and you don't want to be led astray, is that it?'

'Kind of. You see, Rabbi, this woman, she holds a secret. I know about it but I can't forgive it, I can't accept it.'

'Hmmm uhmmm.'

'I want to, Rabbi. I am the last person to judge another, but I feel as if she is right under my skin, you know. I can't seem to break free of her.'

'What are you hoping for? Sunshine and forgiveness? You already said you can't forgive, so *you* stand in the way of your own salvation. There's a good man inside you, all you have to do is bring him out.'

'I can't afford to bring out all the good, Rabbi. My enemies will see it as weakness.'

'Everyone has bad days, everyone goes through it, and for everyone there is hope.'

Mel checked his watch and leaned back in his chair. *Should never 'ave worn this man spanx. It's fucking killing me.*

'So what you're saying, Rabbi, is it's up to me to get past it.'

'Depends on what *it* is, Melvin.'

Mel softened at the empathy in the Rabbi's eyes but was unable to offload. He tried a more general approach, implicating Nick in the process.

'It's not me, it's my nephew. I think he might be batting for the other side.'

There was a long pause.

'What makes you think that?'

'Well, it's just a feeling. Perhaps he should go to synagogue more often, be a better Jew.'

'Perhaps, everyone could benefit from more time in prayer, but if it's just a suspicion you harbour, Melvin, maybe you should let it go. Be watchful, kind, understanding. Show him that he is loved.'

Mel's cowardice to come clean had landed Nick in the thick of it, but Rabbi Weinberg was wise to the bluff.

'Tread carefully, Melvin. Try and be honest about your conflict and then you're one step closer to a solution.'

'It's a head and heart battle, Rabbi.'

'After everything is said and done, you are Jewish first. You may have ham in your belly, drive on the Shabbat, and be living with a man, but feeling something is not the same as acting it out. What you feel is one thing and what you do is something entirely different.'

Mel was relieved.

Mimi is what she is. I'll deal with her my way.

'There's something else, Rabbi.'

'Yes.'

'One of my relatives is struggling. Her husband is very unwell, and I found lots of bills unpaid and her mortgage in arrears. She has not asked for my help, Rabbi. How do I approach her?'

'Tzedakah begins at home. Your relative is hungry and in trouble. Explain to her that it must be tough with all the challenges she's facing and you can help her for a little while. Maybe present it to her as a free loan, a way of dealing with the immediate costs of everything so her pride is not slighted. See, Melvin, how God's message comes through? This is the way for you to reach out to your family and show them your better side.'

Mel nodded and weaved his wobble gut out of the chair.

'Let me know how things work out, Melvin. I'm always available to talk to you. May God bless you.'

'Thank you, Rabbi.'

He left the synagogue and headed straight for Nick's. He found Mrs Stringer nursing her husband Graham with soup and crackers. She was surprised and embarrassed to see him again.

'Let's go in the kitchen, we can talk there.'

'Rebecca, I know this might be difficult for you to admit. You can't be coping well now that Graham isn't working.'

'We manage. Nick helps, and there's my pension and obviously what Graham gets.'

'It's okay, Rebecca. I know you're behind with the mortgage.'

'How do you know that?'

'It doesn't take a genius, Rebecca. Look at the state of this place. The tiles on the bathroom are broken, the gate outside needs replacing, and Graham – there must be so much you have to pay for. It's freezing in here, so gas bills, electricity, the tax on the property … I can see you're struggling, and it's okay, I'll deal with it.'

Her face fell and with it the veil of secrecy.

'Oh, it's so difficult sometimes. Day by day it gets harder and harder, and that's when I worry the most, when I think that soon there'll be nothing left.'

Mel put a protective arm around her.

'It's alright, Becca. Give me the paperwork on the house and the bills, and I'll deal with it.'

'I don't know, Mel. It's very good of you and I do appreciate it, but I'll have to talk to Nick first.'

'Just let me take a look, eh? No harm in that, and I'll come round next week. You, me and Nick can sort something out then.'

'Yes, that would be okay. It's all in the spare room. I'll go get it.'

Mel went back into the lounge, unsure of how to speak to Graham, who was channel-hopping.

'Anything good on, pal?'

Graham was tuned out, staring intently at the horses on the screen.

'I always 'ave a go on the gee-gees too. Nothin' like a bet to get you in the mood.'

'Here's all the documents.' Rebecca thrust a bundle of papers into Mel's arms.

'Good, I'll have Sal the book-keeper look it over. No

need to worry.'

'Okay, I'd better get back to Graham. I need to reheat his soup.' She glanced over at him.

'Yeah, of course. I'll let myself out.'

Mel was silently humbled. *Graham may be in the shitter, but Rebecca really loves him, and that's more than I got. But the day I start opening my heart out is the day I die.*

Chapter Thirty-One: That's Entertainment

Mimi's VW Beetle slalomed to a stop outside Patisserie Valerie on the King's Road. She was smartly dressed in pencil pleats and sling-backs.

'Hi, a large cappuccino and some of those.' She pointed to some choc' iced éclairs.

'Yes, of course.'

Mimi slipped her shades on top of her head, paid the sales assistant, and left clutching the cake box and coffee cup in her hand. She had parked on a yellow, and there was a penalty ticket on the windscreen. She swiped it and scrunched it into her purse, placing the coffee in a cup holder and the cake box on the back seat. She belted up and hit the gas.

Approaching Cadogan Gardens, checking her rear-view mirror, she noticed an unmarked, black SUV on her tail. She pumped the radio and kept her eye on it. Once past Sloane Square, she ran a red and dodged an oncoming Merc. The SUV was creeping up on her.

'Fuck, it really is following me.' Grabbing gears, she spun into reverse and slammed the brakes. The SUV mirrored her move. She mounted the kerb and zigzagged past a school kid and his mother.

'Crap, almost—' Crrrech! Skidding to a halt, she stalled

the engine, splattering the coffee and hurling smashed cake to the floor.

'Come on, girl, come on. Don't fail me now.'

The SUV was inching closer. She jacked the wheel, swerving to the right, and then downshifted hard left onto Battersea Park Road. She cranked the throttle, passing a garbage truck on a blind curve as she wheeled into traffic. The SUV pulled up alongside. She glanced at the driver but didn't recognise him.

Thwat! Thwat! Thwat! He pelted her tyres with one shot. She zoomed down a side street too narrow for the SUV to follow. Mimi raced through the back alleys of the Winstanley housing estate and then bolted the pavement onto a major road. She found a tiny drive jammed between a bookie's and a convenience store. She cut the engine and removed the keys, applied the handbrake and switched on the hazards.

'Oh fuck, that was real.' She let out a deep breath and gulped down what was left of her coffee. She placed her hand in front of her, unable to stop the tremor. She felt weird, dizzy. She was sweating bullets.

'Must be the shock.' She stepped outside and knelt down to check the tires. The back two were shredded. She reached for her mobile from her handbag and buzzed Avery.

'Urgent, call me, been in an accident.' Mimi was irate.

How dare she nearly kill me! It's because of her I'm in this mess.

Blip blip brrr, chirp, brrr, Mimi's phone was beeping.

'Yes?' Yes it's Mimi, and yes you did hear correctly. I was run off the road, and you're to blame. If I'd never got involved with you and your fucking story, Mel wouldn't be blasting his fuse. I've a good mind to go tell him what's been going on.'

Avery was panicky.

'Mimi, I'm so sorry. Listen, we'll pay for all the damage to the car, and if you sit tight, I'll pick you up. You're not hurt, are you? I mean physically?'

'I don't know, there's a scrape on my hand from the friction on the steering wheel, my clothes are fucked – coffee stains everywhere and cake splatter on the back seats and the floor. It needs a valet. I know it was him.'

'Of course, you must be pretty shaken.'

'That's a fucking understatement.'

'Well, look, give me your exact location and I'll be there as soon as I can.'

'Between hell and purgatory.'

Avery didn't answer. She let the comment slide.

'Mimi, please, can we concentrate on getting you home.'

'Wait a second, I'll just check the name of the road.'

'Sure.'

'It's called Lavender Road, it's off York Gardens.'

'Be there in about thirty minutes. Try not to stress.'

Avery tagged Ollie for backup. *Fucked if I'm gonna face Mimi's dagger mouth alone.*

Ollie was trying to transfer his credit card on the phone.

'I'll sort that out for you later, c'mon let's go.'

Ollie had his back to her his head hunched over the phone. Avery tried again.

'I'll do that for you. Honestly, it's easy. You want to transfer your balance to your Visa, right?'

He clasped his hand across the receiver.

'I'm busy, Avery.' She waggled her finger disapprovingly.

'Seems like a personal call. I'm sure your old man's gonna be pleased. Look, I can help you sort out your credit card crap. Just come with me. We're going to rescue a source.'

'What?'

'Yeah, I'll explain in the car. Let's go.'

Ollie hung up and snatched his jacket and keys from the desk.

'We need to let Colin know.'

Avery had frequent cat spats with Colin, the newsroom manager, and wanted to avoid the obligatory third degree over where, why, and what she was using the car for.

'I'll text him – it's an emergency, so we'll do it en route. Blame it on me.'

Ollie scribbled a note and stuck it on Colin's desk.

Luckily he was in a meeting.

It took about twenty minutes to get there. Mimi was hard to miss.

'I've arranged a tow truck. We have to wait till they get here,' Avery confirmed. 'This is Ollie. He's one of our interns.'

'Hi.'

'Good to meet you.'

'Likewise. Is it okay if Avery and I have a private chat – could you maybe go grab us some coffee?'

'Yeah, no worries. I have to call the office anyway.'

Ollie schlepped off in search of caffeine.

Back by the car, Avery was doing her best to calm Mimi down.

'Mimi, I think you have every right to be angry, and I understand, but isn't the point of all this that you want to share your story and at the same time get justice.'

'Yes, but I don't want to get killed trying.'

'I've scheduled a meeting with the editor, and I'm sure we can get you some security as we discussed.'

'I just want it over.'

'I've already arranged a major two-part series, ghost-written by me, inflicting maximum damage on Mel, if you stick it out and talk freely and honestly about your relationship together. We can produce a really good story.'

'I want protection sorted before the end of the week.'

'Done.'

'I want to help, Avery, I do. Sometimes Mel makes me so fucking angry, and then I think of the look he gives. You know that look, it's fucking orgasmic.'

Avery was saved by the tow truck and a slightly out of breath Ollie.

'Here we go ladies. Two coffees, just in time.'

All three rode back to the office making small talk, listening to teen beats and trade ads on Capital radio.

Chapter Thirty-Two: Trigger Happy

Mel was on the phone to Nick, while jamming mint drops down his craw.

'I don't care who's coming to see you, even if it's the fucking Pope. I want you at the club at seven.'

He rammed the receiver down and hollered for Terry.

'Boss?'

'We got young Adam gracing us with his fucked-up presence today. I want Nick fully briefed. Adam's a fucking hot-head. He'll get us all copped.'

'What's Sal got to say about it?'

'He agrees with me. Adam's been running wild for too long. Sal's been out of his mind with worry. It's better this way. Can't take a risk – Adam's too close to the line. Nick will let us know what we're up against and help with the executive tasks of the operation.'

'Right, boss.'

Adam was Sal's first born, an overindulged super brat with an addictive streak and a youth-centric desire for street cred' and infamy. He was widely acknowledged as one of gangland's most inventive junior mobsters, but his off-duty antics were causing concern. Adam had teamed up with hard man Harry Hynes, a notorious cage fighter, and two gun smugglers from Lithuania. Together they had created Boom Bling Ballistics, a preassembled assassin's kit retailing at around £2,000 a pop. The kits had proved so popular with crime syndicates that they were backlogged to around fifty thousand. Each one was loaded with a Baikal handgun, a silencer, two cases of ammo, and a bulletproof vest. Boom Bling Ballistics had become a status symbol in the underworld, boosting Adam's rank and rep. With this new-found fame he had cultivated a caricatured gangster lifestyle that was at odds with his privileged upbringing and family money.

Sal had yielded to his son's appetite for designer threads, fast women, and luxury cars, but when he was sent damning photos of him posing with a Walther PPK flanked by pimps and prostitutes, he figured it was time to rein him in. He called on Mel, who had bankrolled the scheme, for help, and it was decided that someone new would front the biz, letting Adam concentrate on Sal's clothing empire and property investments.

Nick arrived at the club a little after seven, his day marred by Mel's repetitive phone spiel.

'Ah, just the man, just the man.'

Nick cringed as Mel heaved his weight onto him. Mel wreaked of booze and stale Chinese food. Sal was already at the table, his face dinted with unease. He could handle anything life threw at him, except his son. Nick gave him a welcoming smile and sat down. A few minutes later, Adam arrived, decked head to toe in Armani, dripping in gold and propped up by two curvy blondes. Sal gave the nod to Mel as Adam and his boudoir angels approached the table. Tezza slipped the chicks a monkey each to disappear. They slunk off into the shadows and Adam stumbled over.

'Papa, why you spoiling my fun?' he slurred, crusted coke icing his schnozzle and the lines of his lips. His forehead was clammy and he found it difficult to stand.

'Allow me, Sal. This is Nick. He's the new legal whizz your dad and I were telling you about. He's on board and he's smart. You could learn a thing or two from him.'

Nick said nothing. *Fucking moron. What's he roped me into*

now? Adam's eyelids were drooping.

'So, this is wunderkind Nicholas?' He was leaning sideways ready to drop.

'I think you and your dad need some private time. Nick, let's go upstairs and I'll fill you in.' Mel patted Sal on the back while Nick offered him a sympathetic look and then followed Mel into the office.

'It's best served on the rocks.' Mel handed him a whiskey.

'Thanks.' He swigged his drink, sat down and looked around awkwardly.

'Adam runs one of the biggest networks of illegal weapons in the country. We funded the business and he's exceeded expectations, but he's coked out of his brains and is becoming a bit of an embarrassment.'

'Right.'

'My motives are honourable, bubbeleh.'

'I see.'

'Most of the profits from this venture are donated to groups like the JDL.'

'The JDL?'

'The Jewish Defence League- a vital organisation which ensures that all of us can have a safer future free from anti-Semitism and terrorists.'

He's fucking nuts. Let's hear what the fuck he wants.

'The JDL? Yeah. I think I've heard of them.'

'Well, they're very misunderstood. The press shits make up lies about them and disseminates false info on the web. They are committed to protecting our people by any means.'

'I see.'

And so it begins, the nine circles of hell. Where the fuck is this heading? I may buy into this myself. Don't wanna be under the cosh with Mel forever.

'We need you. Need you for a bigger cause. Groups like the JDL rely on us for funding, and our gun-running op raises crucial revenue for our brethren to do what they must to protect us.'

'Hmmm.' Nick was finding it hard not to laugh. He had

never seen Mel so earnest. It was a tad creepy.

'This is where you come in.'

Nick stared directly at Mel's crimson-coloured face, spider veins crawling from left to right.

'What?' He tilted his chair back, his eyes now glued on Mel's neck fat.

'You're ideal for setting up shell companies, so money can flow freely, accounts accessed and so on. Your office is a perfect front for concealing and camouflaging our fund-raising objectives. Your office would be our informal transfer system, bubbeleh.'

Nick recoiled in disgust. Mel was oblivious – he was elsewhere plotting and planning.

'It would be a very ambitious project, Mel. I don't think it's feasible.'

'Yes, but what better way to move money so our brethren can mobilise, develop, and grow.'

Nick was intrigued, secretly angling for a way to cheat Mel out of his cut.

'It would mean turning a blind eye to fake passports, ID documents, customs declaration forms, and creating online accounts for simple transfers with the bogus companies created. Then we could avoid suspicion as it's all at arm's-length. Right, Nick?'

'It's very risky, Mel. Do you have a trusted network so it stays under the table?'

'Of course, the whole biz is tied up. I've greased the officials and have a loyal and dependable pool from the bottom to the top.'

Nick wasn't comfortable with Mel's hard-line rhetoric but saw an easy way to launder cash and make his own profits from the venture.

'Listen, while you mull on that, I also need your legal input on what could happen if everything goes Pete Tong for young Adam?'

'How old is he?'

'Twenty-seven.'

'Not much age difference between us.'

'No, but he's a fucking fool. He's attracted to the gangsta culture – booze, babes and bling.'

'So Adam's the lynchpin for one of the biggest gun-running ops this side of the Thames and now he's heading for the shitter. It's a big game to fail at. Hmmm, let's see now, off the cuff. Conspiracy to possess firearms and ammunition, with intent to endanger life? That's twenty years in the slammer if he gets convicted. It's a long stretch.'

'Knew I could rely on you, Nick,' Mel bluffed.

'Bubbeleh, this is dangerous for all of us. We thought we could trust him to take the business to the next level. He was recruiting salesmen and couriers, forging links with customers and contacts. He turned this into the largest operation in the country and then … bang! He becomes a certifiable coke fuck.'

'And potentially the easiest to bust. With such an obvious public profile, unwanted attention stems from all corners.'

'Exactly, you get it. When he's sober I'll send him to the office for a pep talk, make him aware of a few things – not now, when he's calmed down.'

'Sure, if you think it will do any good.'

'Can't hurt –I told Sal booze and bullets are a no-go. It's worth knowing where you stand before the law though.'

'Yeah, that's true enough. It's always useful to know.'

'Always.'

Why is Mel shoving this shit on my plate? A narcissistic gun runner, that's all I need, another prick to babysit. I have to get out of here. All these shrunken egos, and Mel's latest ploy to use the office as a front to legitimise this heinous crime is fucking outrageous. Yeah, fucking outrageous – and I'm gonna wheel as much out of it as I can.

'I gotta run. We have another hearing in Pau next week and I need to be ready.'

'Glad to hear it, as this time you're going it alone.'

'That's fine.'

'Good, I think that's it for now. I'll pop by tomorrow with all the details for the accounts and the companies. Easy as ABC. One more thing.'

'Yeah?'

'Don't ever think you can fuck your Uncle Mel. It would be like fucking yourself.'

Chapter Thirty-Three: Get Back

Mimi was getting ready for another hook-up with Mel. Like so many T-chicks, she was adept at tucking and taping, a trick that effectively hid her dick. She had been doing this for years, but it was still a little painful. She swallowed a handful of hormones. They made her feel moody and her stomach heave. She used to get injections but changed the dosage. Commitment to ultimate feminisation was a long arduous battle, and the final chapter for Mimi was surgery to get rid of the *man* inside her. She put her hands on her hips and stared at her reflection in the hall mirror. Soon there would be absolutely nothing left of the mild-mannered guy she once was.

'Bye, bye mister, hello Mrs.' She repeated it over, 'Ms, Mrs, Ms. Hello woman.' Three hours of nip, slit and tail in Thailand next week and Mimi's magnetism would be full throttle. As a manmade woman, even the overblown take off of herself was a fantasy that men clung to: Barbie curves, bed head hair, and burst cherry lips. She chucked her keys, phone and make-up in her bag and stepped out.

'Taxi,' she yelled, waving over the cab.

'Allo, darlin'. Where to?'

'Hi, um, 50 Greek Street.'

'Okay darlin'.'

Mimi sparked a smile and settled back for the ride. Her phone rang. It was Avery.

'Hi, I'm on my way to him now, 50 Greek Street.'

'Why didn't you take security with you?'

'They're following.'

'You need to be with them, Mimi.'

'It's fine. They'll be waiting for me afterwards.'

'Okay, let me know how you get on.'

'Yep.'

As they got nearer, Mimi retouched her lipstick and powder-pressed her face.

'Thanks.' She slid a twenty to the cabbie, leaving a five pound tip.

Up in his office, Mel was primed and ready, looking sharp in handmade loafers and a silk shirt.

'Tezza.'

'Boss.'

'Mimi's on her way. Go get some of those little cupcake things she likes. I wanna be nice.'

'Okay, I'll take Mickey with me.'

'Hurry up. She'll be 'ere soon now. What's that reporter's name you saw her with?'

'Avery.'

'Avery? Ain't that a geezer's name?'

'It's unisex.'

'Name of that actor what was in Star Trek he was Avery.'

'Did you get a printout of all 'er stories?'

'Yeah, mainly showbiz glamour stuff. Maybe Mimi's doing a glossy shoot or somefing.'

'Where are the printouts?'

'I'll go get 'em.' Terry went next door and took out a stack of papers from a desk drawer.

'There you go, boss. All boring shit.'

'Thanks, Tez, now jog on while I take a gander.'

Mel read as much as he could stand: A mass of celebrity-fuelled stories with snappy snaps and shock-rock headlines. It was standard tabloid fare. A few minutes later, Terry arrived with three cupcakes, the edge of the box frosted with finger smudges and cream.

'Sorry, boss. It was Mickey. Greedy guts 'ad to 'ave one, and then I 'ad to try.'

'Well?'

'Yeah, they was blindin'.'

'Good, where's Mickey now?'

'Downstairs, boss.'

'Okay, go join 'im. I'll let you know when she leaves, then stay on her like poison ivy. I wanna know when, where, and with whom.'

'Yes, boss.' He darted down the stairs, passing Mimi on the way. He grinned, nodded and left.

Mimi felt electric, her body charged with a sweeping frisson and her mind set to amber. Mel was at the door before she entered. His eyes bolted on her breasts which were perfectly symmetrical and cupped in a u shape.

'You give it off every time. You're perfect. Come on, sit.'

Mimi feigned disinterest and put her game face on. She had to be convincing.

'Always the charmer, aren't you, Mel?'

'It's natural, you either got it or you don't. Now what's this bizzo of yours you wanna set up?'

Mimi was sitting opposite him. It was an open-plan office with wooden floors and modern art draping the cream-coloured walls.

'I've got the business plan here and a list of potential investors.'

Mel stuck his tongue in the corner of his mouth and took the document from her. He flicked through the pages and ran his fingers through his quiff, trying to tame it to the side.

'All these investors are up for this alternative escort agency, yeah?'

'Yes, they all want in.' Mimi was pensive.

'With a new bizzo like this, you've got to get lots of

promo and advertising so the punters know it's out there.'

'Yeah.'

'You got any journo contacts or people in the press who can help out on that side of things?'

'Possibly.' Mel must know about Avery, but was it a fishing expedition or was she in real trouble? She decided to play it safe.

'I was asked to do a piece for a paper. I'm thinking about it.'

'Yeah, that could work in promoting something like this.'

'Yes.'

'Leave it with me. I may bung in a few quid myself.'

'Thanks, Mel.'

'Anything for you darlin', you know that.'

'And what about all the legal stuff, the company papers and everything?'

'Yeah, got just the jobs worth for that. New in the game but a brilliant little worker – lawyer over in Clerkenwell.'

'Right.'

'You can leave this with me, OK?'

'Yeah.'

He took the file and placed it neatly in a desk tray. He scratched the side of his face and waited for Mimi to say something. There was an exquisite carnal friction that steamed the room. Slowly, Mimi got up, her body hot for action.

'Is this what you're looking at, baby?' Leaning over him with her boobs in his face. Mel couldn't help himself. He grabbed her by the waist, drawing her into him, her legs feeling the pull of his stack. His hands were spread across her, squeezing every curve. He worked his way up to her bra, pumping with heat. He slid his fingers underneath her shirt, playing with her breasts.

'Mmmm, that's so good,' she sighed. She reached for his cock as he nuzzled his head in her boobs and nipple fucked her with his mouth.

'You're such a bad girl,' he moaned.

They were in the mix when Mel's phone rang, and their heated encounter came to a crashing halt.

'Sorry, I 'ave to take it.'

'Sure.'

Embarrassed and shamefaced, Mel left Mimi to straighten up. She scrambled herself together and left without saying goodbye.

On her track, Terry, Mickey, and her security.

Chapter Thirty-Four: Renegade Master

'What the fuck were you doing with Mel, Mimi?'

'I don't wanna talk about it.'

'I do. It's fucking risky and could kill the story.'

'Yeah, you're only interested in the fucking story.'

'Look, Mimi, I've sweated shit for you. Got you protection, money, and you're playing fuck and shine with one of the country's most ruthless criminals. You've got to lean back, step aside and take a view.'

'You can't help who you wanna screw.'

'Is that all it boils down to? Mel's using you. He's onto me.'

'No he's not.'

'He is. Before your sleazy little rug fest, one of his cronies went to get all the printouts of my copy. He's watching.'

'Well, there's no way he has any info, because all the stories you've done have been showbiz shit.'

'That's not the point. He knows I'm a journalist who has been tapping you for info.'

'Whatever, I enjoyed every miserable moment.'

'Mimi, just stop with the whole T-girl-I'm-invincible shit.'

'He sends me, Avery. Everything about him sends me.'

'Well, you may be interested to know he doesn't feel the same way. He's just using you, a cheap thrill here, a quickie there. Is that what you want to be, someone's in-between?'

They were scrapping like two barn owls in heat.

'I don't owe you jack.'

'No, but you owe yourself. I know you think I don't care, that all I'm interested in is headlines, but I genuinely believe this story could change things, maybe even change Mel. You deserve better. Someone who actually gives a fuck about you.'

'Thanks, Avery, but I've had my share of pop psychology, and yeah, you really know how to piss on a girl's high.'

'Sometimes, Mimi, it seems like you're in denial.'

'I love Mel, and yeah, sometimes I wish I'd never fucking met the bastard, but does he deserve this?'

'It's not really about what he deserves, Mimi, it's about doing what's right. When you first signed up to this, you wanted to make him answer for how badly he treated you. Now he's reeling you in like a barb carp and it's disgusting. He blew you off for a fucking phone call.'

'Fuck you,' Mimi kicked, her stare stinging Avery into momentary silence.

'I don't want to argue with you. If you want out now, just let me know.'

'If I wanted out, I'd be gone.'

'Fair enough. I just wish you'd see this monster for what he is.'

'Nobody's perfect.'

'Agreed, but Mel's an egotistical jerk who kills for a living.'

'There's some who'd see him as an opportunity. Yeah, he'd be great on TV or in conversation with, or as an art installation.'

'Yeah, he could be tagged *Dinner with Satan.*' They looked at one another for a second and then fell into squeaky fits of giggles.

'Sorry, Mimi.'

'Me too.'

'I just didn't … well … don't want you getting stung, over and over.'

'Dinner with Satan, that's a bit excessive. Do they teach

you that on the paper?'

'I like it – banner headlines always have to be shock and awe.'

'Look, Avery, it's not easy rebuilding his trust. He won't just spill while he's sucking face. He's still ashamed of how he feels, what he thinks of me – of us. I can see it every time he gets close. Every time he touches me, he holds back.'

'I know this is hard.'

'Deep down, I sense he cares a little, but maybe not enough. I don't know. Look, there's a party for a new club he's launching. Esther sent me an email invite.'

'Esther?'

'Yeah, the Grand Dame of his porno chain.'

'Right.'

'Well, I'll send you over the details.'

'And what about the alternative escort business?'

'Yeah, he kept the project outline and says he has a lawyer he uses for everything.'

'Yeah. Mimi, I'm serious, no more afternoon snog breaks. It's just not safe.'

'I can't promise but I'll try.'

'D'ya want a refill?'

'Please, and could I get some lemon water too.'

'Sure.'

Avery went to the counter and ordered. Her intel on Mel was growing day by day, but she still needed Mimi in the mix. It was too early to cut her loose now. As she chunked out her change, her mobile beeped. It was Joe.

'I'm across the road. Yeah, she's with me.' She held the phone in the crook of her neck while juggling the cups.

'One sec.' She let the phone slide and signalled to Pierro to bring over the water.

'Everything's fine, yeah, will do.'

She plopped the drinks and her phone on the table.

'I'm having a meeting with the editor later today. He wants to know where we are with everything.'

'Oh, right.'

'Yeah, it's all good, you know, but the pressure's on to deliver.'

'Yeah.'

'We can't make any mistakes. The press are under fire. Everything we write, everything we report – it's open season on us.'

'Yeah, well, there was all that hacking shit. I mean, what the fuck?'

Avery spun the conversation into another direction. 'What else you got planned?'

'Well, I'm booked for a nip, slit and tuck next week.'

'Yeah?'

'Hmmm, the full shebang.'

'What, the whole works?'

'Yes Avery, I'm getting my dick cut off.'

'Wow, big step.'

'Yeah. I mean, I won't know until I get there, but I'm pretty sure it's what I want.'

'How long does it take?'

'About three hours, and there's a great surgeon in Thailand. They say he has magic hands.'

'Well, you know, if you need anything …'

'Yeah.'

'Wow.'

'I'm ready.'

'Yeah.'

They finished up. Avery slated for the office while Mimi made her way to Richard Ward, celebrity hair guru, for some R and R.

Chapter Thirty-Five: Bitter Sweet Symphony

Nick woke up in a sweat. By his side, a gun, a girl, and a gimp mask.

'Jesus that was some night.' He checked the clip. It wasn't loaded. He lifted the gun cautiously and packed it in his closet. He stared at the woman in front of him. She looked kooky, pretty like Beatrice Dalle meshed with Kurt Cobain. Her skin was alabaster pure. She was dressed skimpily in a black negligee, her legs curled under her with her breasts on display. He tapped her lightly on the shoulder.

'Excuse me,' he sputtered. She had a climbing rose tattoo on her ankle and shaggy blond hair with dark roots.

She didn't move, but he could hear her breathing. He checked her pulse.

'Shit, this doesn't feel right.'

'Wake up.'

She looked spaced-out. Nick jumped up and ran to the kitchen. He poured some cold water into a wine glass and dashed back to his bedroom. He trickled some of it onto her face. Still she didn't budge.

'Wake up! Whoever the fuck you are, wake up!' On the floor he saw a purse, a dress and an iPhone. He gathered it all together and laid everything in front of him. In her purse all Nick could find was a pack of pills, half-empty. He couldn't read what they were.

'I'll call Mel. No, I'll call Matt. No, it's got to be Mel.' Nick dialled 999 instead.

'Hello, I need an ambulance. There's a woman in my flat. She's collapsed.'

As soon as he'd dialled, he knew he shouldn't have. *All those fucking questions*. He rang Mel.

'It's me. There's a girl in my flat. She may have OD'd on something. She won't wake up.'

Mel, Mickey and Terry were there in minutes. With them was an older guy, pot-bellied, with thinning hair and large feet.

'Right, where is she?' Mel pushed ahead of everyone, taking charge.

'On my bed. I've already called for an ambulance.'

'This is Dr Malcolm Crudup. He'll sort it.'

'Pleased to meet you.' He spoke with a muted despondency, as if Mel had taken everything else.

'Likewise.'

Terry and Mickey took discreet snaps of Nick, the girl, and the room.

The dodgy doc checked the woman's pulse, tilted her head to one side and checked under her eyelids. She was unresponsive.

'I'll need to bring her back. She's out cold.'

'Tezza, pull the car round.'

'Yes, boss.'

'Nick, call 999 and tell them you're mistaken. Your friend's okay.'

Nick began dialling while Mel and Mickey hoisted her up into Mickey's arms. Mel slung her belongings into a paper bag.

'Hello, yeah, I called the ambulance for a friend, but it's okay now. Yeah … 63 Theobald's Road … yeah. No, it's okay, everything—'

Mel grabbed the phone from Nick's hand as he stood rooted to the spot.

'Ready, boss.'

'Right, careful. I'll bell you later, Nick. Don't talk to anyone till I get back.'

Nick nodded and saw them out.

About fifteen minutes later, the girl woke up in the car. Baby-doll cute, her eyes were sky-blue like big wheels.

'Mel,' she looked confused and her speech was slurred.

'I told you to take three of those, not the whole fucking bottle sweetheart.'

'Oops, sorry. It all went to plan, right?'

'Yeah, but don't zonk out like that again. It could be a fucking disaster next time.'

'Sorry, I just tripped and kind of fell … all fluffy white clouds.'

'Did you see Nick's face doc? What a picture he was, green with worry,' chuckled Mel.

'I thought the whole thing was jolly mean and in shockingly bad taste.'

'You would Malcolm. You got no fucking sense of humour.'

'The poor boy thought she was dead.'

'So did I,' cracked Terry, puffing on a cigarette.

'Doubt we'll 'ave any bother with Mr Stringer now,' Mel smirked.

'When we get back, we'll take some more shots of the lovely Elaine looking dead as a donut and maybe some blood spilling from her mouf.'

'Boss, I fink you bin watchin' too much *CSI*.'

'Best show there is for crime buffs, Mickey.'

Malcolm was busy scribbling on notes of paper.

'What you up to?' Mel peered over his shoulder.

'Just adding some credibility to this farce. It really is in very poor taste.'

'Oh, keep your hair on, Doc. Or should I say your wig piece.'

'Yes, very amusing. There were many greats before me who were follicly challenged, and I'm sure there'll be many more after.'

'Yeah, like who?'

'In no particular order, I can think of John Malkovich, the Dalai Lama, and the great Winston Churchill.' Mel guffawed mimicking a boxing ring announcer:

'Hmmm, well, all I can say is big hair big teeth and balls of steel maketh the man. I'm thinking of James mutha fucking Brown, king of funk.' They sped off to PT's with Give it Up or Turn it loose on maximum volume.

Nick continued pacing the floor with his head in his hands. He dialled Mel. It went straight to voicemail. Then he texted Matt: *Need to see you. Come now. Urgent.*

At the time, Matt was face-blagging an endless stream of trivia to his million and three cyber friends. He stuck on his jacket and jeans, packed some smokes and headed over. Nick was still in his boxers when he met him at the door.

'You look like you've seen a fucking ghost Nick.'

'You alone?'

'Er, yeah.'

'Come on, quick.' He dragged Matt through the door.

'Wait here.' He rushed into his bedroom and took out the Glock, holding it by the tips of his fingers as if it were a dead rat, and laid it on the coffee table.

'Oh fuck. What the fuck?'

'That's not all. There was a gimp mask and a girl on the left side of my bed this morning.'

'Dude, are you being serious?'

'Yes, go take a look. Go get it.'

'What?'

'Go inside. There's a fucking *Pulp Fiction* gimp mask on my fucking bed. Not joking.'

Matt hoofed it to Nick's bedroom and lifted the mask from the sheets.

'Euh, what the fuck? It feels like it's been used, all sticky and rubbery.'

'Shut the fuck up, Matt. I would never use a fucking gimp suit.'

'You said there was a girl. What happened to her?'

'I don't know, Matt. The truth is, I don't fucking know. Mel came over and they took her away. Shit, it's a mess.'

'Fuck! Mel kidnapped the girl?'

'What? No. She was slumped on the side of the bed, fucking comatose. She was sick. I woke up, found her like that, and I couldn't read her pulse, but she was breathing, so I rang Mel and he came over with a doctor and they took her.'

'You let Mel take her?'

'I was confused, man. I panicked when she wouldn't come to, so I just called him.'

'Where was she from? Did you get her name, anything?'

'No, I don't know. She was just there when I woke up, and I tried pouring water over her. She wouldn't come round, but I could hear her breathing, so I called Mel and he said he'd take care of it.'

'Jesus, Nick, what the hell is going on? Who the hell are you with the fucking gimp suit and the random chick in your bed? And she's been taken – vamoose – as if she never existed.' Matt made an exaggerated arm movement to convey the drama of the situation.

'I know, I know, it's fucked up, but he said he'd call me when things were straightened out.'

'And you fucking trust him?'

'I had no one else, Matt. I dialled emergency services and Mel told me to let them know everything was okay and it was a false alarm.'

'And you did that.'

'Yeah, I fucked up.'

'Okay. Relax. Has he rung back?'

'No, I just tried calling him … nothing.'

'Well, you'll just have to wait it out. I don't trust the fucker. He probably engineered the whole fucking thing.'

Nick folded his arms and crouched on a lounge pouf.

'Can you remember anything at all about the girl, anything?'

'No it's a blank. I went to the club.'

'What club?'

'Mel's got a strip club. I had a few drinks, and the next thing I know, I wake up and there's a blonde on my bed, a fucking Glock, and this.' He tossed the gimp hood onto the settee.

'What the fuck, Nick? Maybe the internet has the answers.'

'What?'

'Yeah, the whole thing's probably on YouTube – probably just a cruel hoax.'

'Maybe.'

'Yeah, well I think we should just chill – no use worrying about shit that may not have happened. I need a drink, Nick.'

'Yeah, there's some vodka in the fridge.'

'Don't worry, she's probably with Mel now.' Matt stood up and stepped to the kitchen.

'I hope so, man.'

'Either way, I wouldn't believe what that fat fucker tells you. He only thinks of number one.' He swigged his vodka neat.

'I'm gonna go get a shower and change. I feel wrecked.'

'Take your time, bro.'

'Thanks for coming, man. ' Nick traipsed back to the bathroom. He opened the window and stared at a lone red fox fronting the street. They drank the dawn away with TV shopping and poker shows on as background to kill the silence. At around eight, Nick left Matt asleep and stumbled to the office in zombie mode.

The sun was caramelising the skies with braids of light but the day was tarnished by Mel's perfidy.

Chapter Thirty-Six: Crossword Puzzle

The newsroom was working flat out on a breaking story. Joe was supercharged, hurling orders to staff and support crews.

'Suzie, we need more hands on deck. Paul, I need you at the printers on five. Get Penny on the line now.'

Penny was the chief subeditor responsible for the final layout and leader copy that would appear on the paper. She had booked holiday time but was on standby if anything urgent cropped up, and Joe needed an experienced set of hands to take control.

'Mr Gander, it's Elliott. I'm already at the print works.'

'Good lad, put Chris on.'

'Yes, sir.'

'Chris, it's Joe. Yeah, we need to put back the deadline and still get the print run in on time so we can do two editions of today's paper. It's been a while, but these are exceptional circumstances. So we'll basically be reprinting the front and back pages only for a later edition.' He put the phone on speaker. 'Great, you're a lifeline.'

After clearing the print run with publishing, Joe took to the floor.

'Listen up everyone, it's gonna be a long tough night, so if you need to let friends and family know where you are, now's the time.'

Ollie made coffee for everyone and double-checked with Addison Lee that they were en route to fetch Penny. A cab had already been dispatched to collect the former senior home affairs correspondent, Miles Althorp, now working in Whitehall.

Ollie was at his desk when Avery called in.

'Let your dad know I'm arriving at the scene as we speak. I heard two loud bangs. It was like cannon fire. From what I can see most of the damage is in the south-eastern wing of Heron Tower on the lower floors. Are you getting this?'

'Yeah, keep going.'

'I can see walking wounded and falling debris. There is a smoke cloud and mounting ash on the pavements. I have no idea as yet, if there have been any fatalities.'

'Okay.'

'I can see special response police teams and a traffic pile-up on the approach road coming east. Wait, I'm at the foot of the building now ... hold on. Okay, about four officers have swooped in and are tackling one man to the ground. From what I can see he is fair complexioned and clean-shaven. I'm heading over. There are now about six armed response units in the area. Be in touch soon.'

Avery clicked off and Ollie ran to his dad to give him the info. Joe sent the office car to the site armed with backup supplies and two seasoned journos, Tom and James.

'When you get there, find Avery. Tell her: excellent work, phone in what she can within the hour. That will make the deadline for the first edition.'

Meanwhile, Penny had arrived and had started to redesign the layout of the page. She went and discussed it with Joe.

'Let's clear the top half for the 600 words and use three lines of header across the top. We won't change the type, keep it standard column, make the picture smaller and then use the second story from Avery to cut in to the remaining space.'

'Yeah, that works.'

'Sorry to interrupt,
Mr Gander. Miles Althorp is here.'

'Miles, come on in.'

'Joe. Just been briefed on this in the car on the way up.'

'What we looking at?'

'Too early to say. There are several casualties from flying glass and building debris on pedestrians, tourists, office personnel and lunchtime footfall. My office will get me the stats after they've made calls to the hospital. The best I can do for you is an official response for the first edition.'

'That's fine.'

'Ollie, more coffee. Thanks son.'

Ollie sped off and Suzie stepped in.

'Mr Gander, I've managed to get the Mayor of London's office on the line.'

'Put them through. Joe Gander, *Daily Post*. Can we get a statement about the explosion at Heron Tower? Who's on the suspect list?'

The person on the end of the line was evasive.

'I'm sorry. We're unable to make a comment at this time.'

'Well, I suggest you hurry up, as every other Tom, Dick and Harry has waded in with their thoughts, and the web is awash with speculation and conspiracy theories. We can hold the page for forty-five minutes. Otherwise, we'll print that no one's available for comment in the wake of a national tragedy.'

Joe terminated the conversation. Within seconds, Suzie got a call back with instructions on when to call for a comment.

'The last big London explosion was a series of coordinated suicide attacks on London's transport system – the 7/7 bombings. Get the background, Suzie, from all our library data and give it to Penny so she can draft an intro to the piece.'

'On it, sir.'

Tom and James were stuck in traffic so they rang in.

'Hi, it's Tom. We're about a mile away. James is going to walk the rest of the way and I'll follow on with the car.'

When James finally got close, armed response units had cordoned off pedestrian access. James had excellent contacts within the force and flashed his press card to officers on guard.

'C'mon guys, let me through, please.'

'Sorry mate, it's a no-go, including press.'

'C'mon, mate.'

'Sorry, it's a matter of public safety.'

'Look, I've got less than an hour to get copy through. There's tons of foreign news crews, why can't I get in?'

'They were here earlier.'

Then he got the break he was looking for.

'Oi, Skegsy!'

A short, podgy policeman turned towards him. He had thick-knitted brows and a pink frowzy face. He waved him through.

'Don't make me regret this.'

'Thanks, Skegs.'

James started snapping shots of everything he could see, including, frightened onlookers, eye witnesses and locals. About five feet away, he spied Avery talking to a distinctive-looking man who had been filmed on the web, helping victims from the rubble. The moment where he saved a toddler from a falling block of concrete was captured on YouTube and went viral. It had already amassed six thousand hits and was rising.

'Avery, we need to get copy in before the hour.'

'Okay James. This is Buddha Christ Mohammed.' She gestured to the man next to her. 'He was here at the time of the explosion and has been helping everyone. Also seems a hit with the ladyeez.' A throng of junior nurses and paramedics were bustling around him.

James started taking pictures, but BCM was reluctant to pose.

A hawkeyed police officer came over looking for answers.

'Can you all make your way to the left? Please, this is a

crime scene, not a backdoor pass to a circus ring. No excuses, please make your way left.' Avery tried being exceptionally sweet:

'We'll be done in a few minutes, officer.' Now the full extent of the horror had become obvious, exit routes and bystreets had been blocked off to the public. First-aid responders, fire-fighters and community chiefs had filled the scene. Avery -that guy the do-gooder: Buddha Christ Mohammed. Are you joking with that name?'

'Yeah, I know, and didn't you think he had this ethereal vibe about him?'

'His name's Buddha Christ Mohammed? Can't we make *that* the story Avery?'

'Yeah, yeah I get it. The three big religions. Look, I've got the first paragraphs done for the early story. Take a look.'

James skimmed the piece. 'Yeah, ring it in and I'll send the pics through.'

Ollie typed Avery's copy straight into the computer as she continued to create the rest of the piece from her notes and reports from eye witnesses at the scene still being interviewed by foreign news crews. Although BCM had rescued several people, already it was the trapped toddler that had caught the public's attention.

Back at the office, the first edition was taking shape. Hospital stats had been provided but the situation was subject to change. Suzie had sourced sound bites from the local MP, a respected Muslim cleric, community veterans, and Whitehall. She gave the revised copy to Penny who trimmed and cut again, this time abandoning an entire unrelated piece, and replacing it with copy on BCM. She ended it with mtf (more to follow). With the first edition approved and headline written, they made the print run just in time.

Chapter Thirty-Seven: C.R.E.A.M (Cash Rules Everything Around Me)

Mel paid off the outstanding arrears on Mrs Stringer's mortgage, acquired her signature, forged it, and filed a fake registration document with the Land Registry. His name was now on the title deeds to her house, to do with it what he liked. Later that morning he had a meeting with Mushi, Tezza, Mickey, and a junior bank manager. It was time to turn up the heat.

'When Mushi gets here, I want you two clowns to play it straight, understand? None of your usual malarkey.'

'Yes, boss,' they answered in unison.

'Mr Greenberg.' Mushi appeared smart and smooth-faced.

'Come on, Mushi, there's no formality here. This is Terry and Mickey. They may look like two slippery eels, but they're here for you whenever you need 'em. They've been grafting for me for over fifteen years and both own penthouses on the river, gold-star birds and enough swag to fill Selfridges. They make money 'cos they believe in the product, see?'

Mushi nodded.

'In about five minutes we got a local bank manager coming, and he sorts out lots of useful letters that go with our product which you can use to impress your portfolio of clients, see? Three easy steps: sell, buy, network.'

'Okay.'

'So I'm introducing you to Handy Andy, the bank

manager that likes to say yes.'

'Right.'

'Whatever you need to show that makes punters plum for the pickings.'

Mushi was iffy.

'You're probably wondering what good a pukka bank letter does, eh Mushi?'

'It had crossed my mind.'

'Good question, mate, good question. Using bank approved letters to go on top of balance statements shows a healthy profit turnover.'

'Oh.'

'Yeah, nothing for you to concern yourself over, but Handy Andy, otherwise known as Andrew Krettsin, allows us to open all the accounts and move money in and out of the bank, see?'

'Yeah.'

Rat-tat tat.

'That'll be him now.'

Handy Andy was a sinewy-looking man with thin lips and small shrewd eyes. He wore a banal grey banker's suit and had stinky onion breath that tanked the air when he spoke through gappy teeth.

'Mel, good to see you again.'

Terry got up and surreptitiously put his hand to his nose.

'Just going to the little boys' room.'

'Me too,' joined Mickey, leaving Mel and Mushi to deal with the stench.

'Excuse them, think they ate something dodgy for lunch,' Mel explained.

'Andrew, meet one of our brightest recruits, Mushi. He's got real potential and a growing customer base.'

Mushi got up and politely shook Andy's sweaty hand.

'New in the job are you?'

'Yes, Mr?'

'Just call me Andy.'

'Yes, Andy.'

'I like to meet Mel's team personally. So if ever you need anything from the bank that could boost business, just ask.'

'Thank you, Andy, I appreciate that.'

'Mushi's one of the new breed, does it all online, but there's a lot to be said for old-fashioned hook-ups, wouldn't you say, Andy?'

'Absolutely, face to face is always preferable.'

'Right then, intros over, back to biz. Mushi, downstairs there's a list of potential clients. You just have to close the deals. They've all been reeled in. So if you go and pick those up, we'll see you outside.'

'Yep, no problem.'

After Mushi had left, Mel changed tack.

'I've got a hundred more ready to sign. Here's 20. I want more letters and an extended line of credit for the company.'

'Done.'

'How's the rest of the bizzo?'

'Ace.'

'Glad to hear it. '

'This Mushi, he seems a little naïve.'

'He'll catch on. Once he gets his commission monies, he won't even think about it.'

'Well, I'm happy to let you have access to the bank's facilities, accounts and names, so long as our arrangement continues without any outside interference.'

'No danger there, Mushi's straight.'

'Well, if you think you can count on him.'

'Yep.'

'Right, let's go eat.'

'After you.'

They headed for Cantina Augusto, a family run Italian bistro on Clerkenwell Road.

'Terrible business that bomb blast, wasn't it?' Mel was making small talk.

'Yeah, they have no idea who it could be, but as usual, Islamist terrorists are suspected.'

Mushi blinked.

'London's always been the scene of hotbed violence – remember the IRA?'

'Young Mushi has a point, Andy.'

'Yeah that's true, but from what I can remember, the IRA always gave a warning. This lot appear to be unstoppable. Did you see the YouTube vid of the geezer who saved the kid? I got it here look.' He pulled out his phone all three watched shots of BCM saving a child. Mushi looked on wide eyed but said nothing.

'Fucking amazing but these Islamists are fucking bad news.'

Mel kicked Andy's leg under the table, warning him to back off.

'Enough of that crap for now. London's been through worse and always gets through it.'

'Yeah.'

'Let's drink to London, the best fucking city on the planet.'

They clinked glasses, toasting their growing business with vino, olives, and a slice of banking bribery.

Chapter Thirty-Eight: Staying Alive

Nick flew into Pau with a guarded sense of purpose. He had arranged to meet Eduardo at the hotel Parc Beaumont and took a cab from the airport. He had booked a room but didn't anticipate spending the whole night there. He checked in and waited for Eduardo to arrive. After about thirty minutes he received a text Eduardo was in the lobby. Nick texted back his room number four five two and opened the window to the terrace. It was a well-furnished comfortable room; modern and airy. Nick rearranged the chairs so they were facing each other. There was a fully stocked mini bar with a sprinkling of assorted snacks and fresh fruit in a basket by the bed. He went into the bathroom and splashed some water on his face when he heard a knock on the door. He dabbed himself dry and went to answer it breathing in sharply.

'I'm glad you could make it. Come in.'

Eduardo entered the room with obvious uncertainty, peering at the fruit and the chairs. He was wearing a navy suit, white shirt and striped tie. In contrast Nick had dispensed with formality altogether and was casually dressed in blue denim, plain tee shirt, leather jacket and sunglasses to cover the bags under his eyes. He looked like an off duty PI.

'Excuse the shades my eyes are sore.'

'Of coursssse.'

'Please...' Nick gestured to a chair. Eduardo sat down half facing Nick with his legs crossed.

'Can I get you anything to drink or?'

'Nothing for me thanks.'

'I appreciate you coming.'

'Your proposal sounded intriguing Mr Stringer.'

'I believe we can do some business together.'

'Pleassse go on.' Eduardo uncrossed his legs and leaned forward.

'The two casualties from Mel's botched up drug run are as you know connected to one of London's premier crime families.'

'I see.'

'Yessss Philip Drummond is the eldest son of Michael Drummond and Philip's fiancée is Lindsay.

The bottom line: we need them both freed if things don't go our way at the next legal hearing. I was hoping you'd be able to offer a solution.'

'I have contacts inside the prison system, who would be able to assist us for a nominal fee and future referral to Drummond.' Nick's face became solemn.

'I must remind you that this aspect of our business is strictly between us. Mel's out of the picture, so I'm relying on your complete discretion.'

Eduardo laughed, a short dry laugh nettled with something sharp.

'I assure you Mr Stringer I will be careful. Like most lawyers I'm a realist. You needn't

worry. Everything between you and I is confidential.'

Nick stood up and handed Eduardo a small leather suitcase stuffed with Euros. With an almost presumptive air he said:

'For your assistance and co -operation.'

Eduardo took the bag and remained seated.

'Arrangements will be finalised by the time of our next meeting – guaranteed.'

'Understood. Thank you Eduardo.'

They toasted their plans with a bottle of whiskey and Nick flew home with a deep sense of relief.

Nick headed straight to Matt's flat.

Outside King's Cross Station Elaine was touting for business– the very same Elaine who had faked death with Nick a few nights before. Dressed in a red mini, thigh high boots and a black jacket she was watching the world go by. Keen on Hennessey, and hand jobs, she had a filthy delicious vibe. Popular with Swedish tourists, bachelor stags and guys called 'Alan', she was scouted for a TV T-and-A show, a reality gig that would beam her into the living rooms of a million people and guarantee her instant stardom. The problem was that the film company weren't paying her for seven days and she was in debt to her landlord, her car company and, of course, Mel. Reluctant to scrounge off anyone, with a self-reliant streak instilled in her from birth, she was scraping the dame to pay her way.

On her beat, oblivious he was in a red-light district, was BCM. She sidled over to him with predatory ease.

'Looking for a good time, hon?'

'No,' he answered with customary curtness.

'You look so dreamy,' she persisted. BCM stared back at her. He made her feel safe – not dirty, just safe.

'You know I wasn't always working the streets, and next week I won't ever have to again.' She felt she needed to justify herself.

'I don't judge. People do what they gotta do. Anyway, some of my best friends are in your line of work.'

'Really? I'm just saying, I'm not strictly a hooker – I'm gonna be a TV star.'

'Great. 'Cos there aren't many hookers in the fame game, right?'

She smiled warmly.

As they yakked on, Terry and Mickey arrived to check Mel's turf. Ever since the bomb blast, London had been on high alert, and rival gangs had swooped in, trying to compete. Mel was taking no chances.

'If you're just looking at the goods and don't actually wanna buy tonight, please jog on as you'll put off the punters.' Terry frowned.

'Apologise to the lady,' BCM replied.

'She ain't no fucking lady, pal. I can guarantee you of that. My advice to you is fuck off.'

'Apologise.'

'I don't know who you fink you are. Riding round with a cape and a rod like a fucking extra from *Lord of the Rings*, but I'm warning you to leave now ...'

'Or else?'

'I'll show you what fucking else.' Terry was about to take a swipe when a local PCSO waded in. 'Hold up,' he said, and turning to BCM he added,

'I saw you on the web helping people in that explosion. Good on ya, mate, well done.'

Terry backed down and let BCM and Elaine get on with it.

'The last thing we need is some 'ave-a-go hero on our balls.'

'Yeah, let's check the others.' They sped off.

Elaine was leaving stripping for good soon so why worry about Mickey and Terry now? She stayed with BCM after the police left.

'I have a small place nearby, nothing fancy, if you'd like to come over?'

'No, that's okay. I'm staying with a friend a short walk from here.'

'Yeah?'

'Yeah.'

'Well then, maybe I could hang with you guys for a bit. Truth is, I've been a little on edge since the blast, and I could do with a some company right now.'

'If you like.'

They made their way to Matt's.

He was playing *Metro Last Light* with Nick: a dark apocalyptic computer game which seemed fitting for the times.

'BCM.'

Matt didn't even see Elaine at first, who was hidden by the shadows.

'I've brought someone along for pizza.'

She unfolded herself from the darkness and raised her hand awkwardly to say hi. Nick glanced up and dropped his glass to the floor, splintering the silence with cries of surprise.

'You, you, you're alive!'

BCM looked puzzled. Matt had it sussed. Elaine was stumped.

'Who would have thought that out of all the places in the world, you'd end up here, alive, all in one perfect piece!'

Nick jumped to his feet and hugged her.

'I'm so sorry. I don't even know your name.'

'Elaine.'

'And you're okay, Elaine?'

'Yeah.' She was completely expressionless.

Nick planted himself between Matt and BCM.

'This is the … er, young lady I was telling you about – the young lady I thought had died in my apartment.'

'Wow, what a coincidence,' Matt noted.

'Sorry,' Nick turned to Elaine, 'but what the fuck are you doing here?'

'I just came to hang out after the explosion, you know, for a little company.'

'Sure.'

'So you two know each other?'

'No, we just met,' BCM explained.

'Oh,' Matt nodded, then looked at BCM and said:

'This is Nick – you know, lawyer, best friend – only friend I trust apart from you.'

BCM put out his hand to Nick, who readily took it, and then they hugged and slapped each other on the back.

'Good to finally meet you. I've heard so much about you,' smiled BCM.

'And you.'

'I think I'll go get some drinks before the pizza arrives. So, Elaine, what can I get you?'

'Just coffee, thanks.'

'BCM?'

'The same.'

'And Nick?'

'Yeah, I'll have a large vodka to celebrate Elaine's return to the land of the living.'

'Nick, can you help me out, mate?'

'Sure, Matt.'

Once inside the kitchen, they began whispering.

'So that's the same woman who was in your apartment, who you thought was dead?'

'Yes, I'm positive. I remember the trailing tat and the big blues.'

'Fuck, did you see her face? She was kind of surprised to see you. I mean, she looked really embarrassed.'

'Yeah, do you think Mel sent her?'

'No, she was with BCM. He must have helped her out with something.'

'Kind of weird though that she turns up here with a total stranger. But then, it was equally weird she was bunked in my bedroom.'

'BCM said it was to do with the explosion and feeling a little freaked.'

'Let's just be on our guard. I don't need any fucking crazy shit going on here.'

'Okay.'

They went back into the front room. BCM was stretched out on the settee, checking DVDs.

Elaine spoke first.

'My little cousin has this game.'

'Yeah, it's perfect for eye-hand coordination.'

Matt called BCM aside.

'We don't trust that girl.'

'Why?'

'We think she works for Mel Greenberg. Just be careful.'

'Okay, but she seems kind of harmless to me.'

'Yeah maybe, but she played dead the other night.'

'Don't worry. I'll take her home in an hour or so.'

They joined Nick and Elaine at the game console. She seemed distracted as if she could sense something was up. Nick probed further.

'So, can you remember much of that night?'

'Well, you know Adam, right – Sal's son – you were partying with him, and the last thing I remember is waking up in the car, kind of groggy and out of it.'

'Whose car?'

'Mel's car.'

'Right.'

'And where did you go? Back to the club or …?'

Nick was sounding adversarial. He kept pushing but Elaine refused to cave.

'You know, it's getting late. If you don't mind, could you get me a taxi?'

'I can walk you back.'

'No thanks. That's sweet, but I gotta get some sleep. A cab will be fine.'

'At least have some pizza before you go.'

'No thanks.'

'Okay.' Nick hit redial.

'About ten minutes.'

After a stilted silence, the taxi honked outside and Elaine got up.

'Great meeting you all.' She looked gently at BCM. 'Thanks for the chat.'

'Anytime.'

After she'd gone, the three of them sat down and finished off their pizza.

'They say three is a magic number.'

'Yeah, three has special qualities.'

'I disagree,' cut in Nick. 'One is the only number. The best number is always number one.

Chapter Thirty-Nine: Lip Up Fatty

'God this is boring.'

Avery drank the last of her coffee and tossed the cup in a trash bag on the car seat.

'Oi! Careful, or muggins here will have to clean that up.' Ollie was chewing on a matchstick, twisting it around in his mouth.

'That's disgusting. Do you have to do that, especially in public?'

'Helps me think.'

'Yeah, but honestly, a matchstick, eeeuh.' She wrinkled her nose in disgust and stared at Mel's warehouse, desperate for signs of action.

'I'm sure even the lovely Avery has some habits she wouldn't reveal?'

'Yeah, loads, but barfing and bunions I keep closely under wraps.'

Ollie threw the matchstick out of the window.

'There, satisfied?'

'Hmmm, here, use this.' She flung him a mini hand sanitiser. 'And honestly, Ollie, if I were you, I wouldn't share the matchstick twizzle with anyone, especially the ladyeez.'

'Whatever. You know, the one per cent dirt these mobile cleansers leave behind is probably trapped on my hand right now.'

'Thanks for sharing, Ollie. I really needed to know that.'

'What time is it, anyway?'

'Time you shut up.'

'This isn't what I expected. You're no fun.'

'We're not in a fucking Hollywood rom-com, Ollie. We're on a stakeout for a British mobster, and this is how it plays. Now keep your eyes on the target.'

'How can I keep my eyes on the target when that's in my face?'

A group of teenage girls sauntered by. They were wearing miniskirts and long socks with cutesy pigtails and sneakers. They were hubba bubba hot, using their new-found sexuality as a dangerous toy. They smiled and turned, checking Ollie out and giggling behind cupped hands.

'That's so inappropriate,' bitched Avery.

'You're just jealous. They were giving me the once over.'

'It's probably the car – anyhow that's seriously pervy, Ollie. You're way older than them.'

'They look about eighteen or more.'

'Yeah, *look*. They were probably only thirteen or younger.' Ollie was unabashed.

'Still eyeballing me. Hot chicks at two o'clock.'

'Didn't you ever go on the mandatory seminar about what's appropriate behaviour in the workplace and what's considered sexist, as I think you definitely need to go on it?'

'I lasted about ten minutes before I jumped. Anyway, that kind of BS doesn't do it for me. I mean, if it were up to the PC police, it wouldn't be appropriate to fart, burp, or use the F-word more than once in public, and everyone knows you can't police public etiquette.'

Avery was stung by Ollie's perceived chauvinism.

'Actually, they do *police* it, Ollie. It's just that you choose to ignore it.'

'Maybe, but that makes me the torch of sanity.'

'Yeah, the torch that's unlit.'

As they stuck it out waiting for Mel or one of his cronies to surface, they saw a tall eccentric looking man hauling a large papier-mâché death mask towards the building. Avery started snapping with a digi automatic.

'I know that face. Now where have I seen him?'

'He looks like a proper artist, bell-bottom flares, flower shirt, long hair and a Dali moustache.'

'Yep, he could have flown out of a seventies' ashram.'

'Check it out. He's wearing open thong sandals.'

'I'm trying to think who he is. I know it was recent … he's got one of those faces you don't forget.'

'Yeah.'

'He's probably just roped Mel into buying that.'

'Yeah.'

'Funny that he's lugging it over there himself though.'

'Yeah, they must know each other. Mel wouldn't trust just anyone to drop box like that.'

'Yeah.'

They watched as he disappeared behind the vaulted door, emerging a few minutes later without the lumbering death mask and a conman's glint in his eye.

'Must have hocked it.'

'Yeah.'

'Hold on.' Avery snatched her bag from the back, took out her trusted Chanel red 39, popped the lid and swiped. She pressed her lips together, gently smudging for a natural bee-stung effect.

'Gimme ten minutes.'

She raced to the opposite side of the road and papped him.

'Oh, you're that famous artist,' she fawned.

Always open to press and publicity, his blues eyes glittered happily as he immediately rattled out his PR shtick. He was a born performer.

'Hi, yeah, you're right. My name's Dick Revel. You may know my father, Alastair, he was the mastermind behind one of the greatest crimes of the century.'

'Yeah, now I recognise you. Weren't you at that showbiz party in Soho?'

'Yeah.'

'My name's Avery Cross, as in – well, Avery Cross. I'm a

reporter with *The Daily Post*. Love to do a feature on your work and your dad and all that. You're famous for doing large-scale death masks, right? Would you be interested in that at all?'

'Absolutely, yeah. I think I've read your column. I've just sold a piece to a very special customer actually. He has some top-notch stuff.'

'Really?'

'Yeah, the whole place – front to back, top to bottom art.' Dick waved his hand in the direction of Mel's building.'

'Wow.'

'Actually, he's having a showing of my work in a privately sponsored exhibition.'

'Amazing.' Avery felt like an art groupie.

'Would you like to come? I'll send you an invite at your offices if you like.'

'Yeah. D'ya know where it might be?' Worried she would be trekking to Boonsville and beyond.

'The Fold, Clerkenwell.'

'Perfect. Well, here's my card. Gimme a call when you're ready. I'll look out for the invite.'

This is great now there's no need to go to the Art Auction with Ollie. I'll let him know.

'Yeah, see you soon.' Dick ebbed along with the flow of midday traffic while Avery hurried back to the car.

Inside, Ollie was slumped on the driver's seat with his head down. He was bleeding.

'Jesus fucking Christ.' Avery was frantic. Joe thought Ollie was safe at the paper not out on a recce. She searched for her phone, her heart screaming.

'Ollie!'

He opened one eye and tried to speak.

'It's gonna be okay, Ollie.'

'He-hello. I need an ambulance right away. I-I'm on the lower end of Saffron Hill. Hurry please. I don't know. My friend's bleeding. I stepped out of the car for a few minutes and I found him like this. Please hurry. I'm at the crossroads in a dark-blue Range Rover, registration mark J17 PST.'

While Avery waited, she called the office, her voice ridged with fear.

'Penny, its Avery. Where's Joe?'

'He's at his desk. Are you okay, Avery? You sound … Avery?' She clicked out.

The squally rasp of the ambulance got closer and closer. Two paramedics were on the scene within seconds of her hanging up.

'Can you tell us what happened, miss?'

'No, not really. I left the car for a few minutes and when I returned I found him like this.'

'Right, step away, miss.'

They lifted Ollie onto a stretcher and carried him to the ambulance.

'Can I ride with him?'

'No, sorry, miss. We'll be taking him straight to St Thomas's and we'll need a formal statement from you there. You're welcome to follow.'

'Yes, thanks.'

Budget cuts meant no ride-alongs for family and friends – everyone for themselves.

The passenger seat was dripping with Ollie's blood. She was careful not to touch anything and left the car parked where it was. She looked around her, frantically staring up at Mel's warehouse. She thought she saw two men watching her from an upstairs window. Avery felt numb. She'd been gone less than ten minutes, but as the car was parked under a large sycamore, it was hidden from the main road and it was unlikely there were any witnesses. She needed to get to the hospital and let Joe know about Ollie. She called a cab and reached the hospital a few minutes later. She waited anxiously in A & E. While she was there, she called the paper again.

'Put me through to Joe, Penny.'

'Hello, Mr Gander. It's Avery. It's to do with Ollie.' She took a long breath, her hands trembling on the receiver.

'He's been hurt. We're at St Thomas's.'

'Is it bad, what happened?'

'I'm not sure, sir. He seems to have sustained a head injury.'

'How? Jesus! I'm on my way. I'll be there as soon as I can.'

'Yes, sir.'

Avery went back to reception to check on Ollie.

Just then, Stevie D was torching the Range Rover in a lay-by off King's Cross. Burnt to a crisp in minutes. The charred wreckage a caustic reminder of Mel's power.

Chapter Forty: Jail Guitar Doors

There it was again, that familiar stench of bleach and desperation that clung to everything – chairs, tables – and that wall of regret. Every prisoner in Pau wanted to jump. Phil had spent the last few days alone in his cell. His body was worn and withered. He was unshaven, coarse brown stubble needling his chin and neck, but his hair was freshly shorn, leaving razor bumps all over his head. He hobbled over to Nick and sat himself down, clutching his sides in agony.

'The white supremacists didn't want me praying the Muslim way, but they're no longer here to hassle me.' He now spoke with a distinct cough, making his voice sound like radio fuzz. His eyes were sunken, pocketed with rancour and weeks of boiled cynicism. He had lost around ten pounds in weight and most of his youthful shine. Nick was eager to wrap this up quickly. An English-speaking guard hovered over them.

'Can you call off the dogs while I talk to my client?'

He moved to the right, out of earshot. Nick nodded in appreciation. He turned to Phil and in a strong firm voice said,

'I've got a plan to get you out of here.' He let it register. 'You and Lindsay released from this hell hole within a week.'

'Yeah?' Phil had been worn down by prison life. He started kneading his arms, using his fingers as knives, chucking nail gunk across the table, a juvenile stab against the rotting docility of his incarceration.

Nick felt dizzy just watching him.

'You know the score – if we lose the hearing and can't come to an agreement with the prosecutors we're stuck here – what the fuck can you do?' Nick ignored the question and sat up straight and stiff he asked:

'Did you ever wonder why yours was the tug car?'

'I figured they made a mistake. Thought my old man took care of it.' Phil's eyes began to water. They were red raw, and underscored by oversized balloon bags. He put his hands over them, trying to press the extra skin away. Nick maintained eye contact.

'Your old man did take care of it, but Mel got greedy, he wanted a bigger take, so he fucked you over – brought you to this.' Nick's hands were clamming up and the back of his neck prickled with sweat beads. Phil was too weak to notice.

'Here, smoke this.'

Phil snatched the cigarette before Nick had a chance to light it. Nick leaned in and then whispered, 'You can get out of here.' He lit the cigarette and handed it over.

Phil drew in tight, so tight he started coughing. He took a drag.

'Why you telling me this?'

'Because you don't deserve *this*. You deserve the truth. You deserve justice. You can turn everything around.'

Phil smirked, his eyes growing wider and wider. Nick kept his cool.

'No disrespect, Phil, but you're just small fry. The bigger catch is outside. All you have to do is give me the authority to speak to your old man. Once I get the green light I can put the plan into action and fix this.'

'I got a message from my old man about a week ago.'

'That was Mel. Said something about an early break blah blah – signed off with the coded symbol of the hangman?'

For the first time since he'd entered the hall, Nick saw a grain of life in Phil's eyes.

'Why should I trust you? I don't even fucking know you.'

'I'm not asking you to trust me. I'm giving you a free pass to get out of here and feel the sun on your face.'

'You've changed – you look different. The last time I saw you … well, you looked fresh off the press.'

'That's what the law does, invites you in, fills your head with idealistic bullshit and then fucks you till you bleed, until you're a ghost. Just a fucking ghost. Now, write down your father's info and the secret sign. I'll do the rest.'

This new Nick was tailor-made for Phil. He had dropped his pseudo legalese and college boy intellect. He was someone Phil could believe in.

'You read me, don't you, Nick?' Phil's upper lip was twitching. He tipped the cig stub into a paper cup.

'I get where you're coming from, but what's more important is where you're going to so let's do this right. No mistakes.'

Phil took the pen and slowly wrote down a sequence of letters, an address in Knightsbridge, a London phone contact, and a sequence of numbers, ending with a childish scribble of a stick man with what looked like the five of diamonds to his left. He pushed the scrap of paper towards Nick and hoisted himself out of the chair.

'You'll be out of here within a week. You have my word.'

Before he left, Nick had a closed meeting with the prison administrator. Then he dialled Eduardo:

"It's Nick."

"You're here alone?"

"Yes it's time. If the prosecutors can't be convinced we need to be ready to get them out.'

'Understood.' The phone clicked off. Later that morning Lindsay and Phil were immediately relocated to a brand new hospital wing utilised by both males and females. Nick was booked on the 9.52 back to London, but he thought it prudent to do all the donkey work from the luxury of his hotel room and cancelled his flight. First he called Mel and fed him some bull. Then he dialled the number Phil had given him.

'My name's Nick Stringer. I've got news on Phil.'

'What's the code?'

'Five of Diamonds.'

'Hold the line.'

Nick was tense, but the voice at the other end was unwavering.

'What's the score?'

'The bird has flown the coop.'

'Meet me two weeks from today lunch time, at Morton's.' The phone went dead.

Fuck that was easy. Gives me plenty of time. Perfect. Relieved it's not the usual East End hangout like the Blind Beggar.

Morton's was an elegantly chic private members' club overlooking Berkeley Square in the centre of Mayfair. As far as Nick knew, membership was limited and by invitation only. Now he had to go and convince the French prosecutors to let Phil and Lindsay go in return for solid intel on a bigger fish and persuade them he wasn't copping a plea deal for his clients. In France, plea deals were still unpopular and seldom used, especially for drug offences. Nick had already had informal discussions about the case with the public prosecutor. If he was unable to win him over with legal arguments, he would have to resort to plan B, a daring prison break timed to go off at dawn in four days' time already planned with Eduardo's help. If he had Phil and Lindsay safely delivered before his meeting at Morton's, he would be bestowed with that fatherly devotion and gratitude reserved for kings and saviours.

Nick's discussions with Eduardo led him to a special network of five inmates and three high-level, prison guards. Eduardo had been quietly cultivating this inside team for years and had already helped dozens of inmates to break free. He called Nick later that evening to go over the details:

'On the outside there will be two locals – they will be on Y wing they work as orderlies.'

'Any anticipated obstacles?'

'None – jail security is weak and all the necessaries have been transferred including ammunition and readymade firepower.'

Nick had used Mel's name to initiate the plan and Eduardo's local knowledge to execute it. No one had thought to question them, and within four days the plan was ready to unfold. They still had a shot with the prosecutors but twenty four hours before the planned break discussions stalled there was no other option but to break them out.

Shortly after 5 p.m., twenty inmates took control of cell block Y, holding prison guards hostage at gunpoint. Phil was freed by a veteran lifer charged with five counts of murder.

'Put these on.' His English was textbook perfect. He threw him a guard uniform and cell keys. Phil hurriedly changed between warring factions of guards and inmates.

'Get down, get down!'

Phil ducked as two fire flares and a roughly assembled explosive shot past them. It blew apart the reinforced steel doors and catapulted them to the front entrance of the prison. On the tarmac outside, Lindsay was waiting with a female inmate dressed as a guard. They walked slowly to the gate, where they found the weekly lorry load of food supplies.

'Five of diamonds,' the driver muttered. Nick had stuck with the same code for the breakout so Phil would take the draw.

'Give me the keys.' Phil pushed the keys in the driver's hand – one of them had a digital reader for automatic locks.

Following behind them were about another ten escapees. The truck pulled out of the prison gates using the electronic tag, joining the A64 auto route. After a gruelling eleven hours, Lindsay and Phil reached Paris the next day and boarded flights for Spain, in disguise, with fake IDs and a case full of cash.

Nick was on his way to mobster stardom and Mel was on the chase.

Chapter Forty-One: Sitting on Top of the World

The newsroom was in sombre mood after Ollie's attack. Fortunately, it looked much worse than it was. He suffered a mild concussion and some cuts and bruises to the back of his head. Told to rest up for a week or so, he'd been lucky. The police confirmed there had been a spate of car jacking in the area, and as Ollie had drawn a blank about who his assailants were, the assault was blamed on random strangers.

Joe was subdued but professional, leaning on his work as a welcome distraction from the nagging worry over who had targeted his son. Producing news stories was an expensive business, and Joe was still being pushed to raise revenue streams. Today marked yet another attempt to do just that, with the introduction of sponsored news stories and articles on all of the paper's apps and hosted websites. They mainly covered art culture and sporting events. Joe favoured this idea above pay walls and advertising content.

Suzie cruised in.

'Just reminding you of your meeting today with Lionel Gellar,'

'What time is it scheduled for?'

'Eleven o'clock, so an hour from now.'

'Okay.'

'How's Ollie doing?'

'He's up and about, playing his computer crap, so he's on the mend, thanks.'

'Good to hear. I'll go check the meeting room's ready.'

'Okay, thanks Suzie.'

He settled deeper in his chair and clasped his hands in front of him as if praying. Questions kept circling his mind over Ollie, but he had no time to search for answers now.

Lionel Gellar was part of the tech wealth elite and had cornered Joe at an industry bash. Lionel had fresh ideas for revenue injection, and, key to all Joe's concerns, quality, or so he claimed. Joe's first impressions of Lionel were positive: preppy neat and tech savvy, he was bouncing with inspiration.

'Joe, it's such a pleasure to meet you again.'

'And you. Please sit down. Would you like some coffee or anything?'

'Just water, thanks. Straight from the tap's fine.'

Joe buzzed Suzie.

'Can I get a coffee and a water, please? Thanks.'

'I'll be very straight with you, Joe. When I first told my nearest and dearest I was planning on investing in a newspaper, they expressed incredulity and thought I must have lost my marbles.'

'Not surprised, Lionel. It's a dying business, so they say.'

'See, I think they've got it wrong. I know how to invest in sinking ships and I'm keen to try. The business model for journalism is flawed.'

Suzie bought the drinks in and set them down on a small tray. Lionel took a long swig and set his glass aside.

'I don't disagree, Lionel.'

'The point is, Joe, we can build profits and productivity by focusing on maintaining the readers we already have and making their digital experience with the paper something they enjoy and look forward to.'

'Carry on.'

'I've been reading the paper ever since I was at grad school. I may be a transplant from the US but I've been living here for years and I know it's the eyes and ears of London. I believe in the paper, so let me make that clear.'

'I'm listening.'

'The first thing I did was check your stats. You're losing readers on a daily basis, but instead of turning to an online version of the paper, they're turning to other sources – competitors, and unattributed web media. Know why?'

Joe wanted to say it was because they were a bunch of uneducated Muppets but went with a sanguine, 'No, Lionel.'

'I'll tell you why. Because once they click, online news is more detailed, more analytical, with no space limits, so you lose them for good.'

'Hmmm.'

'I wanna double-back. Everyone knows you get gossip and tabloid leaders online, it's expected, but a paper's a trusted news source, a forum for ideas and opinions.'

'Agreed.'

'Right, so what you need to do is rebrand, make technology work for you.'

'Hmmm.'

'I checked five nationals and three locals yesterday. Not one featured stories less than a day old. The news is moving constantly. We need to keep up to hold on to your readership. You can't go to print with stale copy. Opinion and ideas, that's what a curated audience wants to read from a paper.'

Joe knew this already with frayed nerves, he let Lionel spout on.

'Are you ready for this? I want to bring the News Bunny back.'

'Sorry, come again?'

'The News Bunny.'

'What the fuck is the News Bunny?'

'I'm surprised you don't remember. It was a supersized rabbit that appeared on Kelvin McKenzie's short-lived TV station. It featured alongside politicians and world leaders. It …'

'Stop stop, stop – this is a wind-up, right?'

'No, the News Bunny was hugely popular and pioneered

a more informal approach to news presentation. I thought we'd go retro with: News Kittens. They could dress up in—'

'Have you been ingesting large amounts of crack cocaine?'

'Look, Joe, you've got to move with technology. My team say—'

'They want to sex up my paper with a hackneyed version of page three.'

'News Kittens, Joe, News Kittens. And as for *The Sun* it's got the largest circulation of any daily in the UK.' Joe's old eyes were frosted with derision.

'It's also the only daily in the world to show naked women. Times are changing. Are you serious with this? You've got to be fucking kidding me … you're fucking insane.'

'A lot of research has gone into this, Joe. People love kittens. But more than that, they love women dressed as kittens.'

'Yeah, and people love the fucking Teletubbies. Doesn't mean they want them dishing out the news.'

'Actually, Joe, our brief research proves, with revamped sections including free regional listings and regional content, London News Kittens could deliver a sense of community to the paper and offer it a fun sexy identity.'

'Hasn't Craigslist killed classifieds?' Joe blazed.

'I think it's the best way to jack up figures and encourage reader loyalty.'

'With regional news pussy?'

'Community-based News Kittens with a key emphasis on local issues, local news, not just free ads.'

'Sorry, it's not happening not on my watch. News Kittens? Behave, Lionel.'

'Joe, you gotta trust me. I believe, as you do, that the cornerstone of news reporting is trust and integrity, but why not sauce it up with the News Kittens?'

'Because it's a gimmick.'

'I don't agree, Joe. I'd like to partner with LSE or another university. I have strong links there. They have an accessible pool of academics and researchers who would welcome the chance to offer informed opinion and analysis on topical issues and news. I think they'd get the News Kittens.'

Joe folded his arms and sighed.

'Lionel, I know you techy types think outside the box and have crazy ideas, really crazy ideas. Sometimes they work, but definitely not this time.'

'The board say you agreed my plan and the changes,' Lionel implored.

'You never had no fucking bunny shit or kitten crap on your plan. I won't allow it. I was told regional news and community demographics were the way forward. A new kind of paper with a local emphasis on serious issues.'

'I'm sorry we can't agree, Joe. I believed we could begin to rebuild.'

'Not with kittens or bunnies or novelty aliens, chimps playing bagpipes, or any of that crap. Now if you'll excuse me, I've got some urgent bizzo to take care of.'

Joe started dialling and let Lionel show himself out.

Chapter Forty-Two: The Marriage of Figaro

'Gimme another,' Avery slurred. She'd been drinking solidly for an hour and was feeling woozy. The bartender poured her a third shot.

'You sure you don't want anything with that? The burgers are good and chef's favourite homemade shepherd's pie.'

'Nope, just as it is.'

'There you go.' He set the drink in front of her and left her alone.

It was lunchtime. The pub was filling up. At the back on a single table she noticed a distinguished man in his late fifties his head in a paper, and a glass of Stella at his side. He was eyeing her in the corner. He emptied his glass, and strolled over to her.

'Easy now.' His voice was thick but had an undertone of kindness.

'Huh? Who the fuck are you?'

'That's no way for a young lady to talk, is it?'

'I'm not a young lady. I'm a journo,' she laughed a haughty catty kind of laugh.

'Oh, the type who spreads her legs for a scoop, eh?'

'No, the type who makes hell for fellas like you.'

'Glad to hear it.'

'Fuck off.'

'Anyone ever tell you your mouth is worse than a Victorian slum?'

'No, but I bet plenty of ladies have told you you're a dead ringer for Clooney.'

'How would you like a juicy story?'

Avery frowned, but her newshound instinct kicked in.

'What kind of story?'

'The best kind, where you catch someone red handed.'

'Who the fuck are you?'

'They call me Ryan.'

'They?'

'You're a journalist, you work it out.' He left his number on a paper napkin and bowed out, fanning the air with a mock salute. Avery felt the sharp sting of the vodka under the pub lights. They reminded her of a low-budget skin flick shadowing the walls with muted bursts of sorrel and tan. It was piss ugly, and she was about to leave when Nick arrived.

'Thought I'd find you here,' he whisked her round, kissing her on the cheek.

'Why's that?'

'It's lunchtime, chance to unwind a bit. I just thought I'd pop by and see if you're okay, especially after that explosion.'

'Yeah, that was intense. I was covering it for the paper.'

'Fuck, glad you're safe.'

'Yeah, there was this one guy, bit of a hero, helped save a tot. That was cool. He had long black hair. Some kind of frickin' New Age guru. Possibly from another dimension.

'He rescued the kid though, right?'

'Yeah, but he was out there, you know?' She waved her arms above her head, signalling another dimension.

'You make him sound like a throwback from the seventies, some kind of hippie shmock.'

'Yeah, he was a hybrid of hippie and New Age. Probably lets the universe make all his decisions and shits peace and love all day.'

'Jeez Ave' let me make a note never to get on the wrong side of you!'

'If you'd seen him, you'd understand. Something about him – weird.'

'Must be really hard covering a story like that. There are so many emotions and variables.'

'I guess, but it's like … action – go, go, go. The newsroom becomes like an operating theatre. Everyone loves a bit of disaster porn.'

'Is that what you guys call it?'

'Just a term I picked up. Anyway, what have you been doing?'

'You mean aside from the usual: gun-running, orchestrating prison breaks and providing dishonest assistance to teenage strippers?'

'You sound like that dodgy lawyer from that gangster movie … what's it called, you know the one with Al Pacino?'

'Every gangster movie has big Al in it.'

'Yeah, you know – the lawyer, crazy, kind of coke-brained?'

'You talking about *Carlito's Way*?'

'Yes, yes, that's what you've morphed into.'

'Ah you got me Ave'! Must be that newshound instinct of yours. Now what you doing a couple of weeks from today?'

'Nothing much.'

'Good, then you're coming to see me and Matt upstairs at The Roundhouse.'

'Great, what time?'

'I think it's ten.'

'Cool.'

'Back to work soon?'

'Yeah, I know I'm smashed, but the paper's having a refit. Nick, I was meaning to ask you if you wanted to come to this art show with me.'

'Who's the artist?'

'Dunno, forget his name, his dad was a criminal Svengali, and he seems to have cornered the market in packaging pre-school plaster of paris as the art world's Second Coming.'

'Think I know who you mean. Has he managed to have a whole show on that crap?'

'Yeah. Anyway, I thought you and I could go as a couple.

263

Like on a date.'

'A date – we've already had four, haven't we?'

'Somehow, I don't think shrooming on your roof, having a drunken fuck after a movie, and eating takeout are like proper dates, and that was three not four.'

'Okay, we'll go as a couple, but you have to see me play.'
'Fine.'

'Honestly, those were some of the best dates I've ever had … underneath the London stars – classic.'

'I want to get to know the real you.'

'Simple. I'm a die-hard Bolan fan who slops out on junk on a Sunday, likes Huxley, Morrison, and of course Schubert's *Ave Maria*.'

'How blissfully elegant.'

'Yeah, reminds me of Anchika- my last girlfriend … well, we were engaged.'

'Never knew that.' Avery looked at him tenderly.

'Who'd have thought you'd be into Schubert.' She rippled.

'Music transcends time and space. Rich or poor, everyone can connect with music.'

'Now you sound like one of those recycled cut-outs from a rom-com.'

'Yeah, but you love it. Every woman likes a little *l'amour du jour*.'

'On that note …'

'Yeah, I got bizzo to take care of.' But Avery was lost in Nick's ardent gaze as he placed both hands on her cheeks and kissed her sweetly.

Chapter Forty-Three: Stairway to Heaven

Back at Matt's, BCM was stripped down to his waist, wearing cargo pants and crystal beads. He had his foot behind his head and was precariously poised in front of a large floor cushion. After a minute or so, he relaxed his body and laid his hands across his chest, breathing in deeply. To his left was a svelte brunette, crouching on a purple mat:

"You okay? I'm nearly done."

'Sure, take your time. I'm just gonna whisk this off and get comfy.' She threw off her sweater and wiggled out of her jeans. 'Mmmm. That's better. They were itchy on my thighs.'

Raven was twenty-two, a college grad from Wyoming on a year-long trip to Europe. She and BCM had met while backpacking in the Amazon. They'd bumped into each other at the local health shop. She sat in a U-shape in a skimpy vest bra and bikini shorts. They looked like models for a neo erotic Pirelli Calendar. Incense sticks and scented candles had been lit up all over the sideboard. A padded frisson hung in the room.

'Okay, I think you need to stretch all that bad shit out, reaaally stretch it.'

She flung her arms back towards her legs and then pushed herself into a series of contorted body poses.

'Oh fuck, I'm gonna fall!' Creeeeech. She toppled over the light stand, and the front door opened, as Matt and Nick were walking in she landed on the floor.

'Arrrh, oh, I hit my leg,' she cried.

'Whoa, what the … who's this?' asked Matt, kneeling down.

'Raven. She … we were practising.'

'Opening our chakras, and, yeah, trying some new yoga moves,' she was, rubbing her shin which had turned bright pink.

'Fuck me, what's going on? It's hotter than a rat's arse in here.' Nick shook his head at the spectacle before him and then loosened his tie and removed his jacket.

'Let me get some ice for that. Wanna help me out, Nick?' asked Matt.

BCM lifted Raven up and laid her down on the settee.

'Ahhhh, I'll just sit here for a bit.'

'Your chakras need balancing Raven.'

'Yeah totally.'

'Visualise your third eye.' BCM was resting his hands across her brow and had a concentrated expression.

'Mmmm, that's soothing, very decongesting.'

Back in the kitchen, Matt had put together a makeshift ice pack:

'Pass me that.'

Nick threw a blue cloth at him. There you go.

'Cheers.'

'Fucking annoying. Two yoga noodles going wacko in your front room. I think this Eastern New Age crap is so overplayed.'

'Don't talk bollocks. You think that's weird? They were doing yoga, not a fucking voodoo ritual. And from what I could see there were no fucking gimp masks in sight. Do me a favour and lighten up, and when we go back in, be nice.'

They went back into the sitting room and Matt tried to diffuse the tension: 'Nick was just wondering what you were up to. He's more of a Zumba guy.' Nick glowered and remained tight lipped.

'Raven was moving from the camel to the crane, or attempting to, and—' BCM was cut short by Nick:

'Sorry, can I ask why it's so fucking hot in here?' BCM smiled gently: 'Good for the muscles. Has to be around 105 degrees, eases all the knots away.'

'I'll just let some air in.' Nick walked over to the windows and flung them open.

Matt placed the ice pack onto Raven's leg.

'There you go, that should feel better.'

'Thank you, the pain's almost gone anyway.'

'Good.'

Nick gave BCM the once over.

'Looking buff man, what's your secret?'

'Mostly yoga and working in construction.'

'Yeah? What exactly?'

'People construction – I rebuild lives.'

'No disrespect, BCM, but both of you were on the floor when we walked in. Seems like you still have a lot of foundations to build.'

Raven shuffled onto her mat in the middle of the room and was plaiting her long black hair.

'I'll just put these on. Leg's much better.'

Nick was crabby. All he wanted was a smoke and a sit down, not a pop sermon from a New Age hippie.

Raven continued talking: 'So, what do you guys do … no wait, let me guess. You must be the musician married to your Les Paul' then she pointed to Nick. 'And you must be the lawyer – you look sort of pissed and pent-up.'

'Ha, got me in one. Got lots on my mind. That makes me pretty pissed and pent up. Sorry I'm not all free and natural like you, Rrrrr -aven.'

'I was just saying, your third eye—'

'Yeah, don't wanna be accused of being a new age Grinch, but I don't buy into all this pagan mumbo jumbo BS. I see perfectly well with just two eyes.'

'I know, but your third eye is unused, and if you free the energy you can make anything possible.'

'I don't need to free shit.'

'Even though I'm the one who knocked my shin, you're

the screw that's loose.'

'Excuse me?'

'I'm very open with my thoughts and feelings too. And believe in speaking the truth Hope you're okay with that, Nnnnnn-ick.'

'Yeah, I'm fine with that, but all this tantric crap – the candles, the incense – it's just not my bag.'

'You're gonna have to excuse Nick, he's, highly strung.'

'Don't make fucking excuses for me, Matt.'

'He's not usually like this. Bad day at the office, Nick?'

BCM cut in:

'I think you have to take a breath and calm down, Nick,'

'Sure, but I'm not fucking pretending that all this yoga BS will open my mind.'

Raven flicked her hair to the side: 'Are you done, because I can sense your third eye and your heart chakra need to be realigned. Sorry, but your mind is toxic. Full of bad endings and ifs and buts.'

Nick's bickering had soured their session.

'I'm out of here.'

Nick stormed off, leaving the three of them to wrestle with the awkwardness of the moment.

Chapter Forty-Four: Dirty Girl

Fiddling with the scrap of paper Ryan had given her, Avery was of two minds whether to call.

'I've been expecting you. What took you so long?

Who-who are you?'

'Your best lead. Come on, you're a journo, let's get this done. The intel I give you is off the record and anonymous. My consideration: Back off Stringer.'

Avery was floored, not expecting *him* to be part of the deal.

'What? Why?'

'Because the only one that goes down is Mel. Stringer doesn't need your kind on his balls.'

'My kind?'

'Yeah, money grubby, power journo with only a dark moral compass for company.'

'Now hold on a second. I don't know how you're connected to Nick, but it's not *your* business to speculate about *my* business. Why Stringer?'

'Told you, Mel's the pit boss, Stringer's a nobody, so keep him out.'

'I follow the story.'

'Yeah, sure you do, but when the shit gets too hard to shovel, you'll be gone quicker than a junkie to a crack pipe.'

Avery paused:

'That's not true.'

'Listen, this isn't celeb crap and chick shit gossip about hair styles, this is the inside story. Lose Stringer or lose the lead.'

Avery pushed her chair closer to the table and in a tight voice said, 'I'll think about it.'

'That'll do for now. You understand that anything I say on the phone is inadmissible?'

'Yes.'

'Good. Sit back, shut up, and listen. Avery turned up the volume on her handset.

'You want the goods on Mel. He's here, there, and everywhere. You won't be able to handle it all yourself. He's a global dope dealer, cyber thief, multimillionaire con man and gun runner. He controls property, land, petrol stations, and once upon a time he even owned me. How'd ya hook a monty-sized fish like him? You follow the money. He's successfully converted all of his illegal profits into legit businesses, making him almost untouchable. Ahhhem ahhhem.'

'You okay? That cough sounds really bad. She could almost see Ryan's tea coloured wheeze.

'Yeah, keep writing.'

'Okay.'

'Regular payments from all of these businesses go to a shell company called MFI Invest. Monies are put into an account in a bureau de change in Victoria. The account is in the name of Melvin London Holdings and proceeds and profits are funnelled through it on a weekly basis. The payments have been made for years. He owns it.'

'Go on.'

'There's going be a drop-off to the account in seven days. I'll give you the address at the Eagle tonight at 10 p.m.'

The phone clicked out. Avery leaned back and took a long slow sip of her coffee. She got straight on to the phone and rang the Legal department:

'Hi Camilla, it's Avery Cross from News and Features. Just needed to pick your brains.'

'Okay, but it'll have to be quick. You can always email, you know.'

'Yeah, it's really simple. Um, what's the view on intercept evidence in the UK?'

'In a nutshell, any wiretap is inadmissible, regardless of how it was obtained.'

'Thought so, okay, thanks Camilla – be in touch soon with copy.'

Ryan knew that for the story to work Avery needed some visuals, so she needed photos of the drop, then all she had to do was follow the audit trail from the accounts to the shell company.

As for Nick. Avery was undecided. She hit nine for an outside line. Scrolling through her phone, she clicked B for Benjie. He was well known in Fleet Street as resident muckraker. If anyone could find it, Benjie could. Cheaper than a PI and infinitely more entertaining, he was fast, discreet, and could muzzle his way through mountains of crap for gold. She had never utilised his services before, but he had achieved cult status with other papers and was the source of some of the most sensational scoops to hit Fleet Street.

'Benjie, Avery. What you up to?'

'Everything, and of course I can't tell you about any of it.'

'Course.'

'So what d'ya need? Who's the subject?'

'A very wealthy entrepreneur. Lots of fingers, lots of pies. Just wondering about his finances.'

'Name.'

'Mel Greenberg.'

The phone went mute.

'Hello, Benjie, you there?'

'I'm gonna have to think about that. He's one of the brothers, and it might be against my principles to dig any dirt on him.'

'What do you mean?'

'I'm Jewish, so is Melvin, and he does lots of charitable

work for the synagogue and the local community.'

'I see.'

'Yeah.'

Well, this was a first. Someone who thought so highly of Mel he refused to embroil him in anything that might hurt Mel's rep.

'Theoretically, if you were on the snoop with another subject in mind, where would you start?'

'Easy, lawyer's rubbish bins. They're like an Aladdin's cave. You never know what gems might be lurking there.'

'Benjie, before you go … another story I'm working, involves a con artist who's fled the country. I heard you might be able to help with sourcing sensitive information. I'm trying to trace some money for widowers and pensioners.'

Avery knew if she mentioned Mel, Benjie would bail, so she made up some BS to tap him for info.'

'He's a Scottish drug dealer who also ran a fake holiday business. Hundreds of pensioners have lost their life savings.'

'Always happy to assist in matters like this. I have the number of a specialist. He can help where others can't. He's highly trained, with very reasonable rates, a lone wolf. No guarantees he'll do the job – 447837042565. If he does commit, I take a twenty-five per cent cut up front. Clear?'

'Yep. Thanks.'

'Anytime, and … er Avery, even a snake can't swallow an elephant.'

Avery grabbed her coat, keys and notepad and headed for Nick's office. Time to get messed-up, bogged-down and dirty.

Chapter Forty-Five: Crow Jane

'Pulled in a massive favour to keep schtum over these.' Mel threw the graphic stills of Elaine onto Nick's desk. She was battered almost beyond recognition, her face, legs and arms capped with bruises, her nose broken and her mouth slashed. Nick swallowed. He said nothing but his lower lip began to tremble. Mel stared at him with calculated indifference.

'You don't get where I am without tying up loose ends.'

'She was alive when she left.'

'That bitch is fried. She was a fucking liability.' Mel's mammoth frame darkened the room. 'Last I heard she was at yours – tragedy, young girl like that, nasty business.'

Nick remained silent.

'The secret is, I always win because I don't rely on anyone. I only back myself.'

Nick wanted to pulp him to a bloody mess, his fingers clenched beneath his desk, his chest tightening. Instead, he just glared at him, wondering if and when a body would surface, until Mel finally got up from his chair, and came round to Nick's side of the desk, placing his big fat arm across his shoulder.

'Heard you got a music thing coming up, and you're gonna be playing at the Roundhouse is that right?'

'Yeah.'

'Showcasing new acts and doing a number yourself, eh?'

'Yeah.'

'Read it on the flyer Tezza bought it over.'

Flashing an evil grin, his eyes blunt and bitter, Mel pulled open his jacket pocket and shoved a wad of fifties into Nick's hands.

'Here's a contribution. Have a good time on your Uncle Mel.'

He marched out of Nick's office, snatching the gory snaps of Elaine from his desk. Despite his outward composure, Nick was gutted.

'Sylvie, stick Sky News on. Check if there've been any murders in the last few days.'

'Okay.'

'And the papers, same thing.'

Nick slammed the phone down and put his legs on the desk.

He needed to be sure Elaine was really dead before he rolled. BCM had her last name so he could easily confirm it via Matt and then check the death register or social security records. A gory kill like that would be front-page news. He scoured online for reports of missing or deceased women that matched Elaine's description. He was stung by the number of random fatalities streaming his feed.

'Sylvie, get me a whisky.'

'Isn't it a little early?'

'Never too early for whisky. I've got a touch of flu. Best way to kill a bug, douse it in alcohol.' As if on cue he started coughing violently. He took out a paper cup from his desk drawer and spewed out a combo of bile, blood and bravado.

'Looks nasty.' Sylvie came in with a glass of Johnnie Walker.

'Ugh, yeah, it's rough.'

'You should check that out with a doctor.'

'It's nothing, just flu. Now get back to whatever it is I pay you for.'

Sylvie was about to close the door when Avery drifted in.

'Wow, you look like shit.'

'Thanks Avery it's flu.'

'You need a break. Lucky for you I bought us everything we need for some downtime.'

'No way, I'm slammed.'

'You work too hard. I made this myself.'

'What is it?'

'I bought us a picnic: chicken, salad, French loaf and a bottle of Sancerre.'

'Does sound good.'

'Let's have it here on the couch.'

'I don't know. It's the middle of the afternoon.'

'So?'

'Ah, you twisted my arm. But best keep the jackals at bay.' He locked the door and then buzzed Sylvie.

'I'm out for the afternoon. Hold all calls, thanks.'

Avery kicked off her heels and undid her ponytail, shaking her inky-blue mane free. She laid the food out on plates and poured out the wine.

'Oh, that's great, mmmm.'

'What?'

'The silence, it's relaxing.'

'Pressure at work?'

'Yeah, but being on the right side never comes easy.'

'Who cares about the right side? It's the winning side you got to be on.'

'Is that you, then, the real Nick, winner at all costs?'

'It is now, by any means necessary.'

'So, what about the old Nick?'

'No one you'd fall for – an idealistic geek with a head full of dreams who believed in justice, freedom and the pursuit of the truth.'

'And now?' She took a bite of chicken.

'Now I know justice ignores the poor, the weak, the disenfranchised and worse justice always buries the truth.'

'Aww, don't be like that.'

Nick uncorked the wine.

'You'd never have given me a second look back then.'

'Well, I might. I used to be a bit of wallflower.'

'Really, Ammmmmazin' Avery ?'

She giggled and nodded.

'Have you always lived in London?'

'Yep, born and bred. You?'

'No, we came down from Yorkshire.'

'Ah, God's country. But no trace of a northern accent?'

'No, but when I visit friends and family I pick it up. When I'm old and grey, that's probably where I'll end up, back in Yorkshire.

'Jesus, that's depressing.'

'Yes, but sooner or later we all have to leave the stage.'

'Until then, here's to the good life.'

Avery sipped her wine and Nick downed his in one. Avery took the glass from his hand and playfully rubbed his cheek.

'You got a spot of something just there.' She went to wipe it off. Nick grabbed her and they fell into a deep smooch.

'Come here.' He pushed Avery onto his desk and thrust his hand up her dress.

'Mmmm.'

Slowly, he kissed her the back of her neck.

'I thought about you in bed last night,' Avery flushed and said:

'What if someone knocks?'

'No one's coming, now …' His hand caressing her inner thigh, she was his for the taking.

'Ave' - why are you really here?' Nick's eyes had become stony.

'What?' She jerked her head forward and pushed his hand away.

'Whoa, I'm sorry. I just want to be clear you're here 'cos you wanna be.'

'Yeah, I wanted to spend some alone time with you.'

'I gotta tell you, I'm under a lot of heat. I've got big cases – people relying on me. I don't have time for sneaky journo tricks.'

'Where's this coming from? I thought we had a connection.'

'Wake up, Avery. Everyone's fucking connected virtually or by six degrees of separation. I'm holding my cards right here.' He patted his chest. 'Since I started this job, all I've been trawling through is shit, and once I get through that, another load is dumped on me. You know what I'm saying? If I take a risk on you, I got to be certain you won't screw me over.'

Avery reached forward and kissed him hard. She bent her head to the side and with a flirty smile said:

'You can count on me, Nick. I will screw you. Screw the hell out of you.'

He ran his fingers through her hair and looked deep into her eyes, both hands on the side of her face, and said, 'Yeah, you probably will.'

They fucked the afternoon way.

'It's dark already. Shit, I got a meeting at The Eagle. Have you got showers in here?'

'Yes, they're on the top floor. You'll need this.' Nick handed her a bathroom key.

'Thanks hon. Had the most amazing time again.'

'I'll call you later, Matt's booked more band time. You can come by and see us play. Remember the gig at The Roundhouse.'

'Yeah, definitely.'

'Mwah.' She kissed him softly, her tongue sliding in to his. Then she scrambled her stuff together and headed for the top floor. She checked her mobile – no messages. She still had plenty of time to prep for Ryan and was out of Nick's office within the hour.

Nick made a beeline for his flat. Before his meeting at Morton's he wanted proof of Elaine's murder.

Chapter Forty-Six: Barracuda

Avery was vamped up. Her slut-walk was drawing cat calls and whistles from the regulars. She found Ryan in the corner of the pub.

'Sit down. Lots of eyes on us. Don't ever walk in here like a brass.'

Being called a prostitute by a gangland staunch was hugely embarrassing. Avery knew she'd overstepped the mark.

'Now go to the bar and get me a Guinness.'

She dodged the herd and ignored the smutty remarks.

'A pint of Guinness, and a vodka lime and soda.'

'On its way. So what's with the scary getup?'

'Nothing, I just tried a different look for today.'

'Oh, what, a hookers-r-us kind of look?'

'Can it. Just gimme the drinks.'

'No problemo.'

She handed over the money and carried the drinks back to the table, clutching her purse under her arm.

'It's a couple of drinks, not a fucking human heart.'

'I'm no good at juggling.'

'Well you'd better learn pronto.'

She sat down, conscious of her spiked heels, her thigh-split skirt, and the blood-red lippy she'd applied to her mouth and the apples of her cheeks.

'See all of them – don't look – they've all got one thing in common.'

'What's that?'

'They're all under my thumb and don't even know it. Now that's smooth, understand?'

'I get it.'

'No, you *think* you get it but the truth is Avery, I got you, I got everyone. I don't need any of these lousy scumbags, but they need me. I work on my own, that way I don't owe anyone.'

'Yeah.'

'A lot of leads in this boozer, a lot of leads, dead ends, and I told you sos.'

She nodded and sipped her drink.

'You need something from me and I get something from you. That's the way a market economy works, see?'

He pulled out a piece and kept it warm on his crotch. Then he dug into his pockets and removed a scrap of paper. Avery lit up like a Christmas tree.

'On here – everything you need to nail Mel and hang him from London Bridge.'

'I'm listening.'

'I need your word you'll leave Nick out of the mix.'

'I don't ever promise what I can't deliver.'

'Good girl.'

'I mean I can try.'

'I won't lie to ya, I've been in this game a long time. I have a golden pass. You know why?'

'Why?'

'Because I never compromise. I take a seed, watch it grow, and the result is respect, pure fucking respect. Once you got that, you have everything. Anyone who crosses the line knows what's gonna happen. Understand me?'

'Yeah.'

It finally dawned on Avery that not all gangsters were the same, and here she was, one on one with an underworld major, espousing the virtues of a moral code.

What a swine – shaming me. Scoop and spread. Heard it from the best and now the worst.

'Good.' He finished his drink, leaving a film of beer foam on the ridge of his lips. He sponged it off with a gent's handkerchief and then pushed the chair away. He gestured her forward. They both stood up, and he left The Eagle, tucking the paper into her pocket without her feeling a thing.

He rang her as soon as he was outside.

'It's in your jacket. Be lucky.'

Chapter Forty-Seven: Crossroad Blues

'I'm sorry. I couldn't go through with it. I eat, breath, sleep it, longing for it to happen, but it's fucking complicated losing part of me.'

'There's nothing to feel ashamed about, Mimi.'

She was sitting head bowed, arms folded in a messy cramped office. There were stacks of books on the shelves, handwritten notes and files piled lazily on top of each other with the cloak of academia trailing the dusty wooden floors.

'Personally, Dr Fitch, I don't give a fuck if I lose my balls – it's the operation that scares me to death.'

'Gender affirmation surgery is a huge step, and obviously, as you've been living like a woman with breast implants etc., we thought you were ready for full transition.' He took out a small tobacco pipe.

'You don't mind do you? It's not strictly allowed but …'

'No, go ahead.'

He packed the pipe with tobacco, pushed it down with his thumb, took out a match, lit the bowl and sucked hard, loading the room with a nutty aroma. As smoke rested on the desk and chairs, an invisible fur enveloped them.

'It takes time, Mimi. No one knows but you when it's *your* time.'

Mimi felt as foggy as the air around her, but was relieved she'd escaped the surgeon's knife.

'I've spent thousands on trying to make this work, doctor

– breast augmentation, pumping oestrogen into me, accessories, wigs, make-up, clothes, and what's it all for?'

'Indeed.'

'No one prepares you for the loneliness. I feel like a jumbo cyclops trawling the earth for others just like me. Ignored by women and detested by men. As if I don't belong anywhere.'

'It's a long road, Mimi, and not everyone will be able to accept you, even if you do have surgery.'

'It's a pool doctor, a pool of darkness, like being drowned alive.' She pulled out a cigarette and leaned in for a light. 'Thanks.' She took a long slow drag.

'Before all of this, ra, ra, burlesque shit, I was a trained architect in a prestigious design firm. I went from making 200k a year to scrimping off tips and recycled smiles. I work unsocial hours, eat dinner from a can, and pick up ageing bigots with alopecia and peanut pricks – that's *my* fucking reality. It was easy functioning as a man. I had a mortgage, a driver's licence, health insurance. I had a life. Now, I survive in the shadows, no identity, and no respect. I'm a fringe curiosity, the novelty joker wheeled out to deliver saucy sound bites and one-liners for people's amusement. I feel like a lab monkey with nowhere to go.'

'It's important to let it out, good to vent, and, of course, natural to mourn the loss of your former self. The financial security, the social status, all of these aspects to your life are gone, and it's good to explore those feelings.'

'Get that bollocks from a seminar on intersex therapies, Doc, while fantasising about your intern at lunch? I need answers, not tick-tack trannie speak.'

'Yes, I see. I know you're finding this process challenging.'

'Challenging? Yeah, you could say that being trapped in a ball sack is fucking challenging when your head says you need breasts.'

Dr Fitch rested his chin in his hands and became quiet.

'Eight hours on the operating table and then what?

Chromosome X, chromosome Y. That's what I ask myself over and over: why, why, why didn't I just have the chop?'

'These dark feelings – they could be a reaction to the hormone pills. I can see from your notes that we've put you on another brand and upped the dosage.'

'This feeling of being caught in a gender trap is choking me, Doc. Like a snared rabbit – just flopping around.'

'I'm going to refer you to another specialist who deals specifically with post-op failure.' He lifted his hand to signal her quiet. 'Now don't go making assumptions over the term, it's a therapy session for transgender people who have been unable to deal with surgery.'

'Right.'

'You can call anytime, night or day, there's always someone manning the lines.' He leaned forward and gave her a card.

'I'm also going to schedule you another session with me in two weeks.'

'I had it all figured out up here.' She tapped her forehead. 'I thought this was the answer, the final solution.'

'You're not alone, Mimi. A lot of people go through this. You don't have to cope by yourself.'

'It's the guilt. I feel like I've let everyone down. I'm ashamed.'

'Of?'

'Rejection. I'm ashamed of what pushes me to express my femininity but not enough to go all the way.'

'Yes, these are complicated emotions. That and the physical fear of the actual operation are all areas we can discuss.'

'You see, Doc, I was worried shitless about infection, bleeding, my prostate.'

'Yeees.'

'I didn't wanna come out permanently damaged with a fucked-up fanny.'

'I get it. Again, it's a common issue that many transsexuals face, seeking physical conformity with gender identity pitted against the fear of loss. It's natural to be confused and conflicted, but to be frank there are more success stories than screw-ups, Mimi, You'll get through this.'

'I feel like Cinderella.'

'Hmmm.'

'Yeah, like fucking Cinderella. When I was ten years old I used to play with my sister's dolls and secretly dress up in ballerina clothes. I kept a treasure chest of lipstick, rouge and glitter pens. I'd walk around in my mother's high heels; feel the softness of her dresses on my skin. I felt just like Cinderella, a draggy servant girl living a fucked-up childhood. I wanted to be pretty, to be saved. I felt I couldn't be me, so I was at one with Cinders. We were both victims, but instead of a prince I wanted to be a real woman with breasts and lips and smooth soft skin. I thought after years and years of noble sacrifice that I would finally achieve my dream.'

'Hmmm.'

'To me, I'm still Cinderella without that fairy tale ending.'

She sighed and headed for the door. Outside the skies were filmed with grey and the song of subterranean Weltschmerz.

Chapter Forty-Eight: Junco Partner

Nick stared at the envelope on his desk for a good five minutes. Still stewing about Elaine, he was in the dark about everything yet somehow believed all the pieces of the jigsaw were slotting into place. Slowly he ran his hands across the top and then shook it.

Bleep brrr bleeep brrr: a text message from his mother. *Please come over asap love mum* xo. He deleted it.

His eyes were anchored on the manila envelope in front of him. It looked fairly impressive with the Law Society stamp smartly embossed on the front. He took a gulp of air, cautiously peeling apart the back.

'Okay, here goes.' His voice was brittle, butterflies wheeling around the pit of his stomach as he carefully read each line.

We are pleased to inform you …

'Yes!' He punched the air, clenching his teeth and tossing the letter aside. Beaming happily, he preened around the room gesticulating to an invisible audience:

'Fuck you and fuck you too. I now belong to the best, the fucking best.' A few seconds later, Fisher walked into his office.

'Congratulations Nick, won't be long till you make partner, eh?'

He clapped him on the back and took out his gold pocket watch, an archaic reminder of old civility, a symbol of the ruling establishment he was now part of.

'There's a bonus in your salary. Take the rest of the day off. You've earned it.'

'Thank you, sir.'

Fisher shuffled out, his mind on other matters. Nick's face was shiny like a waxed lemon. Acing his law finals put a bounce in his step. Finally, he had joined the legal elite.

After a twenty minute cab ride, he arrived at his mother's house, his hands powdered with coke and his eyes pinched from lack of sleep.

He knocked on the door.

'Come in, my darling.'

Her face was frayed and worn.

'It's results day isn't it? Have you heard anything?'

He stood with his head bent and, his hand resting on the door. Then slowly, he lifted his head, his eyes squinting, the sunlight washing the room with yellow dust strobes. He shrugged his shoulders, feigning defeat, until gradually a big smile spread across his face.

'I did it. I passed them, I did it. Let's tell Dad I'm a fully-fledged legal weasel, not a trainee anymore.'

His mother rushed towards him, swamping him with kisses.

'So proud of you Nick. I'm so proud.'

She flung her arms about him and continued her showy display of affection.

'Sorry, Nick.'

She dabbed away the lipstick smudges.

'You've got my respect, boy. All those hours you put in. All that work you did, and today I call my son a solicitor.'

'Of the Supreme Court of Judicature.' He added with excitement.

'You're the very first one in the family to qualify, Nick. Your grandfather would have loved to see this day.'

She linked her arm through his and they went into the sitting room.

'Where's Dad?'

'Sit down dear.'

'Mum, where is he?'

'Your father fell. He's in hospital – just for observation. Don't worry, you can see him later. They say they may discharge him tonight. He'll be so proud of you. Now, before lunch, I've got something I need you to take care of. Nick groaned, rolling his eyes towards the ceiling.

'Don't do that, dear, it's rude, especially to your mother. I know we've had this conversation many times, but today's different. I want you to have these.' She thrust a set of house keys in his hand.

'I've already got these, Mum.' He pulled out an exact copy of the same set from his jacket pocket.

'No, I want you to take ownership of the house, do all the legal work and transfer the family home to your name. It's right, this is your future. I want you to do this now.'

'Mum, we've been through this. I don't need the house. It belongs to you and Dad.'

'Listen to me, Nick. I want you to take it. I'm, well, getting on, there's no denying it. I don't want the burden of huge taxes on my passing. It makes no sense. Now you're a lawyer, you understand the legal implications. I'm trusting you to take care of this and let me know when it's dealt with.'

'Alright, Mum, when I get back to the office.'

'Thanks dear. I've made your favourite.'

They sat down at the table and toasted his success with wine and laughter. Oh how Nick loved the sound of his mother's laugh. It swaddled him with safety and made him think of rose-lit days.

It was around a quarter to four when he returned to work by taxi.

'Fuck you!' He scowled at a hapless hobo through the window. Then he put his head in his hands and started to sob. The cabbie glanced at him in his rear-view mirror.

'You alright, mate?'

Nick sniffed. He looked away from the driver.

'I-I just got some bad news.'

Nick was mourning the loss of his profession on the day he had been admitted to the inner circle. He knew he had no right to be part of the legal fraternity and was bawling like a new-born as he realised that he would never become the man he wanted to be.

'Cheer up. It might never happen,'

'Already has, mate, already has.'

Sometimes you win – sometimes you adapt, but is it a crime to fight crime with crime?

Back at the office, Nick requisitioned the deeds to the family home. Doing an online search of the title, he called Adam as he waited for the results.

'How you doing, big A? It's Nick.'

'Oh yeah, Nick, super prick lawyer man.'

'Let's just use Nick.'

'What do you want?'

'I need a special. Can you do a thousand?'

'A thousand?'

'That's right.'

'Does Mel know?'

'Leave Mel to me. Can you deliver?'

'They'll be second-hand.'

'They still work, right?'

'Yeah, they're all good. When d'you want them for?'

'Within a week or two.'

'I'll need cash.'

'Of course.'

He clicked off. It was easier buying a shipment of guns than a pound of Kobe beef.

Nick waited for the legal forms to download. They provided all the property details including information on ownership rights and boundaries. As he was completing them, he checked the office copies for his mother's full name, wondering if she had put her middle name or initial and was horrified to note that Melvin Maurice Greenberg was recorded on the document as the legal owner of *his* family home. He shook his head in disbelief. Quickly, he executed another transfer and buzzed Sylvie.

'Take this document to Bloom and Co. Get it signed and stamped. Bradley will deal with it.'

Sylvie returned within the hour. Fortunately, Bloom and Co were minutes away. Nick had already prepared a charge in favour of his parents in excess of the value of their home.

'Right Sylvie, I need you to log onto the electronic business service and submit on line.'

The transfer was ready to be lodged with the new charge at the Land Registry. He faxed it there and sent the hard copy by DX for expedited registration. Now *his* name would be on the deeds. Thankful his mother's home was back in safe hands, he checked his messages and downloaded a newspaper report on the savage killing of a London sex worker. The graphic picture confirmed it was Elaine. He would have to box clever and hit heavy. If he was linked in any way to such a gruesome killing it would destroy his legal reputation. There was no way out. It was him or Mel.

Chapter Forty-Nine: Ball and Biscuit

Nick loved a diverse audience: Somali gangsters, a local councillor sucking on a crack pipe and a Victoria Secrets model were all seated in the front row. Avery and BCM were spliffing to the warm-up tunes. Hanging at the bar were Mickey, Terry, and a couple of A-grade hookers.

'This should be a fucking laugh.' Terry had his arm around one of the women. She had bouncy boobs, botox lips and wore a platinum-blonde wig. Her face tinted the colour of toffee and the corners of her mouth crinkled. She had a heavy chesty laugh and was smoking a cigarette, inhaling through her nose.

'Are you sure I won't get into any bother lighting up in here, Tezza?'

'Nah, it's fine. I know the fella who owns the place.'

'Ooh, aren't you well connected. Go on then, you've twisted my arm. I'll finish this and 'ave another Bacardi and Coke.'

Terry nodded at the bartender for a full round.

Backstage, Nick was airing his lungs. If Anichka saw him now, she'd be disgusted. She was in the past, buried with his conscience. Time for the sweet dirty of rock.

Nick hit the stage dressed in stretch leather, denim and mascara eyes. Matt was by his side, tuning his Les Paul, with

Zeb the drummer and Kris on bass, Matt's boho locks topped off by a trilby and cravat. This was their first major gig with Nick in a month. They were cultivating a growing fan base and netting rave reviews from the music press but their lackadaisical approach to rehearsals and gigs meant they were still at the margins of success.

Nick exploded onto the stage, hammered with the mike close to his lips: 'Ever since I was ten years old, I've been wanking off to this!' All Nick had ever wanted to do was perform and now he was steaming the dream.

'Fuck the Stones! Fuck the Pistols!' They struck out their first tune, a dizzy blend of serpentine riffs and grand glam mixed with a stream of eclectic lyrical motifs, featuring politics, sexual subversion and philosophy. Nick was swivel shaking the mike in between guitar breaks. The urgency of his voice rousing the back row into overdrive.

'This is the sound of revolution! What is it?' He held the mike to the crowd.

'Revolution!' They chanted back cheering, banging their beer glasses and whistling their appreciation as Nick slipped into another track.

'More!' Avery hollered from the front.

'Fuck the police, fuck the bankers!' The audience roared in agreement.

The walls were spattered with sweat and passion. The music was loud, rude and boring the hell out of Mickey:

'How long do my earholes 'ave to face this fucking slaughter?'

'Dunno, get yourself a top-up and 'ave a dance like that bird over there,'

'No fucking way Tezza. This is a pile of dross. She's off her head, that one.' They were both gawping at a young blonde rocker, tree-flipping around. Her long arms spiralling the air, her eyes glazed and her body thrusting out of synch. She was spaced – digging the vibe.

'Like it or lump it, we 'ave to report back to Mel.'

'There's nuffing to say, Tezza. It's a bunch of scuzzy rockers bashing out crap.'

'I don't suppose anyfing else will go down. C'mon Mickey We can check back in a couple of hours.'

'Thank God! Let's, get the fuck out.'

With a supercharged audience cranking for more, Terry, Mickey and their respective dates left the raucous vibe of The Round House and its high domed ceilings. Outside, under star-tipped skies, you could still hear Nick's eloquent poetic angst.

'Who'da thought that used to be the home of real music,' sighed Mickey.

'Like?'

'The Ramones, Pink Floyd – fucking epic.'

'Rock royalty indeed. Now, let's go grab a drink at a proper boozer. They'll be thrashing it for ages yet.'

Inside, Nick was driving the beat with searing honesty. Then BCM mounted the stage and Nick threw him a mike: 'Light the way with fire, healing fire.' His voice: a flat fusion of Nick Cave and the swirling hypnosis of Jim Morrison, the shamanic poetics an instant hit with the ladies in the second row.

'These will light the way!' A psychedelic waif threw her lace thong at Nick's head.

'Woo yeah,' Nick grinned, shoving them into his pocket. This spurred on other girls to throw their knickers around and one to flash her boobs to the band. BCM slid back into the crowd.

Nick changed the tempo with another track, his chiffon voice bruising the air: 'Fuck the bankers, they don't care about us, fuck the bankers, sleazy wankers …'

Once the track had ended, the crowd were re-energised and the stage was littered with G-strings and bikini shorts.

'You're all indestructible!' he wailed. He came to the front and reached out with his hands as if he were Moses parting the red sea.

'All of you.' He pointed to random girls in the audience.

'You, you and you, you're all …?' Then he put his hand to his ear.

'Indestructible,' they chimed. Nick had a dark single-minded intensity in his eyes.

Matt put his finger-picking skills on show in the final track of the night, a knotty bluesy combo of simmering soul, ghostly blues and creamy rock. It was dramatic, improvised, and radically different. The crowd were delirious. The house lights went on, and Nick threw tee-shirts and hoodies into the audience.

'Thank you. Remember, fuck the bastards before they fuck you! Copies of our debut single will be 100% free watch this space. Cheers!'

They left the stage dazed and delirious. The music press and two influential bloggers were frantically following them for band interviews and quotes. For Nick it was the beginning of a stellar evening.

Chapter Fifty: This Business is Killing Me

'Wanna take a stab ?'

Mel was working over a third-rate thug with an oversized ego. He had been skimming monies from one of his clubs and pocketing profits from a casino scam. He was strapped to a chair, his face bashed in and his mouth duct-taped. Mel took off his belt, leaving his belly to wobble free, resting his hand on his knee.

'You think you can fuck me?'

The man muffled an inaudible answer.

'Yeah, my sentiments exactly.' He turned to Terry. 'What the fuck are you doing?'

Terry was applying copious amounts of thick white gloop to his left forearm.

'Fink I've got some sort of allergy.'

'What you spreading on there?'

'It's … er anti-inflammatory Zitch Itch.'

'What?'

'Zitch Itch – it's an ointment for my allergy, boss.'

'I'm trying to instil some fucking life lessons here, Tezza. We're not in some fucking health spa in Mayfair so put it away.'

'Takes five minutes to work, boss.'

'Fucking hell, why don't we just get a mani and pedi while we're at it?'

'Sorry, boss.'

'Mickey, get your arse into gear. You're up.'

'Boss?'

'Take a swipe, Mick. Jeez, do I 'ave to do everything today? C'mon then.'

Mickey lurched forward, lost his footing and slipped on a rug, his hand landing on a small coffee table, knocking over a glass of water, and a half-eaten pack of stale Doritos.

'Are you fucking serious? Clean this shit up! Got a pair of fucking panto performers here. What are you two doing, rehearsing for a comedy turn at the fucking Eagle?'

There were glass shards and chip crumbs everywhere.

'It only takes four muscles to smack someone in the head. Can't you even do that? Get up.'

Mickey got to his feet, kicking the glass away while Tezza dabbed his arm dry.

'Now, let's try this again, shall we? My calculations, which are always spot on, show you've been filching funds for over six months. You owe me over fifty grand. My question is, have you got my money?'

The man flopped around in his chair, shaking his head like a sock puppet, his left eye bleeding. It looked like strawberry jam and lemon curd mushed together. Mickey and Terry stood on either side as Mel belted him six times on the face.

'Arrrah arrrah whomp.' The duct tape was flecked with blood oozing from the welts striping his face, his head dangling to one side. Mickey grabbed him and sat him forward. He was drooling and sweating at the same time.

'A good flogging is meant to be very cathartic, lets out all the cobwebs, and what's fair is fair. You stole from me. I gave you food and shelter, paid your mortgage and bought you respectability. It's payback time. Either you gimme the money or I take what's mine.'

Mel clasped his hands together as if in prayer

'Tezza am I being unreasonable? Am I being a fucking prick about this?'

'No, boss.'

'Fuck no. He's the one screwing me.'

Mel swung round, staring at the sunken man. 'It's fucking painful, fucking hurts to be treated this way.'

'Painful, boss,' Mickey chipped in.

'Consider this an interim payment on your debt. Untie him, get him cleaned up, and send him to Sal's.'

There was a piss puddle underneath the chair.

'Get one of the girls to mop that mess up, and I want you both back at PT's in twenty minutes.'

Mel left the lock-up and headed straight for a sauna, steam and rub down at the Turkish baths in Bethnal Green. A smell of ozone and lemon hit him first, along with sea salt and pine needles. There were mostly middle-aged men padding around in white robes and slippers. Mel had been a regular since the spa opened last year. Every other Monday he'd follow the same ritual to try to wind down and ease his aching bones. He slowly undressed, donning a traditional pestemal over his sow belly and carrying a robe and his wash bag into the hot steamy room, which was covered in marble and arched by a big dome. He sat in the middle, alone, awaiting a squat, dark-haired Albanian masseur.

'Nice to see you, Mr Mel.'

He soaked Mel's pink blubber bod' with warm water, lathering him up. Wet and slippery, Mel floundered around like a giant blob.

'Now it rub time, Mr Mel.' The attendant took out an oriental washcloth and started scrubbing furiously.

'Good, Mr Mel?'

'Hmmm, yes, very good.'

Another soapy wash, a rinse with cold water, and Mel was about to leave and get changed when he felt two calloused hands on his neck pinning him to the spot.

'One move and I'll slice you like a piece of tenderloin.'

Mel gulped. Breathless and panic-stricken, he saw a large arm grip his left side. He could feel his head being squeezed. He was trapped in a choke hold.

'A message from Phil's old man. Don't fuck his first

born. Don't fuck his family. You've been on the take for years. Now your number's up.'

Mel was spun around, his body knotted like a lock-twist balloon dog. He keeled over in a hypoxic convulsion and lay still on the tiles.

'Mister Mel!' The attendant walked in just as his assailant slipped out.

Mel was resuscitated. Within two days he had discharged himself from hospital and put a hit out on the entire Drummond family.

Chapter Fifty-One: Senza Una Donna

'How you feelin', boss?'

'Vivid.'

'Boss?'

'Never mind, Tezza. I want you to follow that Avery bird of Nick's. Stick to her like a fucking bad smell.'

'On it, boss.'

'Yeah, got a slippery feeling about her. Can't finger it, but I don't trust her. Any nosey hack is fair game, and I wanna cover my bases.'

'Understood, boss.'

Mel had received a friendly tip-off from Ange, the oldest and most trusted of The Eagle's bar staff, that Avery had been in there dressed like a 'tart' cosying up to Ryan. Mel was on red alert, checking and double-checking everyone on the payroll and everyone off it. He had hundreds of enemies and a sea of smiling yes-men to break bread with but not one real friend he could count on.

I can still remember the screams. He bust her lip and threw her down a flight of stairs. I was only seven years old, but I knew I had to protect my sweet mother from that fucking brute. I tried pulling him off her and he doused me with pepper spray and locked me in the cellar. I can still hear his fucking demonic laugh. It haunted me for years like a fucking death mask. Thanks Dad, I owe you big time. On the outside, everybody loved him, he was always in the eye of the storm. He had women, lots of them. Dragged me into a brothel at fifteen to make a man of me. I sobbed my heart out. She listened. She wasn't exactly Raquel Welch, but when I think back she was a looker. I don't remember getting any goose bumps over her. No, that happened much later. I was sixteen years old. It was Christmas Eve. Dad was running a high-end pawn biz from home. A girl came in hawking her mother's diamond earrings. She was wearing flares and a hippy shirt. Her hair was mid length and fair, just like a girl. Her body – shaped just like a girl. Her mouth – warm, open and gentle just like a girl. Her touch – soft, just like a girl. Dad caught us kissing behind the work shed. He went fucking berserk. What are you doing? That's Tommy's boy! I couldn't move. Shock turned to anger and then disgust. Did you know it was a lad, son? It's an easy mistake to make. I stared shit-scared. His voice got louder and louder. He beat me with a belt buckle over and over until I bled and passed out. We didn't speak again. He never came near me after that, wouldn't play, wrestle or box. We were finished. I was on my own. He never looked me in the eye again, not until his dying day. He said, 'You knew, didn't ya, boy? You knew.' Even on his deathbed he couldn't let it go.

Mel was bent back in a cushy Chesterfield, his eyes half shut. He got up and started rifling through the desk drawer searching for something. He was cut up, like a rancid lime.

'Where is it? I never threw it out. I kept it in between the tax receipts and office expenses.'

He was searching for Mimi's new telephone number. He had tracked her down using Benjie the bin man.

'Ah, gotcha.' He would call her right away. He needed Mimi like a priest needs a sermon. He dialled the number, his fat hands keying the numbers in clumsily. A young child picked up first time.

'Hello?'

His heart jumped. Was that a relative or a sibling?

'Yeah, hello, is—' but he was unable to finish. A harried voice came onto the phone.

'Who is this?'

'Mel, for Mimi.'

'Sorry, you've got the wrong number.'

                'Is that five four seven three two eight?'

'No, you must have entered nine.'

'It's the wrong number?'

'Yeah, I told you, there's no one by that name here.'

Mel clicked off. He felt a wave of relief as he tried again. This time it went straight to answerphone. It was a soft lusty voice, one that he recognised and made his dick hard.

'Mimi, Mel. Hope you're alright. Listen, we got a launch party for a new artist. He does sculptures and shit. I want you to come. Truth is, I miss ya, and I'd like you there. Call me, '

Just before blacking out at the steam baths he'd remembered a summer picnic with Mimi and her face had carried him through it. He wanted it to work between them.

I can't let her go.

Mel had a pick-up to make at the bureau de change in Victoria. He called Sal.

'Sal?'

'He's gone to the dentist for an emergency root canal. He said you take care of it today or leave it till next week.'

'That's fine, Rose, I'll deal with it.'

Mel couldn't wait. He had hundreds and thousands of pounds to collect and no one else to trust except himself and Sal, now at the front end of a dentist's drill. He called a private cab.

'Mel Greenberg, I've got an account. Can you make sure Gary and John come along?'

Gary and John were two 'roid pumpers built like Arnie and Stallone, but they spoke in monosyllables and had shrunken balls, causing them to walk with a pronounced pimp roll. With muscles the size of Texas, they had just enough presence to act as minders and bodyguards for Mel when Terry and Mickey weren't around. After the recent scare at the baths, Mel wasn't taking any chances.

Twenty minutes later he climbed into the oversized Mercedes people carrier, Gary in front, John at the back. They drove quickly to 141 Victoria Street.

When they arrived, Avery was stalking the spot from a café opposite. Terry and Mickey were stalking her and Ryan was stalking all three.

'Look over there, in the Merc. It's Gary and John.'

'Where?'

'Over there, bureau de change, with Mel.'

'Let's call him.'

'Yeah, bright spark. We don't wanna blow our cover and get busted by Avery.'

'Yeah, but Tezza, we should let Mel know we're here now.'

'Yeah, probably right.'

Avery was taking snappy snaps with a long lens. She had all the details of the account and was padding the piece with pictures. She would send her file after publication to the newly formed National Crime Agency. Click, click, whirr Avery was reeling in shot after shot.

'Gary, stand over there a minute while I enter the pin.'

'Sure, Mel.'

'It's fucking bollocks anyway, 'cos I'm taking out a pile of readies from behind the desk, not this poxy cash point. All this fucking verification. Juggling identities is fucking hard, eh Gary?'

'Yeah.'

'Well, one or two is fine. It's when you 'ave ten or twelve when it gets tricky.'

Gary nodded.

'Result. Identity confirmed. Now I got to wait for a piece of paper and give it to the twat with the badge on his shirt who'll gimme *my* money. Fucking palaver innit?'

The machine made some reassuring noises and a square piece of paper rolled down the chute. Mel scooped it up and schlepped over to the desk attendant.

'Mel Greenberg. I'd like to cash that sum, please.'

The desk clerk examined the paper, ran his details through a machine, and then waited for the cash.

'Do you have a bag, sir?'

'Yep, right here.'

'Just needs counting. Then I have to get my manager to sign off on it.'

'No problem.'

It was over a hundred thousand. Once it was loaded, Mel strolled back to the Merc.

'Thanks mate. Jesus, it's heavy.' Mel hauled the bag into the back and propped it on the seat. Terry belled him.

'Boss, we're right behind you. Avery has been taking snappy snaps.'

'Right. Tezza Keep on her. Call me back in five minutes.'

Mel stretched forward and placed his hands on his stomach.

'There's been a change of plan. Take me to my lawyer's office in Clerkenwell. I'll drop this lot off with him.'

'Sure thing.'

Mel's phone was flashing.

'Yeah, we're heading for Nick's. Keep on her.' He clicked out and sat back. Mumbling under his breath:

'Avery is another fucking loose end. Aggro' Avery, let's see what she's made of.'

'What's that, Mel?'

'Said look at this fucking traffic. Can you go down Oxford Circus that way?'

'Yeah, I'll try it.'

His phone rang again it was an international call:

'Eduardo I wondered when you'd surface.' He fumbled around in his pocket and stuck his ear piece in and a toothpick in his mouth

'Nick did a deal with Drummond.'

'Tell me something-----I don't know.' Mel removed the toothpick and tossed it out of the window.'

'Be careful.'

'Thanks for the warning Eduardo.' The phone went dead.

Red lights came into Mel's eyes they were hungry for revenge.

Outside, the skies were folded in pink and gold as evening melted the day away. Mel was grousing for answers and the clock was ticking.

Chapter Fifty-Two: This is England

Michael Alan Drummond was a London legend: discreet, charming, with bourgeois tastes and a soft spot for aristo babes and French thespians. Part of the country's criminal elite, he was involved with everything from share hustles to illegal gambling, prostitution, and drug trafficking. He had properties in the Swiss Alps, Spain, and the Caribbean, keeping a modest home in the leafy suburbs of Muswell Hill. Drummond was in charge of one of London's most revered criminal gangs and had personally gunned down several rivals to keep his throne.

Nick was jazzed. He believed Drummond was the legitimate kingpin of London's gangland and wanted a stake of his bizzo. Mel had bungled the Pau drug run, and although Drummond was no snitch, why be loyal to the man responsible for putting his son behind bars? As far as Nick was concerned, Drummond was ripe for someone new.

Avoiding lunch time traffic, Nick raced along to Mortons and arrived after a twenty minute sprint. It was one of Mayfair's most celebrated landmarks: a stylish Georgian townhouse spread over four floors with a strict members' only policy. Fully renovated to reveal the true glory of its historic pedigree, it boasted panoramic views of Berkeley Square and housed a superb collection of premium whiskies, the converted basement drawing up market clubbers and occasional royalty. His cheeks reddened by the rain, Nick trundled up to reception, trying, somewhat ineffectively, to remove a sticky glob of gum that had attached itself to the heel of his shoe.

He was greeted by a smooth looking clean-shaven man with dark designer -cut hair and perfectly straight teeth. He wore a checked navy suit, sky-coloured shirt and burgundy tie.

'Are you a member, sir?'

'Nope, but I hope to be shortly.'

'May I have your name, sir?'

'Nick … Nick Stringer.'

'Ah yes, found you. Would you like to follow me, sir?'

'Certainly.'

En route, Nick spotted a cool mix of art aficionados and grazing models. Seated in the swanky private lounge, on an Indian red leather settee, was the Grand Moff himself. With his wavy silver locks and sun bronzed hue, he reminded Nick of an ageing screen idol. He was wearing a dove-grey shirt, underneath an Italian silk suit and tan leather shoes. He had a pleasing symmetry to his face and a welcoming toothy smile.

Once their impeccably dressed host had left the room, they were completely alone.

'Please make yourself comfy.' Drummond spoke with an effeminate curl, his words splitting the air with throaty Sauf London flair.

'Thanks.'

'Wanna drink?'

'Please. I'll have a Johnnie Walker – Black.'

'Good choice.'

Within minutes, their orders were taken by a supremely efficient bar steward. There was a relaxed hauteur about the place, suitably out of reach from the working crowds outside but impervious within.

'So, here we are then.' Michael placed both hands in front of him and stared casually at his thumbnail.

'Once took a man out with this hand.' He rubbed his

nose and coughed.

Nick said nothing.

'The way I see it, Nick, there's two kinds of people in this world: those who get fucked and those who control those who get fucked – which are you?'

Nick loosened his tie.

'Yeah, it's best to keep it zipped when you're not sure about where to stick the knife.'

Nick took a swig of JW Black to ease his nerves.

'I just want what's mine. I'm not the forgive and forget type.'

'Once you're in, you're in for life. There's no going back to Mel – are we clear?'

'Crystal.'

'I'll be in touch regarding terms, conditions, and the way we do bizzo. I understand you're part of the legal steal-and-fry crowd?'

'Yeah.'

'We're always interested in diversifying. I'm sure there's lots of common ground between us. Now, did you remember the details of Mel's grand gallery opening?'

'Yeah. The art show this week I wrote it down.' Nick rooted around in his pocket and found a crumpled piece of paper squashed between the ridges of his wallet.

'Ah, here it is.'

'Good. We should be able to set something up for then.'

'That'll bring me one step closer to the big dream.'

'Yeah?'

'Yeah.'

'Well, the thing to remember about dreams, Nick, is if you've got the balls to chase them today, they can come true tomorrow, but tomorrow's dreams can sometimes turn into yesterday's nightmares.'

Nick looked at him calmly and drained his glass.

'I won't forget what you did for my boy, Nick – can't forget what you did. It takes a sharp shot to score that kind of gig with no comeback. Very impressive. Me and the boys are glad to have you on our side.'

'I appreciate that, Mr Drummond.'

'No need for formality. Call me Michael or Mike. I respect manners, though, Nick. Keeps you civilised in a barbaric society. If you catch my drift.' He winked.

'Have you had lunch yet?'

'I did grab something earlier.'

'Then let me show you around the club. It's not as splendid as it once was back in the eighties, but I've been a member a long time and I believe in tradition. This area was popular with Churchill, you know?'

'Really?'

'Yeah.'

'Seen some funny things here too.'

'Like?'

'Ghosts, the area's full of 'em.'

'You believe in that stuff.'

'Let's say I don't dis-believe.'

'Hmmm.'

'Yeah, this place is full of surprises.'

They ambled around the elegant venue, Nick struck by the wealth of original artwork gracing the space.

'There's that line, Nick.'

'Yeah?'

'If you get too close to that line, you're on the other side before you know it and then it's too late.'

'I understand.'

'Everyone wants what they can't have. Some people get away with taking it all, and some take a hit. That's how it's always been.'

'Guess so.'

'You've made the right decision, Nick. You can count on us, but if you cross that line, you'll be shitting blood for weeks, understand?'

'Yeah.'

They walked to the balcony overlooking Berkeley Square, a romantic vista of trees and fountains.

'Glad we got that out in the open … to new beginnings.' Drummond raised his glass and Nick did the same.

'New beginnings.'

Chapter Fifty-Three: Vicious

Mel called Terry from his mobile.

'Pick me up in five minutes outside Nick's.'

The Merc skidded to a halt. Mel hauled the bag out and waited at the kerb. A few seconds later, Mickey and Terry pulled up with Avery on their tail in plain view. Mel ignored her.

'Wanna hand with that, boss?'

'Yeah, thanks.' Mickey lugged the bag to Nick's, and they all piled into the lift.

'How long's that nosey hack been on our case Tezza?' asked Mel.

'She saw everything at the bureau de change, so she must have been on us for at least twenty-four hours,' he replied.

'At least,' Mel concurred. 'Let's drop this off with Nick. He can stick it in his safe, and then I think it's time Avery and I got properly acquainted.'

Finally they reached the fourth floor. Mel stomped past Sylvie and left Mickey and Terry in reception. Bursting into Nick's office, Mel found him with his legs on the desk leafing through some official-looking papers. Startled, Nick swung his legs down and propped himself up in his chair.

'Mel.'

'Expecting someone else, eh?'

'No, not expecting anyone. You never rang ahead so ...'

Nick blustered.

'Yeah, well, expect the unexpected. Stash this lot in the safe. '

'Okay.' Nick nodded.

Mel was still on his feet. He inched closer to the desk, plonking himself down on the corner, his eyes glued to Nick's.

'You must want *it* very bad.'

Nick lowered his gaze but said nothing. 'My question is, why be a small time dodgy brief, when you can be master of the fucking universe?'

Nick was thrown.

'I've been doing this since you've been popping zits and jacking off to *Playboy*. You think you got it all figured out, but you're new to this game, Nick, like a seal cub in hunting season.'

Nick stared abstractedly at the wall.

'Look at me – listen, I'll only say this once.'

Nick sighed chewing his bottom lip he kept his eyes on Mel.

'Any lawyer can bend the law. A good lawyer can change the law, making it work against all odds, but only a great lawyer knows he must never be caught BREAKING the law else he's no different from any slugger on the streets. Don't become a cut-price thug, Nick.' He rubbed his hands together as if he was getting rid of rubbish and then he stuck his puffy red face right next to his and laughed so hard his eyes became wet.

Nick looked pale and worried. He got up and in a small voice said, 'I'll just put this away.' Mel strode after him.

'It's not too late. I can see you've had a taste. Guilt's a jealous whore, she never sleeps – fucks the weak every time. Follow the rules, son, then nobody can touch you.'

Right now I'm better off following the yellow brick road- follow the rules – Mel's rules what the fuck gives him the right to lecture me. Guilt – fuck that.

Nick squared up to Mel and spoke quietly. 'I didn't turn

into a cut-price thug, I already *was* that thug.'

Mel threw him a look of disgust spat at him and left. Nick lugged the bag to the safe and sent Sylvie home.

Outside Nick's office, Avery was on the opposite side of the road waiting for their return.

'She's still with us, I see,'

'Yes, boss,' Terry sighed.

'Fucking impressive, that bitch could be an ace stalker.'

'Yeah, probably has those kind of leanings, boss.'

'Well, in order to track and trace, you have to have a certain kind of personality, you know what I mean, lads?'

'Yeah,' Mickey nodded.

'We'll take a short cut to PT's, carjack the bitch and bring her home for some tea,' Mel chuckled. 'She can write all about it once she's recovered, and in the spirit of reality TV and all that fucking bollocks, we'll tape the whole thing and send it to her editor.'

'Nice plan, boss.'

'Yes, Tezza, then we'll dump it all on Nick's lap.'

'Yeah.'

'How long before the art opening Mickey?'

'It's scheduled for seven tomorrow evening.'

'Perfect. Gives me just enough time to work on her and go to the party. Tezza, did you send invites from Nick to Drummond's crew?'

'Yeah, boss, done. Got that Sylvie bird to do it for a bag of sand.'

'Good. Everything's falling into place.'

'Boss?'

'Yeah, Mickey.'

'Do you believe in God?'

'Now what kind of a question is that?'

'Just askin'.'

'Well don't.'

'Sorry, boss.'

'To answer your question, look at that.'

Ahead of them the sun was setting, red floaty clouds over a red sky with broken streaks of grey and yellow.

'Now stick the radio on.'

Mel smiled as the beguiling buzz of Lou Reed's 'Perfect Day' broke the airwaves and another soul was lost on the highway of life.

Chapter Fifty-Four: Let Her Down Gently

Mel's lock-up was crammed with vacuum-packed dildoes, inflatable rubber dolls and dozens of rainbow coloured rabbit vibrators. Mickey had taken delivery of buckets of sex toys for a new venture he'd started private T parties for Hedonists. There were cobwebs on the ceiling , a stack of disused broken furniture , a large stash of unopened radio equipment , and an assortment of weapons on show including a Heckler and Koch 9mm.

'What the fuck's that?' Asked Mel dodging out of the way as a monster-sized purple rubber cock smacked him in the chops.

'Sorry, boss, it's stock for my adult-themed party bizz. The city boys annual bonk fest.'

'Not exactly Hugh Hefner, is it Mickey? Bloody yellow butt plugs ! All this tack feels like I'm in a Taiwanese brothel sadly, without any of the talent. Get rid of this shit now. And put those straps away .'

'Yes, boss.'

'Tezza, bring the lady in. But before you do stick that on.' He shoved a *Ronald McDonald* mask in his mitt . And make sure she's covered up completely before she sets foot in 'ere. Mickey you get a choice of Michael Meyers or our very own face of modern protest Guy Fawkes.'

'Decisions , decisions do I opt for our beloved anti hero Mr Fawkes or a psychopathic murderer idolised by slash artists and serial killers world wide . Hmmmm. Yep .Gotta be gunpowder Guy.'

Mel shook his head. 'Just stick the bloody thing on. By the way the company that knocks those out shift about 100,000 a year a little rebellion can turn a tasty profit eh ?' He walked over to a chair in the middle of the room and waited for Tezza to return .

Avery had been forced to wear a *Bride of Chucky* mask. Her hands were tied and her hair shoved roughly behind a thin piece of elastic.Tezza was dragging her forward by the shoulder .

'Ah, it's the audacious amazin' Avery,' Mel boomed, his nostrils flaring making the whites of his eyes bigger.

'Sit her down fellas, on that chair.'

Avery was struggling, trying to break free like a trapped bird.

'Easy, don't want a pretty little thing like you getting hurt now do we?'

'Fuck you.'

'Tezza, get me that tape from the other night. It's in the passenger side of the motor.'

'Back in a mo.' Terry went and got a small tape recorder. Inside was a recording of Avery that Mel had paid Benjie the bin man for.

'Here you go, boss.'

'Okay, fellas , now step outside while Avery and I can get properly acquainted.'

Mickey and Terry left and stood guard in the driveway. Mel slid another chair over and

sat opposite her. 'I tell you, Avery I'll be honest with ya , I'm sick to death of this game. Sick of the long nights, the lying, the cheating, the hypocrisy. You got supersized authorised corruption with wanker bankers , sex scandals in Whitehall , power pricks pedalling scum and then there's the loneliness I'm sick of it .You can't trust nobody . But I keep going cos I'm good at it and I make it fucking work.'

'You think you'll get away with this?'

'Already have. You're a clever girl Avery you know I've got more fixers in my pocket than you've had hot dinners, and I'm here to give you some good old fashioned advice.'

'You're a fucking nobody. Just a sleazy well -oiled con artist.'

'Ha, ha. Is that so? Can't say I'm impressed by your crass depiction of me as some kind of bob a job villain. Don't be fooled darlin' I'm the genuine article.'

'Everyone's going to be looking for me.'

'Course they are. You're top of the list after Kim Kardashian's arse , a viral video of a stray kitten playing with a ball of string , a love rat celeb who's been bagging rent boys and your favourite soap star confessing to a crack habit . You might get a mention in your local gazette. You and all those other hacks created this titty gossip masquerading as news . You'd probably nab your fifteen minutes headlining the local news, but truth is Avery you're just a number a bit of filler squashed in between adverts for haemorrhoid cream and car insurance   but by breakfast you'd be forgotten. A cheap reminder of a sleazy night.'

'Fuck you.'

'No Avery, fuck you. Stick to the script. The five W's and the H, aren't they the cardinal rules of investigative reporting? Who, what, when, why, where and how? But you, Avery, you prefer to the Mata Hari school of intel' gathering , don't you eh?'

'Huh?'

Mel slunk up to her only inches away and placed his hands on her legs. She kicked him tried to push her chair away . He got up and circled her chair laughing viciously .

'Relax sweetheart. You don't do nothing for me . Even if you spread 'em for a story. Brings a whole new meaning to seal the scoop eh? Very noble of you.'

Mel ran his fingers through his hair and spat out his stick of gum.

'I don't know what you mean.'

'A hooker has more honesty than a scheming news hack

like you. She spreads her legs and we climb into bed, but you people are far too clever for such an honest trade, aren't you Avery?'

'I don't know what you're talking about?'

'Let me see if this jogs your memory.'

Mel laid the tape recorder on a wooden crate and pressed play. Avery could be heard talking to a man in a harsh flat voice.

'You couldn't afford me,'

Mel pressed pause.

'You know what follows next don't you, eh? The big payoff, and here it is.' He continued shaking his head, letting the tape run.

'Nice doing business with you – that's a hundred with fifty on top. Now I'd appreciate it if you closed your investigation. Quid pro quo.'

Mel walked over to the chair and removed her mask. He looked straight at her. Avery was ashen, the colour drained from her face, her eyes resting on the seedy sex toys and the dusty floor strewn with boxes and bags. He was inches apart from her when he said:

'You're just as crooked as I am.' They both looked down at the floor as a spider darted out from beneath a stack of crates. Mel let it linger by his big broad foot and then squashed it to a cruddy pulp.

'Now correct me if I'm wrong, Avery, but isn't that the CEO of Frieze Industries?'

'You haven't got the full facts. You're distorting the truth.'

'Whoa, the truth! What the fuck do you know about the truth? A double dealing meth addict knows more about the truth than a scheming little news slut like you .' He shook his head.

'No, Avery that's not news gathering, that's bribery, and I understand from Mr Macintyre you continued to tap him for cash for three months, blackmailing him over his affair with his PA. What a piece of work you are. You're downright nasty.' Avery crossed her legs. 'There are always victims, Avery, but your role has been overplayed in this little drama.'

Mel rang Terry.

'Yeah, bring the recording set-up and send the whole thing to Nick's email.'

Mickey and Terry were back in the lock-up in minutes with a small digital camera and recording equipment.

'Stick the mask on her.'

Terry pulled her mask down.

'Scoop before the truth, Avery. You're such a fucking disappointment.' Mel coughed. His facial muscles tightening. 'You want us to think you're watching from the side-lines, an innocent bystander to the system, but the *truth* is you are the fucking system. You're the one doing all the screwing.'

Terry and Mel started taking shots from every angle.

'Now get ready for your close-up.' Mel lifted up her mask. Her face was pink and roughened by stress. Sweat trails around her hairline and chin gave her a fevered hue.

'I need the loo.'

'You'll 'ave to wait,' Mel replied. Then he spoke to Terry. 'Take her upstairs, side entrance.'

'Got it, boss.'

Terry lifted her up carefully and walked her up a flight of stairs. Outside the toilet, he undid the rope letting her hands free.

'There's nowhere to run, so don't try anything silly.'

Terry left the door open while Avery squatted on the loo. Terry looked away. Avery straightened herself up and washed her hands.

'Right, all set. Let's put these back on.'

Just as Terry was about to tie her hands, she punched him in the groin. Terry tripped back and fell to the floor. Avery made a break for the door and rushed down the stairs, only to land in the hands of Mickey, who was waiting with more rope and another mask.

'Mel thought you might try somethin'. Now be a good girl and hold still.'

He had his hands across hers, cuffed her, and then stuck an alien mask on her. He walked her back to the lock-up.

Mel was sitting on a chair.

'Go and make sure Tezza's okay.'

'Yes, boss.'

'As for you, Avery, your sell by date's approaching.'

'I wasn't blackmailing him. I was trying to get to the truth.'

'You took the money. Threatened to tell his wife about the affair, and stopped investigating.'

'How long are you gonna keep me here?'

'You'll know when we're done.'

Terry came limping in. Scowling at Avery, he became sheepish with Mel.

'Don't wanna hear it, Terry. Don't wanna hear how you let some half-brained skirt get the better of you. Lucky I sent Mickey over there. Sometimes, Tezza, you're such a dumb mug.'

Terry turned red and waited for Mickey to kick off. But he just shrugged his shoulders, staring at the cobwebs on the ceiling.

'Right, have we got enough footage?' asked Mel.

'Yes, boss, we've taken the pix shot the film, saved it to a video file and it can be uploaded to the web in minutes.'

'Good, stick it on that USB.' He gave Terry a USB stick. Terry transferred the images and recordings in seconds.

'All done?'

'Yep.'

Mel looked at Avery. 'Well, it's up to you, this is your baby. How you gonna go?'

'You're all full of shit.'

'Yeah, and you got cankle ankles. Now what's it gonna be?'

Just then Mel got a phone call. It was Sal. The VAT man from the tax office was nosing around.

'You two babysit. I'll be back in an hour.

'Right boss.'

Avery was on her own, skirting for favours, and time was running out.

Chapter Fifty-Five: When You Got a Good Friend

'Everything's sorted.' Nick spoke slowly, his brows jammed close together and his shoulders sloped to the side. His chair was swivelled to the right and opposite him sat Drummond, smart enough to win it all, his gently bronzed face shining in the dim office light. He spoke in a cold monotone voice:

'Make sure everyone's on time – Mel always turns up late. In order for this to work, timing is key.'

'I understand.'

Drummond slid his chair back, sun strobes buttering light into his pale red rimmed eyes. Nick's green blotter was covered in papers and coke crystals from the morning. He brushed it clean with his hand. Drummond kept his eyes firmly on Nick as if he were turning everything over in his mind.

'He'll play worse than the devil. We've got to be prepared for anything he swings our way,'

'I know.'

'He'll do whatever it takes.'

'I'll take my chances.'

'Good, well then, see you midnight.'

'I'm ready.'

Drummond left, pinching his thumb and forefinger, the vertical lines on his face creasing together. They were all in the hole now.

Nick stayed in his chair, making mental calculations of

how much he would make on Mel's demise. He was surprised by his clinical pragmatism. Just then, as he scribbled down six figures, Sylvie knocked on the door. It sounded urgent.

'Sylvie?'

'Yes, Nick, I got this USB stick from reception. There's a note with it.'

'Thanks.'

She hesitated before leaving.

'I-I hope you don't mind, I read it.'

Nick looked up at Sylvie's face.

'It says you have to watch this first, before the party tonight. It's time sensitive.' She trembled, her mouth twitching and her eyes watering.

'You've seen it, haven't you?'

'No, I tried to – I tried to watch it, but I couldn't.' She shook her head and turned away.

'Don't stress it then. Take the day off.'

'Are you sure? I don't want you to be on your own.'

'There's nothing you can do, Sylvie. It's too late.' He cleared his throat. 'Everything's going to turn out just as it should.'

Nervously, Sylvie straightened her skirt and left the USB stick on his desk.

Nick let it lie there, a wall of silence building around him. He was about to upload it when the sound of someone in the corridor stopped him.

'Niiick!'

He knew that high-pitched whine. It was Adam, most likely boozed and coked to the bridge.

'Fumph!' Adam had kicked open the door and was rocking from side to side. His greasy mop of black curls smelt of sex and smoke.

'Jesus, what happened to you?'

'Fucking bitch took it all,' he garbled.

Nick steadied him upright, guiding him to a chair. Adam's face was childishly pink from the alcohol and he was sweating hard. He had loosened his tie and was still swaying left and right.

'Hold on a second.' Nick tried to stop him falling, but it was a moment too late. Adam slid to the floor, knocking his head on a solid glass paperweight that fell off the table.

'Jesus fucking Christ.'

Adam lay on his side, his tongue poking out, his eyes frozen. Nick checked for a pulse. Adam's head was oozing blood, chunks of glass wedged above his brow and in his hairline.

'Jesus fucking Christ.'

Nick checked his pulse again. He reached for his cigarettes. The weather was turning, sheets of rain pounding the windows and the stench of cheese and blood congealing the air. Nick sat there for several minutes just surveying the dead corpse in front of him. He inhaled, shivered, and picked up the phone.

'Matt, you've got to come over right away. Dial 411 on the key fob.'

He blinked, staring at the clock and waited for Matt to appear. All the partners had left, it was approaching 6 p.m. and now hailstones were rapping the window panes. He got up and locked the office door, dimmed the lights and shut the blinds. He went back to his chair and stretched his legs out on the desk. He had forgotten all about the USB stick, which still sat undisturbed on the jotter in front of him. His mind on the cache of guns he'd ordered from Adam. Hopefully they were in transit somewhere. He couldn't dwell on that now. He put his arms above his head, his eyes glued to the wall. It only took Matt a few minutes to arrive:

'Ratttattat Nick. It's me open up.'

'Be right there.' Nick unlocked the door and let him in.

'What's up? Why the fuck is it so dark in here?'

'Ssshh.'

'What the fuck, man, turn on some lights. Are you storing vampires in here?'

Nick exhaled and pulled Matt nervously by the arm.

There on the other side of the room, in front of them, lay Adam's lifeless corpse.

'Jesus Christ man, what the fuck happened?' Matt's eyes popped wide open.

Nick sighed. 'It wasn't me. It was an accident. He just slipped, hit his head on the paper weight.'

'What the fuck. Who is he?''

'I swear I didn't do it. He's Sal's boy. He fucking slid and hit his head – next thing I know he's fucking dead.'

'Sal as in Mel's right hand?

'Yes.'

'Why aren't we calling an ambulance, or the old bill at this point?'

'Even if I could explain this to them. I don't have the time.'

'True enough. There's a guy with a smashed cranium on your office floor! Jesus I mean Jesus what the fuck Nick – *I* don't even believe you.'

'My point exactly, so we have to get him out.'

'What? Gimme a minute. Let me think, let me think this through.'

Matt was pacing the room with both hands pulling his hair. He reached for a cigarette, burning his fingers as he tried to light it. He gave up, breaking it into pieces, and throwing it on the floor.

'Why the fuck are you doing that? Don't want that shit on my floor!'

'Dude, you got the goddamn Jewish equivalent of Vito Corleone on your *floor*. Why are you freaking over a lousy cigarette?'

'Yeah, okay. Point taken. What the fuck are we gonna do?'

Wait -I know this guy.'

'Which guy?'

'Does weird things with bodies … dead bodies. We can have him cremated and then crammed into a shot gun or rifle shells.'

'Are you out of your fucking mind? Seriously, are you fucking tripping? Why not just turn him into a fucking human firework?'

'Actually, there's a company that does just that. They mix human ashes with combustible powder and then bam!'

'Hell yeah Matt, why not add a fucking Metallica soundtrack while we're at it? Look, we don't have the time or the logistics to put those wacko plans into action.' Matt spoke slowly.

'Well----- there is Nadine.'

'Who's she?'

'The queen of cremains.'

'Cremains – what the fuck is that?'

'Cremains as in remains Nadine she –well - makes stuff out of dead bodies.'

Nick frowned. His glum stare transforming into an ominous glower. 'Why don't we do that, Matt, make a fucking art project out of Sal's dead son and list him as a rare fucking collectable on eBay? After all, I'm sure his organs are worth a pretty penny. What's the going rate for a kidney these days? What the fuck is wrong with you, Matt? We need to deal with this quickly and simply without creating a fucking event about it.'

'Fuck Nick – I don't know. It's the first time I've ever had to help in the disposal of a corpse before -and I can't fucking think straight. What about dumping him in the Thames?'

'Too risky. We'd have to get him down, haul him to the car, and then drop him in. There's people all over Waterloo.'

'Have you got a basement?'

'Yeah, and it does have an incinerator down there, but it's a shared space with other buildings so you never know who might be around.' Matt continued pacing the floor:

'I got it – this might work. Let's take him up to the roof and throw him off. He was a known coke brain, he could have easily stumbled and slipped.'

'Yeah, that could work. He had gambling debts that I'm

sure Sal was aware of, and it's kind of plausible. Every time I saw the guy, he was always wasted. He could have taken the lift to the roof and then just—'

'Yeah, make out it was a random accident – drunk as a skunk and then splat.'

'He was totally trashed when he came over. He's a regular at *Secrets*, the strip club down the road. He's well known in the area and it would have been perfectly natural for him to stop by.'

'Yeah, but everyone's gonna ask the same question. What the fuck was he doing on the roof in the first place?'

'He was shit-faced Nick, maybe he went for a smoke like you said to do some blow, or just to get some air.'

Nick was hesitant. Matt put his hand to his mouth as if he was going to vomit.

'I think we should concentrate on getting him out of here and onto the roof. We can go through the detail later.'

Nick checked his watch. Soon the bars and clubs would be filling up. If they wanted to get rid of his body, they'd have to try now in the lull period.

'Yeah, okay. I'll go check the hallway, ensure no one's around.'

Nick rode the lift down. They were the only ones left in the building.

'You were gone ages.'

'I had to check everywhere, make sure the offices were empty. Fortunately due to some staff shortages Security's clocked off early. The last thing we need is for anyone to connect us with Sal's number one.' Matt smoothed down his curls and tied his hair up with an elastic band. He wandered around Nick's office muttering nervously:

'Let's write a note.'

'What?'

'A suicide note.'

'What the fuck are you talking about? If it was an accident, why the fuck was he writing a note? Anyway, why go to a strip club, then come here to top himself? He could just as easily have stuck one of his hundreds of shooters in his mouth and – kiang – all done.'

'Hmmm, good point, Grissom.'

'Yeah, let's just keep it simple. No fucking note.'

'I don't know Nick, it has to look convincing, at least there should be some drinking paraphernalia and some extra contraband on him.'

'I'll jam some coke in his pocket and douse him in a little of this.'

Nick went to the drinks cabinet and took out a bottle of Macallan's Scotch whisky.

'We'll dump half and leave the rest on the roof.'

'Don't you watch any crime dramas? We'll dunk him in the whisky, keep the bottle here, and we'll throw it in the dumpster later.'

'Okay, you lift him under his shoulders and I'll grab his ankles. Wait a minute, Matt, set him down, let's pour this over him.'

'You do it.'

'Fine, I didn't know him that well.' Nick took the bottle and sprayed it on Adam's neck, clothes and hair. Then he put it, half-empty, back in the cabinet.

Propping the body between them, they hauled it to the lift. Nick held the door open with the dead man's hand until they managed to get him inside. Then they rode the lift to the roof. Awkwardly, they tumbled out and dropped him like a weighted sack of potatoes onto the concrete.

'Jesus, Nick fuck, hang on to your end!'

They dragged the body on the ground. Nick looked at the London lights and the azure skies. He remembered his shroom trip and how beautiful the city had looked, as if she were alive. He had fallen a long way since then. Bad thoughts flooded in.

'How the fuck did I end up here?'

'How you got here isn't the thing. We got to get him off and get the fuck out.'

Nick looked pale and angry. They shuffled to the edge of

the roof. Adam's clothes reeked of whisky and stale perspiration. There were damp spots all over his jacket trousers and shoes.

'Still can't believe this. Fucking hell Nick – what the fuck?' Matt's face was twisted with confusion and disbelief and his voice was shaky.

Carefully they propped him up, Adam's lifeless head swinging to the side, his body wobbling over the edge. Matt peered at Nick, his eyes now toughened and cold.

'On one.'

With a breath they shoved him off the roof.

Chapter Fifty-Six: Pop Goes the Weasel

Mel, Terry and their full crew rolled up to The Fold Gallery. Already there were Drummond, Dicksta and a smattering of liggers and art fucks who were holding court over a rather large sculpture of Niki Minaj's derriere. It seemed fitting for what was about to go down. In the bathroom Sal was trying to call Adam, when he spotted Nick at the door and cornered him.

'I'm worried. Haven't seen my son for days. It's not like him to just disappear.'

'Sorry, I've not heard anything, but I'm sure he'll turn up soon.' Nick feigned nonchalance and avoided eye contact. He washed his hands and started to mingle.

Outside, the press and paparazzi were lining up, jiving for quotes, celeb pics and as much daytime trivia as they could handle. Nick scoured the pavement for Avery, went back inside and nodded at Drummond and his guys. Drummond waved him over, a cigar in one hand, a drink in the other.

'Good to see you, son. Everything's gonna be fine.'

'Hope so. I dunno where Avery is.'

'She your Mrs?'

'Kind of. She's a journo. I was banking on her being here when things play out.'

'Well trust me, when the shit hits, everyone's gonna want a front row seat.' Drummond glanced over at Mel, who blanked him completely. Nick made his way through the crowds to Dick and found Matt by his side.

'Well, we made it.'

'What's this?' asked Dick.

'It was a rough night, but somehow me and Matt made it to the other side.'

'Sounds cryptic,'

'Let's just say it was a real bonding experience Dick. You can never know how far you'll go till you get there, right?'

'Right.' They drank to friendship.

'Excuse me, I need to see Mel.' Nick walked to the opposite side of the room. Mel, Terry, Mickey and Sal were standing behind a roped cordon looking at a huge pair of sculpted lips, Mel's spongy frame throwing wide shadows across the line.

'Nick.'

'Mel.'

'See you're getting cosy with big D?'

'We had a little bizzo.'

'Good for you. Been meaning to ask, you got insurance?'

'What?'

'Life insurance.' Mel rubbed his nose as he spoke, in an overly casual tone.

'I don't need it. I'm fully comp.'

Mel's hoggy face had a purple hue, his neck fat, and cheeks blurring into a blobby mess as he tried to force a smile. He moistened his mouth with some gum and wrapped his chubby hand, crowned with gemstones and gold, around Nick's back, squeezing him close.

'Be careful who you mess with. No one sells me out Nick.' Mel's breath was touching the nape of his neck and he smelt of stale aftershave and mint chewing gum.

'It's been terrific, Mel.' Nick patted him on the back and filtered his way through the crowd.

'Nick, long time.' BCM had made it after all. His presence reassured him for some reason. Maybe it was his Zen-like tranquillity or his long tresses. Whatever it was, Nick welcomed him with an open smile and warm hug.

'Peace and power,'

'Peace is power.'

Nick gave him the peace sign and turned to the door. Everyone was agog. Mimi blew in, hot and slinky, her soft loose curls salon fresh. She wore a stretch caddy silver satin evening dress that clung to her like a second skin and open toe glitter pumps with sky rocket heels. She was accompanied by a Jared Leto lookalike with Jesus locks and a honey tan.

'Wow,' Nick mouthed.

Mel caught Mimi's eye as she waved and winked with a self-satisfied smile.

Still there was no sign of Avery. Nick redialled her number and left another voicemail.

'Hey it's me. Big turnout for the art show tonight. You should be here. Miss you.'

He tracked back to Matt and the Dicksta.

'Stop it, your eyes will pop out your head.' Matt was ogling Mimi's centrefold curves.

'Sinful.'

'You are aware that's Mimi Deepridge, yeah?'

'What?'

'Hold on, look.' Nick pulled out his Blackberry and googled her name. He stuck the images, Instagram pics, and Twitter feeds of transtastic Mimi under Matt's nose.

'Fuck, wow!'

'Yep, she sure does.'

'The Dicksta missed a trick here. He should have done a sculpture of *that!*'

'Think he's working on it.'

'It's the best of the sexes.'

'Bit of X, bit of Y, mix it all up.'

'Third eye, third sex,' cut in BCM.

A right-handed waiter armed with a silver tray sailed around them. They all opted for the mini sliders.

The waiter combed the room and finally spotted Mel. They exchanged a look of action and when he was within arm's reach he stopped and Mel looked sharply into the waiter's eyes. Then, in a firm voice devoid of emotion he said: 'Do it now.'

The gallery was filling up with partygoers from another London hotspot. There was a noisy hum as people jostled around from one exhibit to the other. Drummond jostled through the growing crowd to speak to Nick.

'Everything's in place.'

Nick nodded and beckoned Matt and BCM over.

'You guys wanna smoke?' He wanted them out of the gallery before the hit. They followed him to the exit.

In the basement of Mel's lock-up, Avery was wrestling with duct tape and shock. Left alone while Mel and the crew had raced over to The Fold, her hands were still tied and blistered with pink bumps. She dragged the chair towards the door and searched for something to free herself. Face to face with a giant sex doll, she pushed the chair back and eyed the room for something else, something sharp. Outside she could hear the ebb and flow of normality: cars, voices in the distance.

She tried shouting for help, but she was unable to make a sound. It just hung in her throat. She could feel crawling, creepy things around her feet, scuttling onto a damp spot under the chair. She tried to prise her wrists free, but they were sore and bloody now, the pain too extreme to keep going. She heard the door unlock, and froze. She could hear the thump thump thump of her chest and she had a splitting headache.

Is any of this real? Her fingers were numb, and she was ready to give up, when she glimpsed Ryan through her mask.

'Now what've I told you about picking up strange men? Hold steady, this may hurt a bit, but I'm sure you're strong enough to take it. If you've had a Brazilian, that is.' He removed the mask and peeled off the duct tape, leaving a sticky imprint on her lips, which were now pink and swollen.

Her pretty face was dented with worry and she'd developed some stress spots around her cheeks.

'R-R …' She couldn't finish the sentence. She was hoarse and raw inside.

'Yeah, gonna hurt for a bit.'

'How-how …'

'Easy, take it easy. Let's get your hands untied first, shall we?'

Dried blood and crusted skin flakes dusted the floor.

'Can you get up? We should get out of here now.' Ryan had his eye on the door. 'Mel could be back any time.'

He helped her stand up.

'Need to treat that with some antiseptic.'

'Yeah, but first I have to call my editor. Mel's at the art show. If I hurry I can make it.' Avery used all her strength to get the words out.

'I'll drop you off after we've seen to that.'

She nodded and pointed to her bag. 'Could you?'

Her treasured leather Birkin had been flung to the far side of the room, but everything was intact.

Her breathing was still laboured.

'Thanks, Ryan. I owe you.'

'I know.'

Back at the art gallery, a single spotlight shone on the host who stood alone on the stage. A tall willowy redhead with refined angular lines, she wore nude lipstick and heavy kohl accentuating her eyes. Dressed in black Georgette and strappy stilettos that lengthened the curve of her calves, she oozed sartorial simplicity. She spoke to the crowd in an over-theatrical way as if delivering a Shakespearean soliloquy. Anywhere else it would have seemed contrived.

'I want to thank you all for coming to this …'

Bang! Thwat! Bang! Bang! Bang! Three gunshots could be heard outside, startling the already inebriated crowd and causing them to run helter-skelter, left and right.

The show's host was tripped off the stage in the melee

and emergency lights kicked in.

A health and safety official appeared from a side door. He had a large microphone and kept repeating the same words over and over:

'Would everyone please form an orderly queue and exit the building. There is no danger. I repeat, there is no danger. Would everyone exit the building ...'

Hanging out of the passenger side of a vintage Merc, a masked shooter wielded a semi automatic. Bullets sprayed the pavement, and Matt and BCM ducked as another round hit. There was the sound of breaking glass and an icy howl like metal scalping stone. Matt looked down and saw blood pools trickling towards him. Nick had been shot in the stomach and his left arm.

'Hang in there.' Matt was clammy, his hands grappling for something, anything – a cloth, a handkerchief – to stem the flow. He looked around but there was no sign of BCM anywhere. Maybe he had gone for help. Matt turned back to Nick, resting his head on his jacket and then scrambled for his phone. Nick was in bad shape. Matt called 999.

'Hello.' He was shivering. His voice uneven and trembling. 'My ... be-best friend's been ... shot. There's blood everywhere.' He gasped and bought a breath. 'Hurry.'

'Caller, caller?'

'Yes ... here.'

'Can you give us your location please?'

'The Fold ... Gallery, Clerkenwell. Please ... hurry.'

Matt clicked off. Nick's blood was all over his hands and trousers, inking them red.

'Stay ... with me, Nick ... stay,' he sobbed.

Nick's eyes were clouding over, half-shut, half-open. He could see swirling shapes of yellow and green above him and felt the sky lift and fall. He heard the blood singing in his nose. Waves of nausea hit as he reached for Matt's hand.

'No more coins.......for the jukebox. I wanted to be the man to push the button ... thought I owned it, thought I was on my way … but I'm the one who got played. Mel's mechanical puppet … scanning the hit list….. for one last song. I'm a twelve-bar cliché of greed. All my dreams torched and no way to bring them back. It doesn't matter, if I had a hundred tomorrows left or lived a thousand times before. Truth is, I fucked up … got gold in one hand and mud in the other … in the end it's the same for all of us. We go out the same way we came in … alone.'

THE END

Coming soon from Saira Viola on Fahrenheit Press:

Crack Apple And Pop

Printed in Great Britain
by Amazon